Dear Reader,

The book you are holding came about in a rather different way to most others. It was funded directly by readers through a new website: Unbound. Unbound is the creation of three writers. We started the company because we believed there had to be a better deal for both writers and readers. On the Unbound website, authors share the ideas for the books they want to write directly with readers. If enough of you support the book by pledging for it in advance, we produce a beautifully bound special subscribers' edition and distribute a regular edition and ebook wherever books are sold, in shops and online.

This new way of publishing is actually a very old idea (Samuel Johnson funded his dictionary this way). We're just using the internet to build each writer a network of patrons. At the back of this book, you'll find the names of all the people who made it happen.

Publishing in this way means readers are no longer just passive consumers of the books they buy, and authors are free to write the books they really want. They get a much fairer return too – half the profits their books generate, rather than a tiny percentage of the cover price.

If you're not yet a subscriber, we hope that you'll want to join our publishing revolution and have your name listed in one of our books in the future. To get you started, here is a £5 discount on your first pledge. Just visit unbound.com, make your pledge and type **nativity5** in the promo code box when you check out.

Thank you for your support,

Dan, Justin and John
Founders, Unbound

A Dark Nativity

This edition first published in 2017

Unbound
6th Floor Mutual House,
70 Conduit Street, London W1S 2GF
www.unbound.com

Text Design by Ellipsis, Glasgow

A CIP record for this book is available from the British Library

ISBN 978-1-78352-434-1 (trade hbk)
ISBN 978-1-78352-436-5 (ebook)
ISBN 978-1-78352-435-8 (limited edition)

Printed in Great Britain by Clays Ltd, St Ives Plc

1 3 5 7 9 8 6 4 2

A Dark
Nativity

George Pitcher

Unbound

I was deeply touched by the generosity of friends and strangers who supported this book. The full list of honour is at the back, but there are special shout-outs that I want to make here, to five people who, between them, put up more than half the crowdfunding total.

Guy Weston's intervention last Christmas was a game-changer. You're beyond kind and generous, Guy, and even paid for lunch that day. I look forward to our pilgrimage. And special thanks to my fellow travellers Richard and Alison Cundall, to Will Lewis for blind confidence in me, and to Melvyn Marckus, who has generously edited and read more of my writing than is strictly healthy.

I'd also like to thank the Rev'd Charlotte and Bill Bannister-Parker, Richard Bridges, Sarah Macdonald and Sian Kevill of MAKE Productions and Sir Kenneth and Lady Warren for their generosity, variously of wealth, spirit, lunch and Oxford.

Thank you all – I couldn't have done it without you.

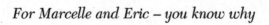

For Marcelle and Eric – you know why

In darkness, and in secret, I crept out,
My house being wrapped in sleep.

– "The Dark Night of the Soul",
St John of the Cross

Part 1

Prologue

We were helping Israel to close its borders, to turn in on itself. As word had spread through the Samarian hills to the east, a pathetic trickle of Palestinians, a fresh generation of refugees, had grown into a crowd more alarming as families sought the security and health services of the Sharon Plain. I heard Hebrew as well as regular Palestinian Arabic.

We were young then, Sarah and me. I think we believed in humanity. How long ago that seems. We'd been co-opted to offer humanitarian support between Bat Hefer and Tulkarm, just by the reservoirs, and provide some order for the crossings of the new fence.

The border guards were a mixture of Magav police and military and were meant to defer to our UNRWA bibs – it stood for the UN's Relief and Works Agency, but we said it was "Rather Walk Away". They kept directing families of all ages into a holding pen, a high flat-wired fenced area about the size of an English suburban garden, complete with a shed at the bottom end, where shamefully there was a single chemical latrine, some emergency medical gear, such as stretchers, as well as a metal chest of flares and, we always suspected, mustard gas.

Sarah had started to warn the men as the air grew more still towards evening that the pen was growing too crowded. Sarah was always firmer than me. I may have burnished the image in the intervening years, but I picture her now standing brace-legged in high-waisted khaki trousers, her field phone sticking above her blue bib like a badge of authority, leaning slightly in to a Magav officer on her walking stick and telling him what to do with her question: "Are you going to seal the muster station and order open process?"

I tried to remember what I'd read five years before about crowd-control errors at football stadiums. There were some children pressed up against the fencing with older siblings behind them. But they were only curious, not being crushed. I smiled at them and they stared neutrally back, running the wire between dry lips.

Sarah heard the cry first. She swung round with her eyes to the distance, as if she was looking at the mountains. Then I heard its second, louder version, somewhere between exhalation of fear and an imprecation.

"Shit," murmured Sarah and ran with her loping gait to the UN jeep.

She unlocked the med box with the bundle of keys at her waist and pulled at the handles of a bag, about the size of a rolled sleeping bag.

"Follow me," she called, heading for the gate of the pen.

She was dodging bodies and catching shoulders. We made it to the back of the pen, where a woman in a blue silk weave lay, her knees splayed like an open oyster. A boy knelt beside her, too young to be her husband. A brother, perhaps.

How had Sarah known? Maybe she'd seen her arrive earlier. But she always seemed to know things before me.

The ground was wet. It was never wet unless the boys pissed in the holding pens.

"Roll up her robe."

She was a large woman, hair matted, crying and juddering. She was past caring for her modesty, but the boy looked desperate, frozen. Sarah leaned across and slapped him across the face and barked something huskily in, I thought, Arabic but it sounded strange, more like a Hebrew patois. He lifted her robe back like a tablecloth and I gently pushed him to one side to provide some screen with my back, for some dignity. Up nearer her head, he grasped her hand and held it to his chest.

Sarah moved round, still kneeling, and lay her walking stick across her lap and the woman's legs over it to either side of her. She cupped her hands, as if in homage. Or prayer. The woman threw her head back, arched her spine and cried again, a primal howl that filled the valley and made the men stare away.

"Oh Christ, she's delivering," said Sarah, to herself.

She rolled aside and tore open the Velcro strip of the med bag.

"Nat, get where I was and hold the head – don't pull, just support."

I knelt in the ruts her knees had left in the earth.

Then I felt a warm, firm hardness fill my palms as the woman shrieked and the boy whimpered. Sarah leaned across her with a syringe and surgical scissors between the fingers of one hand. She tore the antiseptic seal off the blades with her teeth and spat them aside. She said something to the boy again. I caught it in Arabic:

"Hold her ankle towards you." But then she seemed to repeat it in her strange dialect.

He didn't move. She slapped him again and the message was clear in any language. "Hold it!"

Then, softly, like the sudden mood-swing of a madwoman in an asylum, she ran the ball of her thumb across the forehead of the woman to shift the hair from her eyes and spoke in English.

"It's all right, my love. You're going to have a baby."

The new face appeared sideways in my palm, still in its caul, features squashed and pulled down like a tiny bank robber with a nylon stocking over its head. The blue-grey mass barely filled my hands.

Sarah dealt with the cord like she was wrapping a gift in a shop, but the baby, freed of its caul, didn't wake. Sarah held it face down in the palm of her hand, and rubbed its back. The head rolled, the mouth opened noiselessly and a little fist twitched. Then, blinking suddenly through rubbery folds, it cried. There was a wave of acclamation in the throng behind us. God was still great, apparently.

The baby was swaddled in bandages and a gauze arm-sling from the med bag and given to the boy to hold on stiff, clumsy forearms. The woman took some minutes to deliver the placenta and get cleaned, then leaned against the hut.

Sarah handed her the bundle with the little dark face.

"Here's your daughter," she said. "Every happiness of her."

The woman smiled and thanked her, the boy grinning. "He has a sister now," she said.

He also had a fast ticket through the processing station. It would take no more than an hour or so for a UNRWA ambulance to take this fragment of a family down to the Laniado hospital in Netanya. That's why they smiled too.

Later that evening, Sarah and I sat on a ridge and looked down across the plain towards the coast, drinking tea spiked with vodka from a Thermos and sharing a cigarette. Most of the new arrivals had been processed in threes, even if it broke up families. It was a pointless exercise, because even if they were denied access across this new border point, they'd make it through the urban streets on either side. It was all for show, though it heralded the wall that was to come. The pen beneath us had room for families to sleep now in some safety, even if others arrived in the night.

"Good gig today, Sarah," I said, out of nothing.

"I wonder where the dad is," she said after a moment, blowing smoke into the night. "Whether he knows."

"She's alive. Pretty sure that's better than the alternative."

Sarah didn't reply.

"Why were you speaking Hebrew to the boy, Sar?"

"It wasn't really Hebrew," she said. "It was Aramaic. It's what they sometimes speak up in the north. They may have come down from Syria originally."

"There's another one in the family now. Another mouth to feed. Wouldn't have been if you hadn't heard her."

I could see she was drawing hard on the cigarette. Sarah never gave much away, but I knew when she was close to the edge. She screwed her eyes to see into the dark. I leaned across to take the fag and, in a girly way, started to sing.

He bought me a banana, I made it shake, he brought me home with a bellyache.

It was a hopscotch song from our childhood that we'd corrupted for the primary school girls when it was our turn to look after them. Smoke came from her nostrils like a dragon and she turned and grinned at me, then slapped me across the ear, playfully, not like she hit the boy.

So, Sarah. Sarah the Jew, whom we mocked at school and whom I came to love. Always the cleverest of us. She was always Sarah Curse at school, full name. Funny the things that come to mind when you have too long to think. We've always spoken with a quick frankness, as those who have grown up together do, not always really friendly but without the dishonesty of the casual acquaintance.

Once, after we'd left school, I told her suddenly that I'd always coveted her name, that it had been so cool, and she confessed that it had been made up, though not by her. It had originally been Cruse; her grandfather had changed the spelling as a refugee in England to make it easy to say, but also because so many of his family had been shipped out of northern Italy by the Nazis to die. They had been from the Savoie border regions of Italy and France. The name was probably a corruption of Crose from the Italian word *croce*, which means cross. Crozier is probably another corruption.

The awful implication was that forebears of the Jewish Cruse family had probably been baptised French Christians, before reconverting to Judaism in Italy.

I told her that I'd longed to be called Sarah Curse. And we laughed, rather ruefully given the darkness of Sarah's family history.

But also because my name is Natalie Cross.

And this is my story, not hers. I'm telling it because it keeps me alive. That's literally true, as you'll see. This is not just an act of therapy, it's my life assurance, as a dear lover in Lebanon once told me. A record of crimes against my humanity. Names changed to protect the guilty, but they can and will be named if I come to any more harm and they know that. So that's why I'm telling this story: it's my security. So long as it's told and heard, I'm safe. A testimony, really.

1

So come with me through the places that make me who I am. From the executioner's block to the dhobi-room, where I try to scrub out the bloody stain on my priestly alb. But it keeps coming back. I offer it all up and sometimes, for a heady, transcendent moment, I am healed, and yet the gash returns, like an ill-sewn seam bursting open, like Lancelot's ever-wounded side, bleeding for Guinevere, that can't be healed this side of his king's forgiveness. And, God knows, I'm the wrong side of forgiveness.

At school, Sarah came into her own. And her own received her not. We were at our comp in a vapid little suburb to the south of London. We thought she'd had something like polio, I reckon, or some sort of congenital muscular-wasting disease. Later, she told me it was Perthes' disease, a hip-joint thing she'd had surgery for, but was getting better all the time, though she'd get arthritis later in life.

We never asked about it when we were young. We were never told not to talk about her condition, but it was implicit in the form teacher's introductory injunctions when she joined the class in the middle of the academic year.

"Sarah uses aids to walk and sometimes will spend time in a wheelchair when she needs surgery," she said, as Sarah sat in the front row, displacing someone to the square window alcove. "So she needs our support. Let's all make her very welcome."

I wondered at the time whether that entreaty was a play on words. She had crutches, this girl, but she needed our support too. We were to make her welcome despite that. I wondered even then whether we should have made her welcome *because* of that. The boys, amounting to around a third of our class, generally did, but they were nicer than us.

Sarah used to form a bulwark in the corridor as girls leaned against the walls, learning to fold our legs and doing the jabby push that accompanied shrieks of faux outrage at the mildest social observation. We had our roles in this girl-gang: the happy frump, the lippy, the hippy, the thoughtful and the dykey, the tarty, the outré and the nerd.

I was the quiet one. Not really shy, not, I think, insecure, but remote and I was comfortable with that. I was looking in on their play. I was the audience to their performance. So I watched the drama unfold.

The young girls at the primary through the fence played a hybrid form of hopscotch and their improvised sing-song carried through windows flung open to expunge the stench of school-dinner vegetables. It was the soundtrack to that time.

I met my boyfriend at the sweetie shop, he bought me ice cream, he bought me cake, he brought me home with a bellyache . . .

Sarah would lean on her crutches, white forearms braced in the horseshoe rings. Her upper body pitched forward like an awkward mannequin. One winter half-term in the sixth form there was a ski-trip – I was the only one other than Sarah who didn't go, and we were knocking around together a bit by then – and I saw photos of

11

the grown-ups leaning like that on their sticks at the top of the slopes and I wondered why, if they wanted to look athletic, they should also want to look like Sarah.

It was difficult to spot when the mood changed in the girls' corridor. The microclimate of a gang of girls shifts with imperceptible signals. It's like the distant curl of a cloud that a mariner might spot, or a fresh breeze to the face, the first indications that a storm is on the way. These are gentle and apparently harmless signs, not seeking to draw attention to themselves, sinister only to those who know what they portend. The dark twist on the horizon was a conversational shift.

I couldn't have attributed the initiative to any one girl in the pack.

Maybe Tarty said "spaz". Maybe Outré said something about it "really getting on my tits". Perhaps it was Sulky: "All she wants is pity."

But then someone said: "If you bent two of her forward, you'd have a pantomime horse."

And the troupe came together in a spontaneous caterwaul that was like energy expanding, noxious fumes filling the corridor as if there had been a gas explosion in the science lab and a wall of ignited fuel was rolling towards the fire doors. They howled and rocked as they struck pantomime poses against a torrent of released vocabulary – cripple and hunchback and legless.

Mummy, Mummy, I feel sick, call the doctor, quick, quick, quick.

I watched the smile on Sarah's face die, like a head relaxing into sleep, as she absorbed that her friends were now laughing delightedly at her and not with her. The illusion of friendship had evaporated in the heat of the tribe's ridicule and nothing could be the same for Sarah at that school again. I watched from my safe distance.

Doctor, doctor, will I die? Count to five and stay alive . . .

It never occurred to me, as an act of conscious kindness, to reach out in her defence, to stand by her and to try to reclaim the innocent time before our gang had given themselves permission to mock her. The relief of honesty was, in any case, too great for them – they were venting what they really thought and the serpent could never be returned to its basket.

I suppose I felt that it was better for her to know the truth. People are nasty; they hate you. That's the default position. What we do is cover that up with a sentimental carapace of generosity, whether that comes in the shape of religious example or shared humanity. It's selfish really – I am kind to you in these circumstances because it makes me feel better.

Sarah had moved to one side to sit in her wheelchair; I guess to make a quicker and more dignified exit. I think it was that no one offered her a hand as she awkwardly negotiated the transition from sticks to wheels that prompted me to do something. Or it may have been that it was all playing out at excruciating length. Whatever it was, I stepped into the crowd that day and stood beside Sarah's wheelchair. The braying laughter subsided briefly to accommodate me in the tableau.

"Shut the fuck up," I said. "You stupid little bitches. She's worth ten of any of you."

I had nothing else. I had to get us out of there. I moved behind Sarah and pulled on the handles of the wheelchair. She jerked violently like a crash-test dummy.

"You have to let the brake off," she said and did so.

The jeering followed us down the corridor. I've learned a bit about pushing wheelchairs since, like turning around to go backwards through swing doors, but I knew none of that then. I used Sarah as a battering ram to get outside.

We went down the old driveway beyond the playgrounds and away from the little girls' songs, me leaning back and slipping on old grit. If I'd let go she'd have ended her run in the stream at the bottom. I sat beside her, behind the groundsman's sheds, and pulled two cigarettes from what was left of a packet of ten. She held hers ineptly. I think it was her first.

I looked at Sarah not with pity but with contempt.

"You stupid bloody fool, Sar. How could you have thought those girls were your friends?" I said at last. "The truth is that they're grateful they're not you. Get real."

"I don't think they're my friends," she said. I had expected her to be crying. But she was smiling faintly at me through the smoke.

If I'd been older I'd have liked to say, "They despise you for reminding them of what they are – able-bodied but still useless. They can't take you into their lives as anything other than a burden. That's the truth, Sarah, and it's just sad and pathetic for you to delude yourself that they think any better of you for making them feel superior. You're a cripple and they want to laugh and point." As it was, I just said, "They hate you."

"I know," she said. "But thanks anyway."

I pushed her back up the hill. On the steep bit, I started to miss my footing on the grit again and to slide backwards. With my head down between the handles of the wheelchair, I began to laugh helplessly. We were immobilised.

"What are you doing?" she said from the front.

"Nothing," I managed to say. "I'm stuck."

She pulled the brake on and I helped her out and on to her sticks, and I pushed the empty chair up slowly beside her, watching each of her careful steps.

In truth, I ignored her for a while after that, just as the other girls ignored me, leaving her behind as an amusing but failed emotional experiment. But I remember she often looked tearful and pained at the end of lessons and of the day. It seemed to be her rightful lot, and I tried to shrug it off inside.

We were both outsiders; I see that now. I started to fetch the wheelchair when it was elsewhere. Push her between classes. Help her with her lunch tray.

I imagined she wouldn't live long – I don't know why, as her disability wasn't that great. But even the teachers let that assumption prevail. And far from fading from my mind, she kept recurring, like a persistent musical phrase.

2

My descent into faith started with a note shoved under my door in a student hall at university. I kept it for a few years. I don't really know why. Maybe I knew it was an important letter. Maybe I was keeping papers for my biographer.

I can pretty much remember it in its entirety.

Hi dear Nat . . . Don't leave us. Please don't leave us. We love you and this is REALLY important, because it's about the <u>most</u> important thing for all of us . . . YOUR ETERNAL LIFE IN LORD JESUS. You may think you're just turning your back on us, but really you're turning your back on HIM. So it's HIM begging you to come back, not US. So we're just praying that you will come back to us – and be saved, like us, by His Grace. Pleeease Nat!

In His Love Forever, Noel

It was written on a piece of A4 file paper and had a crucifix drawn quickly as a kind of logo in the top right-hand corner, the hanging figure on it a couple of expertly turned curls.

Jesus Christ. Is that the best you've got, I thought, sitting on the edge of my tiny bed in a shared flatlet on The Vale, an Elysian undergraduate estate. I should have screwed it up and binned it straight away, but there was something so exquisitely naff in those hundred or so words that I wanted to keep looking at them. I didn't know enough about it then, but I do now. The condescending conflation of authentic discipleship with their little tribe. The offer of salvation like it was their gift. The pleading and the capital letters. The word "just".

This was about a month, maybe less, into my first term. I'd gone to Birmingham and Sarah had gone to Oxford. I went to the Freshers' Festival at the student union, a Victorian U-shape throughout which were stalls and hawkers selling clubs and societies. I wasn't lonely, because I don't do that, but I did feel oddly detached, like I was watching everyone else have fun, as if they were putting on a show for me. Less further education than further alienation, really.

I didn't want to go scuba-diving or demonstrate against Thatcher's cuts, though I did hang around the craft stands, especially the woodwork and carpentry. There were some rubbishly turned finials and I knew I could do better. I took a leaflet.

"Lineker shoots – Jesus saves" said the sign as I walked into the next hall. I didn't want to talk, but I'd been spotted reading it.

"Hi, fancy taking a shot at Jesus?" The boy held out a plastic football and pointed at a large chipboard hippy with a headband, with his hands out in large gloves. "If you get it past him and into the fishing net – admittedly a mixed metaphor – you get free fish and chips at our next Friday fish night." He leaned in conspiratorially. "Otherwise it's 30p."

"I'm rubbish at football," I said.

"Yeah, but you're good at something. We just want to know what it is." And he threw the ball from hand to hand.

"Who's 'we'?" I asked.

"The Christian Union – we put the uni in union."

He seemed nice enough. "What does a Christian Union do? Make sure vicars get overtime if they pray too much?"

"Indeed," he said, and smiled. "What's the leaflet?"

"It's from the carpentry club," I said.

"Jesus was a carpenter!" And he held his arms out like the ludicrous icon of his saviour behind him.

"I know," I said slowly, from under my eyebrows. I can deploy a devilish eyebrow, not least because I have a scar through one of them.

"I'm Noel," he said.

"The first, I presume," I said. He just grinned and nodded and looked down at his football boots. "I'm sorry, I bet you get that all the time," I added quickly.

"First today," he said. "What do you want to do?"

"What, right now or with the rest of my life?"

"I have the answer to both," said Noel. "But let's start with now."

"I . . . want to find someone who does voluntary work overseas."

"Where?"

I shrugged. "Ethiopia?"

"WorldMission," said Noel, throwing the ball to his fellow Striker in Christ. "I'll give you the phone number. Run by our brothers and sisters."

"OK," I said and lingered.

He handed me a flyer. "Come to Fishermen & Chips anyway."

And I did. It was in some old gymnasium and we were counted, then sang a couple of songs to guitar and piano during which the food magically arrived, wrapped in greaseproof paper in a big cardboard box. I didn't much care for the singing, and the rocking from side to side wasn't for me. I suppose I knew then it wouldn't last. But the fish and chips were good. And it felt a bit like a family and I suppose I wanted that. So I went back on Sunday for more songs and swaying. No one I knew would see me.

It lasted as long as any of those early university things do. I was hanging out on a cheap beer night with a crowd from my course, drinking lager in plastic pints, and wondering where to go on to. I knew Noel and his group were having a party at a little house some of them shared in Selly Oak. There would be food. So we set off with a couple of bottles of wine, about six of us.

It didn't go well. Noel's sidekick answered the door. I could go in, but the others weren't welcome. Odd, because they weren't even particularly rowdy.

"Why only me?" I asked, genuinely inquisitive.

"You're one of us."

"No I'm not. Is Noel there?"

"He's out the back. You can come in and see him. Just not the others."

"But these are my friends."

We bought a Chinese takeaway, went back to The Vale, and sat in one of the common areas, drinking wine out of mugs and eating chip butties when the pork and rice ran out.

"I don't know how you can stand all that patriarchy stuff, Natty," said one of the girls when we'd exhausted the "not very Christian" line.

But that was just it, I realised. I had wanted a father figure. I'd had a father, but he didn't figure.

The note arrived under my door when I didn't show the following

Sunday. And Noel caught me up in the University Square one damp morning.

"Nat, please don't be lost."

"I'm not," I said. "I know where I'm going."

"You don't understand – if you commit to Jesus, you're truly free, not like this wandering journey you're on. And bring your friends to him."

"Noel, it's been real. But no thanks."

He stopped walking. "Nat, why are you doing this to us?"

"I'm shaking you off my feet."

I was pleased with that and didn't turn around. But he tried again. He was doing Mech Eng, which wasn't far from the History block. He told me that I only knew the Lord a little and needed to know him more. I told him this time that I'd report him to my course leader for harassment. And that was it.

But I reread his note. A kind of rage gathered in my chest. And here's the thing: I started taking a bus to a Victorian church in Moseley. I started to argue with Father Trevor there, a middle-aged priest with a bad haircut, about what we were meant to render to Caesar, if anything, about who the poor were, and we made up a story about what happened next to the woman taken in adultery. They ran a night shelter and I started to help out with a soup kitchen, the first time I'd fed hungry people. But the turbulent little ball of rage that Noel had put at the base of my ribcage never went away. I have it still.

At the end of that first term, I switched to joint-honours in History and Theology. At the end of the year I dropped the History. I called Sarah in Oxford and visited her a couple of times in her beautiful college and then in a town house she shared, with not too many stairs. It was easier for me to visit her, but she was improving and came to Birmingham once, where she seemed an anomaly, just not part of my life there.

I also called WorldMission on the number Noel had given me and spoke to a nice woman called Sally.

"You're a Christian organisation, aren't you?" I said, not disguising the accusation in my tone.

"Yes, we are," said Sally. "Our mission is based on the principles of Christian faith. But our volunteers are forbidden from evangelising in the field, unless someone asks. And they do ask."

"I'll only come if I can bring my friend," I said. "She walks with crutches and isn't a Christian."

I got the forms to fill out and that's how Sarah and I started, with an internship of about thirty of us that long first summer holiday, doing mainly backline logistics stuff in Ethiopia. I think they took Sarah because she'd already developed a bit of a reputation with the UN network through the Refugee Studies Centre at Oxford. Anyway, she spoke to Sally herself and her forms looked bloody good.

We were always pros from the start, Sarah and me. No bleeding hearts. No charity. No celebrities. Those were the rules. It was a good bunch, that first gig. I remember on the way back coming across a load of Live Aid trucks up to their axles in sand, remnants of "Do They Know It's Christmas?", which seemed a very long way away to the north and west. Wrong supplies, wrong place. A load of us started rocking with our muslin scarves held high between our hands, in a pastiche not just of the song but of the whole rock-festival philanthropy sketch.

"Feed our eee-gos," we sang happily. "Let them know we're rich and famous . . ."

The drivers smiled behind their aviator shades. The anthem had been everywhere, but not in the desert.

I think Sarah and I knew that we became aidies because we had to. There was no choice. We used to tell people we did it for a laugh and watch their faces freeze. And when we cried, we cried together, but never emotionally, more as catharsis. I certainly started to feel that I was at home out there and that it was Britain that felt foreign when I got back.

When I came back that first time, I gave talks to the church and argued some more with Father Trevor about why Samaritans were thought to be bad and who exactly our wealth enriched. I fell in with a campaign for women's ordination. I was aware that I was being gently held up by the congregation. No, offered up.

So it was natural to do a post-grad course to be a deacon. I liked that there had never been such a word in Greek as "deaconess" in the early Church. Just deacons. Men and women. And when women were ordained priests in the Church of England, I was sent to a ghastly selection conference for that too.

First, there were a load of interviews with the Diocesan Director of Ordinands. He was a thin man with a ponytail who asked me why I thought I wanted to be ordained into the priesthood of the Church of England. I said I wasn't sure I wanted to be, but I thought I was called to be. That seemed to be the right answer.

I was never very sure what a vocation felt like. It was a kind of giving in to drift. Perhaps the truth was that I'd never felt a sense of calling, though of course I didn't give that impression at my examination in Ely, the three days when I had to jump through the spiritual hoops that were held obligingly in front of me by earnest but actually quite uninterested church people, whose job it was to recommend ordinands for priestly training.

There had been underfed men and over-fat women who had spoken of their moments of epiphany in college chapels or on Derbyshire ridges, or of an incessant celestial nagging that had told them that this single-storey motel in East Anglia that smelt of stale pastry was "where God wants me to be".

I knew none of that. All I knew was that I'd spent more time in famine zones than most people of my age. Sarah and I had been to east Africa four times by then, Sudan as well as Ethiopia, and had graduated from being backline flunkies to distribution and medical support at the sharp end, leaving WorldMission behind us as Sarah became more involved with UNHCR – the United Nations High Commissioner for Refugees.

The politics that caused the suffering we witnessed out there made us both mad. A faith in something bigger helped me with that, but Sarah didn't need it. I may not have bothered to identify it much at the time – too busy, I suppose – but I needed the one simple voice that spoke of a hope of freedom and the ludicrous notion that the loose components of a wasted human being in my arms in the scrub, the genderless child who had already vacated its place in the human order to become meat for flies, was as worthy of the existence it was being denied as the hordes outside our coffee-shop windows in London, as entitled to the stroke of the back of its mother's fingers as them, as much of an agent of world change as the banks and the law firms and the churches.

Anyway, I constructed a case for my ordained ministry from that insight. I made one of my male examiners weep, while I stayed resolutely dry-eyed. He revolted me. How dare you cry over the starving, you worm, you pathetic sentimentalist, sitting in an over-heated meeting room on the outskirts of a provincial cathedral town. I bet you give your children's clothes to Oxfam and make up a shoe box of bewildering northern-hemispherical gifts at your parish Cristingle service and then go and play six-a-side with the youths that you wish you were still among, preparing them for the secular lives that you didn't dare to try. Instead, thin man in casual wear, you sit in front of me in a chair for old folks while indulging your feminine side, reaching for the carton of tissues that were meant for me, as I spare you no morbid detail of how a child under five in southern Sudan could not even know that they had a right to life.

I was asked again about why I thought priesthood was for me by a woman examiner who seemed more preoccupied with whether the male applicants were gay. This time I said: "Because I've touched the hem of his cloak and I'm healed." Which I thought, at the time, was true. And maybe it was.

Anyway, it worked. They recommended me for training.

I used that examiner to get what I wanted, of course, to be a signed-up rep of the only truly durable world movement in history that was available to a Western white woman, founded by a strange figure who had stood by these nameless and worthless creatures and told them they were whole human beings. They presumed I loved Jesus of Nazareth, as they signed my paperwork for my Diocesan Director of Ordinands. But I was prepared to use Him too – though, of course, we are required to talk about that the other way around – by standing in his number against the pointless little games played out by political scientists and bankers in bunkers and marketing men and aid workers and moist little volunteers in easy chairs in malodorous conference centres, all of whom in their busy little ways starve babies to death, or at least let them die.

And so I had a career. I was employed by the Church of England, but my ministry was in foreign aid. I became something of a poster girl, I suppose, for women priests without a proper job. And I liked that too. It was who I was and who I still am.

Years later, Sarah and I met in one of the City chaps' wine bars in Paternoster Square, dark inside, but pleasant enough outside under the awning when it wasn't too cold, close to one of the autumn's first-lit gas burners. She was scooping hot Camembert on to toasted focaccia while I toyed with an anchovy salad.

We'd laughed about how we'd graduated from the Kentish Town greasy-spoon we used at the agency to a place that sold Petit Chablis for twenty-three quid, which, to be fair, only Sarah could afford.

I remember watching as she looked at her prematurely wrinkled fingers and swollen knuckles. Her nails were good, I noticed, not dirty and cracked as they'd been when she'd been in the field.

I'd just asked her a difficult question. If the Nobel-aspirant Russian oligarch she was working for now was so keen on finding a solution to Palestine, why was he using American dollars?

"It's just the international currency."

"How many of them?"

She looked at me for emphasis. "About a billion."

It was the first time I thought she might like money and it shamed me.

"Is that a thousand million or a million million?"

"Does it matter?"

She popped a lump of bread and molten cheese in her mouth and sucked her finger. We were girls again and it was fun.

"I don't do money, Sar, you know that," I said. "It sounds like a job for suits. It'll be one of those ghastly gigs with name badges. Davos with matzoh balls."

"It needs to be done."

"Does it? I mean, does it really? What difference can money make when people hate each other?"

"They can hate each other in more comfort. They can hate each other as social equals. Money makes people forget they hate each other anyway. They can despise each other's garden furniture instead."

"So your man's an economic engineer."

I looked out across the dazzling lake of new paving stones towards the Temple Gate.

"Engineering's part of it."

"I think we want people to stay poor. Keeps us in a job."

"The Church or Aid?" asked Sarah. She was always so easy to talk to. "The poor are always with us."

There was a pause as she tore off some softer bread from the basket and wiped her bowl with it. A young Baltic waiter came and poured more wine.

"I really want you to come to Jerusalem, Nat," she said. "We get to be peace envoys. With the Centre's money. And I'll be there. What's not to like?"

I was silent, as if considering it.

"Ade and I are finished," I said. She was looking at me and

chewing at half speed, so I paused for dramatic effect. "I mean Adrian."

And we laughed out the tension of the moment.

"He bonked who?" she asked, after I'd given her the highlights.

"I don't know. Someone from the office."

"Don't you want to know?"

"What difference would it make?"

"Then it's settled."

"What is?"

"You have to come to Jerusalem. An away-break to save the world."

When I think of my own investment of trust and self-deception in my marriage, I often recall Sarah and her dark epiphany back at school, that she was physically disabled and despised for it, which marked the end of the denial of her little truth. In my case, I pretended my life with Adrian was something that a little honesty would have immediately shown that it wasn't.

Adrian had been part of a tribe too. He was part of a warrior class set against world poverty and deprivation, coordinating and sometimes leading a private army of the irrational from the proud Western democracies to attack the wicked insurgencies of famine and drought in our former colonies. We were underpaid mercenaries, I know now, not so much working towards heavenly reward but for our daily bread. We were offending a system that depended for its riches on the desolation of Africa. We were a disruption to the natural order – as Sarah was – and I came to depend on Adrian's living witness to our alternatives.

None of this gang culture meant anything, of course. But while it lasted I was happy to believe that I was part of the gang, that it contained me. Actually, my commitment was built on contempt, just as those schoolgirls' was, but I'd never have admitted that so long as I was captivated by the power I exercised over Adrian's relative inferiority.

When I caught Adrian bonking his assistant director of probation – on the job, as I believe the boys call it – I was surprised by two of my reactions. First, I recoiled from the scene not in horror or hurt, but – now get this – because I felt I had intruded on their privacy. It was allegedly my house, our home, but my instinctive reaction was that I had violated their intimate space. I've dwelt on that feeling since, even cherished it.

The curtains in the big front drawing room were closed. Nothing unusual in that. Adrian would have been watching some dismal sports channel into the small hours and may have gone up to bed at about two, with a glass of skimmed milk, and then left for work, after a run, without touching this front room, an empty can at the foot of the sofa like an abandoned sentry box. So it was in that familiar morning half-light that I saw the two figures through the hallway arch, struggling out from behind the sofa. I seem to recall that my first thought was that we had repairmen, then rejected that, since the curtains were drawn. Then burglars, but as my eyes adjusted and I held the front door to facilitate an escape, it was clear she had a white, scalloped blouse, open with bra in place, and was scrabbling for the discarded shrink-wrap of tights and tangled pants. He was lurching out on the opposite side, rather comically yanking up the charity-shop trousers I'd given him for his birthday.

Her touching desperation to retrieve her underwear left her leaning over the back of the sofa, and it was clear, in that forensic snapshot, that this was how their sex act was being performed. It didn't take long for me to assess the scene – what, four to eight seconds? – but I know now, knew then, that it wasn't revulsion and hurt that made me spurn this vision and propelled me to the other side of my own front door and into the cobbled enclave outside. And maybe I'm even wrong too about their privacy, maybe it wasn't my good manners, a well-bred sense that I was witness to an intimacy that was not my own. Perhaps it was the simple pathos of the event, the pantomime routine, a silent movie, or perhaps the mannered attempts of a French-farce pair of lovers to retain dignity through reclaimed clothing. No, it was pity that drove me away, like turning away from a humiliated child.

I was surprised also at the lack of shock. I suppose it would have been right to have been shocked. But, walking back purposefully to St Paul's, I found I was smiling at my liberation, for I knew in that moment that my life was changing into a journey without Adrian in it. He had, strangely and unintentionally, taken the initiative himself and our life together which had started and, in a way, ended in adventure, with a protracted period of mundanity in the middle, was drawing to its close. Our love-making had grown routine, but in truth had always been indolent, invariably in bed once we had acquired one, as though sex was something for the poorly. 'Sex' makes it sound hot and dirty and that hardly works if it's a duty performed, a grunting act of prone service, a household chore that we shared like a modern couple should. Little wonder that they call it missionary; I might as well have been offering him sanitation and scripture.

Our life as a couple had started in excitement, but that was all about the work we did. We sparked off on saving the world, not on

each other. Any attempts on either part at an awakening of spontaneous passion, in a hotel bathroom attached to a conference centre
where we weren't staying over, say, or in a warm gazebo on a summer's evening at a diocesan retreat, had left him feeling vulnerable
and me bored, tugging on the short length of rope that was our
marriage.

Yet, here he had been, in his shirt tails, taking a dumpy colleague with hip cellulite – I don't know if she was really the deputy
director of probation, I made that up – doggy-style on our soft
furnishings. So, surprised, yes, but not shocked. It occurred to me,
astonishingly, that it must have been his idea. I made for a chain
coffee shop in Paternoster Square, which I knew staff didn't use
because there had once been a dispute over the authenticity of its
Fairtrade coffee. I thought of sitting outside and smoking, but
decided against it in case I was spotted by passers-by and I didn't
want to engage just now.

I'd returned a day early from a conference in Cambridge on
women's ministry in Muslim countries, which we'd abandoned
when the final keynote speaker had phoned in sick, and I'd jumped
a fast train and made straight to the house. No one knew that I was
here. Except, now, Adrian and his tea lady, or whoever she was. I
sat for about half an hour, drank a cappuccino with an extra shot
and pretended to read the paper I'd had on the train, to attract no
attention.

It wasn't long after eleven when I'd arrived at the house. Adrian
sometimes took an early lunch to go to the municipal gym when it
was less crowded, but this was mid-morning, for goodness' sake. I
guessed that they'd both slid out for their tryst, perhaps attending
a cancelled work meeting somewhere. That and being partially

clothed in the sitting room meant that she hadn't been an overnight guest. Adrian wouldn't be leaving me, I knew that. That would involve too much initiative. They used the house because they were too poor or mean to use a hotel. She was either married or lived too far away, or both, though that was of little real concern to me. So what was of concern to me?

I resolved, after staring listlessly at the weather forecast in the back of the newspaper, that I wasn't going to throw him out, at least not immediately. It was too high-maintenance an option, would mean transfer of belongings, too much talking, and I had a shedload of work in submissions to General Synod on provision for those opposed to women bishops, which already had to be compressed by the conference I'd just co-organised. In those days, I thought that was important. On such prosaic considerations were my life decisions made back then.

So I suppose I decided to forgive him. Or tolerate him, which is pretty far from forgiveness. But we're in the forgiveness business, Christians. Given all that unfolded subsequently, this was Jonah bound on a calm sea for Jaffa before being flung into the belly of the whale.

I met Adrian in the crypt cafe of the cathedral early that evening. He was largely silent as I knew he would be. He had the grace not to offer excuse or apology. He sat, staring up the cavern of mausoleums towards the military dead, and said at one point: "I don't know what's going on. I never wanted any of this."

I let the ambiguity of that hang in the musty air. Then told him we'd live separately in the house for a while. It was a big house. We'd look at each other from a bit of a distance and see what was left of us to salvage. It was an aggressive version of giving each other some room, which was the kind of expression we were taught in priestly training.

"I don't know what happened to us," he said.

"We hung out and got married," I replied.

He swung aside in his seat. Then he stood and slowly walked out, giving me time to catch him up, which I didn't.

Adrian's not the sort of man women notice, but he had a quiet commitment that I took for strength when we worked in our overseas aid outfit in Kentish Town. The regular cast passed through. Earnest young women making a difference, young men with shaven heads ameliorating the plight of the proletariat, distracted girls filling in before marriage; our generation's spare parts finding no other purpose for themselves in the nation's economy.

We pitched ourselves as The Fed, a charity started a decade or so earlier by Jake Sorresen, one of those self-starting hipsters with a thirst that couldn't be sated on peace and love. He was alpha-male meets folkie, Surrey goes to Lindisfarne, long and languid, loose and smiley, hair like metal wool tied behind a monkish pate, his clean-shaven, weather-beaten face set against the power-beards of the big foreign-aid charities, with their centralised executives and bibbed chuggers outside the Tube stations.

His was a flat organisation, a federation of autonomous cells in Britain and the US, which commanded their own relief missions, the only resource from central office being intelligence. Famine or floods, we were quick. Jake's office would call for resource and like a mini-cab firm putting out a fare, a team of two or three could be in the field within thirty-six hours. These pathfinders would assess and advise, calling down the right response, very often from the big agencies. Yes, it was exciting.

Sarah Curse passed through. She was by then working properly for UNHCR and was seconded to the Russia Centre in Cambridge. She came to us on a kind of internship for three months, but really it was to see whether we were good enough for UNHCR recognition. On the day she arrived, she waved her stick – just one stick now – across the office at me and said she'd heard I worked there.

"What does the Russia Centre actually do?" I asked her in the Italian coffee shop we took to using in Fortess Road, a Formica anachronism with big glass pouring jars of sugar.

She shrugged. "It funds Middle East projects mainly. Infrastructure projects commercially. But philanthropy too. Trying to support a two-state solution."

"Right," I said, flopping back in undergraduate, post-ironic style. "Not money-laundering or trading American passports then."

"I don't think so. Sergei Sarapov is – or was – close to Yeltsin, but he's one of the good guys. His wife was killed in a gangster hit in Moscow and he lives in Vienna now. It's in Cambridge, I think, because that's where his daughter went to uni."

"The charidee oligarch," I said, determined not to buy it. "I must send him a begging letter."

"Stop it," she said with a quick smile that showed her neat teeth. "Whatever it takes. That's my view."

"Yeah, whatever it takes." I looked out of the window at the grey people.

Sarah sat next to Adrian in the office, but they never talked much. She spent most of her time on a laptop and directed questions at Jake or me. I'd sit on the edge of her desk sometimes and triangulate between her and Adrian. I think he was intimidated by her easy intellect.

Adrian had worked there for a couple of years before I arrived. I must try to look at him objectively at that time. I suppose he grew on my younger taste buds because he was purposeful, without seeming to impress his purpose on those about him. Dear God, is that the best I can do for him now? Well, sorry, looking at him dispassionately is exactly that – perhaps there never was any passion.

He would fill his day effortlessly, just doing one thing after another with the same paced intensity, without apparently noticing that he was doing it. He never seemed to whine about his rent like the rest of us; or what to eat, his lost travel card, the cold when the office heating failed. He was just relentlessly Adrian. We called him Ade, and inevitably Foreign Ade and Relief Ade, even Christian Ade when I discovered he went to church, though there was precious little evidence that faith was his motivation, other than what he did for those luckless enough to be born into the worst cesspits of the world. He didn't really notice money, but he would give a fiver he couldn't afford to rival causes if he thought it would buy someone a clean drink.

I can probably pin our beginning to a bright and sharp September evening, sitting out on the decking beside the return of the terraced house that was the London office, after fixing a supply of maize to Addis Ababa, I think, and drinking cider from cans. He had finished his and was thumb-tipping the ash from his cigarette into the empty. It had been a highly charged day, when the hours hung on to what we were doing. He'd have gone on with the phone calls into the night and beyond. But he'd cracked it by late afternoon – I'd found a supplier in Notts and Ade had persuaded them to deliver without VAT if he provided the transport, which we could, and the task had blown away into a rolling, grey London sky like bonfire smoke. We could stop, suddenly.

It was just the two of us in the back room. I ran to get cigarettes and cider from the Bangla corner shop and we sat out the back in our self-righteous hiatus. In other circumstances, it could have been post-coital.

I said something inane like, "Why do we do it?"

He had replied in the first person: "I have to. There's no option. There's a war on."

After all that came later on, and the pathetic creature into which he evolved, it's hard to imagine him as I saw him then. It's like looking at old photos of yourself in implausible fashions; you can't feel the body under the clothes any more. But Adrian was like a young man who had failed to get commissioned in the armed forces in a great war, perhaps through colour blindness, or a con-genital abnormality, or perhaps because he had some great gift for martial intelligence, and so he was expiating his guilt in some brightly lit bunker on the Home Front, punishing himself with one brief after another, birching himself with administration so that some fewer of his comrades might die in the field. Pale and under-nourished by sunlight, his attitude remained that of the front-line combatant. His life was forfeit, but as long as he had it he would commit small acts of defiance in the face of the unseen enemy and, so long as his friends did the same, by tiny increments we would one day prevail.

Ade was at war with poverty, with disease and dispossession, marshalling weapons at our disposal against them, so that those crushed under the oppression of hunger, dysentery, malaria and those random acts of Ade's God – the hurricane, the earthquake, the flood – might be liberated.

Our joint enterprise in southern Sudan was yet to come. But on the splintered decking of NW5, by a damp, untended ivy trellis, with the taste of dry cider lining my mouth and the sun setting on my first realisation that there was a war on and that he was a warrior in its theatre, I suppose I thought I fell in love with Adrian.

3

There is a final moment, I think, when the old life ended and the new began. Through a glass darkly, I remember. Me, standing in the bathroom shower, the time directly before my exile. There's a chasm between me then and now and, if I look down dimly into its depths, I can see the shadows of people and acts that make me scream silently, as in a dream, numb to virtue and stripped of any capacity even to feel guilt. Guilt requires some small measure of responsibility and I never asked to be here, on this side of the bottomless pit.

It's funny, because a detail of the start of that day is very vivid, as when the victims of a disaster, like an air crash or the outbreak of war, recall the tiny, prosaic images just before it happens. As when you look away from a running child and its image is frozen for an instant on the mind's photographic plate. Adrian had said that the computer had crashed, or the broadband line had gone down, or something. I was in the shower, the steam of the day's first hot water rising.

"Did you use it last night?" Adrian was shouting through bubbled glass, his head and the collar of a pink shirt presented in large blobs, as in a Derain painting.

I remember watching him from my steaming geyser. I had one

foot on the side of the bath, and had just dragged a razor deliciously up the side of my calf. I recall this detail, because it was my razor; I had bought it at a new little convenience store on Ludgate Hill. I had bought it because Adrian had complained that I was always using his. He had thrown his razor away, saying he didn't need it because he was going to grow a beard now. I recall thinking that it was all about stopping me using his frigging razor. That's the way I thought of him then, but we pottered along.

"What?" I called back with an irritable edge.

I had heard him perfectly well. But I looked at him through the panel of mottled glass. His forehead was close to the door, inclined so that the stretch of his balding pate was exaggerated, the bubbles of the glass picking up the line of his recently cropped, greying hair above his ear. His dark eyes, made more beady by the new austerity of the top of his head, were disassembled like molecular diagrams. I could recognise from his posture that he was pushing his lower lip together into a crease with the fingers of his right hand, a habit that was used to indicate both his self-control and irritation.

"The computer won't work. I can't log on. It says my user name is invalid."

He stressed the first syllable of invalid, to make it sound like a sick person.

"Have you tried rebooting it?"

This exchange continued in the liturgy of a million middle-class households, more usually, I imagined, between parents and children. I told him to use my laptop if he just needed to look at emails. The old PC on this first floor, bought way back from my theological college during an IT upgrade, had become his by custom and practice, and he tended to tuck himself away up in what was now evidently his study, reading council papers without interruption. The wild man. He always had to start again if he was interrupted, he said.

"I wish you wouldn't use it."

This was about territory, not internet access.

"I didn't," I replied, calmly now, in our customary rhythm of de-escalation.

"Well, somebody did," he was saying as he turned away and disappeared into the invisible world a foot from the door.

"I expect it was the Archbishop of Uganda, looking for homos in the diocese," I murmured to my shin.

I remember this and other little conversations because this arid domestic trivia, from which any nourishment had been sucked, was to be the last of the normal that Adrian and I really had.

I dried, dressed and made for the cathedral, a hop and a jump away. As I left the house, two figures stood just across the cobbles from my front door. One was familiar, hands thrust deep into a navy donkey jacket, a grey beanie pulled over his ears, stamping his feet though it was far from cold. The other was new, pale and younger with a black beard, maybe Turkish, two cameras slung from his shoulders, one of which he now focused on me.

"Hi, Tony," I said, walking up to them, ignoring the whir of the camera's motor-drive. "What's up?"

"Want to talk about Sudan, Nat?"

I let my shoulders drop wearily and turned my head to express scepticism. "What about Sudan?"

"Oh, y'know, Nat. Nicked any Aussie trucks lately?"

I sighed a laugh. "You know I can't."

Tony was the most persistent of the press pack that had pursued me after the last Sudan trip. He was freelance, but had made me his project for some reason, turning up in Amen Court periodically to ask the same questions. I'd made him tea and brought him sandwiches when public interest in me had meant that he staked me out most days and much of the evenings, but I never invited him in. There was a protocol to be observed.

"Why the snapper?" I indicated his new colleague, who was examining a shot of me on the back of his camera.

"This is Mirac," said Tony, and Mirac grinned and raised his weapon again.

"I said why, not who."

"They say you could be up for a big job. One of the first women's bishoprics or something."

"And a paper's paid for a photographer? Really?"

"He's agency and a mate. Well, he owes me a favour. Y'know, if I got the exclusive interview with new Bishop Natalie, I'd have the pics too."

"Oh, come on, Tony, you're having me on," and I laughed. "That'll be ages off yet. It wouldn't be a scoop. It would be a guess."

"But have they talked to you about a bishopric? I mean, they couldn't, could they, until the old Sudan job was cleared up?"

"I don't know," I said.

"What does that mean?" Irritation had crept into Tony's voice.

"It means I don't know anything. I haven't heard anything. And you shouldn't believe everything you hear in the newspapers. I'm late." And I waved a hand airily over my shoulder.

Off past the hideous new Paternoster Vents, a stainless-steel installation which wafts smells from some kind of substation through what are meant to look like angel wings, to the Chapter House. This place was the purpose of my existence at the time; both an escape from and a justification for the home with Adrian.

From behind the heavy door, when I'd shouldered it aside, Jay said, "Morning, Natalie. They're upstairs today – you're not quite late yet."

Jay liked me, I knew. She was comely, wide-faced, big glasses, a colourful wrap thrown across her right shoulder, both shawl and wearer from Nigeria. I dropped the almond croissant that I brought her in a paper bag on to the desk. "Sorry about the greasy bag," I said, but she waved me away with a laugh.

Climbing the three flights of formal stairs was nasty, their steps shallow in pitch and long in the tread, built for cassocks, making them difficult to skip up. Coffee and tea at the top, in large white china pots, unlike the plastic screw-top Thermoses known to every parish in the land, next to plates of khaki biscuits, with nauseating fillings. I took a coffee, black, and pressed the saucer into the palm free of paperwork. I liked Jay's coffee and I miss it.

I entered the big state room as I always did, pretending to have difficulty managing both coffee and papers. This little deceit saved me having to look at the assembled men for a moment. There were a couple of "Ah, Natalie" greetings, of the bouncy-syllable variety to demonstrate faux welcome, and one "Hey, Nat" from someone who wanted to be my right-on friend.

You don't need to know who these people are – nobody does – but there was Dean (never "the Dean"), in the middle and silhou-etted in the light of one of the three long sash windows that face the cathedral. He was between the Canon Precentor, a better

41

harpist than administrator, and Dean's secretary, jolly and over-weight. On my left, against the ridiculous columned fireplace and under a huge, dark painting of an early Victorian cleric whom no one could be bothered to remember, were the tall and beaky Canon Treasurer and Hugh, our Canon Pastor and the only one, including me, in an open-necked shirt without a jacket. The legal secretary was sorting papers further down the table.

All were men and they mostly wore the full-wrap acetate clerical collar, except the secretaries, the only laypeople present. Dean wore his crushed silk vestock and starched linen collar, somewhat presumptuously with a large pectoral cross, made of nails.

"Always those nearest who are last to arrive," said Dean, grinning but not kindly.

"Actually, Hugh lives closer," I said, wincing into the light from the window.

Hugo, Hugh for short, Huge to me, was my neighbour in Ave Maria Court, the small enclave of house-for-duty Georgian homes, and one door closer to Paternoster Square, like it mattered.

The Chapter House had survived the Blitz and had dowager-duchess status among the local postmodern architecture. It sat incongruously next to Temple Bar, Fleet Street's ancient gate to the City of London, which had been rescued from ivy and nettles in the park of some stately home and dropped like a last-minute conversation piece into the redesign. It fitted in only in so far as it was a folly.

I sat at the table, facing the windows and beyond them the north walls of the cathedral, as the meeting lurched along between self-interest and exhibitionism. These meetings were easy enough to play. Just stay in touch, drifting a little off the tide of the conversations, offer my own agenda items and make about three considered interventions into those of others. Job done. I stared out through the long windows, as though considering the issues of budgeting for art shows in the north transept, or the policy on charging tourists who said they wanted to access the cathedral to pray, but really considering the uselessness of these two houses: the home I shared a few hundred yards away with a man who couldn't manage his own email and this politburo of ecclesiastical bureaucracy.

The great walls of the cathedral rose terrifyingly outside, so large they looked closer than they were. It was right that they had put the old Temple Bar next to it – this was our Temple in the old scriptural sense, the Temple at Jerusalem, the old order, and no number of new committees could expunge its corruption.

I imagined it as a great steam liner in port, we in some sort of stevedores' office on the jetty. I had heard somewhere that Christopher Wren had deliberately built the edifice from every bit of its entire base upwards, like a ship raised from the keel, to avoid the king suddenly ordering something smaller to save money. Then I imagined the great ship sway in some remote ocean, pitching slowly and irresistibly in the swell, then quite still in a glassy sea, perhaps the north Atlantic in April, a huge foundering metaphor for the Church of England.

As I watched from the Chapter House, my cathedral-liner began to settle at its east end, its bow out of sight from me, but the horizontal lines of its ancient architecture imperceptibly tipping in that direction and then occasionally taking a more definite lurch as a bulkhead in its vast crypt gave way. Its great west-end stern began to rise from the water and the tourists who had sought sanctuary there began to drop, screaming, into St Paul's Graveyard. Finally, the great vessel started to swing to the perpendicular, the proud dome breaking free and crashing into the City offices of Cheapside. It stood there a moment, its lights extinguished, then shuddered and roared as it began its inexorable plunge into the depths of the ground, leaving a chaos of flotsam on the surface, smashed choir stalls, events leaflets, regimental flags and a Pre-Raphaelite painting, bobbing on the vacated surface of the City of London, as the screams died away.

Well, shall we leave it there.

"Well, shall we leave it there?"

Dean was wrapping up. Chairs were pushed back.

"Natalie, would you spare a moment," he said down the table.

I nodded and smiled.

"Just give me five minutes and then come through." And he glided out, the trunk of his body still, as if on castors.

We called the Dean of St Paul's "Dean". That may seem obvious, but the most senior cleric of a cathedral is usually only called that, without the definite article, to his or her face: "Yes, Dean, the regimental flags in the transept will be laundered ahead of the Lord Mayor's choral evensong." Elsewhere it would be "The Dean wants the bloody flags washed."

But we called ours "Dean", rather than "the Dean", behind his back too. Like it was his name. Everyone knew intuitively that you couldn't think of a name demographically more inappropriate for the spectacularly patrician Rt Rev'd Dr Algernon Crowhurst. Algy was Winchester and Oxford; Dean was a plumber's mate.

If you're going over to the dark side, you have to visit Dean. He is not lightened in any part of himself by popular culture. I imagine his evenings are accompanied only by the rhythm of a marbled mantelpiece clock and a carefully chosen operetta on the wireless (never the radio). He would read papers that contained Latin extemporisations, without translations. Forty years ago, he'd have smoked a pipe confidently, a straight one, held proudly level by a square jaw.

He reminded me of a drawing of a clergyman I'd seen in the vintage catalogue of the clergy outfitters in Westminster, which, like Dean, was on life's slow train, stopping at all stations. I had been collecting my cathedral vestments, and the quietly clipped lady sales assistant had brought out the museum file of old catalogues, the pages now in plastic sachets for protection. There was an ink sketch of a clerical figure – male, of course – in a "short summer cassock, with breeches and stockings". The illustration was probably from the 1930s.

I could imagine Dean Crowhurst wearing breeches and stockings, and not just for private recreational purposes. He was tall with deep-set eyes and lean and sunken cheeks, but not unhealthy; a metabolism that was apparently unchallenged by intake. He ate, but only for fuel. He could only be attractive to a woman without natural juices. So that would be most female Church of England congregants then.

"Come in, Natalie," he said, bending his abnormally long frame to sweep some self-satisfied City glossies off the low round table next to a faded moss-green sofa. "Coffee?"

Of course he'd have a pot ready. He'd have had a fresh pot sent up at exactly the right time. Two cups, I noted. We were on our own. Some effortless pleasantries out of the way, Dean placed his elbows on the arms of his cheap winged chair and rested his fingers together like a spider on a mirror. He started with his ritual update on the legal action against me for nicking a truck in a famine zone, which had been dragging on for years.

"I hear that the Sudan business may at last be coming to a satisfactory conclusion," he said. "I'm glad of that. As you know, I've always been frustrated that I can't assist. But no doubt the Bishop knows best. I can only hope the lawyers have supported him well enough. He will speak to you, and I gather that Lambeth Palace wants to be in at the kill."

Dean had always smarted that the Diocese had insisted on running my case rather than the Chapter, which had a cosy concord with the City's law firms.

"If that's the case, then it may be that we can finally close this quasi-criminal file of yours and you can prevail as a free clergy-woman without a stain on your escutcheon. I have to say that I've always held that a disciplinary procedure for you would have been quite inappropriate, given the public interest. I'm hoping that you'll have come out of it rather well."

"If that's the case, I'll be glad it's over too, Dean," I said. "Thank you."

"Somebody said the other day that your file had been retitled GTA? I didn't follow."

"*Grand Theft Auto*," I said. "It's a computer game."

"Indeed," he said. "How charmingly informal." And he shifted slightly in his chair to indicate a change of subject. "I thought today we'd just touch on the progress of women bishops at General Synod," he continued, his lower lip rising like a fender.

So here we bloody go, I thought. What I hadn't told Tony on my doorstep that morning was that some muppet on a Sunday newspaper had been in touch to ask if I would be included in a wildly speculative round-up of the likely candidates to be the first bishop without men's bits. I'd learned that you didn't talk to journalists about other journalists, or there'd be a feeding frenzy. But she'd suggested I was the "wild card", given what Dean called the Sudan business.

"I'm happy where I am," I'd said to that reporter, but I was aware that was a churchy reply. It's meant to imply that the nature of religious vocation doesn't have the same structural aspirations as secular life. That might have been true in my case, but generally it's nonsense. The upper reaches of the Church of England are a hotbed of morose entitlement, as venal as any commercial body.

"If parliamentary time can be found towards the end of this session," Dean was intoning, "we could plausibly see the first female names on shortlists by spring next year. Normal rules of meritocracy will apply, but the CNC may well be anxious to ensure that, in an environment of recruitment that isn't exactly, ahem . . ." – he was doing what he imagined was roguish theatricality – ". . . accustomed to executive search in this quarter of the Church's human resource, it would want to be sure that likely candidates were being properly identified. And . . ." – pause for imaginary effect – ". . . were likely to accept the sacrament of consecration."

The Crown Nominations Commission, the office that forwards names of likely bishops to the prime minister and ultimately to the monarch, makes a Freemasons' Lodge look like a drop-in centre. It wears its secrecy like fetish gear and gets off on the confidentiality of its deliberations. I wondered who Dean knew on it. I didn't really know where he stood on the issue of women bishops. I imagined he played by the book, with a dollop of disdain. General

Synod, the Church's parliament made up of houses of bishops, clergy and laity, had voted decisively for removing the legal obstacles for women, already ordained priests, to be made bishops. There was an irresistible rationale to that, even among most traditionalists and the predominantly male-gay Anglo-Catholic wing, to which Dean belonged, who nevertheless grew weepy over the theology of fatherhood.

In the way of the glacial Church, it had taken several years and would take several more of self-flagellation and hand-wringing about how to make provision for these lachrymose bachelors, but for now the legislature looked like it really might put a ladies' lav in the House of Bishops. I smiled at Dean with practised humility and pleasantly enough, I thought.

He tucked his chin behind his collar and continued.

"I think I can anticipate where you are on this and, of course, in many important respects, we shouldn't be treating women candidates for episcopacy any differently from the male of the species."

"Differently?" I asked, cocking slightly to the right. I can do coquettish. Men like Dean liked it even – especially – if they were gay.

"Well," his hands opened, "there is at least meant to be some element of surprise in the approach from the CNC. But I thought it was only fair on you that I ask."

I paused for a beat or two, looking at the carpet, pretending to choose my words.

"I have no desire to be a bishop," I said evenly. "And I don't suppose there is much desire among the entire company of the Kingdom of Heaven for me to be a bishop. More to the point, you won't want a bishop with damn near a criminal conviction for foreign-aid food theft and lorry hijacking."

"As I say, the general feeling is that that could be something of a public relations triumph."

"I'm happy where I am," I said. "Maybe some parish ministry is called for. But I'm not a symbol of unity. Or an administrator."

"There's a prophetic tradition in the English episcopacy too," he said calmly. He was talking someone else's book.

"Or a leader of men, then," I added.

I let the phrase hang in the air. I'd enjoyed the reference to the Kingdom and now I knew I'd brought it bang down to earth. But elegantly, as Dean would appreciate. The corner of his mouth was raised, in the semblance of a quizzical smile.

"I understand that. But, in any event," he too paused for a beat, "they have asked me to sound you out." Well, I never, Dean, good job you pointed that out as my silly, ditzy brain may not have grasped it. "I think they're very keen, you know."

"Is there to be a lavender list?" I asked, doing the cocked head thing again.

"Oh, I don't think there'd be anything so formal." He leaned forward in his chair and shot his cuffs. I realised now we were being collegial. Men had done this stuff in senior common rooms and the tea rooms of parliament for generations, but it wasn't a body language in which I was fluent. "I think it's more a case of the House of Bishops being asked to get their ducks in a row, as it were."

I resisted the temptation to change the vowel in duck. So I confined myself to: "And if I look like a duck and quack like a duck . . ."

"You develop the metaphor with a self-deprecation I hadn't invited. But precisely."

Dean was smiling at me now in a manner that he must have imagined was kindly. I sensed he was enjoying this more than he had expected.

"Anyway, the Bishop would like to see you on the matter of the formation of your ministry too. I'm sure if you tell him what you've told me he'll be grateful."

His use of the word "formation" was interesting. It's what they talk about at theological colleges before ordination. But he turned conversation to my work at the cathedral and I understood his agenda for this encounter had been concluded.

Outside, I found Hugh in his small office on the first floor. It smelt caustically of lilies. In his most inquisitively camp way, he went straight for the debrief.

"Just some rubbish about whether I should ever want to be a bishop," I said, noting privately that I was playing Dean's confidentiality game. It was infectious. I needed quarantine.

I took a mouthful of tepid coffee from a mug whose rim was too thick and which was painted with a childish pig.

"And why are church coffee mugs so shite?"

I didn't want to talk about bishops. I liked Hugh and didn't want him to think I was on the make.

"It'll be the finest porcelain for you soon enough, your grace."

Hugh made to prod me with his ginger nut.

"Sod off, Huge. I really can't bear this whole sketch. It's either smarmy pussycats like Dean trying to do me a favour, or weepy, fat old faggots – like you – at Synod treating me like the Antichrist. Anyway, I don't have any parish experience."

"Sweets, don't be so naïve. They'll stick you in some gig in the City for six months – or St Mary's in Elizabeth Street is free."

He rolled his eyes roguishly. St Mary the Virgin was a very high church, where women knew their place.

"And purple would so suit you. Or maybe you could get away with mauve. Do it for me, darling. We've got to have a bishop that nobody minds men shagging for once. What happens next?"

"I'm seeing Londin next week, Tuesday."

Short for Londinium. Bishops style themselves in Latin.

Hugh made a sound and gesture like he'd taken an arrow to the breast. "They're so lining you up, dear. What time? Promise me you'll meet me straight afterwards in the Cock."

"Three."

"I have choir at four. Cock at five."

You didn't contradict Hugh when he was on a gossip roll. I remember smiling at how much I loved having him around. How I trusted him completely. I would instinctively not talk about this stuff to anyone else. Not Adrian. But Hugh was metabolically incapable of letting me down. It just wasn't in his make-up. I wished then that we could have worked together until we were two hundred years old. He would have kept me clean, if I'd let him. If I'd just hung out with Hugh, nothing would have happened. And not much comes of nothing.

4

I first met Toby from the Foreign Office some weeks before the Bishop introduced us, at one of those pointless debates about women bishops – pointless because the same people always came, not unlike Sunday church. We weren't telling anyone anything they didn't know already and everyone came with their irreversible ripe-soft or rock-hard opinions on the subject. All they want to do is to roll the stone over the tomb and let nothing out that might change them.

But you didn't dare fail to turn up, because that might hand the initiative to the other side. I'd thought of withdrawing from the women debate, because I'd already said what I wanted to say so many times that I recited it involuntarily, sometimes as I cycled or walked, rather like that schoolgirl hopscotch rhyme. It had become a chant, a plainsong, with such a familiarity that you could think of something else entirely as you said it. But I kept coming back because you can't leave the floor unguarded, and apparently we'd all invested too much time and effort in it.

As I took my place on the altar steps, the floor that night was depressingly full. It's my experience that the conservatives and traditionalists – or misogyniks as Hugh called them – got their act together far more effectively than the liberati. When we did a soft gig to supporters, preaching to the liberal choir as it were, all we got was a sprinkling of pale vegetarians in scarves and the odd librarian doing a masters in gender politics. By contrast, the righties always whip themselves in through social media like a Tea Party laced with coke.

We were in one of those City churches, which, whatever the show-off Blue Badge guides say, all look the same, even if they've been bombed. Dark and dull just about covers it. At this one, a war bomb had taken out the east end, which was replaced by a white marble altar in-the-round, with a vacuous sculpture as its reredos, a lump of rounded white stone supposedly "cradling" a smaller one. It looks like a lozenge mothering a jelly bean.

We sat in chairs just too small to be comfortable – a church leit-motif, that – on the steps in front of this smug installation, the early evening light illuminating the lazily squiggled coloured-glass windows. I was looking down the original nave, which was dark wood and smelt of death, laid out collegiate-style with those raked pews facing each other, across an aisle full of loose chairs facing forwards. These were now filled with the retired, carrying fussy bags full of papers, which evidently needed chairs too. For all his apparently innovative genius, Christopher Wren built places where today the bourgeoisie collated notes.

I was alongside Gerry, one of our male-priest camp followers, who wore a fixed grin and, with his forward-combed fringe that was almost a quiff, looked like a bit-part actor facing a first-night house for a post-performance discussion. To my far right (a gag I'd leveraged all too often at these events) was the opposition, Angela Vincent, the traditionalists' trophy wife, who knew her place in the Church and it wasn't in its sacraments, and David Buxted, from the oxymoronic Free in Faith, all high clerical collar and florid jowls.

Angela had a talent for crossing her pale-tighted legs seemingly two or three times at the calves, as if no man, or woman for that matter, this side of Phrygia was going to part them. She wore a crimson suit, in contempt of her tightly tied-back red hair, with a Seventies silk scarf. She looked like an air hostess. Between us was a celeb-columnist who had once been an editor of a newspaper, exuding a patronising bonhomie like a chat-show host. Two women on a panel of four and he still made it feel like tokenism.

Our introductory five-minute set pieces were OK, so far as they went. I was the first up to the lectern, with a thoroughly well-worked routine about our divisions being like tennis nets over which we tried to deliver polemical ace serves. Sometimes our shots were ruled out, sometimes faults were called, but the net was low enough to shake hands, even hug, at the end. And when the match was won, I hoped the victor might jump the net like they did in the old days to join the vanquished where they were, on the same side. It's a middle-class and twee routine – it's what's required – and it was a trite little spiel about Christian division and made it all sound like a game, which is how the Home Counties like it.

Angela went with the headship of the Church (St Paul and all other men) not being about seniority and Mary being the Mother of Heaven. Gerry talked about scripture being used down the ages to endorse a flat Earth and the slave trade. Finally, the jowls reddening to magenta over the high collar, we heard from Buxted about honouring God's creation of fatherhood and motherhood as enshrined in the teachings of the Church on the incarnation.

Then a short colloquium, during which our old hack got to

showcase his abilities as a charming and quick-witted anchorman for any broadcast producers who might have been present. As if. And the panel got to repeat several times what we had just said.

Then the floor had it. Surely Jesus chose twelve male disciples? If I'd had a pound for every time I'd heard that we'd go somewhere nice for dinner, sir. Surely women were persecuting their oppressors? Nothing wrong with women priests, but they should know their place. All the Catholics want is legal protection from offensive radicalism.

Angela was enjoying herself. "In many respects, Natalie and I are the same – we're both serving Jesus Christ in His Church."

Amazing how some can actually pronounce His with a capital H. I started to look forward very much indeed to a drink with Hugh with a capital H. I usually stay as silent as possible during this part of a debate. I hoped it might look Christ-like. What is truth, after all.

Then a fair and solid young man stood and took the roaming microphone.

"Toby Naismith from the Foreign and Commonwealth Office," he said.

None of the others had introduced themselves or their occupations. It went something like this: "I'd like to ask the Reverend Cross the degree to which she feels not so much persecuted but isolated and marginalised, like so many other Christians in even more uncomfortable parts of the world" – I liked that word "even" and remember it particularly – "I think, for example, of the Christians in what we might still call the Holy Lands, who to all intents and purposes are increasingly being denied the opportunity to worship. Does she feel that she is denied? Is women's ordained ministry like being a living stone?"

It was a reference to the First Letter of Peter, written to first-century persecuted Christians. Peter, stones, get it? The "living stones" are these days used as a metaphor for the churches in the Middle East, a dwindling physical link with the original witnesses to the risen Christ.

"It's a dramatic analogy," I said, playing for time.

Then new, fresh words came to me, expressions I hadn't used before.

"We're all the warp and weft of faith, the fabric of the Church. But some, by gender, are denied connection with apostolic mission and that's a direct denial of access to Christ's ministry. Like being given a different part of a church to sit in. Our web is severed from the loom. Is that what you mean?"

It was a neat scriptural shot to his baseline. But he was still on his feet.

"Are you saying that your bones are dry – your thread of life is snapped?"

Some of the grey heads turned to look at him now. But he was smiling and his head was inclined quizzically and courteously towards me.

The chair-hack wasn't about to be out-smartarsed.

"Are you quite all right? Sounds like osteoporosis," he said and some of his audience laughed as if along for a cruise-controlled ride.

"It's Ezekiel," I said evenly. They were all still listening and I was surprised. "It's true. Women's priesthood in the Church of England does feel like a kind of Babylonian exile."

This brought a derisive snort from chair-hack. "It's not so much being in exile from the Church," I continued, "it's losing hope that our Church may ever return from its self-imposed exile from women's original witness of the Christ, which is well attested in scripture. That's as dispiriting as being in exile myself."

Angela leaned in.

"If I may," she said. She's rattled, I thought, by this whole scriptural authority riff. "It's really a very grave error to suggest that women's ministry and witness has been denied by the Church. Down the centuries, women have been venerated, women have been sanctified. From Mary Magdalene to Mother Teresa."

"I don't think that's what the gentleman means," I said. Why are they always "gentlemen" when they're in audiences? He had sat down again, but I could feel him watching me through the sea of grey. "I think the suggestion is that we're in exile from women's first witness of the Christ. We need liberating from that exile."

"You're not suggesting the women at the Cross – Mary the Mother of Christ was one of them, you know – you're not suggesting they need liberating by the Church. We're liberated by God, by our faith," said Angela.

She was flushed and her mouth had tightened.

"I'm suggesting we're cut off from the experience of women at the time of Christ," I replied with what I hoped was measured calmness. "The Syrophoenician woman, who thought she was a dog for wanting crumbs from the Christ's table. The Samaritan woman, who had slept with more than one man so she had to fetch her water in the midday sun to avoid the scorn of the Jews. The bleeding woman, who tugged his robe."

"You're making the women sound more special than the men,"

Angela shouted, and there was a murmur of ironic laughter from the chairs. "I mean, you're suggesting that there's something different about the women whom Jesus healed from the men. They are – we are – all the same disciples, we just have different roles."

"But only men can exercise priestly ministry," said chair-hack, detecting the mood.

"We can all exercise our ministries. But let's not bring gender politics into it. There are no gender politics in the Kingdom of Heaven," said Angela, firmly regaining control.

"And that's what we're trying to build," I said. "But there are plenty of gender politics in this world."

"Well, let's keep them out of the Church," said Angela, looking straight ahead. "Natalie just wants to turn this into a socio-political argument and I don't see the gospel in that."

"You're right," I said. "I think politics only properly liberates when we bring our faith to it. And faith is nothing unless it liberates."

"I'm glad you concede you're a politician. May I remind you, Natalie, that we're called to fulfil the law, not to destroy it."

There was a pause as this gospel injunction was ingested. Then I blew it. I don't know why.

"Angela, I hope you're not having your period at the moment. Because if you are, under Levitical law, you shouldn't be sitting with these men."

I'd like to say there was a frisson. Actually, there was a honk of disapproval from the nave and I'd lost the audience. Chair-hack changed the subject matter, like a teacher stumbling across a Shakespearian profanity. Angela pursed her thin lips and left as soon as it wound up, claiming pressing "pastoral" demands.

I hung about for the drinks, if only to demonstrate that I hadn't done a runner like Angela. I wanted to be ostracised a bit too. I enjoy people being uncomfortable in my presence. I soak up opprobrium like a Scientologist.

Tight-arsed Christians struggle with their disapproval of people like me, because they know they're not really meant to do hating. But they do. So do I, but the difference is I admit it. To them – some of them – I'm a woman dressed as a priest and still an odd outsider. But it's more than that. I'm an icon of the overthrow of their clubby little structures and good offices, where only men wear frocks and the women do Marian obedience.

Ever notice what really gets them going at the Feast of the Annunciation? Not the divine ravaging of the child-bride's womb, not her sheer bloody fear, but Mary's flipping obedience. I've only ever seen one painting, by Lotto, I think, where Mary looks like she's wondering what she's eaten to be having this hallucination. The Archangel Gabriel even scares her cat. Otherwise, even the Pre-Raphaelites do obedient. Behold the handmaid of the Lord. Well, you can argue I might be that, but I'm not your bloody hand-maid, you jerk, you in your blazer and bifocals, with your little plasters over your shaving cuts, dabbed into place by your minis-tering Mrs Minnie Mouse. There, you've set me off.

I stood and talked to the verger for a minute, a stocky chap in a livery gown who wanted to go on about the acoustics being poor, though I think not hearing me may have been a positive advantage for him. I'd had a glass of astringent Argentinian white and avoided the white-bread grated-cheese-and-pickle sandwiches – it's not authentically C of E unless the catering's third-rate – when our man from the FO slid sideways through bodies and stood in front of me. He was shorter than I'd expected. I noticed he had a paisley-patterned pocket square.

"I thought you won on points. And you might have had a knockout in the final round if the ref hadn't stopped it."

"Hardly a heavyweight contest," I said, just graciously enough. "Actually, it was tennis. Do you think I'm a heavyweight then?"

"Only polemically."

Toby introduced himself again and gave me a card.

"I was on the Middle East desk when we did some work with your people on Lebanon relief. I think we used to speak to Adrian. When were you out there?"

"Not long after Israel started closing its borders," I said rather gratuitously. "Well done on that, by the way."

I like getting to the point.

"We're actually much more supportive than you might think. It's the Christians that are the great concern out there now."

"Why's that? Aren't they all Russians trying to get American passports?"

I wasn't about to be patronised by a diplomat.

"We're not too bothered who they are. We're just anxious that they don't get pushed out entirely. Christians provide the balance out there."

"Is that right," I said flatly. "Actually, I don't think it matters if there are no Christians in Palestine, does it?"

"They're crucial for peace. They have a role to play. You've had that role to play. You've always been there for us." It was unclear whether he meant me specifically or Christians in general.

"There were no Christians at the crucifixion," was all I said.

He was smiling again and that annoyed me.

"We'd like to talk to you more about it. I wonder if I can introduce you to my boss, Roger Passmore? Perhaps you know him. Can I reach you at the cathedral?"

"Sure, it's the big building at the top of the hill," I said.

He called the following day. Apparently contact had already been established with the Bishop's office. That's how we'd link up. The Bishop would bring us all into the loop. From such banality does evil grow.

5

The Old Deanery is tucked down one of the capillary lanes that track the sclerotic web of medieval thoroughfares to the south of the cathedral. It's a gently beautiful seventeenth-century house behind in-and-out gates and a cobbled courtyard, with a twin flight of stairs up to its black front door. As with all these places, you buzz "Bishop's Office" to be let in and there's a large hall with grey carpet over an uneven floor, some iconic gifts and a model of the cathedral to keep you amused while you wait.

For the posh-boy visitors, it must be a bit like waiting to see the headmaster. I remembered that feeling even from my school and pressed my thighs together as I sat on a chair to see if I could still get that schoolgirl sensation in my hip muscles. His Cerberus, an elderly lady, more tired than retired, with dyed honey hair, occupied a desk at the front window of this room, through which you can wave rather than use the buzzer if she's at her station. We'd exchange some listless pleasantries about the day, which drove me to take a pad with me and affect to make some notes of preparation.

The Bishop had just "had someone with him", Cerberus said, and opened his heavy carved door for this previous guest, a grey little chap with dandruff on a shiny navy jacket with a tiny, smug

Christian-fish badge on its lapel. The Bishop never gave it the "Have you met?" routine and we guests just smiled an acknowledgement of our change of shift, and this worthy administrator of some church-outreach initiative was gently dispatched to his further ministry, with the afterglow of a little episcopal affirmation.

"Natalie, how good to see you."

He took my hand, less in a shake than an embrace. I wouldn't have objected in this instance to the quickie English double-cheeker, because the Bishop didn't occupy your space and knew when to abandon it. He was warm, without cloying. I liked him then. I don't know if I could like him in the same way now. I don't know that I could like anyone like that now. But actually I can't be sure how much he knew of what he was letting me in for at that time, or even now.

His office is a modest room at the back, with fading magnolia walls above panelling, some intimidating bookcases, heavy embroidered vintage curtains, his laden desk facing a window on to the backyard. We sat in a three-piece by the marble fireplace. He always took the upright upholstery by the firedogs, back to the working door, his face lit from the only window. I took its opposite number, eschewing the threadbare and somewhat subjugating chaise-longue. The Bishop has a fop of grey hair that he pushes back regularly, more in distraction than affectation, and kind blue eyes behind rimless spectacles that engage rather than simply examine you. He was filling out a bit, I noticed, as he sank a bit in the chair, a little pot developing under the shimmering purple shirt.

"How are you, Natalie?" he asked plainly, neither a platitude nor a piece of bleeding-heart pastoral ministry.

I assured him I was fine, referenced my brief at the cathedral, and, just before it became too routine, he lobbed in a couple of mild indiscretions about Dean, rolling his eyes in a post-adolescent way. It didn't amount to much – something like ". . . in that particularly exhibitive way he has made his own" – but it served to show we were on the same side.

"I hope the Dean indicated that we're in the endgame of your little unlocal difficulty. It looks at last like we can say that there won't be criminal charges. At any rate, the UN's administrative tribunal seems to have lost interest in taking your case any further. The lawyers will send the paperwork to me and their letter will be copied to you. As expected, but good news nonetheless." He coughed. "There will have to be the odd quid pro quo. While the Archbishop of Sydney no longer wants to make a martyr of you, they'll want something to save face, I suppose. We're now at the level of negotiating a settlement for you, so I'm hoping that it's all about money rather than about something more vindictive like punishing you."

"We've established what I am – we're just discussing the price, right?" I said.

Some months previously a columnist in the *Daily Mail* had called me a media tart.

"That's about the size of it, Natalie," said the Bishop, ignoring the reference. "But I can't be certain they won't want an ounce or two of your flesh in some form or other. A grovelling apology or something."

"And at the ICJ level?" We'd originally been threatened with the International Court of Justice when the Sudanese government was involved.

"Always too heavy-handed. It's been a long haul at the diplomatic level, but I think that's over. For appearances' sake – and because it's technically an Anglican Communion and not just a Church of England matter – it'll have to be finished off at archbishop level. So it's been knocked upstairs and you'll have to go down to Lambeth and see the team there, I'm afraid. But after that we should celebrate."

"Thanks for all your support, Bishop."

"Now let's move on. I think I may have something rather interesting for you, Natalie," he said fairly quickly. I was conscious that Cerberus had this down as a half-hour slot, rather than the full hour.

"I do appreciate you're not under my authority these days." He chuckled and arched an eyebrow. "As if you ever were. But I was talking to a chap at the ADC, who tells me that DFID has made some progress with the Foreign Office and Number 10 in getting some proper support for the Palestinians in Jordan, Syria and Lebanon."

A translator would have described how the Bishop had been briefed by an emissary from the Foreign and Commonwealth Office in the margins of the Archbishops' Development Council. This was set up by the offices of Canterbury and York around the same time as the Quartet – the UN, the US, the EU and Russia, the foursome that had spent the best part of a decade wringing its hands and providing money-laundering services – allegedly to coordinate global Anglican efforts in aid and development with reps from government agencies.

"I need hardly tell you, of all people, how important that could be for the Palestinians," added the Bishop.

I smiled in the face of such rank flattery. Silly boy, I thought. What I said was: "It's been a long time coming. Why now?"

"It's all wrapped up in the peace process of course." Well, stone me. "I'm presuming the Quartet have brokered something when it comes to the repatriation of refugees. As you know, that's a huge sticking point."

And I thought I'd come to talk about women bloody bishops.

"What, money to stay where they are or to return home?" I asked eventually.

The Bishop paused just long enough to acknowledge "home", clocking what was effectively my position statement.

"A mixture, it seems," he replied, setting aside some paperwork from his previous meeting. "There would be money to raise conditions immeasurably for those who decide to stay where they are – and you'll know how much that is needed. But then, crucially, vast investment for those who return to an unoccupied Palestine. As I understand it, the Western partners would effectively be subsidising an infrastructural rebuild of the West Bank and Gaza that, with some cooperation from the Israelis I might add, would bring living standards up to those of the settlements."

I snorted in affable derision.

"I know, I know," he said, holding his hands aloft and swinging his lowered head in theatrical disbelief. "I'd have thought there was a greater chance of the entire Knesset galloping through the eye of a needle than seriously examining the prospects of Arabs living the lives of Israelis behind 1967 borders, especially with American money. But there you go."

"American?" I turned one ear towards him.

"Apparently so. Well, it's UN money, funnily enough, but you'd look to three-quarters of the Quartet for its source. That's who is really behind it."

"No Russian money?" I asked.

"Actually, there is some," he said as if he'd just remembered. "But it's private, not state, capital. They wouldn't want to be left out."

"I have a friend who works with the Russians in the Middle East," I said. "She may know."

He said nothing.

"How much in total?" I pressed.

"I don't know. I really don't know." He was swinging his head again and spoke softly. I wondered then and I wonder now if he did know the sums involved and just wasn't letting on. Those in Whitehall who run bishops train them well.

"Anyway," he said more loudly, suddenly sitting up and swinging one, short-socked ankle over his knee. "The Foreign Office has, again as you'll know, quite a collateral interest in the plight of Christians in the Holy Land, such as they now are. And this chap I saw at the ADC thought that we should be talking about how the Christian voice in the Middle East could be speaking up for the peace process in general and this scheme in particular. That seems to me to be rather a good idea. And," he cleared his throat lightly, "of course I immediately thought of you."

The Archbishops' Development Council was one of the interminable talking shops that the Anglican Church gets off on. I'd always rather enjoyed the sense of superiority I felt from having served in the field when it came to overseas aid. I thought of saying so, but kept silent.

"You'd be ideal," he continued. "You know the region, you can speak to the issues and, er, you're quite high profile."

"You mean I've been in the newspapers."

"I mean you know how to handle the media."

"I stole a lorry," I laughed. "And they took photos of me. That hardly makes me the acceptable face of the Anglican Communion."

"You gave your all in one of the toughest places on earth to have to serve a ministry. People relate to you. And to your motives. It's easy to trust people when you know where their heart is."

He's good at this, I thought. But he did like me, I knew that. He'd backed me as soon as the UN's heavies had come after me. Us. It wasn't just the threat of prosecution over the lorry business – it was the way I'd played out in the media too. I knew that the prosecution of me by the Aussies and the UN would have been a whole lot worse if the Bishop hadn't come out publicly in my support.

"This is a matter of enormous regret and we take it very seriously," he had said at the time. "But foreign-aid workers work under great stress and at great personal risk to themselves. And there is no greater risk than that attached to serving the innocent victims of a war zone."

Yes, I remember it verbatim. I liked him too, for standing in my corner, and I thought that as I watched him try to persuade me to go back to the Middle East.

"Would you like more coffee?" he asked.

I'd entirely forgotten the half-pool of milky slurry that remained on the small table beside me. I flicked up a hand from the arm of the chair in deferential refusal.

"I wonder if you'd meet our man from the Foreign Office. His name's Roger Passmore and he carries a brief for the Middle East desk. In any event, I'd really value your take on the whole thing."

I sensed our meeting was drawing to its close.

"If you could come back here, I'll introduce you to his young aide-de-camp, a nice boy. But Natalie, if you do get involved – and I do hope you'll go and see him at least, no obligation to buy, as it were – I want this to be purple-stole business. It's far from clear that any of this will happen. I don't think it's any more than a radical flyer at the moment. And with all the delicacies of the peace process and our roles in it . . ." He trailed off. "We really need to keep this tight, yes?"

Our roles in it? *Our?* But I nodded: "The seal of the confessional."

"Good!" he slapped his thighs. "I'll need to introduce you to the Foreign Office people. And then perhaps you'll come back and tell me how it goes."

We started to amble across the office.

"How is Adrian?" he asked. I said he was fine too. He was good on partners' names, less good on knowing anything useful about them. "And how is the monstrous regiment going? I hope the trad jazz isn't winding you up too much."

"The usual mix of hormones and politics," I said. "I think most women who would make bishop have lost the will to fight and I'm guessing that's a position that doesn't keep an established Church awake at night."

He stopped short of the door. "I hope you haven't lost the will to fight, Natalie, nor the will to live. We need you."

It was the sort of thing he said on the way out, the anteroom

salutation, but I did wonder how much it was a thinly veiled deal
– do me this favour, Natalie, and there's a bishopric in it for you. I
hoped not, because he was a friend and it would mean he'd developed a different, more formal and manipulative approach to me.
But it was demonstrable that this hadn't been the meeting that
Dean had anticipated we were going to have.

As I walked up the lane towards the worker ants of Paternoster
Square, I knew I couldn't share this agenda with Hugh, and it irritated me that this was an issue that was changing two friendships.
I didn't have many – never had. With both the Bishop and Hugh,
I'd always talked freely and we'd built a decent back catalogue of
protected confidences. And then there was Sarah; I couldn't ever
see her as my contact with the Russians. But after that conversation it all felt very different, like I'd been taken into an inner
sanctum. I was aware that I was responding in a new way. Or perhaps I was just pondering all these things inside, in heart rather
than mind. For one thing, I hadn't responded at all when he mentioned Roger Passmore's name and I couldn't work out why.

Hugh was right. I was called by an antediluvian churchwarden at
St Mary the Virgin, Elizabeth Street, and was asked if I could
"help out at all" during its interregnum, the hiatus between incumbent vicars when the laity run the church. We settled on Trinity
Sunday in May. It's always difficult to find a priest to preach at
Trinity. The doctrine of the Trinity – Father, Son and Holy Spirit
– is complex and incumbents invariably want to swerve it.

"Will you preach?" he asked.

"Yes." Of course I'll bloody preach. Women do that too.

I prepared something on the word "if". If God is three persons, what does that mean? "If" is an enormous word for its size. It's loaded with so much hope and expectation. Trouble is, nobody notices it much these days. It's a cheap little word. Kipling must take the blame for that. Mention the word "if" on its own and your mind defaults, like an internet search, to that ridiculous phallocentric verse.

I didn't say that in the sermon, of course. I just said I visited his house once, an unfinished Jacobean pile in Sussex, with a colleague from a teaching agency. It was a sad place. Kipling had known so much of the world, created his own universes, was so very rich, and it came down to this rather poky, rambling house, surrounded by his books, where he grieved for his only lost son whom he had encouraged to go to war with the world. What would the Almighty know about that, eh?

That's how I dealt with the first two persons of the Trinity. What I didn't say was that I hate the poem. If you can take all the shame and disappointment that's thrown at you and make a decent fist of pretending it's not really there, then you're a real man, my son. What do the little ladies do, I wonder – throw themselves at this lantern-jawed bovine, splattered with his own blood and disappointment, I suppose. Yes, Kipling really did for that word.

But it's bigger and better than that, I said. It's what our fantasy and faith hang on – and what separates one from the other. And that's the Spirit. That's what I thought, anyway. If this story is true, in any real sense of that word, then it's the hugest thing that has ever happened and can ever happen. If it isn't in any way true, then it's the most unimaginably vast con-trick perpetrated on us in human history. Either way, that's a great story. For the time being, by which I mean this mortal life, I opted for the former. It just made more sense.

"Will you cense the altar?" asked the churchwarden, who would have been called cadaverous by anyone who hadn't worked in Sudan.

"If you'd like me to," I said. Hugh had told me that they'd want "the smelly handbag", the thurible in which we swing the burning incense.

My private vestry prayer at St Mary's was a kind of alternative sermon. If there's a God – and please God there is – this church isn't about him, this vacuous act of self-reverence, aerated only by the bubbles of human endeavour: music, scripture and thought. Here it was Elizabeth Street, in what's known by the lisping churchwarden as "the cheaper end of Belgravia", but this emptiness pervaded the whole Church of England.

I had been put in a light cope, suitable for the slight shoulders of a lady, to process in behind the choir, whose tenors were now making a manful stab at a canticle. There was one tall and pale one, loose folds of skin marking his weak jawline, whose head rocked from side to side as he concentrated on marking time with his scriptural words. A lawyer, I thought, or a chartered surveyor. A Pharisee.

Dear God, I remember thinking, I'm the least in touch with the divine here, I feel no godly nexus as they apparently so effortlessly do. The way out of this thought pattern at critical times like these, I had learned from better-read colleagues, was to wager with Pascal that there was no God, but that this ritual at least made life bearable for those present, even joyful if you hit the right notes in the choir. Sitting in the sanctuary is difficult, watching His loyal servants at a distance, gathered together in the whimsy of the vain and ancient language of prayer and music, filling the void that He has evidently vacated.

The cherished Anglo-Catholic former incumbent of St Mary the Virgin, Father Tristram, had retired and the abandoned but lavishly pensioned congregants were searching for a replacement, some witless cleric to serve out half a dozen years inadequately in the shadow of his illustrious predecessor.

"There's a woman dressed as a priest in our chancel," I imagined Father Tristram saying.

From the embarrassed smiles of some of the regulars, women as well as men, heads snapping forward to stare non-committally into the middle distance as they felt me process past them, I guessed that their default position was rather more Catholic than Anglican. We must make her welcome in our household of faith. But what to say? We'll ask her if she knew Father Tristram and tell her how lovely he was.

The women were the gilded trophies of flushed, pretend-busy men, who would escape to offices where they encountered other women only in servile roles, or else in the safe, faux-male stridencies of peer-group female colleagues who, they presumed, had sacrificed their womanhood on the altar of Mammon – who was a man, obviously.

To all of them here, men and women alike, sacramental ministry, if they knew the term at all, was a post of implicit and cunning authority. A priest had magic hands and a cool and assured manner for the "manual actions" – they really call them that – over the Eucharistic elements of bread and wine and it was the kind of cupped-hand movement that went with oratory, not cooking. Here they were, on this Sunday morning, to celebrate their sameness, not the infinite variety of creation, not the other, scandalous foolishness of a faith that dared to suggest that a leper, a paraplegic, the terminal baby, the shoplifter, the rioter, the migrant, the loser, the candlestick-maker of the centrepiece of their dinner table, or, indeed, even a woman, could bear the same image of God as they bore.

I sat in my sanctuary stall like a latter-day Pope Joan, failing to display the correct genitalia for cardinal inspection. There's an apocryphal story that new popes have to sit on a loo-seat contraption to show that they have the right tackle, viewed from below. But this lot looked like I was flashing them.

I would distribute the communion wafers in a little while, but I knew I would look up afterwards to see those women and men who had sat fast in their pew, not through any sense of unworthiness on their part, but on mine, for my gender would have contaminated the Body of Christ with a chromosomal impurity that they couldn't ingest into their own.

Well, stuff them, I thought from my privileged place in the holy of holies, beside the patten and the chalice and the veil and the purificators. If they don't share the same bread as me, they're not part of the same body as me. I despise their isolation. They're neither hot nor cold, but lukewarm, and I spew them out. I knew I had to get away.

I'd heard a woman priest like me, one of my sisters I suppose, speak at the General Synod, wringing her claws as she entreated us to reach out to those in pain who cannot accept our priesthood. Way to go, girl, that's really gospel. But when they refuse to reach out, intuitively, not to me, but for what I'm holding, the taking and the offering, the tearing and sharing, then all they're doing is standing silently by, like soldiers I saw in Africa, who stood smoking while children slipped away in strangers' arms. Or like those who stood silently beside others whose bloodlust had overcome them in the praetorium and shouted "crucify him".

Lambeth Palace, where the Archbishop of Canterbury lives and works when he's in London, occupies its own time and place, its own bureaucratic Narnia. It looks accessible and easy to reach, just over the Thames from the Houses of Parliament. And it's like you have to walk away from it to find a bridge, Lambeth or Westminster, to walk back towards it. There are no train stations near it and even the buses seem to avoid it.

I approached from Westminster, across the bridge by Big Ben, turning right down the steps and along the river walk under the Victorian gables of St Thomas' Hospital, crossing the lethal junction by the boat cafe on the south side of Lambeth Bridge.

You bang a heavy knocker on the little door beside the huge one in the red-stone medieval gatehouse and the keeper lets you in. Then it's across the circular driveway, past gardeners tending lawns, towards the Palace front door. It's like an Oxford college has been dropped into central London in some children's sci-fi thriller, a parallel universe, a rip in the fabric of the metropolis.

"Why are you going?" Adrian asked that morning, as I put toast on the table.

"I told you. The lawyers want to wrap up Sudan."

"But why Lambeth?"

"I suppose it's where the lawyers want to be. The client is the

Church. Headman's office. Maybe the coffee's better. Do you want an egg?"

I avoided the usual destination of this dialogue. Over all the years that we'd talked about it, I knew Adrian had never had a satisfactory answer from me. Why would I steal a lorry on my own? How could I have driven and navigated it a thousand kilometres through the Sudanese bush without help?

"Let me say that I came with you. Let me say it was my idea." It was his constant refrain ever since I'd told the UN's Stasi that I'd acted alone.

Several times Adrian had asked me why we couldn't say that he'd had taken the lorry, why it couldn't have been him that had acted alone.

"If one of us has to take the rap, why not me?" he'd say. "You could still get busted for this."

"So?"

"Jesus Christ, Nat, we live in this big house – you want to be here. They might want to make you a bishop one day." He'd look desperate, like I was deliberately misunderstanding him. "I was the nutcase, the guerrilla who wanted to feed the world. Everyone said that at the office, remember?"

"You're in the public sector. If they came after you, they could come after the government." It was my standard reply. "And they'd just throw you to the wolves. Leave it with me. I'm to blame. Leave it as a Church issue. It looks after its own. Plenty of evidence of that."

Adrian would throw down cutlery or slam a door. "You just want all this to be about you. Your bloody drama. Your bloody heroics."

"Is that what this about? Look there's no point in us both going down, which is what happens if you fess up now. Let the Church handle it. They sent me, they can sort it. Anyway it's done now."

Maybe it was finally done now. I was beginning to believe Dean and the Bishop. Truly, it was a legal action that was dying of boredom. After the early media interest, the Australians wanted me hung out to dry. Vehicle and property theft (the latter a class action on behalf of several aid charities), criminal damage, endangering the lives of others, contractual fraud.

And maybe Adrian was right. Maybe I liked all this attention. The martyrdom. I'd acted alone, without Adrian, and I liked that story. It's the one my doorstepper Tony had run in a Sunday paper and I'd liked it: "the fallen angel of mercy" he'd called me.

Perhaps they were both right, Tony the reporter and Adrian the husband. I'd flown too close to the Sudanese sun and was burned. I'd been summoned to the boss's big house, the one behind impervious walls, bombed in the war, rebuilt and resilient, to be sacked. Well, I knew I wasn't going to be sacked, but Adrian still thought I might be and I liked him thinking that too. It had been a real possibility at one time. I can't say I'd ever cared much, other than Adrian had told me I would be fired and he'd have been proved right. I'd always known I'd find somewhere to live though, maybe abroad. He'd have to come with me.

When you enter the front doors of Lambeth Palace, there's a flight of red-carpeted stairs directly in front of you, less of a stairway to heaven than a celebrity airstair. At the top, turn left for first class, the holy bits, drawing rooms and chapels. Right for the rough trade, admin and staff. I was turned right.

A large library at the end on the left. A huge bay window, overlooking gardens and Parliament's terraces beyond. A conference table the size of a Thames pontoon. This had been the archbishop's study until a predecessor had decided it was too grand and should be more widely used. It amused me momentarily that an archbishop should think that he was wasting space.

There were already two of the lawyers I'd met several times before, a woman and a man, in their forties but looking prematurely old. The Palace's chief of staff slid into the room through a door concealed in the bookcases that covered one wall. And a nice young man from Church House, our civil service function from the north side of the river.

And there was another woman already in the room. In the shadow, by a cabinet on the right of the window. She had a slim ring-binder open in front of her and she looked up when we came in, but didn't move until the chief of staff came in, then she walked down the room and handed him the file. She was short, with a grey untended bob, and she wore a floral blouse, open at the neck revealing a modest string of pearls.

"Thank you, Cara," said the chief and Lambeth's Moneypenny smiled briefly at everyone except me and trotted out. I bet they think I don't remember those details, but I do.

We settled to it at the window end of the table. The gist of it was that the Australians would settle for aggravated damages, including the replacement of the damaged truck, amounting to some $400,000.

The male lawyer did most of the talking. "As we know, the good news is that we avoid a UN tribunal, both expensive and wearisome. We can probably get them down on damages."

"Insurance will pay," said the chief of staff, turning to me reassuringly.

"The plaintiff has, as you know, always wanted to come after the Church Commissioners, who were technically your employers at the time of the incident, rather than The Fed," continued the lawyer. "That's partly because we have more money – cleaning out a small charity is neither lucrative nor edifying. But it's partly because they're also demanding that in settlement a CDM is taken against you, Natalie, as principal party."

Not quite the absolution that the Bishop had promised. A Clergy Disciplinary Measure in a consistory court, almost certainly meaning the suspension of my clerical licence, so no job with the Church any more. It wasn't what I had been expecting. Naturally, a CDM had been mentioned in the past, but only in the context of it being unnecessary because the Church was essentially my co-defendant.

"Why, if they've got their money?" It was the chief of staff again.

"They're accepting that Natalie acted alone. I suspect it's their principal witness, James Adaire, whom I think you know, Natalie?"

"Jimmy. Yes, I know Jimmy," I said. "Blimey, he still wants his revenge after all this time. I thought the drift of it was that they'd climbed down. I thought my crucifixion was off the agenda."

"There's still another way," said the lawyer, shifting on his seat like he was coming to the whole point. I looked hard at him. "Now they're talking of settling, we don't need to go to court. But if we were to refer Natalie for a psychiatrist's assessment, it could be treated as a pastoral rather than a disciplinary matter."

It took a moment for the horror of that to sink in.

"No," I said. And left it there.

"Listen, Natalie, this needn't be arduous or intrusive," said the chief of staff. He'd clearly been prepared by the lawyers. "But you were in a very post-traumatic circumstance. The Bishop said as much. If you needed some treatment, some counselling, that's not just good for the case, it's good for you."

"No," I repeated. "I'm not mad. You can't make me see a doctor this side of a criminal trial. Anyway, it sends the wrong message after everything that's been in the papers. It's not mad to want to feed people."

They variously looked at their files.

"I can't see that we could get the damages down or avoid a CDM if you're sure you're refusing that path," said the lawyer.

"I am sure. I'm not mad, whatever a shrink might find, and I'm sure they can find something, anything, in anyone. Is that what you want?" I'd turned to the chief of staff and he looked kindly at me. "Anyway, I can't see that it works. Either they find I'm mad and you have to defrock me, or I'm not mad and we're at square one."

I could tell it was a good point, but not one they wanted to hear. In practice, it's very hard to remove a priest's holy orders, but if I was sick in the head, I could be on long-term suspension being looked after. Some of them would like that, I knew.

The meeting broke up shortly after that.

"Take care, Nat," said the chief at the top of the stairs.

"I'm sorry this has taken so very long. I've been a lot of trouble," I replied, looking away down the corridor.

"The Archbishop sends his love," he said and retreated into the dark.

That evening, Adrian leaned against a kitchen unit, eating cereal. "What did they say?" he asked.

"They said it's over if I pretend to be mad."

Adrian snorted. "Really? And are you?"

"No. I said I wouldn't see a trick cyclist."

"So what now?"

"I suppose I may have kept the case open," I said sadly into a cupboard. "I wasn't prepared to pay the price."

I knew what I'd done was going to cost the Church a whole lot more money. And then there was the disciplinary action against me. That could cost me my ministry, whatever the newspapers and the Bishop said.

"So it's not over," said Adrian.

"It is finished," I said emphatically. "They didn't want to know if you were there or not."

6

So, Sudan. Time to tell the truth. One time – the time I'm going to tell you about – I stole a lorry loaded with maize and beans and drove it into the bush. Well, we did. Over the half-dozen trips I made there, I watched skeletons that were alive, in a way, though not fully human. I held children with absurdly huge heads as they died. You know the sort of thing. It's not that you're providing any sort of comfort – there's no time for that. It's just that they're easier to dispose of if you're holding them as soon as they're dead. And it's more hygienic than leaving them on the ground. Their families, if they're not too weak themselves, will very often try to hold on to the bodies for mourning, or seek to bury them in their own shallow graves, where animals might dig them up.

Sometimes we kept them alive and I guess that's what people call job satisfaction, isn't it? But you need to understand that a famine is as irresistible as a tsunami. You can't stand in its way and hope to live. You're always dealing with the aftermath. The killing is inevitable. It just is, whatever your charity adverts might say. We'd keep them alive to die next time. The only way to stop famine is to open the money valve from north to south, stop food trading and kick out crap African governments. But that's not going to happen, is it?

There's a Dinka lament, sung by the men as they drive stakes into the arid soil to secure torpid oxen, which repeats again and again that the gods of a new harvest will come to them in the husks of the dry crop seed that they are forced to eat. It's a wail that hangs in the air of Bahr el Ghazal in the evenings as if the world has been stilled to listen. If only. The cycle of fighting and oppression over so many decades in southern Sudan had made starvation a commonplace. What conjures a sort of phosphorescent burning in the well-fed bellies of aid workers, those of us with our seven barns filled to the rafters with grain, those of us who are the self-satisfied refuseniks from late capitalism, is that we can't slow the Monopoly board games, the market's measure of success by excess. We're treating the consequence in Sudan of the economic glut way north, in Europe and the US.

But enough. I've been in distribution camps where we've measured starving children with a stick: tall enough and they take their chance; small enough and they are fed. It's a form of selection. OK, not as gratuitously bestial as a Nazi death camp, but it was still a kind of system of selection for death. Less industrial, but the consequences for the luckless were the same.

The big relief charities ranked themselves by tonnage, while we smaller operators just got by on easing the processes of death. But The Fed's founder, Jake, had been a charismatic figure in the early days of the aid business and it was he who had eventually, with Sarah's help, secured a UN accreditation for evaluation and assessment. So we punched above our weight for a small outfit. And we got right on the tits of the big aid charities.

The fashionable rubric of our times was that fractured and fragmented interventions in sub-tropical African famine needed holistic management. Reaching the living bones of God's forgotten people meant first negotiating the possibilities of charitable co-operation. We were the scouts, the pathfinders for the deployment of international aid.

I was to discover that that so often meant not so much feeding the hungry as analysing their plight. It was as if Screwtape himself had whispered in Wormwood's ear and The Fed had been recruited as an unwitting double-agent for the devil. We withdrew our open hand from the mouths of infants in favour of trying to deploy big aid more effectively. But in reality that meant turning away to doff our cap to the great grain-mill owners of international development.

We flew into Nairobi and from there to Lokichogio in the north-west of Kenya towards the end of the second millennium, significantly enough for us. If there was a millenarian in me, I see now that we were approaching our end times even as we began. Ostensibly we were to establish where the hot spots of famine were in Bahr el Ghazal and identify "critical paths" to supplying them with British-sourced support. In practice, this meant naming who could realistically be fed and who was beyond reach. It's a classic Western, neo-liberal approach and when we work with the market model, it's always a mission of despair. But perhaps I didn't know that at the time, or perhaps I just denied it.

We transferred to Juba and then to a dispersal camp in northern Uganda close to the Sudanese border, blagging a lift with UN transporters, as if we were on some kind of ghoulish pilgrimage to the living relics of Sudan's starving. The air is thick with diesel in a transportation zone, but there was a smug little village of white plasterboard thatched cabins that had been purpose-built to house aid workers and crews. It was like the staff quarters of a holiday-let children's camp. I presumed we'd get up the road into Sudan to witness what we were here for, but an administrative ritual had embraced the days of the camp. Soon after dawn, debates began about who had the most pressing need for telecoms, which was a field-phone affair patched into the UN system somewhere else. You could sit on the front deck of a cabin – some had proper verandahs – and place your call. Most of the boys, many of them Australian, evidently enjoyed the insouciant command structure of this palaver. There was a good deal of testosterone involved in being first to the phone, a locker-room rivalry between the various charities: our aid workers can beat up your aid workers. Ade made some desultory bids for the phone. But it wasn't clear what he wanted to tell the office. Maybe just that we were there.

The next push of an aid operation was being run by a bumptious Australian in a branded charity T-shirt. There were a lot of those blue T-shirts. Corporate identity is an important factor in delivering emergency relief. On the third morning, when Ade was helping with some smaller supply trucks, I lit a cigarette and hung about on a porch as the Aussie charge-hand, a self-consciously unshaven ocker called Jimmy, made his calls. Apparently there were trucks that were ten days late, probably raided in Uganda's bandit territories in the north, I imagine. And he was dealing, like a Sydney commodities trader, with three competing haulage firms for replacements. He was swinging around on the parapet fencing of the porch, saying things like "That's forty-eight flat rate and if you want to go it alone, you'll get stuck when the rains come and we'll have to come and pull you out like we did last year . . . screw 'em."

He hung up. I asked why we didn't use some of the small flat-beds that Adrian was fiddling with.

"They'd never make it, honey. Roads are too rough. We need the big boys."

We certainly do, I thought.

As it happens, the rain started that night. It banged up the dust and flattened the thatching. It had come early, but still too late for crops further north. All this rain was going to do was cruelly extend what they called the hunger season. I watched the liquid air form a constantly tearing gossamer veil from the edges of the roofs and imagined bulging Sudanese eyes in brittle-boned skulls turned to the sky. It's over, I remember thinking, when I'd felt the rain on previous trips. It's back to the European breadbasket for me.

I slept in the following morning and was only woken by wildly gunned engines, a familiar dawn chorus on wet, unmetalled African roads as axles are lifted from muddy little trenches. But the rain had stopped and the engines had been started a little later, the grey low mists of a rainy season pre-empted by high broken clouds as a capricious wind swung around. It was a window in the rains, an early warning of the soaking to come. But I knew there was still time for a run.

I walked out into freshened air. There were five or six oppos hanging about, Aussies and Yarpies, more than you'd expect to see when there was the daily business of warehousing to be done. I recognised one of them, Jimmy's deputy, Jo, and approached her. She told me Sudan was opening three airstrips for three days.

"We're shipping as much as we can – maize and supps mainly – to Loki to airlift it in by UN."

I'd once heard a station manager, with English understatement, call the opening of airstrips a mixed blessing. Starvation was the Sudanese government's weapon of choice for southern Sudan, to tie up the SPLA rebels in a famine zone. The airstrip closures, or no-fly zones, were officially to hinder rebel troop and arms movements. But in effect it was a means of controlling the food supply. Yet more unspeakable were the temporary reopenings of these supply strips. The distribution of food when it arrived would act as a draw to the local populace and the effort of long treks in emaciated frames was effectively a cull of the weakest. Thus was the subtle turning on and off of the Sudanese genocidal tap.

I went to make coffee. Adrian was down in the truck compound, where they were loading what they could of the big bags on to smaller trucks, muscular black bodies, sporting bandanas, whitened by the mist of escaping flour, swinging 400 kg bags on to flatbeds until their tyres touched the wheel arches, then they'd take a couple off.

By early afternoon, the ground was firm to the tread as the heat of the day hit the mid-forties. The loading had to stop. The metal of the trucks became too hot to touch. Staff were listlessly wandering around the encampment, splashing themselves from troughs, when a deeper mechanical rumble than any of our smaller trucks could manage shook the ground. The first of the big artics swung into the camp, a massive leviathan pulling a trailer, its dark-windowed cabin sealing the artificial climate of its crew. Six more followed. They were greeted with no cheers. We stood around, hands on hips, as they lined up on a levelled muster point, purpose built for the transport elite, and their engines idled then died, pulling human voices back into the air. The wiry and paunched drivers and crew tumbled from cabs like birds leaving elephants' heads and they shed clothing as they hit the heat.

"Back to Plan A," I said to Jo as I walked back into the shade. She said nothing, but winced back into the brightness of the lorry park. She seemed preoccupied, nervous.

"We can go with a road delivery now, right?" I pressed, trying to make eye contact with her.

"I don't know," she said.

I sought out Jimmy: "What are you going to do?"

"Get these loaded up and over to Loki airport just as quickly as bloody possible, before the Sudes change their minds."

I didn't know where to start. Faced with the fatuously stupid, you have to backtrack into territory so facile and self-evident that for a while you can't get your bearings.

"But it'll take you two days to get these loaded and to Loki, and you don't even know whether the airstrip will still be open when you get there."

He started to turn away like his clipboard was telling him more than me. I followed.

"You don't even know if you have planes, for Christ's sake."

"It's the quickest way before the rain comes – I'm not getting seven forty-tonners stuck on the road for the SPLA to pick off."

"Jesus, Jimmy, you've got seven trucks and a dry road – just get them into Sudan."

"Listen, Missy, I don't know what kind of authority you think you have here. But I say it's zip. Understood? You don't work for me and I don't think you know how this works." He smiled, like he was patiently explaining to a child. "So it's my way, not your highway."

I felt that hot phosphorous rage, but I noted I was under control, which made me feel confident. I was in the grip of a terrifying calmness. I never wore a dog collar in the field, far less held a service. It was a hangover from the WorldMission days; the only sign was what we did, not what we said. But here on the baked earth of northern Uganda, I knew I was talking the Church's book, rather than The Fed's best interests.

"You don't need to know who or what I am, or who I speak for," I said. "Food in Sudan, anywhere in Sudan, is better than food warehoused at Loki for the hunger season."

He returned to his clipboard. "It's not going to happen."

I tried reason. "Listen, I don't want an argument. Surely all that matters here is that people get fed? So let's take lorries into Sudan."

"No."

This was a power play. Nothing to do with facts.

But the burning inside wasn't going to make me angry. Rather the opposite – it was feeding me. So I went for the challenge to his manhood.

"You're bottling it, you friggin' useless little cock."

The pen froze over the clipboard. He didn't look up straight away but took four paces towards me, so his face was very close. It was small and bristly.

"Listen, you dried-up little bitch, I don't know or care where you come from, but you get right back there or I'm going to screw you good – you'll walk bow-legged for a month."

He held the stare, letting the silence and my lack of reaction establish his authority. I just chuckled ironically and held up a cocked little finger. He walked past me, catching my shoulder. I felt a coolness over my skin, tingling and insulating me from the heat. I looked down at my hands and stretched my fingers. They were like waking hands, not shaking, steady and purposeful.

It took the night and most of the morning to load the big lorries and it was early afternoon before the convoy shipped out. The drivers weren't contracted for Lokichogio. Jimmy had five drivers, including himself, so in a further grotesque absurdity, he left two loaded trucks, with the promise that they would return for them, or find a further two drivers by radio along the route. I hissed to Adrian not to say that he was licensed and insured. We weren't going to be part of this dilettante exercise. But in the event Jimmy didn't ask. We were contaminated and even the prospect of shifting more of the supplies than he would otherwise be able to into a temporarily open airstrip wasn't going to encourage a rapprochement with The Fed's reps.

In an alpha-male roar, the five trucks swung out of the compound, heading east, a driver and one crew riding shotgun in each cab. If anything, it was hotter now. I looked south-east; no cloud bank. It could be a week before the rains came again. The whole encampment was strangely vacated, like a school after speech day. The only people left were the stevedores, the contracted loaders in their whitened scarves and sawn-off khakis. Somewhere there would be the cooks and ancillaries in their branded T-shirts and the compound managers and some armed security. I found Adrian in the shade of a baobab tree, swigging from a bottle of water and flicking the pages of a truck manual.

"Adrian," I said. "Ade."

He looked up.

"Adrian, we've got to do something." I couldn't think how to convey the awful dystopia that I saw around us. It was like I was the only one who could see it. "We've got a chance here to do something. It mightn't ever come again. I don't want to look back and think we didn't take it."

"What do you mean?"

"Adrian, we've got two fully loaded and fuelled trucks and an empty camp." He turned his head, wanting more. "Adrian, please, we'll never have a chance like this again."

"Who for?" he said and his tone was blank.

"Oh, for God's sake, Adrian, this isn't about my ego, or yours. We're here to do stuff, not just move stuff about. What did you say you'd joined up for?"

I was invoking the back garden in Kentish Town and I could see he knew it.

"Don't you know there's a frigging war on?"

We fell silent. He looked off west, towards the falling sun.

"So it's Bonnie and Clyde," he said.

I sighed and dropped my shoulders. "If you like. Come on, Adrian. This will never come again."

There was a long pause. I had nothing else to say. Then the surprise.

"How do we get the keys?" he said, standing up.

So Adrian went in the office hut while I leaned on the door jamb trying to look nonchalant. A somnolent Ugandan staffer kept vehicle keys on a hook board. Adrian said he had to move the trucks down to the sealed area. They were contractors' trucks, I heard him say, and insurance didn't cover them being left outside a locked compound, and, yes, we know nothing's going to happen to them in a semi-deserted camp on the Ugandan side of the border, but we've had enough trouble with contractors already and I'm not about to give them another contractual breach to use for bargaining.

He was good, I'll give him that.

Adrian swung the first and slightly less loaded of the big lorries down towards the fences, dust and exhaust billowing from its sides, while I ambled to the far side of the other truck. I was a schoolgirl dodging a lesson.

I heard the engine die in the distance and there was an extended pause, like the whole camp was waiting for something to happen. I thought he might have changed his mind, gone back to our hut or bumped into someone with one of those clipboards, a compound manager maybe. But he appeared, admirably casually, striding up the centre of the camp track, examining the other set of keys as if there was some mundane issue with the tag. Perhaps there was. Maybe Adrian really was wondering whether the registering systems for transport could be improved. I pulled myself up the steps on the crew side as I heard the central-locking clunk on Ade's door and we sat into the high seats simultaneously.

For the first time, I thought Adrian and I were making common cause and it felt good.

The engine fired and, without a word, he swung the tractor unit around, air-brakes hissing, and followed the line of his first short trip. Then, at the top of the encampment, as if it was natural, as if a forty-tonne truck can saunter and whistle carelessly, he edged us left, instead of straight down to the sealed compound and joined the main thoroughfare through the scrub, north-west, towards Sudan.

"Seatbelts," I said and we laughed, nervously, like we were taking the piss.

I'd say the first thirty kilometres of that ride were the happiest time I can remember. The sheer thrill of straddling this monster that obeyed our illicit will, the self-righteous kick of breaching the fuss-body bureaucracy of the aid machine, the electrifying charge of danger, rolling at a steady 60 kph on a dust track, achingly slowly from the captivity of the distribution station and teasingly slow towards an unknown destination and known dangers.

I opened the drop-down compartment on the dash and took out the map and compass, which all trucks carry as part of their administrative payload, ticked off on those clipboards as a pilot would check his plane.

Neither of us spoke much – it was so damn obvious what we were doing. We were constantly leaning forward and back to check the wing mirrors, our silent, mutual assents over the drum of the engine that pursuing motorbikes or jeeps could yet frustrate our joint venture. It was like that until we put about a hundred kilometres and several forks in the road between us and the rightful owners of our pirate ship.

As for that rightful ownership – how virtue added to the headiness of our banditry! And there was sweet irony. This machine, powered by diesel refined in the rich Western nations, was powering our nourishing cargo to those to whom it rightly belonged, by virtue of their crying need, if need can be a virtue.

We're coming, I thought sentimentally, hold hard.

We drove north-west, following the valley of the White Nile, crossing the border north of Moyo, towards Kajo-Keji. In those days, you'd be unlucky to be stopped and searched. Relief lorries were obvious, there was nothing much to smuggle, and refugee traffic was all one-way, north to south. They probably thought we were stragglers from a convoy heading to Juba. Once in Sudan, we quickened our pace as Adrian grew accustomed to the varied bass ratios of the gearbox. I pulled the scarf and bush hat from my head and ran fingers through my matted hair.

Astonishingly, now I look back on it, given the tension of my heightened consciousness, I began to doze, head lolling like a home-brew drunk to the random jazz rhythms of the rutted road.

We'd decided to head up towards Rumbek, in the withering heart of Bahr el Ghazal, where the convoys now bound for Loki-chogio would originally have headed, to identify local distribution stations where we could. At dusk, the base of my spine dulled from constantly counter-balancing the swaying cab, we pulled over in the scrub, ate some of the three-day emergency rations in tinned packets from under the seats, and as the safety of the night shrouded our great beast, we slept in our bags head-to-toe in the back of the cab.

We woke to a quiet that I don't think I'd ever known before, a holy stillness that held within it secrets of the new day. Rolling from the cab, I stood facing east, my breath clouding in the remnants of the night air, watching a fading vermillion of dawn behind the hazy hills and across a rolling morning mist.

If I've ever felt blessed, just wholly at the centre of everything, an alpha and omega, it was then, as the dawn both required my attention and honoured me with its presence. I was certain in those moments that what we were doing was sacramental, as I stood there in the moment, in the lee of the sleeping lorry, witness in a barren landscape to the cornucopia that it carried, God's holy gifts for God's holy people.

After a short while of this communion, perhaps less than ten minutes, the driver's door opened and I heard Adrian pee against the great wheel. He emerged stiffly around the vertical wall of the engine cowling, blinking blindly into the light and zipping himself up.

"Good morning," he said, without looking at me.

"Yes, it is," I replied.

It's difficult, but I want to explain that this was a moment, more intense and real with someone than anything I'd had before.

And I want to be honest. It was deeply affecting and I believe I was in the presence of a great, limitless love. I'm not foolish. I know how the sun's rays of light refract through the moist and warming air. I'm not taken in by a bag of nature's tricks. But I was held in the palm of that morning and I knew all manner of things could be well. It made me smile that this had happened only after my ordination. It felt like affirmation rather than vocation.

So it wasn't all bad with Adrian. It was good, there in that moment. And I took his hand and smiled up at him.

There was an awkward pause.

"Better have a quick coffee and something to eat and get going. If we look broken down, it won't be long before we attract attention."

"Ade," I said suddenly and he turned back. "Thank you for coming."

He smiled and shook his head, looked at the ground and kicked a stone.

"I don't think we were offered a choice," he said, his voice dropping at the end to indicate conclusion.

"So let's go now," I said. "We're on a mission. We'll eat and drink later when we have some miles on the clock," and I ran to the driver's side.

"Are you insured?" he called.

It was one of the funniest things he ever said, because he was sending himself up, whether he meant to or not.

We'd done about eighty kilometres before I pulled over and then it wasn't because we wanted to brew coffee and get some sort of carb and sugar hit from dry biscuits. A small skull-and-crossbones sign nailed to a teak tree by the side of the way indicated that the road had been mined at some stage in the ebb and flow of battle between the Sudanese government and the southern rebels.

Young sappers of the SPLA were swinging their detectors like suburban lawn strimmers in the road ahead. I pulled on to the gentle banking on one side and hissed the air-brakes to a standstill. The SPLA boys in their desert fatigues would be no trouble, so Adrian and I made some coffee. They approached us and, in response to one mildly curious question, Adrian said we'd had engine trouble, fallen behind our convoy and were now catching up. I said we had a radio in the cab and were in constant contact every fifteen minutes, just in case any of the half-dozen soldiers had ideas for our transport.

The commander nodded distractedly and winced into the distance. Nobody here cared about paperwork. While we waited for the all-clear, we ambled about separately, sipping sparingly at water bottles from the small refrigerated box in the cab that we couldn't get to work properly, so the water was mostly tepid.

Leaning against one of the great tyres, hot to the touch like a burning skin, I saw Adrian crouching about a hundred metres down the road, watching something low and a little in front of him, a lizard perhaps. But he stayed there and was staring. I walked in his direction and saw that he was kneeling now, his backside on his heels, his hands resting palm-upwards on his thighs. As I walked softly up behind him, I saw he was fixed on a pile of maybe a dozen or fifteen skulls, human, in the drainage ditch by the road.

They were sun-bleached white and scavenged clean. Most had no jawbone. They were probably all that was left of a government garrison in retreat, jumped by rebels along this remote road, and I expect the skulls had been kicked into the ditch by the sappers to keep the road tidy for purposes of their sweep.

But someone had stacked them respectfully, so that they were piled upright, a sightless audience to the passing. Adrian had been looking into the little caves of their eyes. I realised he was praying.

We drove. We stopped. We drove again. The journey continued like this for a couple of days. No more sappers and skulls, just great tracts of driving, Adrian and I taking turns at the wheel and otherwise dozing in the back, the odd navigation conference and calculations of the rations left aboard the lorry. And our odyssey punctuated by little vignettes of the horror that the civil war had visited on inhabitants luckless enough to live in this ruined Eden: a burnt-out farm, its fenced and empty animal pens still standing; a pile of cattle carcasses; abandoned machinery, its bright yellow paint echoing a hopeful time, now evaporated in the heat haze.

We drove for hours through forests of teak, which along with the stratum of oil somewhere way below, in some benign fantasy of another economic world, could not only have fed the people now fled, but sent their children to brand-new schools to become doctors and engineers and teachers and aid workers to other desperate regions. They could have gathered in the sun on their school runs, like parents from the Home Counties to the Emirates, to complain that they'd had to wait half an hour to see a doctor in the flagship new hospital or to sneer at how hideous was the new superstore.

No, in truth the tribes of southern Sudan are too noble for that Western model of existence. Maybe that's what made them so vulnerable to the ravages of civil war. The population of a country spoilt by prosperity is harder to oppress.

The Dinka herd oxen and watch the sun rise. They were always going to get walked over by those with American guns who would fight Western wars, even if they didn't care about the rich seams of black gold under their plains.

We stopped at a tight little settlement beyond Amadi. It was still standing but was strangely vacated. "Ghost town" didn't do it justice, for that implies abandonment. The ghosts were very present here and some were still walking about, in a semblance of remaining alive. There had been a hospital. That's why government forces targeted it in a deliberate act of apparently wild vengeance. There were children in the wall-less building now, some sitting on metal-slatted beds, others lying, with dirty-bandaged stumps and the blank expressions of those who invite no sympathy, because there is none to be had that could mean anything.

We were told that the settlement's rudimentary shelter, a trench with wooden beams and corrugated iron bearing a load of replaced earth, had taken a direct hit. The forty or so inside, women cradling their already gaunt children, some men pathetically shielding them, had been eviscerated, like the first turns of a kitchen liquid-iser through soft fruit.

Back on the road, we encountered some Baggara militia, Arab tribesmen armed by the government. They stood in the road, like children pretending to stage a checkpoint, but what they really wanted was a lift on the truck. They had probably tired of raiding villages, killing the men, enslaving the women, the everyday work of mercenaries.

I kept telling myself what we'd learned, in the rudimentary training of listening to more experienced operatives; that the over-whelming likelihood was that we'd be OK if we stayed in a locked cab, talking to them through open windows. The convention was that aid lorries were proscribed from providing transport for the armed of either side and, other than those crazed by blood-lust and drugs, the fighters on both sides had some deeply buried code of honour that aid workers were to be allowed free passage.

Still, this was no place for a woman to carry a bag of gold and a child and expect to survive. My bag of gold was the truck – and my child was Adrian, if you like – and we were, by our own account, a lone and wounded straggler from our pack. Adrian, somewhat unnecessarily, kept repeating to me to keep my voice calm and to maintain that we were assured of free passage by the UN. I rather wished he'd have spent more time doing so from his own window, but most of the talking fell to me, and I could feel them start the mocking routine from the foot of my door, a worrying prelude to objectifying me and turning violent.

As it turned out, it was only the height and relative precarious-ness of our load, I think, strapped down with tarpaulins that offered no purchase for ascent, that discouraged our hitch-hikers and after avaricious glances to size up the lorry and its attractions as loot, they retreated down the road we'd travelled without looking back at us. We were the discarded and already forgotten husk of an opportunity.

On the third day, we hit the vicinity of Rumbek, nothing that could be described as outskirts, far less suburbs, more a simple increase in shacks, tribesmen by the road with skeletal oxen and more vehicles swerving to avoid our truck, like fishing boats around a great dreadnought. At a long-disused garage, with absurd piles of tractor tyres and rusting jeeps on bricks, we asked for a route to the airstrip, alongside which we knew there would be a distribution station. We finished the last few miles by late afternoon, the heat beginning its reluctant collapse into night.

The figures by the wayside grew in number, the stronger of the Dinka gathered in small groups around their animals, some singing the laments that went with the dusk.

Finally, the word "airstrip" next to a red cross on a sign, with a crude emblem of wings. Adrian swung the truck in next to a huddle of cabins and faded green tents. In front of us the ground fell away towards a plain and there, silently, was a crowd, stretching away into the middle distance, and makeshift shelters and carts like floating debris on a sea of humanity. The predominant colour was dusty black from a mass of exposed skin, yet the colours of women's shawls, the stripes of yellow and orange on brown lent the scene a grim gaiety, like football shirts at a massacre.

No one looks at you, I'd learned, and no one moves towards a supply truck at this stage of a famine. The alienating ennui of starvation has set in.

We left the cab to look for distribution staff. In the first cabin were some men lying on mats, one holding his abdomen and retching, dysentery perhaps. Then a cabin, still bearing the name of a civil engineering contractor and possibly shipped here from some wound-down oil development, bore a large, red-painted cross, its horizontal axis running rivulets, like blood or tears.

Next to it was painted the single word Lancelot, a medical relief outlet. Inside, an improbably well-fed Sudanese woman beamed at us and indicated for us to sit on a bench beside a desk with some paperwork. She bustled out, presumably to find someone. We waited, sitting, then wandering about the room, our feet echoing too loudly, looking out of windows that showed nothing, other than the back of another shed.

A while later, a tall, young white woman swung through the door. She didn't smile but said "Hi" in a neutral, unhostile manner and shook our hands. She wore a linen shirt, baggy against her slim frame, and fatigue trousers under a sleeveless porter's coat – plenty of pockets – and I saw from her wristband she was a doctor. Her dry fair hair was tied tightly back, showing coffee freckles running up from her neck to her temples. We told her we had a lorryload and what we carried.

"Great," she said, with neither contempt nor joy. "I'm Miriam."

We moved the truck across to a distribution yard, where strong, young, local men and a couple of English public schoolboys on a gap year broke up and assigned our load, bagging up smaller pack-ages to be carried long-distance on foot. Adrian and I slept beside each other that night, on the floor of a tool shed, under opened sleeping bags, feeling some body warmth, cherishing nourished flesh.

Early the following morning, we went down to see if we could help with distribution. A mixture of aiders and local hands were farming out the smaller sacking bags of maize to those strong enough to make the treks back to frail families. It was as well ordered as ever – that's what always surprises journalists and celebrity visitors – and apart from sorting out some obvious "mallies" for redirection to the medical tents, there was little to do.

So I wandered in the direction of the camp, where the listless throng sat with their emaciated offspring. This is no place for tourists, even semi-pros like me, and I wasn't about to wander aimlessly among the protracted dying, but Miriam, pinned down with diagnostics and prescription in a medical tent, did need some help with prioritisation of new arrivals at the margins of the camp who wouldn't have the strength to move through the grounded crowd. I could rank-order the critical stages of starvation and come back for a couple of the local med staff as necessary.

It's not difficult work. They barely see you when they're semi-detached from their surroundings, their bodies turned in on themselves. They have eaten their insides and are entirely internalised. There is no crying out for help here. Nor is there self-pity. The world is just as it is; it contains life and death and the margin between the two has been so eroded that the wait for death is just negotiable territory between existence and absence, more part of belonging with the dead than the living.

The quick and the dead are judged by omniscient aidies, the former redeemed so far as is possible, the latter disposed of hygienically. But those in limbo have given themselves to being taken either by us or by the stillness of the ground. We call ourselves relief workers sometimes, but part of that is about the quiet acceptance of our mutual exhaustion, knowing absolutely that relief is coming in one form or another. We're telling them: you will be fed or you will die.

Life isn't cheap in a famine zone. It's understood. It's death that comes cheap, not life.

At the edge of the muster, the groups thinned and I stopped by a small gathering still sitting in the sun, no shelter yet rigged, or no will to rig one. There's a very particular aura to the locus where someone will soon starve to death, and you come to feel a kind of beat in the air which marks the fading rhythm of living organs.

A young girl, maybe twelve, maybe more, was standing, alongside the matriarch, shawled and proud, her skin like hide, hardened by the sun. A younger mother squatted, her high cheekbones marking the contours of her skull, holding what was left of her child, a boy I think, in her lap. He no longer had the strength to be cradled, lying across the creases of her skirt like he'd fallen from the sky. The oversized head had fallen back, the flies around his eyes not flitting, but taking their fill from the ruins of his eyes, like cows at an oasis, watched from the air. A twitch of those eyes, which barely degenerate in starving children, was the only movement on him.

Reporters always say the skin is like paper, but it's not. It's like the last inedible membranes on cooked joints of meat that have been fully carved. All subcutaneous tissue had dried up and withered below his ribcage, which looked set to split from his chest. He had no bottom or hips and would never move his legs again. His mother's arms, the last of wiry tendons pushing their veins to the surface, fell either side of him, as though he was an offering. She stared without focus and I knew she was no longer absorbing images. But she could be saved.

I knelt beside her. We learn to remain expressionless if we want to communicate. It's a kind of sign language, needing none of the extraneous baggage of human contact, which requires wasteful energy to handle. But in this instance no contact was strictly necessary. The man had in all likelihood gone looking for shelter, or was dead, hatcheted maybe by government security, and these women would have walked for days with their dying infant cargo. The girl and her grandmother would survive, along with the mother, I could see that, but the boy child would soon be dead.

A plastic bowl of maize and water mush lay beside the mother, and the girl picked at a square of flatbread that lay in it.

These survivors would need medical attention, vitamins, supplements and the dying child would be in inaudible pain as his vital organs started their final collapse, so whoever had brought the holding sustenance should have attracted the attention of one of the medical corps who were moving through the crowd. I knew they should really get to one of Miriam's tents – this woman's strength could be supported once she had lost the burden of her child, its body despatched for incineration. I called past her to the sky-blue clad figure of a med scout and he glanced up briefly from another patient to acknowledge that he would work in my direction.

I reached for the little bowl of nutrients, tore a corner of the bread and dipped it in the mix, held it to the mother's lips to suck. She didn't move her head, but her insect-hand rose to take the morsel. Then the other arm rose like a crane jib. She was looking at me now.

"Take this," I said in one of the few Dinka phrases I'd learned.

It was a pointless command. But I needed her to suck on something rehydrating, get some moisture in her mouth.

"Do this," I repeated, holding the bread in front of her face.

Her hands took it and she separated it, the damp piece went in her mouth and, fixing me now with a blank stare, held out the remainder to me. I straightened slightly as I realised what was happening. She was sharing it with me. I took it quickly without smiling and looked up, not without petulance I think, at the standing girl and grandmother, who listlessly and without emotion looked down on our tableau of the living and the dead. I put the scrap of bread on my tongue.

A light transporter plane came moaning through the haze that afternoon, putting up what little dust was yielded from the rock-ground as it landed away from us. As it idled back towards the cabins, I saw sacks held in netting through its open side-doors, their blue roundels confirming that they were from the same source as ours. We had long unloaded, but I glanced over in the direction of the vehicle compound, where our truck would have been. I knew that this could be the start of a narrative of consequences for stealing a supply truck.

But the UN gofer who clambered out showed no interest in the bureaucracy of supply chains. Adrian stood in the sun, convincingly playing an old hand at Rumbek, and debriefed the pilot. This was one of three tiny planeloads that made it out of Lokichogio and had been allowed to continue from Juba. The Sudanese were closing the airstrips again, the latest step in its programme of controlled starvation clearly completed. The rest of the shipments we'd last seen at the Ugandan border would be laboriously distributed by road through south-western Sudan. They were further away than ever now.

As I heard the story and watched the sanguine acceptance of it on the part of the station staff, inured to chaotic disappointments and to whom one small shipment was just what it was, a kind of manna from heaven, I could picture Jimmy with the officials of Loki airbase, hands on hips, mirrored aviators reflecting his resignation to the business of famine administration.

And I knew that we, Adrian and I, were affirmed and vindicated in our piracy. I was glad, of course, for some bodies had been fed that would otherwise have disappeared. Some bags of food had already started their slow, determined journeys back to villages. I knew the horrors of under-supply: too little and we were only delaying, not interrupting, the processes of starvation. Some say the cruelty of that is ugly, but I don't buy that. Perhaps a very few would live who would have died but for our truck. Maybe our one load had made a difference. We could never know for sure.

But, God help me, I was glad for another reason that had nothing to do with famine. I'd proved that little jerk Jimmy wrong – a truck convoy had been the way to go. I wanted to seek him out and spit in his face. We'd only got one stolen truck through, a grandiose, token gesture that probably achieved nothing in the overall scheme of things, but I knew Jimmy's wrong call had let people die. And I realised I was pleased that we'd brought our truck here and he'd taken his to Lokichogio. It felt good, almost as good as arriving with a full convoy. I went to find Miriam, whom I knew would be signing off paperwork for the plane in the office cabin, where Adrian and I had arrived the previous day. It seemed longer ago. I wanted to ask her what best we could do for her back in London, more for moral support than practicality.

She was alone when I got there, leaning back against the desk and rubbing the heels of her hands up her pale cheeks, pushing the crinkled skin around her lower lashes up and over her green eyes. When her hands reached her forehead and flattened back over her hair, I saw she'd been crying and her top teeth emerged to bite her bottom lip hard.

I made no move towards her, but didn't look away.

"I'm sorry. It doesn't often happen," she said. "I'm just so bloody tired."

"I know," I said and just stood there for a moment, a small act of solidarity, I suppose. "I'm sorry too."

I tried to think of something else to say.

"Thanks for not grassing us up," I said eventually.

She smiled briefly and I left the room.

We hitched a lift on the plane. It was returning to Juba to refuel, then north to Khartoum, where some of the distribution of aircraft was being centralised, depending on which strips were being opened and closed. The whole pretence was about "security", but really it was just about further government control of supplies.

Before we left, Adrian disabled the truck, on a pretext of servicing it. He just disconnected the fuel lead or something. It would be easily fixed by anyone reclaiming the truck, but meanwhile would prevent any of the more able-bodied, or ambitious militia, using it to get out to remote villages. We couldn't take the risk of what might be done with a lorry that must have been reported as stolen. Besides, rogue transport is dangerous in a famine – Sudanese tribes have a touching but self-destructive culture of sharing all they have. Some of the food that had been walked back might last a month, but less than a week if a truckload of extra people turned up.

Back in Khartoum, I felt weird, like I was watching myself in a performance. I felt like I occupied a bubble, like no one else could see me. Adrian and I evidently looked like a proper item, as they say. We scrubbed up at a foreign correspondents' club, trying not to show our passes, though no one seemed to know anything of stolen trucks, and we were fed vegetable pie and potatoes. We got some cash at the embassy and went out into the cooling evening air. Sharia still held its grip on Khartoum, so there was little for Westerners with a post-zone thirst to do in the dusk, but we walked around the top of the airport, watching the lights of planes coming in from the north against a salmon sky and headed towards a cafe near the British Council, where the Blue and White Niles convened towards Egypt at al-Mogran.

This was where Brits hung out and we sat on a small terrace, separated from the gritty road by a metal fence, a little too large and heavy for the informality of a street cafe. It was soon clear why it was there; children and a few of their elders came begging, pushing their light palms through the bars at our ankle level. Occasionally the proprietor came out to curse them in Sudanese and take an optimistic swing with his foot at the skinny arms, which shot back through the railings like eels into rocks.

We drank coffee and iced crushes and smoked small cigars, picking at olives and oily vine leaves, as the bar began to fill from the Council and its surrounding hostels. We'd turned our branded gilets inside out, so that The Fed's logo – with its "Feed the Body" motto – didn't show, in case word was out for two lorry hustlers. But we still attracted the odd inquiry about where we'd been and the state of Bahr from the English-speaking young men and women who came in for kebabs and cola.

Adrian had a decent knack for dealing with these encounters, a friendly but economic exchange that conveyed information without freighting it with energy and, importantly, drawing no one in. Or maybe he was just like that – another thought is that he never had much conversation. We must have entered that period of decompression for aidies that follows a drop or a "mercy", as some of them called a station placement, a period of no more than an evening in failing light as you reconnect with the living, thriving world. That process was seasoned this time by the illicit nature of our operation, so there was even less to say to strangers than to each other, the opposite of how these rehabilitation sessions usually worked. We'd been outside Rumbek, we said, up from Uganda.

A draped string of light bulbs, with tin cans for shades, flickered on to illuminate us and we attracted the attention of a small group – perhaps five – of earnest young ex-pats with very fair skin and short haircuts. Their leader, a tall lad with a crucifix ostentatiously hanging around his neck on a leather bootlace, presented himself. This one was going to be harder to shake. After Adrian had delivered his standard replies in monosyllables, he moved on to me.

"Natalie. I'm Natalie."

"We're an educational project. Mostly building schools."

I nodded. There was something of a pecking order in aid. Famine relief ranked high. Schools didn't.

"I see it as a struggle between good and evil," he was saying.

I nodded again. Right so far, though I imagine he didn't mean local dictators backed by Western bankers versus starving farmers.

"The challenge is to keep them trusting in God, so they don't revert back to witchcraft."

"Uh huh. We just try to feed them, I guess."

It's difficult to join in this sort of conversation without sounding rude. And he was leading off now, a one-man mission. Once the act of evangelism is started, it must be made complete.

"There was a school building, brand new. But they were still meeting under the trees. They needed to cleanse their school. And they couldn't afford an animal for sacrifice."

"Or they'd eaten them all."

"Ha, right," he said, showing his teeth. "I told them that God had given them the school. In His grace – it was OK. And Jesus Christ had already made the perfect sacrifice, the only one that matters. Anyway, I got them to join hands around the schoolrooms and we said a prayer of blessing. Then – and this is the funny bit – I walked up to the wall of the school and patted it with the palm of my hand, saying, 'God bless this school.' And when I turned around, all these Sudanese kids were doing the same, patting the walls."

I deployed an exhalation of tobacco smoke into the night to mark the moment.

"And I told them, we've got to trust in the Lord. That's what I truly believe."

"I don't think you do," I said.

I was looking up at him, this gangly man with his simple answers, God's displacement therapist for the horrors of Sudan. I wasn't about to pull rank with my priesthood. That would have just been a get-out. Better to stay undercover.

"I don't think you truly believe that at all," I repeated.

"Oh, so you don't have a Christian faith," he said with faux disappointment, warming to his task of conversion. "So what motivates you to do your work? I bet it's the love of Christ, same as me, you just call it something different."

"I didn't say that, but God is what you fall back on when everything else has failed."

"No, it's not like that. God is everything that never fails."

"Is that so?"

I was smiling up at him now, as a benign heretic, not a priest. I went for the line that was most regularly put to me by aidies who interrogated my faith: "You don't feel that he may have let the people of Sudan down a teeny bit?"

"It's the world that's let Sudan down, not God. We're doing His work in putting that right." Those capitals again. "I really hope you let Him reveal Himself to you."

"Oh, I think He's done that all right," I heard myself say.

"So you're coming to faith? That's really great."

"I don't think anyone comes to faith actually. I think faith comes to us. Sort of squats like an annoying friend. For me, it came for a night and now I can't get it off my sofa."

"You're funny. I love it. It's just wonderful how Jesus works in people."

"I didn't say that either."

"I know. I just did. How would you put it then?"

He'd clearly been on a mission training course.

"Probably that I've reached out and touched the hem of a

passing garment. And it's not me who's bleeding any more. It's been twelve years, you know."

He stood grinning at me, his mind hanging like a crashed computer screen.

"Luke? Chapter eight? That's me," I said, then added: "It's not what you believe, bro. It's what you do."

I stood to go before I knew I'd made the decision and Adrian followed. He took my hand as we walked back to the billet, I remember that. The following morning, we got a message that UN lawyers had been in touch with head office and we were to return immediately. Tickets were transferred to the embassy. So we flew back to London.

Shortly afterwards, I married Ade. It seemed like the right thing to do at the time. It can't have been the common cause with the lorry, because I started to tell everyone that I'd acted alone and I rather preferred that narrative. I told him that was the story we were going with, that he'd left keys in the truck, I'd started it and he'd tried to stop me. Somewhere up the road he'd jumped from the cab and made his way to Khartoum to raise the alarm. Now I think about it, one of the reasons for marrying that we discussed was that it would mean that he wouldn't be required to give evidence against me, so he wouldn't have to perjure himself under oath.

Sarah didn't like the idea at all. It was the first and last proper row we ever had. I was round at her place in Hackney – by now quite smart – and we'd drunk nearly two bottles of Chilean white while she cooked a paella.

"Why would you do that?" she said. Note the conditional.

"Why wouldn't I do that?"

"Because he doesn't need anyone."

"I don't need him."

"Then why are you marrying him?"

"Why are you hanging out with a mopey Russian gangster?"

"Don't be ridiculous. I'm not marrying Sergei."

"You might as well. He's lost one missus. What's the point of wringing out his damp hankies if you're not going to get the money?"

"Is that what you think, Nat?" She'd turned from the hotplates, holding a spatula and I noticed suddenly there were tears in her eyes.

"Just being honest. We do what we have to."

"That's foul. I work for Sergei because of what he can do for peace in Palestine. You and Ade are great aidies. Doesn't mean any of us have to marry each other. Even if we want to and I don't."

"I'm marrying Adrian. You marry the Mob. You tell me which one if us is selling out."

We ate rice and prawns and chorizo, but something had changed in the room. I didn't see much of Sarah socially for a long while after that.

Some repatriated aid workers complain of the genteel ordinariness of life back at home, like returning war veterans, and for me I suppose it was the boredom, an endless drone of days that made me want to shout in defiance at the death rattle that passed for human exchange.

And then the business of the stolen truck took over. The newspapers had made me out to be some sort of renegade heroine, the Joan of Arc of international aid. A crinkly pop star had backed me:

"This heroic young woman should be given a bleedin' medal not a bollocking." I wanted to get away from all that again, abroad, and I suppose part of me wanted to prove to the UN I could still do a proper job, not just make headlines with potty stunts.

There was also a cold little knot of sadness lodged in my chest, just behind my sternum. I can point to it and I recognise it now, the kind you see the truly desperate fold little fists against and collapse into, with a small rising whine rather than a sob. I managed to resist that, but I was bloody unhappy – no, I was bloody and unhappy. I can see that now. And it was because I knew then that nothing was bloody good enough and never could be. I started to endure and prevail, but it wasn't living, I was making a decent enough job of the face I presented to the world, a brassy kind of armour that affected that I was battle-hardened, dry of wit and soul, had seen it all and was willing to sit through the repeats.

Most of all, I realise now, I was already bored with Adrian, with his silent strength and quiet faith, which together provided his placid conviction that the world could be changed and that, one day, we'd all trade fairly and everyone would be fed.

But I married him after we came back from Sudan that last time. Other than the legal implications of the lorry affair, he was my lot, a kind of matching option, in the way that you would choose a rug to go with a chair. Another couple, looking in, might have said we had much in common, a backstory full of oddball anecdotes that might have been told in one of those regular slots in a weekend colour supplement. But the truth was that he was my dreary base into which to fasten my hidden despair and I was his release from a buttoned-up little treasure trove of dreams.

We married in his childhood church, a whitewashed hall of a

place in south London, where chairs make scraping noises like recurrent coughs. Sarah said she was out of the country and maybe she was. It was a settled but soulless place, miles of Edwardian terraced houses where no one knows their neighbour. Though people live decades in such places, they don't dwell there, far less abide. The minister – and registrar – had a beard of course and smelt of patchouli oil. There was a band of Ade's mates, with a bassist who swung the neck of his guitar like an exercise machine. I lifted my skirts and did a little jig after the acclamations and our small congregation clapped, both in time and celebration.

And for a moment there I confess I was happy, because if you look happy then you are. We drank afterwards in the back room of a local pub called The Woodman and the room was free if we spent a hundred pounds at the bar. It was all too bright but kept the dark out and the landlord let us have it all night – I think he was a Christian – and we left at dawn, a bunch of tired aidies with nowhere to go. Even from the beginning, sex with Adrian was prematurely middle-aged, lazy, practised.

And, for him, the war was over. He joined the Home Front of the struggle against poverty and for social justice. Like any demobbed soldier, it emptied him. He started to look for a job that would pay the rent – rather sweetly, he was, I think, setting up home – and I almost immediately started the search for one that would get me away. Local government for him, and for me, after The Fed, an NGO delivering social-support services to displaced populations. That's what it said in its shiny little brochure. These days it would have delivered migration solutions. For me, the important thing was that it did this abroad as well as in the UK and offered plenty of foreign trips.

7

The next time I saw the Bishop he had Toby with him.

"Natalie, this is Rupert Naismith, whom I think is what is commonly known as a Foreign Office Flyer, though there is nothing common about him," said the Bishop.

"No, it isn't," I said. I looked at Toby and he just shrugged. It was self-deprecating and that appealed, against my better judgement.

The meeting was brisk. Clearly it didn't occupy diary time and the Bishop's sole purpose was to despatch us, like children running an errand.

I came later to know that they're all nicknamed Rupert, the officers and ex-officers of Guards regiments. I suppose he may as well have been called Rupert and I'm not sure I ever really knew his real name. Who cares? But he'll always be Toby to me. Perhaps Rupert was his "cover" that day. Perhaps the Bishop really did think his name was Rupert. I have no idea whether the others I met told me their real names and again I don't care. They were just avatars in my alternative reality.

We'd met in the Bishop's office, so that he could introduce us, then I was to allow two hours for Toby to take me to meet his colleagues. I noticed more about him this time. He wore a pale yellow-and-white striped shirt, the collar of which seemed a little high, like I remember my father wearing. Or I may have seen it in a television revival of one of those intense boardroom dramas, in which men in such shirts did barely restrained anger all the time. The shirt fell loose at the front. He didn't need to worry that his correct collar size might show his stomach; nothing inside it touched the shirt and, when he sat, you could still see his belt all the way round.

He wore a lilac tie with snail motifs on it. He wore it on the two or three times that I encountered him in these formal circumstances, though now I come to think of it, there may have been one with giraffes too. But, surprisingly for a spook, he dressed so you noticed his clothes. I remember his young pink neck too, scoured with shaving. The dimpled chin and the flush of cheeks that came with health that didn't need exercise, ginger-blond eyebrows, balding at the top of the forehead, a stubbly outcrop at the front, like seaweed finding purchase on a freckled rock. Tortoiseshell glasses with top-frames. Lashed azure eyes and fair hair cropped up the sides. No earlobes. Yes, I think I could pick him out of a parade.

We left the cobblestone yard of the Old Deanery and walked up the narrow lane, with its barber shop and wine bar, little changed in function, I imagine, over the past half-millennium or so. It's a dark little passage – the sun only shines on the new world.

"Are you Toby or Rupert, then?" I said, breaking into a trot to keep up with him.

"Call me Toby," he said and smiled. "Because it's my name."

"Why then? Why the business with the name?"

"To tell the truth, I think the Bishop was just a bit confused. We'd just been talking about my army years."

117

When we reached the traffic, I squinted up towards the cathedral. It was eighteen minutes past eleven.

"Shall we get a cab?" asked Toby and stepped towards the pavement edge. I noticed how elderly his natural posture was. He was so naturally fit, but held himself in that manner of the old moneyed classes, bent forward from the waist, his shirt collar emerging tightly from his suit lapel.

His hand should really have held a tightly furled umbrella as he hailed a taxi. I wasn't inclined to follow his burst of military energy and stayed by the glass of the sandwich shop on the corner. The taxi passed and he stared after it indignantly. Another was passing in the opposite direction, its window open. I lay my forefinger and thumb on my tongue and whistled hard. I can do that, always have been able to, and it's handy in the field. The cabbie glanced across his resting elbow and swung around. Toby smiled at me.

He barked something authoritatively through the cab's front window and then turned, holding the door. His right hand performed a little swish towards me, as if sweeping me into the back. Momentarily, I wondered how many luckless bankers' daughters had been swept along similarly in the outer reaches of SW postcodes. Swept off their feet, he probably imagined. What a knob.

Inside, as the cab swung left at the Circus for Victoria Embankment through a knot of office workers out for sandwiches, I thought Tobes was leaning forward to shut the sliding plastic window to the driver. But he was just jerking the flap of his double-vents on his jacket from under his bum.

"Is the Foreign Office the big marble one with the murals in Parliament Street?" I said, wanting to sound informed but uninterested.

"Ye-es, I expect so," he said, attempting a patronising smile that made him look like he was going to sneeze. "But we're not going there."

An irritating pause, into which I was expected to contribute.

"So where are we going, Sherlock?"

Looking back, how I wish that I'd just asked the cab to pull over and let me out. It was sunny, I could have walked for a bit.

"We're going sarf of the river – to sis."

"We're going to visit your sister?" I imagined a snake-hipped redhead with an Alice band and freckles. Clapham, probably. I was glad he'd attempted an Ealing-comedy accent. It put him further into my classification.

"No, not quite. I don't have a sister." Ah, actually that made more sense. "S-I-S. PO Box 010. Six." He turned towards me for the first time. "Vauxhall Cross."

I looked out of the window at the tourists around Big Ben, in what I hoped was a "whatever" kind of way. On Millbank, I expected the cab to turn left over Lambeth Bridge, crossing the Thames at the Palace, where I'd been for the legals not long before, but Toby leaned forward again and called for the cabbie to drop us just the other side of the roundabout, on the north side of the river.

A tenner through the window, some change, a receipt, then another come-on swish across the traffic and through a huge arch, decorated high above with gilt roses, in a great, light-grey granite slab of office block. Doors to be swished through, plastic identity card shown, turnstiles to be thighed through, the odd "she's with me", but apparently no need for me to tell anyone who I was, no desk-diaries with an elastic band across today's date for me to sign.

You'd have thought I would have to prove who I was, but being in Toby's tow was enough.

Then a lift. Down. If I'm honest, this really was a surprise. But perhaps we were going to a bunker. Or a theatre.

The lift gave out on to a white-bleached, concrete corridor with the lighting ducts in piped conduits. Swing doors and a little platform, next to a rail-track of a small gauge. It had more in common with a mine than London's Underground network.

"Hi-ho," I murmured.

No response from Tobes.

"How sweet," I added. "Do you have clock-golf too?"

"It takes us under the river to our office," said Toby, flashing his card in front of a reader again. "Saves anyone being seen going in and being compromised. There are two trucks, one at either end, with passing points in the middle, so a train is never more than five minutes away. Like a ski-lift."

"Or a tunnel of love." I was beginning to enjoy this.

The driverless funicular rattled into our chamber station and we got in. It was blue, surprisingly modern, big windows, sliding doors. It hummed into the illuminated darkness. I decided to try being nice.

"Is this your normal commute, Toby?"

It was still slightly mocking, but I said it with a smile.

"No, I live in Clapham. I take the bus in and use the front door."

Ahh. I felt slightly sorry that I'd mocked him now. Perhaps he was just a fresh-faced boy who knew no other world. But I was chuffed I'd got Clapham right, even if I had got the sister part of it wrong. He would live in a shared terraced house, close to the common, with a knock-through living area, with friends who knew what he did for a living and were quietly impressed, though they would pull his leg too. So he was used to it, but knew his job was quite cool, even if he'd applied for it, like everything else, on the internet.

The partner train flashed past – I saw no one in it. Then a more modern little station, more space, a flasher lift and into a corridor that felt high. I caught a view of the Thames sliding by, as if in the opposite direction now. Some big swing doors, open-plan behind tinted screens, staff at computers. A meeting room with two tall slit windows, facing only another wing of the same building, with similar slits. A fat-faced, smiley woman at the door.

"Would you like coffee or tea?"

I went for water, Toby held a hand up and said he was "good".

I wandered away down the length of the table: "Who are we meeting?"

"Middle East desk. I don't know who. I'm just the bag carrier." He looked at me and grinned. "No offence."

The room filled suddenly, led by a pale and skinny man, probably prematurely aged at around fifty, with blotched skin and a closely shaven balding head. He smiled a crinkly eyed grimace that gave his lids the texture of foreskins and shook hands, having dumped some buff folders.

Behind him was a younger woman, tallish and slim, with sensibly managed hair, a pale blue suit about a decade out of date with a beetle brooch on her left lapel. She sat and opened a red and black notebook and a small laptop.

The third was another woman, shorter, with an unattended bob, showing grey streaks that weren't highlights. She wore a ready, broad and rehearsed smile and leaned in to shake my hand warmly as if she knew me. She came too close with her greeting, wanting to convey that she was my friend and colleague in this troupe. When she'd moved from behind the others, she'd have known the first thing I'd notice was her dog collar on a navy clerical shirt, under a charcoal sleeveless cardigan.

This little triumvirate had been together elsewhere, I thought. They had gathered before I arrived for the purpose of this meeting, and I wondered what they'd been saying about me and what was on Miss Buttoned-Up Oxbridge's laptop, as Toby, suddenly deferential, slid by wall-side and out of the room, closing the door without any acknowledgement from the new arrivals. This wasn't apparently a display of rudeness; they all knew each other too well for that.

"Roger Passmore," said Baldy, nodding in affirmation of his own name. "This is my colleague Catherine and I wonder if you've met Cara Carrington, who works in the mission division of Church House?" Cara. Of course. From the big meeting room at Lambeth Palace. But not bustling out this time.

I could have arrived for an interview, which in a way I suppose I had.

"I don't think we have," said Cara, tilting her head and furrowing her brow, which I recognised as the universal pastoral signal that "I'm happy to know you – please trust me with all your secrets."

No doing, sister – I hope to Christ I never looked at anyone like that. "We were in the same room once at Lambeth Palace," I said. "But we weren't introduced." I saw a flicker of insecurity cross her face and that was satisfying.

We sat at the phony, walnut-style table, Passmore at the head, the Rev Cara by Catherine opposite, so she was on the edge of the meeting, having to lean in on her forearms to show her engagement with me.

I remember there was a sort of washing-up session at the top of the meeting. Passmore was clearly used to this kind of recruitment exercise and was nothing if not a stickler for detail. He delivered a smooth preamble on the Official Secrets Act as if barely listening to himself. He said it was generally misunderstood and that we didn't sign it so much as be bound by it permanently, like any other law.

He made what may have been a previously successful gag about some people exercising their right to opt out of it in favour of Her Majesty's hospitality – even Rev Cara didn't laugh – and wound up by saying that "in any event", he found it easy talking freely with clergy because his work "in all kinds of ways" suited the confessional.

Rev Cara smiled fit to burst at this. I mentally cast her as a circus act called Seal of Confessional, balancing a ball on her nose and slapping her short fins together.

"We just wondered if you could help us with some analysis we're doing of the peace process in Palestine," he said.

That's what he actually said, I remember now.

"The difficulty we have is ensuring the safety and security of aid workers in occupied territories in Palestine, particularly Christians."

Oh yeah? You don't give a damn about the safety of aid workers, I thought at the time. But that's not what I said. What I said at the time was all quietly expert and thoughtful.

"Why would you have to?" I asked. "My understanding is that

aid workers are there at their own risk, with the UN supposedly providing some blanket cover."

I knew from my own time in Palestine that we were meant to invoke the United Nations for free passage, but that it was useless in the field. It's hard to invoke international law under mortar attack or with a muzzle in your mouth, though I'd been lucky. I'd heard stories. There are more aid workers killed out there than you ever hear about in the Western papers, mainly because so many of them aren't European.

Rev Cara interrupted, her voice soft but firm. I bet life was tough for Mr Rev Cara.

"Much of the work we've done there has been facilitated by the Foreign Office. The government has a duty of care to those who work there. I'd like to think the Church does too."

What textbook did she get that out of?

"The Christian population there is dwindling, as I'm sure you know," said Baldy Roger. "Most of them are Russians now, looking for an American passport. But the Christian axis continues to offer a crucial arbitration between Israel and the Palestinians."

I didn't need to hear all that stuff. Baldy even asked if I knew Palestinian Christians are called Living Stones. Yeah, I did actually. And Israel was trying to get blood out of them. But I didn't say that.

It went on like this for a bit, the usual old rubbish about the Christians keeping the peace by being the *via media* between an Israel that occupied the entire region and a Palestine that wanted to wipe it from the map.

After a load of this, I asked the big question: "So where do I fit in?"

"Ah," he said, taking this as encouragement that I would want to. "We want to hold a conference out there. A Christian conference, one that reaches out to the other faith communities, that provides a neutral platform for speakers from all three religions, a bridge across the conflict that both shows the importance of the Christian presence but which really sweats its unique opportunity to be the catalyst for a lasting peace in Palestine."

I promise you he did talk about "sweating" the Christian opportunity.

"We'd love you to convene one of the three days of the conference. We'll have the Archbishop of Jerusalem, of course – and we hope we'll have Canterbury too – but we really thought it would be helpful to have someone who knew the region and its problems at ground level, as it were."

"And a woman," said Rev Cara, with a concerned face now.

"An aid worker, a Christian priest, someone who could speak authentically but wasn't just one of the big figureheads of religious leadership," said Baldy and Cat (as he called her) patted this profile of me into her laptop.

"Right." I sat back and laughed at the three of them. Not unpleasantly. I was doing charming, like I did on my women's committees. "But why are we here?"

They sat still. They didn't surely think I was making an existential point?

"I mean, why are we sitting in intelligence services talking about this?" I'd wanted to say: why are we sitting in this hollowed-out volcano like Bond villains? But I didn't want to offend them. Not yet.

"Why are we here, Cara?"

Again, I wanted to say, why are you here?

They all looked at Baldy, but he didn't speak, so I went on. "You know how this usually works. Some bloke from the Foreign Office has a word with the Archbishop's Council, then suddenly the Anglican Communion's office is organising a conference in Israel. Why not that? I'd never have known the difference. Why the spooks?"

"We indirectly cooperate, as you know, with a number of arms of government and the intelligence service is one of those and it's a two-way street. . ." Cara began to drone on, colouring slightly and taking the subject seriously for the first time that afternoon, I thought. Baldy let her finish.

"All that Cara says is right," he said. "Much of the coordination for a project such as this would be done through the Middle East desk here. Nothing odd about that. It's where the expertise lies. And then there's your expertise, Natalie. We'd want to dovetail into that. It's a question of excellence." Oh, my Lord.

"And . . ." He paused for effect. "There's something else we'd like you to do for us." We all stayed quiet, so he had to carry on. "And this is where this meeting departs from its formal agenda."

Cat, I noticed, had stopped tap-tapping into her laptop.

"Thank you, Cat," said Baldy. She stood without a word and left the room. Such economy, three swift movements and she was gone.

"The women priests now outnumber you," I said to Baldy, but what I was really wondering was why Rev Cara was still here.

"Cara has been putting much of the conference together for us. And she suggested you as the ideal candidate for this role."

"Role?" I was struggling again to take this seriously.

"We wondered if you'd be kind enough to run an errand for us."

Baldy was talking like a geography teacher taking an orienteering exercise.

"What sort of errand?"

"We simply need an envelope swapped with another envelope in Jerusalem. It's quite safe and simple. It's a simple exchange of contracts. Letters of undertaking on both sides to abide by the protocols that establish the Church in Jerusalem as a mechanism for a peace agreement. Not so much as arbitrators, not that proactive, more acting as the clearing house."

I snorted slightly and shrugged.

"Why would you want me to do it? Why me? Why don't you just email each other? Or why not have Cara be your postman?"

"It's just about a degree of anonymity, Natalie. For right or wrong, people who have worked closely with the Foreign Office are perceived as people who might . . . unhelpfully recognise people on the other side of the argument. Cara is one of those people. They will similarly send someone who has had no background in negotiations or discussions. It's just a way of acting in good faith."

"It's really not a big deal," said Cara suddenly. "It's just that both sides have to behave in the same way."

"And what would those sides be?" I asked. There was a pause so I filled it. "Let me take a wild guess – I suppose I'm not running your errand for dispossessed Palestinians?"

"We're hoping that Hamas will respond in kind to the initiative we're holding out."

"It would be a tremendous service, if you could help us," added

Baldy Roger. His forearms were on the table. He'd finished his pitch and was now sounding supplicatory.

"No," I said, gathering myself to leave, "that's well above my pay grade. You have ways and means. I'm an ex-aid worker, that's all. And one who's in trouble for nicking a lorry at that . . . but I expect you know all about that. I'd play with your conference, but I'm not about to start fronting the next American–Israeli peace process, or whatever it turns out to be. I wouldn't know what I was doing. It's a daft way to do it anyway."

"Well, I hope you'll think about it. You're ideal and it would be a huge help," said Baldy and Rev Cara looked sad. "But let's talk about the conference anyway. We'll be in touch."

And after a bit more chit-chat I left. Toby was curiously already waiting outside in the corridor and delivered his Persephone back through the underworld. That night I looked Cara up in Crockford's, the clergy reference log. Leeds Uni, then Westcott House, Cambridge for her training. Parish ministry in Derbyshire, then mission work for the Archbishops' Council. That was it. It obviously didn't tell her story. But then my entry looks as innocent as hers, too.

8

Funny, isn't it, how looking back you remember incidents that change everything, but you don't notice at the time how they're changing you. These slower swings in direction are more like slow changes of season; I'd discover after a while that the climatic conditions I lived in had dramatically altered, without identifying a particular moment when my second spring had taken me to priesthood, or when autumn became winter in my marriage.

Then there are those life changes that combine the sudden and the seasonal. An event that changes everything for ever, so that we can see later that we were different people either side of that moment. I was a different woman with that ridiculous little team in the bright and shiny Vauxhall Cross office, with the forced flora under its twenty-four-hour lighting, than the woman I was subsequently. But that change wasn't incremental. It came in a single moment. That moment of change, after which nothing ever looked the same, was just after I'd found child pornography on Adrian's computer.

More precisely, it was the moment right after his denial. This is how it happened.

Looking back now – and it's weird – I see myself entering my house as in a movie, an atmosphere charged with a sense that there was something waiting to be discovered. Waiting for me, to be discovered by me. I realise I'm writing that back into the story now, giving the build-up to the hideous little discoveries a greater sense of anticipation than I had at the time. There were no portents of things to come. But those things did come, so the events that led me to them are freighted with a sense of foreboding.

Still, it has to be said that I stood in the hall of my house for a moment and felt the intensity of silence around me, the still air taking on the soupy quality of someone else being with me. Mystics and mountaineers have talked of sensing the presence of The Other. Perhaps that was the trip I was on. If not, why did I call out "Hello?" Then, feeling idiotic and slightly insecure, "Adrian?" It felt like there was someone in the house.

I knew he'd left for work, as always, at about half past eight. The mug was in the muesli bowl above the dishwasher, an arrogant little assumption that I would put it in because he had a formal, contractual start-time of nine and my commitments varied. It was 10.15, I remember, and I was just back from taking the duty matins and binning correspondence in the Chapter House.

Whatever it was, my issue wasn't with the ground floor. I was calling upwards, towards the study and bedrooms, where a classical radio station was playing softly. We never listened to classical radio.

I started upstairs as if I was in a cheap movie horror scene, not exactly scared, but moving briskly and wearing a bewildered expression to assure anyone I found, or if no one then myself, that the atmosphere was normal. On the landing, silence again. I must have known I was alone, but still pushed the door of the study open as if I was intruding. The desk light was on and I remember the door hitting the bookcase-end behind it. There was no one behind the door but, childlike, I still looked.

The desktop computer was on, its fan turning a little whirlwind of dust in the morning shafts from the window. That must in some way have been playing into the stillness of the house, changing its mood, as if there was someone still here after they'd departed. I'd have muttered some sort of dissatisfied expletive as I turned the lamp out and shook the mouse to shut down the screen. Adrian's email from his server connection at the office shone out and I reduced it. Behind it was another page, a deep red background, a primitive masthead stamped across the top with "dotcum.com", a small screen to the right streaming a loop of some monstrous organ penetrating an anus like a Victorian mill piston. I let out an abrupt little grunt and scrolled down. Lots of doll-like painted faces with improbable names under them, improper nouns like Summer and Lolly. I shut the site and went to Recycle Bin. Nothing. To Tools and History. A gruesome litany of babes and bangs and sluts between the codes and forward-slashes. This time, I was surprised at how calm I was, how I moved the cursor around the screen like I was shopping or looking for directions. I clicked on a couple at random, black screens started to download, little wheel-clocks rotating to show that moving images were being downloaded. I shrank them to the bar at the bottom of the screen, like foul genies going back in their bottle. I carried on clicking, bent towards the screen as if an invisible, incompetent child was occupying the chair.

Then up came some apparently random coding, and after a blank white screen for a moment, the machine matter-of-factly delivered the image that made me exhale as if punched, the air drawn in a short gasp, knocking my ribcage upright, my hand over the bottom half of my face as if holding the living breath in, so that nothing could escape from me, not a cry, not a word in response to the scene in front of me. If I made a sound, it would be a response. That would mean I'd engaged and I could not. The eyes. The insane bewilderment of the grin. The plaits in the hair.

Then I had to get it away, out of the room, out of sight and out of mind, out of me. The hand that reached for the mouse wasn't calm any more; it had that robotic, anticipative shake of someone traumatised. I knocked it down, but didn't delete, scrolled down the history. There were many pages from the same site. I couldn't, wouldn't, open them, as a vague notion of self-protection returned – this was my session now and it would record my choices. Could I explain that? I wondered what planetpuck might be, or sodasiphon or icescream.

I shrank the history to the base bar and threw the mouse behind the phone as if it had stung me. My God, my prints were on it. Don't be silly, it was my computer, our computer, why shouldn't I have touched it? My hands were at my side, not covering my face or anything. I was suddenly interested in my calm. The initial shock was gone. I could do what I wanted. I picked the mouse up and placed it carefully on its mat. I turned and left it as it was, like I was abandoning a failed tumble dryer. Downstairs I felt safe, the atmosphere had returned to something approaching normal, the exaggerated clatter of my movements in the kitchen affirming I was functional and human, making some coffee, the teacher who had cleaned up the messy child, the nurse who had changed the dressing on the wound. I can do anything, I told myself again.

I assessed the legality of having the computer upstairs with active downloads. They had been opened by me. But the log-in was Adrian's. What was running was evidence of a crime. To that extent, I was helping police with their inquiries. These were material consequences. Elsewhere in my consciousness I was recognising incrementally that nothing would or could ever be the same again. I had ruptured a membrane to hell in my own house. Its gates were open. It was like I'd unlocked the beast in the study upstairs. It was still belching noxious breath with its gentle fan, poisoning the air of my house. Was that what I had felt and smelt in the house, what had led me to the desktop there in the first place? I don't know, but I had been led, hadn't I?

Contingency planning, they call it in the field. Think what could go wrong – with supplies, with militia stealing the food – and eliminate the possibilities. What if I died this afternoon, electrocuted on a household appliance, brain haemorrhage, bludgeoned by a burglar? That stuff would be found on the computer and I'd never have a voice. Adrian wouldn't confess. It couldn't harm the dead, he'd reason, even if I was despised for my secret life. He was nothing if not pragmatic, as his internet cache strangely showed, with its neat cataloguing. What if the house was raided this afternoon? I'd look like his winsome accomplice, like those passive partners who are stage assistants to rape and murder? It was like there were cadavers of the innocents on the floor above me.

But, again, I was surprised that I was calm. The involuntary shake in my forearm had gone almost immediately. I realised it was the shock of the moment, genuinely and only the moment of realisation. There was no aftershock; it hadn't possessed me. Indeed, I was self-possessed. My breathing was shallow. I was the expressionless cleric as I passed the large, fitted gilt mirror in the hall that had come with the house, pale, offering no signals in my face because there was no one there to offer them to.

I did some paperwork, read some cathedral project proposals for art exhibitions, wrote some standard letters to donors. But I phoned the women-bishops group and made my excuses, flat-voiced and administrative, for not attending a briefing in Westminster. I wasn't going to leave the house. Not in the state it was in. Not with the bodies in the study. I couldn't yet leave the scene.

I rehearsed what I was going to say, I remember. Not for the purpose of delivering an effective speech. I needed to build my case, to identify and articulate what I thought, so that I was normal and right. On the side of the angels, I suppose. I made a small split-bean salad, enough for one, with some pitta bread and hummus. The afternoon wore on. I drank tea. I was normal; I hadn't been to the edge of the abyss after all. And I waited, not with impatience. I was curious to know how it would turn out.

I turned on the television for the news and turned it off again. Put the radio on and the evening news magazine was running. Made more tea. Read a book on female witness in the gospels that I was to review for a theology periodical and noted with satisfaction that I could concentrate on it, make notes. It's what I did then, before I found the deeper abyss.

And he arrived home – though, as I write that, I know now that I'd stopped considering it home, even then – at a little after six. He must have worked later than five, or had a quick drink with one of his mousy colleagues, maybe the one he'd had here. I heard the key and my mood didn't alter, no start at the base of the throat, no gall rising. Briefly, I wondered if this was how violent episodes started, placidity turning to a sudden red mist, the sort of event we read about in the papers and never have a clear idea what really happened. One of us left dead.

But no, the surface remained as calm as my interior. It was a strange atmosphere but I wasn't inclined to break it. I was in the kitchen at the end of the hall, a cavernous and heartless chamber that had presumably been a garden room when the kitchen was in the staff basement. I could picture the scene as he saw it: the gloaming of the hall, the brightness of the kitchen, the radio on softly, me sitting at the table with book and notes. "Hi," he said, from the door.

"Hello." I looked up. But didn't stand. Just stared at him. Not with disgust, actually completely thoughtlessly, taking nothing in. A pause.

"What's up?" he said, sensing something.

"I think you'd better tell me what's on your computer."

"What do you mean?" he said, straightening up.

"I think you know. You left your browser open. Something to titillate at dawn. Your Daily Office, as it were."

He took a step into the room and exhaled like a collapsing tent.

"Oh, Jesus. It was only a bit of curiosity. Some pop-ups came with some spam and I clicked them. I'm not interested in that stuff, just clicked to see what it was."

I was on my feet now.

"Interested? What the hell do you mean? I don't care what you're looking at with your pants round your ankles. But if you're an illegal pervert – and you are – you need to be banged up and you're not taking me with you, *capisce*?"

This was unplanned. Where had it come from? I wasn't angry. I was still calm. But why was I doing this and where was I going with it?

"Hey, don't do this," he said, his voice rising over mine, one hand out, palm down, conciliatory, reasonable. "It's just a bit of porn. It happens. A stupid mistake. I don't get off on this stuff. If I was used to it, if I were a user, I'd have concealed it, wiped my history. Come on. It was just a couple of curious clicks."

I'd walked towards him. That surprised me. I hit him on the upper chest with the palms of both hands, like one of those percussionists with a circus troupe, smashing dustbin lids together. He staggered back, a blank fear on his face for what might come next.

"I don't give a damn what you do with your mind and body, but you bring it in my house and I'm going to call the police. Which is what I did this afternoon."

I looked for a reaction to this lie. His brow broke.

"Police?" He grunted a disbelieving laugh. "For God's sake, Nat, I can see why you're angry, but this is way overreacting. Have you never seen this stuff before?"

"Dear God, Adrian, don't tell me you think this is in any way tolerable. It's still up there. I've done what I need to do. Now get up there and get it out of my house. And then get out of it yourself."

He was back at the door, staggering back under the force of another thud from the balls of my palms. He turned and lurched from the room. He was like a humiliated child as he stumbled up the stairs, not sure where or why he was going, but I had no pity. Humiliation was what I wanted.

I sat again and began to process his reaction, what he had said. I turned the radio off, but not really to hear what was going on upstairs. It was like inside me something was speaking to me, and I needed to listen, to concentrate anyway. But I suppose too that I wanted the atmosphere to be sparse when he returned. I wanted him to feel he was facing his judge, not a probationer. No, that's not quite right, I wanted him to be entering his condemned cell.

Right now, he would be learning quite how much I'd discovered, I thought, hoping that I'd just stumbled on some fetish or adult site, if adult is the correct alternative to what was up there. I imagined him closing his eyes and dropping his head as he raised the images from the download bar, not so much out of the shame of discovery as the disappointment that this was indeed what I had found. Maybe he'd sit for a moment on the sofa in there to prepare his response. Maybe he'd kill himself.

It certainly took some time for him to reappear. Longer than I expected anyway. Perhaps he'd thought I would follow him. I heard a foot on the landing, then heavy steps on the stair. They bore the weight of guilt, I thought. I was sitting again and he came further into the room this time. I said nothing. If I'd smoked at home, I'd have been holding a cigarette.

"Nat, that stuff," he started and his voice was weak. "You can't believe that has anything to do with me. Can you? It doesn't. Really. Please."

As the words started to come singly, I noticed he was even paler and there were tears in his eyes. His jawline trembled. I had expected denial; I hadn't expected self-pity. I felt nothing.

"So who got them up, Mrs Pug?"

Mrs Putt was a weekly cleaner provided by the Chapter. She had a squashed and wrinkled nose. This was engagement and I immediately regretted it. However absurd, I'd let an alternative possibility into the narrative. He jumped on it and started forming sentences. They tumbled out as if their quantity gave them credibility.

"I swear, I have never ever looked at child stuff. I never, ever would. That's just vile." He struggled for other words. "You must know that. Anyway, I just looked, just now, and it's from behind a paywall and I've never paid for anything like that – you can check my credit card if you like, if you must. The other stuff, the tame stuff, the stuff I checked on in the spam, must have linked to the other pages somehow, I don't know. But I had nothing to do with that stuff. Oh, for God's sake."

He half-turned away, sighed and stared at the ceiling. The humiliation was complete. I stared at him, waiting for something else. It didn't come. I think he was waiting for some comfort, for some evidence of anything between us that could bridge this. I didn't feel sorry for him, but I did feel some sorrow for him, I see that now. I see also that, had I felt something for him, I really might have stood and taken his arm in some sort of gesture of familial solidarity, shared the pain, offered some grace, if not forgiveness.

But I knew then that I wasn't that person, we weren't those people, and it came as no surprise, as I'd known it all along. It couldn't compare with the shock of the discovery upstairs, after all.

And something else. Something more mildly shocking, but of the moment and this room we were in. The something that changed everything. To my surprise and shock, I wanted to believe him.

An alternative narrative began to form. I examined it briefly, turned it over to make sure it wasn't counterfeit, satisfied myself that I wasn't indulging in wishful thinking.

"Have you also taken to listening to Classic FM on the radio upstairs?" I asked softly.

"Of course not," he said sulkily, his back still turned. "Why would I do that?"

"I know," I said, by way of cold acknowledgement. I said it calmly, the energy sucked out of our confrontation by this new banality. The kitchen was still to this little epiphany and I realised I could hear, or could imagine, the whirr of the computer fan again upstairs.

The revelation continued to unfold itself to me. I examined how every part of it fell into a well-formed place. How everything previously now looked awkward and ill-fitting, how this new idea had brought order to all that before had been random and chaotic, how it made all things new.

"I really can't believe that you believe this of me," Adrian was saying, or something similar.

"I know it's not you," I said in my new voice. "I'm sorry."

He looked at me. He must have been surprised. I know I was.

"It's just some ghastly internet download error."

"No, it's not," I said.

"What do you mean?" He was looking down at me, with concern, I expect. I may have been pale. I was staring through the wall.

"It's a warning from hell," I said.

Finally, I looked at him and focused. I could tell he wanted to ask the same question again. Instead, he just said, "I wouldn't do that."

"I know," I said.

9

When the bombs went off on the London Underground in July 2005, I was in a stockbroker's office, talking about funding mission in the City, and Sky News was running on screens suspended from the ceiling, a silent pantomime of a major "power failure" on the transport system. Do us a favour, I thought. The dark truth we suspected surfaced when we saw the lid blown off the bus and the faces of survivors, white, black and red. I can remember wondering what I should do, whether I should be somewhere, visiting the injured, comforting the dying, that sort of thing. These were promises I made when I was ordained, but my instincts had been nurtured in Africa.

As it turned out, the decision was made for me. Hugh called my mobile and told me I'd been allocated Aldgate tube station, under the London Diocesan Crisis Plan. I didn't know we had a plan. I walked quickly up Fenchurch Street, the sound of sirens the only augur that this wasn't a normal City day.

My dog collar was all that was needed to penetrate the police cordon and, as ever, I'd entered a brutish new world, devoid of anyone without a fighting role to play, like a war zone. In a small, hastily erected marquee, I was given an identity card to fill out, simply name, function and employer. In the final category, I wrote

"God". When I ran an errand later and had to show it to an officer at the tapes, he laughed. It is a laugh, really.

At the church, St Botolph without Aldgate, a light and airy seventeenth-century rebuild next to the Underground station, the incumbent staff and clergy were doing the best they could to become a field station for the emergency services, mostly an elite crew of fire and rescue firemen trained for bomb carnage.

I smiled. The atmosphere of suppressed desperation was very much like Africa, but we were fulfilling our caricature of old England. We were making tea.

"We must get them something to eat – to keep up their strength," I said to a tall police officer in a hi-vis jacket. He took me across the road, traffic lights signalling dutifully to a road blocked by parked ambulances. Opposite, there was a City sandwich mini-mart, evacuated of its staff. They'd left in a hurry. It was unlocked; the swing door gave listlessly to my shoulder. Tight little gondolas freshly filled with tempting gourmet sandwiches and salads for a lunch hour that the local money men and international currency dealers would now be spending in the bars to the west.

"Help yourself," said the policeman. "It's OK."

He held a cardboard box, while I randomly reached for salmon, couscous, all-day breakfasts, yoghurts and crisps.

"Better not take too much ham," he said. "There may be Muslims."

I filled plastic carrier bags too and we crossed with our booty back to St Botolph's. The church was filling now with a shift just up from the dark underworld beneath. Big men in almost paramilitary gear, they stood about with mugs of tea and coffee or sat uncomfortably in small groups in the pews. I started to do what I do. I fed the hungry.

I've often found violence surprisingly easy. People don't realise that. You just need to get started. Once you've hurt someone, really injured someone or just hurt them emotionally, you wonder, frankly, what all the fuss was about. And then it suddenly makes sense of all those assaults you hear about, the ones that make you wonder: why didn't they stop to think for a second just before pushing the knife or pulling the trigger, like most of us would?

But you don't think, you see, because it's easy, because you've done it before and it's over before you realise you've started. That's why it makes no sense to people reading newspaper reports in their conservatory extensions. They see someone on death row or facing decades in prison and think, how stupid, all for a moment in which they could have weighed the consequences and made a different decision. Never mind thinking about the victim – why didn't they think of themselves? Then they wouldn't have ruined their lives too. But it's not like that. You're resentful, you're angry, you even hate and then you do what you do, the opportunity arises so you just do it. Oops.

The first time it happened to me, it was all over before I knew I'd taken any kind of decision. I suppose I was a little surprised I'd done it, but I knew in the instant of seeing what I'd done that I could do it again. I can't say that I wanted to do it again, but I'd lost my violence virginity and, rather than remorse, all I felt was relief, like a rite of passage. Any mystery was gone and I could do it again and again if I wanted. I'd hugely injured another person, but I didn't care about that of course. As for me, it was no big deal, really.

This is how it happened. My dad struggled not so much with the functions of bringing me up – that is, feeding and educating me, and I suppose being there for me, bless him – but with the logistics. He was a single parent, having lost Mum to cancer just as I was starting secondary school, and he had to get around his job and get me around mine, or so he thought. He'd take me to the cinema most Saturdays in term time and take care about what he took me to see. I suppose he was anxious not to patronise me – he'd raise the subject on Wednesday or Thursday evening, the local paper open on the kitchen table. He'd avoid the U certificates and go for the 15s, which was sweet. I noticed he took me to an 18 once when I was sixteen, but he must have asked his mates at work. It was a spy movie, with some violence and loads of swearing, but no sex to speak of. I guess that would have been toe-curling for both of us.

That's what makes all this so disappointing, that he tolerated me being sexually abused. I can't really forgive him for that.

It came about because of a mild little dad-like inadequacy. School was three miles away and the school bus went nowhere near us. The public buses were the other side of the park and Dad wouldn't have me crossing that, especially not on dark evenings, which is ironic given the alternative he came up with.

There was his cousin. Actually his cousin-in-law. He was married to Dad's uncle's daughter, I think. But you don't really concentrate on those family connections when you're young. They lived on the other side of the park and he worked at a shoe wholesaler out on a light industrial estate the other side of school. So he'd pick me up and drop me at school in the mornings. Then he'd usually pick me up at whatever time I finished. I did wonder how he could finish work at my school times; sometimes it was 4.30, sometimes six or seven, if I had activities or the occasional detention.

They call it abuse and it was quite serious abuse. But I used to think it didn't mess me up, then or afterwards. I know it sounds stupid, but I did feel in control. I've always felt in control.

He always said I looked nice in a smarmy way, and then – I can't remember when it changed exactly – he seemed to concentrate on my legs, always going on about my black school tights, how "shiny" they were and how "shapely" my legs were, which made me sound like something out of my dad's old magazines. I don't think they were shiny at all. We weren't allowed shiny tights at school.

I just stared out of the window most of the time, not really looking at the overfamiliar route home. The first time it happened, we were stopped at the traffic lights, his hand left the gear-stick and he ran his knuckles up and down my leg, between my knee and the hem of my skirt. I thought later that this was how I'd have described it, the vocabulary that I'd have chosen, with a prissy degree of exactitude, to a sympathetic but clipped woman police officer, if it ever came to that. I guess I'm meant to say now that my stomach knotted and I was scared and wanted to get away from him. But actually I just felt this strange sense of detachment, simply watching, while listening to his stupid mutterings as if from a distance, as if he was in a different place.

It became a routine. No touching on the way to school. Then the hand on the knee, moving to the thigh on the way home. After a while of this, he'd stopped talking as much and seemed as bored as I was. It was just a habit. I even wondered if he really knew he was doing it, staring out through the windscreen and idly stroking my right leg between gear changes.

Then suddenly it got worse, when I switched from art to woodwork for exams. The Head, a bouncy little freak called Pander in the way that we had to have at least one teacher who had a silly name, was very keen for her girls to do woodwork and metalwork. I welcomed the opportunity to get away from books and classroom and do something practical at last. I liked the curl of the shavings and the smell of glue and resin.

Cousin Derek had a shed in his garden, on the back of his garage, and was into lathe-turning. It was suggested by the weedy but kind man who took our classes that I might turn a couple of chair legs for my project. The rear legs of my chair were to be curved but squared, but the front legs could be turned, under proper supervision. Well beyond what was required by the syllabus, but there'd be a good grade in it.

I had a strong sense that I was performing an act of acquiescence in going to the shed. In truth, I wanted to do the carpentry. But I knew it looked like "consent" for Dirty Derek, even if consent doesn't work for the under-sixteens. Sure enough, as I held the chisel to the lathe to get the feel of marking wood on the turn, he would run the palm of his hand down my bum. If I was in my school skirt, he lifted it and stroked through my tights. If I was in trousers, he was firmer, dipping down for little raids between my legs. The conceit, I suppose, was that I was concentrating and so didn't notice – busy with my hands, I had abdicated ownership of the rest of my body. This happened a couple of times or more, an absurd routine in which the upper halves of us conducted

145

carpentry tuition, while apparently entirely unrelated sexual activity developed under the bench. Then his breath shortened and his words cracked and faltered as he told me where and how much pressure to apply to the wood.

Derek made his move. His right hand left my bottom and reached over my shoulder and took the chisel from my hand. He turned me by the shoulders towards him and I realised he'd taken himself out. "Exposed himself," I'd have told that kindly and imaginary police officer. He directed my hand downwards and I'm afraid to say that it's funny, it makes me smile now anyway, to recall that I was wearing rubber-lined gloves. This evidently was sufficiently sensuous, however, and he wrapped my fingers around him and started to move his hips back and forth. I made no movement myself, didn't even tighten my fingers, he applying the pressure with his own hand around mine. I just stood there, staring into his overalls. This didn't go on for long. He didn't quicken the pace and didn't finish, at least I don't think so. But after a couple of minutes, he was breathlessly telling me some crap about how beautiful I was and how he would look after me and that this was our secret place. He ran his hand through my hair.

After that time, I told Dad. I think it was the next day, at supper. "Derek's trying to have sex with me." Dad did look properly shocked, to be fair. Not the sort of shocked that people do when they want you to know they're shocked. He did the expressionless, pale version that people do when they've evacuated their faces and moved inside to handle the horror of what they're being confronted with. I've since seen it on the faces of people seeing someone starving for the first time.

I filled the silence. "He touches me. He's started to make me touch him." It sounded like a voice coming from elsewhere, like I was possessed. Now I'd said it, it was real for the first time and I wanted to cry. We ate a little more. Spam and beetroot, I think.

Eventually he said, "I'll sort it out immediately. I'm sure it's nothing."

Those were his exact words. I thought he might hug me, but he didn't. Perhaps he thought I'd think that was the same thing. And he didn't sort it out. I was back in the shed the following week. I know now that those few days changed me and Dad for ever. I never went to the cinema with him again anyway, always busy when he suggested it. Perhaps he thought I was growing up, but it was an odd way to grow up. I think I hated him for putting me back in that shed. And, in the end, I sorted it out myself, almost as if that was what Dad had meant for me to do.

Derek seemed bolder. It seemed as if carpentry had become an excuse to get to the shed and that we'd both signed up to that understanding. As soon as we got there, he was rubbing himself against me from behind. He turned me and took off the glove of my left hand this time, wrapping my stiff little fingers around his engorged tool.

I could see where this was going. We were going to have sex and I didn't want it to start that way and I knew I was going to have to make a radical intervention, a game changer, as it were.

As I understand it now, of course, he was going to rape me, but that wasn't a legal distinction that bothered me at the time. He was panting, his eyes closed, thrusting urgently. I was looking around, as if distracting myself, like some child prostitute trying to displace herself. His left hand was steadying himself on the bench, gripping the base unit of a round saw that fell across a kind of safety guillotine, his long, crinkled fingers across the locating groove in cast iron, bolted to the bench. There was usually a little safety grille around it, but he'd removed it for easier access. The round saw unit was hinged and of great weight, so that it didn't move easily and could be guided into wood without splintering the grain.

Nothing was planned. I just saw the simplest logic of cause and effect and there's a beauty in that.

So I reached out with my right, available hand, pulled hard on the handle and the round saw block swung a quarter arc, gathered a blind and irresistible momentum under its own weight and fell with a metallic clunk, not visceral at all, across the middle and forefinger of Derek's fist. He exploded away from me and doubled up. Then came his cry, a deep, primal howl, and he fell past me at waist height, through the door and rolled on to the grass of his lawn. The wooden door flapped anxiously as I watched him, caught between holding his injured hand and fumbling defensively with his trouser flies.

In that moment, I could see everything perfectly. The clarity was overwhelming and peaceful. Derek would talk of an accident. My father would know the truth from my cold calmness, but he would never speak of it and it would be an impassable barrier between us until he was dead. And I was free.

I looked at the round saw. I heard later that his forefinger, which had lain where the curve of the saw left the block, was still attached by some sinew and stitched back on and saved. But his middle finger, the one that had dipped between my thighs in the car, lay there on the bench, turned on its back, lifeless. It looked, of course, like a little willy.

❖

148

I learned a lot at Aldgate that warm summer's day in early July. I learned that the paramedics who are first at the scene of a bomb explosion have a code system for the mortally injured. G1 for those with the best chance of survival who are to be removed immediately. G2 for those who have to be treated on-site before they can be moved. And G3 for those who aren't going to make it. They're filled with morphine and left to die while others are prioritised. G4 are dead already.

When we got back from looting the mini-mart, we started to distribute to the crew that had completed the first rescue shift. I wasn't surprised that they were hungry – I've never had any trouble eating when I've been in famine zones – but I was struck by how little blood was on them. But then these were the boys with the axes and the coded stickers. The ambulance crews were now down below, in that Orphean hell.

I figured sugar was what was needed most. So I brought hot sweet tea. Then I took round a box of chocolate bars I'd taken from the shop, after they'd got some carbs down in the form of sandwiches and baguettes.

"I shouldn't really," one of the youngest said. "I've told my mum that I've stopped eating those."

"Well, she's not here, is she?" I said. "And I won't tell her." He laughed and took one. I could have been at a church fete.

The other priests were in black cassocks, because this was their church and it gave them a clear identity. The phone was ringing off the hook upstairs in the office. The *Daily Mail*, *The Times* and ITN reporters trying to find out what was going on.

"Tell them to fuck off," said one of the older priests.

"They only need to know what's going on," I said. "Then they'll go away."

I took three of the calls.

"Who am I talking to?" asked the first.

"It doesn't matter," I said. "Just say I'm one of the priests here."

I realised I didn't want my name in the papers again. Not this time.

Downstairs, the shift was changing. I heard the priest who'd taken the aggressive media stand on a mobile phone.

"Are you all right, love?" he was saying softly. Turned out his daughter had been on the Circle Line through the City that morning. Different time, but he couldn't be sure. She was safe at home. He hadn't mentioned it before. I wanted to kiss him.

There was a big bloke standing slightly apart, his tunic loosened at the neck. He was doing that stare into the middle distance, unfocused. I poured a mug and put three sugars in. "Tea?" I said. He took it. "I'm Nat."

He didn't look at me, but I'd given him permission to say something. So I just waited.

"Sometimes you wonder if they'd be better off dead. There's a girl down there. Can't be more than twenty. Both legs gone above the knee. Sometimes you think they'd be better off dead," he repeated. There was a long pause that neither of us filled. "I thought she'd be better off dead."

Ah, there it is. She must have been borderline G3. And he'd wished her dead. He needed somewhere to put the guilt.

"Well done," said the police officer at the door when he'd moved away. "They're told to talk about it quickly afterwards. There's some counselling too, but it's pretty useless. It's the other halves who get it all in the end. They're the ones who find them whimpering and wet with sweat in a corner of the bedroom in the middle of the night."

I went outside and sat next to a priest on a bench in the churchyard. He talked amiably about suicide bombers and newspaper reporters. I noticed one side of his face bore the scars of an old burn and I wondered how it had happened, but I didn't ask him. We sat and looked out over the empty streets and listened to London in the distance, a shortened lifetime away.

"Why would you want to do that?"

"Do what?"

"Punish yourself?"

I looked at Dr Gray as he slumped in his button-back chair, corduroyed short legs crossed and away to one side, silly maroon-patterned socks in scuffed slip-on brown shoes.

"Well, I thought it was your job to tell me that." That was quite an answer for a fifteen-year-old and I was proud of it. It was the same sort of approach I took some years later when I went to that selection conference to be a Church of England priest.

I'd never had an eating disorder. We'd been through all that. Dr Gray, a bumptious middle-aged man, seemed so fixated on me having anorexia or bulimia that I'd wondered for the first session whether he'd got his files mixed up. This would have been around my third session and I only went about six times.

"I told you. I cut myself."

"Well, that seems a very unpleasant thing to do."

He was so useless, I wonder today whether he was qualified at all. I'd told him I self-harmed out of pity for him really. I needed to give him something. He had a consulting room in a mock-Tudor parade of shops, with net curtains and cursory ornaments, scruffily piled books on a cheap self-build bookcase.

"Shall I tell you why I do it?"

"Go on, then."

"I want to see what's inside me. It's hard to explain, but I also feel a pressure in me that needs to be released."

I would drag the pointy end of a pair of scissors up the loose white of the inside of my forearm, or the flank of a thigh as I sat on the loo. If you pull with little more than the weight of the blade, as a harrow might bounce over stony, dry earth, little red beads pop up in its furrow, like beads of blossoming vegetation. The trick is to extract blood that can be wiped away, leaving a blushing pink trace, but healed, as easily dried as tears.

"How often does this happen?"

"Most days. On the way to school. In a corner of the bus. Sometimes in the loos at dinner time. Even on a couple of occasions in class."

"Oh dear."

"Yes."

Scissors were good, but those little plastic white knives from supermarket snacks had a useful little serrated edge that helped with applying exactly the right pressure, and I liked the red against the smooth virginal white. Even the spike of a geometry protractor worked, though it lent itself to jabbing with an angry clenched fist. I was never into jabbing.

"So why did you come to see me?"

"My form mistress noticed. She thought it might be drugs."

"Do you take drugs?"

"No."

I had to tell this child therapist something, so I told him about my cutting. It made the sessions easier for both of us. There was something to talk about. But he didn't seem to know much about it. I embellished, extemporised, being sure to do it earlier on the day I saw Dr Gray, so there was a fresh pink-grapefruit streak for him to notice.

"Why do you think you want to hurt yourself?"

"I don't know."

"Do you feel depressed?"

And then I stopped and that seemed to please everyone, which is all I wanted to do at that time really, I realised. Pleasing people is easy, like passing exams, as easy as wiping away blood on soft toilet tissue, or on to a sanitary towel to make it look like my periods had started.

"Are you all right now, Natalie, do you think?"

"Yes, thank you, Dr Gray, I feel much better."

"Good. Now are you having any trouble with food? Do you find it disgusting to eat at all?"

Towards the end of the afternoon, the church had got quieter, the paramedics gone. Most of the crews were now in and out of the entrance to Aldgate station, providing access for forensics and the traffic to mortuaries. I decided to take a tray of tea and cans of fizzy drinks over there.

When it was made, I swung easily over the low churchyard wall and started towards a couple of police officers on the far side of the entrance. But at that moment there was a flurry of activity from within, two or three paramedics moving quickly, almost at a run, towards open ambulance doors reversing in our direction.

A short stretcher emerged between two bearers, something blackened and indistinct on it, under reflective silver blanketing, like a burnt Sunday dinner in tinfoil. My first instinct was that this was a child, but later I deduced that this was a shortened adult body. They have smaller stretchers for that?

A policewoman followed and stopped about three yards in front of me. The action and raised voices had moved to the ambulance, her role complete. She held her fists under her nose suddenly, then turned towards me.

I let the tray fall, cups and tea spilling and smashing across the pavement, and held her as she buried her face in my shoulder. Her peaked cap tilted absurdly upwards as if in a raised salute. She was only there a moment and there was no sob, just a stiff little body, tight all over. Then, composed again, she pulled away. She had mousy hair and poor skin.

"Sorry, Vicar," she said, gesturing at the tea and broken china. "Bad day at the office." And she was gone, back on the job.

I'm told the security services recruit broken people for the dirty work. The Church certainly does. I wondered if they knew this stuff. Incredible if they do, from school reports or doctors' notes or wherever, because I barely know about this stuff myself. The psychopath doesn't know she's a psychopath, right? Obviously I tick some of those boxes.

Everything looks so normal, dull even, from where I stand. Then I look at what I've done and it's not like anyone else's stuff. And it looks like someone else did it, but I know it's just me, the one who can present this normal front to the world. Is everyone like this? I hope so, because then that makes me part of a mass of humanity, like anyone else.

There was a boy at school. Jon. After I humiliated him, I could see he'd been crying and that was good, because it showed he cared. I heard later on that he'd failed a load of exams and I wondered if that was my fault. But I can't say I cared. I wish I could.

He was square, but not short, not really shy, but diffident in that way boys have in their mid-teens before their character kicks in, if they have one. We were paired in some physics experiment, latent heat or something similarly forgettable. He stood there a bit like my assistant at a cookery demonstration, holding the thermometer and a stick of candlewax and glancing between the whiteboard and the apparatus, not much bothered that I appeared to be doing all the prep. I was always practical, always did the heavy lifting.

Anyway, the wax in the copper pan began to form an inflating dome before us and we stared at it with a kind of fascinated detachment. Then it burst open with a koi carp pout, splattering hot foam over the front of Jon's trousers, and subsided into itself, a retreating monster.

With a voice I hadn't heard before, Jon said in a nasal, officious tone: "Leave him, doctor, there's nothing more you can do."

It wasn't as if it was that funny, but it burst the tense piety of the physics lab. I gave an involuntary snort and sprayed our submerging creature with spots of saliva, which hissed on the pool like a geyser for a second. I was shaking, with one hand over my mouth and the other on Jon's thermometer-bearing forearm. He had bowed his head to conceal himself behind the row in front and was hissing rhythmically.

Some arcane, distant instructions from Mr Paton, the teacher, made matters worse – I couldn't breathe and felt a small emission moisten me down below. I turned for the door, hand still self-suffocating, as the adult words, "Are you all right, Natalie?" followed me through the door and into the corridor.

The loos were a short skip away and in that sanctuary I howled, joyously, abandoned, like grief in a war zone, watching my distorted image in the cracked mirror as the peals turned to moans and I regained control. It must have been ten minutes later, school-maximum eyeliner restored and the door clatter of lessons ending to an electric bell, that I emerged, hyperventilated and lighter. Jon ambled along the wall against the tide, his files hung at the hip, naturally, not trying to be cool – I liked that – and asked, "Are you OK?"

"Yeah, sorry, that really got me." I ran a finger under one eye to demonstrate my recomposure.

"Do you mind if I ask," he said, as we walked and he pointed to his own eye, "what did you do to your eyebrow?"

"No, it's fine," I said. "I had a cyst removed. It weakened the muscle and made that eyebrow droop."

"It's nice," he said.

In an American high school we'd have dated, right? As it was, I usually walked with Jon between lessons. And, I promise, I really honestly did get something in my eye. The wind funnelled between temporary school cabins and picked up crisp bags and leaves. Something slapped into the corner of my eye like a tiny fly, just wedged against the bridge of my nose. It was my bad eye, the one with the scarred lid, and I felt the separated muscles in my brow buckle. It felt perfectly normal to hold my face in Jon's direction, eyelids lowered, and he carefully and surprisingly gently flicked it away.

That was a moment, wasn't it? Or it would have been for a normal girl. But already I was feeling stupid and there was a welling resentment that something trustful was forming, some dependence on another that exposed me and took account of his place in the world.

And that's what I don't understand. I can't even ask myself why. I don't have the answer, but I don't have the right question either. If I knew where you were, Jon, I'd say sorry. Not because I am, in truth, sorry at all, but because I carry this burden of self-loathing for having led you to believe you were my friend in the first place. It would be easier to say sorry to you, Jon, if there was some way to explain the way I am. Maybe it has something to do with the woodwork project in my father's shed. I don't know.

There was a hoodie playing an orange and white traffic cone like a clarinet in Leicester Square once, slow jazz between his knees, and I gave him a two-pound coin because it could have been you. He made me think of you anyway, Jon. I let you into a bit of my life, so I had to make you suffer, you see. It's the way it works in my world. Maybe it was because you made me laugh like a girl.

It was a sunny afternoon around exam time. We walked down the grassy banks beyond the hockey pitches and into the woods, where the less self-assured went for cigarettes they didn't know how to smoke properly. I sensed a new nervousness in you, like you were assimilating the real circumstance with an idea. So I pushed you up against a tree and kissed you hard, a long slippery one with teeth grinding together. When I broke away and looked at you with that expressionless passion I'd seen girls do at dances, your breath had quickened in little pants and you'd hardened against me.

I rolled a kiss around your cheek to your ear, which I nuzzled in my mouth like a calf on a teat, and then I started to whisper clearly and deliberately: "I'm not going to let you, Jon, I'm not going to let you, and you know why? Because you're pathetic and you make me sick. You're pathetic, you hear?"

Then I broke away completely and stood in front of you with a calm and conclusive defiance. You were doing the bewildered expression, half-smiling, because this was a joke, right? And you hadn't asked for any of this. You shook your head slightly and tried a laugh, one eyebrow dipping quizzically, and for a moment I considered accusing you of mocking my disfigurement. But no, this wasn't a catty row, it was a statement.

So I said, "I don't want you Jon, so leave me alone, you creepy cock. You're pathetic." And I slapped your crotch, where you were still tight against the cheap school nylon. And then I turned and ran, ran up the banks like a warrior princess, and across the fields to school, hardly touching the ground. I could have run for ever, free and exhilarated again.

As I burst through the swing doors of our block, ribcage heaving to supply me with the power I craved to kick and yell, I didn't know who I wanted to see or what I would do next. But I wanted someone, a witness, anyone with whom to dance and shout.

The hallway was empty, but for one presence. Sarah was sitting in her wheelchair, looking at me intently. And she was smiling, just faintly.

✻

Towards the end of the afternoon, it had become apparent that there was no more to be done at Botolph's. Those coming in and out now were firemen and police looking to use the loo, and the demand for tea and food had disappeared. We could leave it to the incumbent clergy and their staff. So they thanked me and I left.

The sun was lower, winking between the high-rise office blocks, and it was peaceful as I headed for the top of Fenchurch Street again. A quick word with the officer at the tapes – the one who had laughed at my identity card earlier, but he seemed bored now – and I stepped out of my parallel universe.

The office workers were finishing for the day and were tripping out and on to the street. Some of the younger ones held squash racquets or bike bags. The transport links were down, but the sense of apprehension of the morning had gone and the City had moved on.

I felt invisible, as I sometimes had when I'd returned from an aid trip. I could stare at people without feeling that they could see me. But down by the Bank of England, it was if I'd never been away. I checked my phone. A load of missed calls from numbers rather than names in my contacts list.

But there were two names there. Adrian and Hugh. Adrian had called about six times in the morning. I phoned Hugh first.

"You OK, love?" he said as soon as he came on the line.

"Yeah, I'm fine," I said. "Busy day at the office."

"The Bishop is beside himself with pride. Never has he had such cause to be grateful for our partnership in the gospel," said Hugh, invoking one of the bishop's favourite pay-offs. "Did you have to do any last rites?"

"Nah, wasn't like that, Huge. Emergency-services pastoral, mostly. Any messages?"

"Your husband called several times. Wanted us to guarantee that you weren't doing anything stupid. I said it was a bit late for that and he bit my head off, sorry. He wanted to be sure you weren't going underground."

"No danger of that either," I said and smiled.

Then I went to dial Adrian, changed my mind and texted him. I told him I'd make supper.

10

Adrian had been very anxious to find out how the child porn had got on his computer, though he may have been further signalling his innocence. He'd made a huge fuss with the internet provider, but seemed to assume that it was solely a failure of technology. So now it was down to me to interpret its real provenance.

I sat in a coffee shop on Ludgate Hill, watching the quantum of humanity on the pavements and a shunting line of traffic edging down to the Circus. There was a cold and low sun. Neutral tones. Chidden of God. I was at a small brown table, with a cappuccino cooling, beside the glass wall that separated me from all the atom-ised energy outside, witnessing the chaos theory of commercial life. A matching brown stripe made a horizontal bar across the window, the cafe brand printed on it next to me, presenting itself to the world beyond. It was my fourth wall and I watched the street performance beyond it, entirely alienated.

It was like being in a tranquillising advertisement for coffee – like one of those in which everyone in the background moves faster than the heroine. I remember wondering, as I waited, whether this was depression. I was barely thinking. I did have a sense, I think, of being washed along on a tide. I'd thrown the rope ashore.

In an overpriced coffee shop in east-central London, my feet were losing their purchase on the silt of a slippery seabed and I was being carried away by a current. And I was letting it happen, willing freely to be washed out to sea.

So when Toby arrived, I was surprised by my serenity. My neck moved my head only slowly as he approached, yellow and navy college scarf hanging loose in the collar of a smart new grey coat that I guessed his mum, not a girlfriend, far less a wife, had bought him for Christmas.

He stood for a moment, smiling inanely down at me. No, thank you, I didn't want another coffee. I didn't think I'd ever want another coffee again.

"I'll just get something," he said and bounced to the counter.

I resumed watching the world perform its quantum mechanics for me.

"Thanks for calling and sorry I couldn't speak to you," he said as he tore the top off a narrow sugar sachet like an aidie opening a swab. "How are things?"

I doubt this easy-going intro was part of his training. It was just the way he was.

"I've changed my mind. I'll go to Israel," I said.

I hadn't actually planned to get straight to it. But I was in a kind of meditative trance and it was as if the words bubbled up naturally. Maybe I was speaking in tongues.

He expelled one beat of a surprised laugh.

"Really? Well, that's fabulous news. I'll tell the office right away. They will be pleased. Well, after we've had coffee, I'll tell them, huh."

He could have been a salesman winning a photocopier contract.

Then he talked about speakers at the conference and I didn't listen. I waited until he'd finished his flapjack.

"It'll be great working with you," he said.

Clearly the little matter of the extra job as a postal service didn't merit a mention. It was all part of the same mundane package to him.

When he fell silent, I asked: "The people you work for, Toby. How far would they go to get me to do it?"

He cocked his head in one short half-turn.

"They wouldn't pay you, if that's what you mean." He overemphasised his words to show he was joking.

"That's not what I mean," I said sweetly and smiled. "Would they put child pornography on someone's computer?"

Toby sat back slightly and pursed his lips against a thin line of coffee foam. Then he wiped it like a boy, on the back of his hand.

"What?"

"They put child pornography on my husband's computer."

Pause. "Who did?"

"Somebody at your end."

He tried to look like he was taking the allegation seriously.

"Why would anyone do that?" he said.

I smiled and let a little silence run out.

"Never mind," I said. "It doesn't matter."

He stared at the table and drew the corners of his mouth down, rubbing his palms slowly together, in a praying position. I took this to indicate not so much disbelief, but that he simply wasn't prepared to go there, not into the deranged dysfunction of a client's married life.

"It's OK, Toby. I'm not paranoid. I'm sound. But it's true."

He looked like he had something to say, took a decision and leaned in on the table.

"Look, Natalie, they don't do that. They wouldn't know how to. We just want you to speak at a conference. And to help us a little with a drop." He paused, then he said: "I'm sorry."

I suppose he was being sympathetic, breaking it to me that he couldn't offer me a way out of the discovery of Adrian's horrific online habits.

"I believe you, Toby," I said, because actually he wouldn't know. Too young, too unworldly, and that was some sort of comfort. "But it doesn't matter. That's not why I'm doing it. I'm doing it because I want to. I want to go. The time is right."

I realise now that that's the truth of it. The men from the ministry were offering me an escape, an exit from a life that wasn't just wearing me down, it was killing me. I do wonder whether I'd have gone even if I'd known how it was going to turn out. The awful truth is that I suspect I might. No, I know I would have gone anyway. It was no longer about what I wanted to do. Something bigger and stronger than me had taken over. All I had to do was obey. I was no longer in control.

Part 2

11

I was wearing the half-smile of the incredulous, palms upwards on my knees, jaw slightly dropped. Toby was weaving in his hatchback through the Jerusalem traffic like a native. He was shaking his head.

"I tell you he came on to me, Toby."

"I just don't believe it."

"Is that you don't believe me as in you think I'm making it up, or as in you're amazed and can barely warrant it?"

Toby carried on shaking his head and hooted at a cyclist.

I'd come strangely to like the boy Toby. We'd flown out via Switzerland, where we'd had an overnighter to collect a briefing from some UN worker bees – they don't like to be called drones – about the projected $10 billion aid budget for the occupied territories. That was so I could speak "with some authority" about it at the conference. I took that as a clear signal that I was meant to talk their book.

I didn't mind that, if the money was real, and I guess Zurich was meant to show me that too. I'd emailed Sarah, who was already in Jerusalem, and reckoned on her telling me what to say. I was obeying her and, now that Adrian was finished, I reckoned we were back on the same page.

We seemed an odd couple, Toby and me – he the young spook, me the washed-up aidie – to have this geopolitical power play performed just for us. It was like some silly case of mistaken identity, or like we'd won a competition to see how the peace process worked. I couldn't or wouldn't take it too seriously, especially in our down time and would send it up to Toby. Did he think Tel Aviv would get a Disneyland? Were we on commission? Could I get a photograph with the cheque – perhaps one of those giant charity ones – at the Shrine of the Holy Sepulchre?

"I'm just saying Americans don't do that kind of thing. They're too worried about getting into trouble. It wouldn't happen."

"But I'm telling you it did, Toby. Maybe he couldn't resist me."

"Now you are making it up."

"Well, thank you very much, Tobes, you're a gent."

I didn't care whether Toby believed me or not. In fact, I rather suspected that he was required not to believe me, otherwise he'd be in possession of salient information that he may have to report. So it was probably easier to keep it at the level of regular banter. For Toby's sake, I didn't tell him that I'd damned nearly crippled the American jerk. Maybe ruined his reproductive prospects.

We'd been introduced at a networking event ahead of the conference. Toby had taken his responsibilities as my escort very seriously, installing me in one of his office's low-rise apartments in a leafy enclave of suburban Jerusalem, and had rarely left me alone as the conference approached. It was convened at the Mount Scopus campus of Jerusalem University, to the north-east of the city – a sort of white concrete affair that could have been one of England's more modern universities. We'd sat in the sun on a low wall outside the complex we were using for the conference, next to a small evergreen tree set in a huge concrete planter at an incongruous angle of some forty-five-degrees, so that it had to be supported with a wire hawser.

"Incapability Brown been at the weedkiller?" I said, or something like that.

"Best not say that to anyone else," said Toby. "It's a monument to nine who were killed in the cafe here in a Hamas attack, mostly Israelis but Americans too."

"Sorry. When?"

"A few years ago."

Mine was to be the middle day of the conference. The media would come for the mid-morning set piece, my little keynote largely drafted by UN staff, then some photo calls. It was during one of the seemingly interminable breaks for coffee and cakes, during which Toby would circulate me around the various conference catchments – Palestinian Arabs, other Arabs, academic Israelis, political Israelis, UN officials, visiting bishops and archbishops, Quartet reps, the party of the junior minister from the Foreign Office, media. And this one American that I counted, called Kevin Schreiber.

"Is he CIA?" I asked Toby.

"No, he isn't CIA," he answered with a cod weariness that I didn't understand. "He works with our office."

"The Foreign Office?"

"Yes, sort of."

Schreiber was tall and thin with neat white hair, fit and quite handsome in an uninteresting sort of way. He talked easily and fluently, if in a rather monotone fashion. It seemed odd to talk in such a matter-of-fact way in a crowded room about the little bit of street diplomacy that had brought us together.

"It's really very straightforward. Toby will bring you to my hotel tomorrow and we'll run you through the briefing. There's nothing to it." I've run through this time and again since. It was all meant to be so simple. And, in one respect I suppose it was.

Toby drove me over when the first day of the conference finished. Schreiber was staying at the American Colony in East Jerusalem. Of course he was. It's a discreet old hotel, built in the Ottoman style, and just right for a sleazy diplomat like Schreiber. Toby pulled up at the front and my door was opened. Toby stayed put.

"Aren't you coming?"

"Not my side of the business. Do you want to get a cab back, or shall I wait?"

I said I'd get a cab. Schreiber had what I imagined would be called a Junior Suite. Everything with dinky little arches – the windows in clutches of three, the separation of his lounge and office area from the bedroom. He poured white wine as soon as I arrived without asking if I wanted any, and we sat next to each other on the sofa looking at his laptop. That should have given me a heads-up – it all felt too intimate from the start.

The briefing was laughable by any standard. It consisted of a single photograph of a cafe with red signage in Arabic that I didn't recognise and a Google map of some East Jerusalem lanes, to which he pointed with a pencil. The address on a piece of paper handed to Toby would have been fine. But Schreiber wouldn't have been able to practise his Boston charm that way.

I had to laugh in his face when he told me solemnly that "I

cannot describe the man you will be meeting, because I don't know who he is."

"Well, that's rather the point, isn't it?" He must have thought I was flirting.

"He will know your name and he will be looking for a woman." He refilled my glass. "Do you mind if I ask how you got that scar across your eyebrow?"

"I was in a car crash."

"It's really very attractive."

"It speaks very highly of you too, Mr Schreiber."

He leaned in, leering, and I could smell white-wine breath.

"Where do I get my envelope?"

"What envelope would that be?" I rolled my eyes and moved away up the sofa like a coy maid in a play. "Oh, that. Toby will give it to you."

"Then I guess that's all I need to know." I stood and grabbed my jacket.

"Need you really go? I thought we might have a drink, get to know each other better." He exited the other end of the sofa and barred my way to the door.

"No offence, Schreiber, but I think I'd rather die."

"Aw," he pulled a little baby reproachful face, "that's not very Christian," and he moved in on me, pushing me against the wall.

I looked up at him and placed both hands on his shoulders for balance. Then my right knee found the inside of his thigh like a locating rail and glided its delivery into his slack little sack, like a kitten in a purse. He hissed through his nose and stood back, his arms hanging as if in a paralysed dance move as he fought the urge to grab his groin. In truth, it hadn't been too hard a jab.

A gasp. "You little bitch."

"Now you're on the money, Schreiber," I said and swung out the door.

And that, more or less, is what I was telling Toby about as we drove past the Colony for my errand the following day. We were in good spirits, the boring conference was over, I was looking forward to a few days off in Jerusalem and, though I wasn't going to say so, knocking around with Toby for a while.

"What are your plans?"

"I don't know. I may visit some aidie friends. I've got some working with the Bulldozed." I'd tried to call Sarah but she hadn't replied. Nor had I seen her at the conference centre. I should have thought that was strange, but I suppose I just thought she was frantically busy. She probably was.

"Where's the envelope, Tobes?"

Toby theatrically slapped his forehead like he'd forgotten it and I sharply palmed his shoulder. He pulled a manila one from his inside pocket. It had nothing written on it, but it was no bigger than a private letter.

"Is that it? I was expecting something larger, Tobes." It was an attempt at innuendo.

I watched the white sprawl of affluent inner-city Jerusalem passing. The new Jerusalem, the unholy city, dressed as a whore for her pimp. Could this be where it all began and would end? For me, maybe, but I didn't know that then. I was still somewhere safer and, as Toby drove, something in the high Holy Land light made me think of being happy in other trucks, my feet on the dash, like the one in Sudan, or like the one in Beirut, one hundred and fifty miles or so to the north.

If I hold my nose, I can still taste the dust from breeze-block buildings caking my outer lip, there in Lebanon, when the Church started to send me on missionary work. The smell of fruit and urine as I walked the hopeless alleyways, one foot either side of the central-running drain, laundry drying high enough overhead to catch some of the sky. The narrow-lipped children, eyebrows raised at the Western woman in clean, pale cotton. And I smiled into the deadpan faces, with their pastel-shaded charity clothing, and the brilliant white light of that sky, pinched by the narrow alleys, occasionally illuminating their bare walls, but never cleansing them. I remember how they hung their clothing over corrugated-iron shutters, painted blue. Blue paint was what they had.

This bit is Yusef's story. It isn't really mine. Without Yusef, I wouldn't be here now. The first time I knew Yusef was just six weeks – some forty days, as it happens – and I know now he was my salvation.

Yusef was, and very probably remains, and may he always be, a teacher originally from the West Bank. He was assigned to my beat in Syria, Lebanon and Jordan. He was from an exiled Palestinian Christian family, and I think that's how he had picked up work with us. I was notionally coordinating the efforts of local educational associations for the Palestinian camps, with a brief for skills training for women. There were women heroically managing their communities across the camps and I'd developed an interest in their workshops on gender and family issues. The rank poverty of some of the camps had fomented grotesque domestic violence – who'd have guessed? No work, no hope of deliverance, a black hole of human deposit, against which some of these women were offering pay-groups, chiselling away at the rock face of illiteracy, organising collective projects among their alloy folding tables and stackable white plastic chairs. It was an impertinent little joke at oppression's expense.

The conventional view of these women in Europe is of scarved heads hanging washing to dry on bicycle wheels. Bless. But then Europeans also think that these camps are like Bedouin tented communities, or the kind of medical and feeding station we parked our stolen truck beside in Sudan. Listen, people, how many decades do you think they've been there? This isn't temporary displacement – nor are they shanty towns so much as ghettoes, where Palestinian families have been raised and have rotted since the ethnic cleansings of Israel in 1948 and 1967.

I worked across twelve such camps in Lebanon, out of a base in north Beirut. The nearest was Burj el-Barajneh and I spent most of my time there, quickly learning that the other camps had their specific characteristics: there was Beddawi, edgy with its youths tattooed with Arabic slogans. Al Jaleel in the Bekaa Valley was an old French barracks, where the mountains rose towards the Syrian border, as rooted in its history as the ancient ruins of Baalbek. Then there was the big Burj el-Shemali camp at Tyre, with its cordon of Lebanese security and ring of red oil drums, with sandbagged bunkers to stop building materials from getting in. And Mar Elias, the smallest of the camps, populated with Christians expelled from Galilee in 1952.

And there was this well-built man in his early thirties, tall with a wavy burst of dark hair and a ready smile. Yusef would drive me between the camps, making connections, patiently explaining background. In the heat and the dust and the smell of diesel, with a hint of lavender, I came secretly to cherish our drives along the rudimentary dual-carriageways of the coast as we dodged ancient grey Mercedes, stunted palms marking our way in the central reservations. I wore sunglasses I'd found on an airport seat and put my feet on the dash of Yusef's 4x4 and imagined we were in a low-budget road movie.

I liked him for his sense of silence between bouts of effortless chat. We'd chew gum or smoke for half an hour, then talk about the cleverness of a Roman viaduct which now ended abruptly by the road like some pointless ski-jump, or about how the woman we'd met that morning was the sole survivor of a Phalangist mortar attack. I sensed that Yusef had previous, as ex-pats in the region had come to call it, but then so had I, and neither of us felt compelled to delve.

I'd just been checking out educational resources for primary children in Barajneh and we were heading back towards Beirut when Yusef said, "You must come home for tea."

I laughed. It sounded more Home Counties than Lebanon. "Is this how Arabs do a first date? Are you asking me home to meet your family, Yuse?" I said. I'd started to abbreviate his name and he seemed to like it, sometimes calling him Yuseless when I pretended to be cross with him. He smiled when I said it anyway.

"I suppose so. They're there anyway. How much have you seen of how we live in the camps?"

I knew his challenge was right. I met women's collectives in day centres and schools and UN officials in offices and at the consulate. I didn't actually know much about everyday life in the camps.

"I'd like that," I said, afraid that I may have offended him with a glib response.

"You'll like my uncle's cake," he said.

So, the next afternoon, I walked up the little alleys that were cambered higher at the sides to run what was all too often raw sewage down the gully in the middle, around a couple of breeze-block doglegs, which I took to be stopping child cyclists getting up too much speed, and we were at Yusef's stable door. His uncle leaned against it from the inside, smoking a filterless Gitane.

"You're late for a goy girl," he said, one side of his mouth breaking to show shiny teeth in a guileless smile.

"She's out of your class," said Yusef, in English for my benefit. "And don't speak Yiddish in my house. Come inside, Natalie."

A leathery old lady I took to be his mother sat by a cabinet in a rocking chair that looked absurdly out of place. French, probably. She was holding a cat in a shawl and was about no other business. I would learn that she sat like this endlessly, with a studied detachment from her surroundings, but not without contentment, her place a simple statement of presence. "Her name is May," said Yusef. "Say hello to Natalie, May." May held up a hand, nodding and smiling.

Yusef had a son, spare and skinny in a clean white vest and nylon tracksuit trousers, Western-branded. I could hear the relentless ricochet of a plastic football against concrete as Asi played with his friends out in the yard, shushing them if they shouted, as he had been told. He was ten.

Yusef brewed some tea and poured a couple of chaser shots of a clear, home-distilled spirit that tasted of pastis, only far stronger, and we sat in the little front parlour, his mum smiling distantly over the cat and never rocking her chair. There was a framed poster of a Renaissance Madonna and Child above her. The whole place smelled strongly of a kind of industrial disinfectant that was commonly used for family hygiene. The towels and underwear drying in the kitchen showed that this was the bathroom too – I knew from conversations with young mothers that there would be a communal loo out at the back, shared between three of four households. These would be kept as well as they could be, but the sheer volume of family waste backed up, which was a recurrent nightmare for women raising children. I made a casual resolution not to have a second cup of tea, worrying needlessly about germs. To the left of the reinforced frosted glass in the back door that led to the latrine would be the bedrooms, perhaps two of them, the boy sharing with his grandmother, would be my guess.

Noticing my assessment of the property, Yusef said, "Money comes in from the West in cycles."

"Guilt cash," added his uncle, leaning in over the stable door, rubbing his thumb and fingers together in a pastiche of the Middle Eastern money-grubber.

"It means the camps turn filthy over maybe three, five years and they fear cholera, so then we get some investment for electrics, plumbing, hygiene. It's not so bad."

I could tell Yusef was a little shamed and I wanted to tell him that he so didn't need to be. "The street at the top has been replumbed and wired." He smiled and looked off into an imaginary distance. "It'll be good enough for the Lebanese to move in soon."

Uncle said something in Arabic and Yusef snorted. I cocked a quizzical eyebrow. Yusef waved an explanatory arm. "He said . . . how would you say?"

"There goes the neighbourhood?" I guessed.

"Yes, kinda."

Uncle just chuckled and drew on his stub-end. If I hadn't been there, I was sure they'd not have used the Lebanese as the butt of their joke. It would have been Jews. But a Westerner's presence made them watch their manners and mask their prejudices. So they showed me that they accepted their lot cheerfully, and it was a relaxed banter, only somewhat forced, that marked my visits, which became regular after that first tea and firewater.

I started dropping in on my own when my routes took me through the area, and sometimes when they didn't. I was driving myself around more now, while Yusef accompanied a new intake of volunteers. I'd bring milk or a small sack of chickpeas as a contribution and sometimes we'd make matsos and hummus to share, whether Yusef was there or not. I barely spoke to the old lady, but squeezed her hand as I left and she'd smile.

One afternoon, I was there with Uncle and the boy was sitting on a chaise reading old American comics he'd found somewhere, when Yusef returned. It felt good. It felt like we were family. I made tea and we sat on an old bench seat from a car in the front compound and watched the water – and much else besides – as it ran down the centre of the alleyway. Uncle went to look for fresh water as the plumbing had gurgled dry, though I suspected he was off to play backgammon with his mates and lose a little money.

We smoked Uncle's cigarettes in silent communion and I didn't think about asking before I said, without looking at him, "Yuse, where's Asi's mum?"

"She's dead," he said, without pause or tone. "She died."

"I know," I said. "At least, I assumed, I guessed. But that's not what I asked is it?"

He turned towards me and his eyes were smiling. "What you mean? Is she in heaven? Yes. Maybe. She's in a plot we have – we Palestinians – down on the edge of town. At least most of her is."

He exhaled smoke and stubbed out his cigarette end on the ground between his knees. I said nothing, but waited and looked up at the sky between the drying washing hanging outside the upper windows across the street. There was also washing hanging on a bicycle, I remember.

"She was killed when Amal shelled the camps. She was visiting friends in Sabra and Shatila. She used to help out with social work there. They had made it to a kind of shelter, but it was hit, a direct hit. It was a phosphorous bomb, made to kill, to fry. She hadn't taken Asi. He was only a baby then, but she did sometimes take him with her in a papoose. That trip, she left him with his grand-mother."

It had been what they called the War of the Camps, when Shi'ite resentment of Palestinian refugees had boiled over. Amal was the Syrian-backed militia, but they had been supported by Maronite Christian Phalangists, meaning Yusef's wife might well have been killed by Christians.

Yusef had jerked his head back towards his front room in an indicative gesture as he had spoken of May. I looked past the stable door. "That's your mother-in-law?"

"Yes."

"I thought she was your mum."

"She is now."

"What was your wife's name?"

"Ella."

I cupped his shoulder with the palm of my hand and looked away up the rise in the lane, away from the pain, rocking my hand almost imperceptibly back and forth. Yusef broke the silence. "We have a wreath-laying on the anniversary. Some music, some prayers. It's soon. Will you come?"

"Yes," I said, taking my hand away. "I'd like that."

So I went with Yusef that day. It was a strange dislocation of time and place for this Brit girl, because it was not unlike some brass-band commemoration in a northern English town, except for the brilliant white light of the sky. There were PLO uniforms and wreaths and a marble pillar to rest them against, their petals already curling in the heat. Yusef was calm, detached, a light smile fixed on his lips. He didn't bring Asi, he explained, as it felt too military and he didn't want him to be "part of the war". Not yet, he added to himself. But he had to come, he said, to mark the event.

"Our people won't be forgotten, of course, so long as we have hearts for them to live in. But it's important that these events aren't forgotten either. We're making our history."

We sat and drank dark, gritty coffee just off the memorial square afterwards. I watched Yusef grimacing into the light as he tugged urgently on his cigarette, much like Sarah used to. His serenity at the memorial had gone. I think I asked him what he was thinking. And now he smiled again and looked distant. "I see strangers in my country," he said, "selling stolen fruit."

We walked back up the hill, towards his Palestinian quarter, flags marking its entry point, and it was as if all the laundry hanging from the windows had turned like the flags to green, white and black, each shirt with a red chevron scarf, hanging lazily, defiantly. He was talking, almost idly, about the Great Catastrophe of his grandparents' generation, how Galilee was cleared – "War of Independence," he laughed with a snort – and how more of his parents' generation had poured over the borders in 1967, how his family had left their village hours before the militia arrived to drive them out, leaving everything, even breakfast on the table. He told me how those who stayed were massacred. Israeli families were moved into the homes; they liked the high ceilings and cool rooms of the Arabic houses.

"You'll go back," I offered and immediately regretted my Western reassurance. He stopped and looked at me.

"I don't want to go back. Why should I want to go back there? This is my home now. It's nasty, but it's where we belong now." He started to walk again, back towards his new Eden. "No, I don't want to go back. But I want them to pay for our land. They should pay."

When we arrived at the house, the stable door was open and May was on her feet, the first time I'd seen her out of her chair, clutching a blue muslin cloth to her face and rocking on her heels soundlessly, her creased eyes twinkling with tears. Yusef rushed to her and held her shoulders, turning her to face him; there was a rush of colloquial Arabic, but only a few tremulous, broken sentences from the old woman. I stood at the door, watching this tableau like it was a mummers' play. Yuse sat her down, firmly but gently, returning her to her place as one might tidy a room.

"What's up?" I asked from the door.

Yusef's head stayed down and he spoke past his shoulder. "It's Asi. Someone's taken him."

He came to the door, his hands shoved deep into the back pockets of his combat trousers. He looked like someone whose train has been cancelled and he was wondering what to do next. And his lips drew apart as if he had backache.

Asi had gone down to the scrubland that separated the camp from the Lebanese side of town to play football with his friends. Yusef didn't like him leaving the camp, but Asi usually took advantage of his absence to find some more space, like a grazing cub, as Yusef put it.

Further details were erratic – May was something of an unreliable second witness. But some kind of flatbed truck had pulled up, carrying young men and bigger boys. Six, maybe more. They had started spoiling the game, then roughing up Asi and his friends, shouting and jeering. Yusef had already told me that Lebanese boys called them Canaanites, but these were the kind of resentful, more dangerous Lebanese bully-boys who called them "little outlaws" and had been going "tick-tick-tick" with their fingers in their ears. A scuffle broke out and Asi and another boy were dragged on to the back of the truck and driven away. We had this from the other friends, who had run straight home. One father had found Uncle, who had gone down to the makeshift pitch.

"Do you want to go too?" I asked as I sat on the car seat next to Yusef, who was thinking hard, rubbing the palms of his hands together. It was strangely cool now that the sun had gone. "I can stay and look after May."

He shook his head. "There's nothing to see at the football pitch. They won't be there."

I wondered if Asi was dead and then wondered if Yusef was thinking that too. It felt weird, because we were behaving normally, discussing options as if we'd lost a wallet.

Three small girls came and stared at us from across the street, through the gloom. Strange, how children can sense family crisis and want to witness its drama. Behind them, a man painted a blue door with black pitch.

"I could phone the office," I said. "See if anyone can help."

Yusef snorted derisively, then worried that he might have seemed rude. "No, really, thanks – there's nothing anyone can do."

"They could call the UN – see if there have been any security reports," I offered.

"No." I'd clearly pushed the offer too far. "There's nothing they would know or do. It would only make things worse."

I just sat then. My silence seemed to affirm the circumstance, the lawlessness, hopelessness, the errant nature of refugee freedom. When it was dark, Yusef said he was going to talk to the other missing boy's family. "Shall I come with you?" I asked.

"If you like."

It wasn't far. Uphill through a maze of alleys, the odd dark dart of a cat or rat in the alleys. They lived on the second floor of a soft concrete block, the steel rebars jutting through where the blocks crumbled. It was like an abandoned civic car park, where chipboard had been used to fill out the wall space. The father, gap-toothed and lanky in a white vest, was holding a small girl who played with his mop of dark hair. Behind him, his wife was putting two more to bed. They ignored me as they talked and I smiled at the woman, who dipped her head in automatic supplication. I guessed it was her eldest boy who was missing.

The other father was throwing his head back in agreement of something and we left, the door shutting sharply behind us against the now cold night air. We headed back by a different route to Yusef's house.

"Any news?" I asked, almost scampering at Yusef's heel.

"No. But he says he knows where the truck is from."

"Where then? Who took him, Yuse?"

He didn't answer, but there was purpose in his stride.

"Yuse, where did Uncle really go?"

"I don't know."

Back at the house, Yusef disappeared into the back and I point-lessly made some tea. May was rocking very slightly in her chair and she took a cup. Yusef emerged and he had changed. He was wearing a dark keffiyeh, secured with a single-cord agal, a bulging leather jerkin, and his calves were tucked into leggings above sturdy ankle boots. He was pulling on fingerless sheepskin gloves.

"Where are you going?" Even I was growing tired of my questions.

"To look for Asi." He was commendably patient, I'll give him that. He pulled what looked like a heavy torch out from a kitchen cabinet.

He bent and kissed May's forehead. There was a sharp rasp, more of a push, on the door and a shout. Yusef called out what I recognised as "OK, coming". Then he turned to me. "Is it OK for you to wait here with May? We won't be long. But if you need to go, that's fine."

"We?"

Yusef opened the door. There were four men outside. Three were in the background, young, one dressed like Yusef, two others wearing short bishts, the black woollen cloaks. At the door was the other father we'd visited, still in his sandals, dressed as I'd last seen him. One of the young men was shuffling under his bisht as if he had a lining caught and as I peered out into the dark, it fell open. I saw his right arm flanked with the shiny shaft of a semi-automatic weapon. I turned to Yusef, no longer the compliant visitor, the innocent abroad. I was young but I suddenly felt very much like his boss.

"What the bloody hell are you doing?" I said through closed teeth, hoping those outside couldn't hear, hoping also to keep a separation between Yusef in the light and warmth inside and those in the dark outside. He didn't say a word, to me or them, but just walked out and down the hill, the three young men following, the other father lingering for a moment. This man smiled briefly in at both of us, nodded and walked slowly back up through the alley towards his home.

I closed the door and looked down at the old lady. She was looking hard at me through rheumy eyes. I went to take her cup, perhaps to fetch more tea, but she held my forearm with a hard little hand and pulled me towards her. She smiled now, in reassurance. She pointed up with her other hand at the rounded, ochre face of the poster Madonna on the wall beside her then, releasing me, clasped her hands together and sat up straight in a childish pastiche of prayer.

I paused, not knowing what to do. But I knelt beside her, on one knee, and put my fingers together, in the pointy spire we'd been shown at school, and started to whisper, just blowing articulated air through my teeth and watching the old woman. I was saying nothing, it was the wordless whispers of the kind that children fake, pretending to tell secrets. But, through my fingers, she looked quiet, and her tears dried.

It was almost dawn when Yusef returned. I think I must have dozed in the leatherette armchair, because May was looking kindly at me, in that motherly way that old women have when they've watched someone younger asleep. Yusef walked in alone and went straight through to the back, where I heard the clank of the latrine bucket and running water. He re-emerged without keffiyeh and jerkin.

I said nothing and didn't get up from the chair. I realised I was cold, distant. I hadn't planned to be.

"You OK?" asked Yusef. "Did Mother behave?"

I sat up. "Where's Asi?"

"I don't know." He shook his head and I suddenly felt sorry again, not just for him and for Asi, but also guilty that I had been superior, judgemental. "But we've done all we can."

There was a long pause and I looked at May. She was smiling calmly. "Well, let's keep hoping and praying," I said and went to heat up some bread.

I don't know what time it was that Uncle appeared with the boy at the foot of the alley. The sun was high, late morning, I guess. Yusef had slept for a couple of hours and was now moving about the house doing odds and ends, cleaning. His body was looser than it had been before. He murmured that it had been Shia, maybe Druze, bully-boys who had taken Asi, but he was no longer haunted and the atmosphere of prepared bereavement had dispersed.

I had drunk too much coffee and felt sick and had gone out front to sit on the car seat and stare back at any children who stared at me. When I spotted them, Uncle was walking in a sweeping slow-step to keep pace with Asi, his arm across his shoulder, the boy walking with a showy limp, clasping his knee with his left palm. I called "Yuse!" just once and stood back from the stable door, allowing the light in from outside and for the boy and his great-uncle to stand in it. May threw her hands up in her chair and ululated a chant, and Yusef strode from the kitchen and knelt to hug his son, who stood spare-limbed and doll-like, as children do who don't know how to respond to adult emotion.

Uncle stood grinning and lit a cheroot. "Where is Nadim? You looked after him?" Yusef was talking close to Asi's face.

"Home," said Asi. "He needs a new football. They took it."

Yusef stood and patted the boy's backside sharply to propel him to the kitchen to wash the cuts on his knee and shin. We followed in an act of welcome and I dabbed his leg with wet loo roll. Then we walked outside again and took the proffered cigarettes from Uncle.

But it was Yusef who spoke. "They just drove them around a bit, waved some guns, then threw them off the truck," he said. "It happens."

"Are you OK?" I asked.

"Yes. Sure."

I paused just a beat. "And the boys who took him?"

He looked at the ground for a moment. "They may not be so well." Now he looked at me properly, as if trying to think of something to say. "Thank you for staying here."

I slapped his upper arm in a satire of manly acknowledgement and said, "Please be careful, Yuse."

I hugged Uncle, hugged Asi like he was mine, kissed May and

headed down the alley and towards town to find the guarded compound where I had left the 4x4, what felt much longer ago than just the day before.

I returned to England only about a month later, the local UN desk having absorbed much of the administration of the social and education projects we had set up. Through the good offices of the NGO that had sent me in the first place, I took a job administering a teaching-support charity in north London. It was only part-time, three days a week, but it was something to do. It wasn't where I was going. I started at The Fed shortly after that.

The interview was perfunctory. I'd worked in Sudan and I'd worked in the Middle East. But they did ask me why I'd been ordained as a priest.

"Is that where your compassion comes from?" Jake had asked me.

"No," I'd replied before I'd thought about it properly. "No, I don't think it's about compassion actually. It's more about justice. I think it's more about anger than pity."

Jake had cocked his head in attention to this. "But I suppose it's the Christian's imperative to love our neighbour as ourselves, no?"

"Yes, but I think it's ambitious to suppose that that brings peace, for other people or ourselves," I'd said. I was a bit on a roll so I went for it. "He also said that he hadn't come to bring peace, but a sword."

Looking back, I see that by my mid-twenties I was carrying a sword, rather than a cross. I didn't know how to use it then. Indeed, it was probably piercing my own heart. But I would learn.

12

The job Toby drove me to in Jerusalem was utterly banal, with no shadow of the horrors to follow. He parked a couple of streets away and I walked maybe a half-mile dogleg of streets. There were a couple of dusk drinkers sitting outside in the orange light. Inside, everything was dazzling white plastic.

Two young men in bomber jackets were sitting at the bar and turned towards me as if I was expected. I pulled the envelope from my pocket and ran it over my knuckles, raising my eyebrows to the young man who was now standing. He flicked his head as if to beckon me and put out his hand to his colleague, who produced an envelope from a black leather shoulder bag. It was an A4 envelope, folded double. The envelopes passed each other briskly and without fuss, no tugging, no ceremony of laying them down together.

"Thank you," I said, and he flicked his head again and grinned.

I walked briskly back to Toby. He was parked in one of those herringbone Jerusalem bays, reading a paper. I went to his open window.

"There you go," I said and passed the envelope through the window.

"Splendid," he said. "Jump in."

"Do you want to know anything about who I saw, what they looked like?"

"Nope. No offence, Nat, but they're people like you. Or me. Just doing someone a favour."

"Aren't you going to open it?"

"Above my pay grade. Come on, get in."

If I had, if I'd gone for a drink with Toby, maybe some supper, I wonder how things might have turned out. I doubt it would have altered anything; they'd have got me later, is all. As it was I made it easy for them.

"No, you go on. I'll walk back to my digs. It's a nice enough evening."

That's what I was doing. Swinging along between the low shrubs beside the main road, heading west, about a kilometre from my conference apartment, when I heard my name barked from behind me and turned instinctively. A dark vehicle with dark windows was pulling up next to me. Arms on my arms, a large heavy hand on the top of my head. I was in the back of the car before I'd seen who'd called me.

And there was no dwindling dusk, no gloaming to which the light of my day submitted. Light straight to dark. I was alive and then I might as well have been dead. Breath still inflated me, but imagination and consciousness were gone, like my own hard-drive had crashed.

I was plunged from the light of my day into the dark of a nylon hood, as I lay across the back seat of a saloon car, bucketing like plane baggage in turbulence. I can't say what I was thinking about, if I was thinking at all. So I can't claim I was violated. More like invalidated. Tough as it is to concede, all that surrounds us defines us. We have no other identity. I amounted to Natalie Cross, Anglican priest, inadequate wife, minor canon, sometime missionary. That's me in London, or Africa, or the Middle East, floating but anchored to a deathless litany of functions. From this moment, I had no purpose other than those defined by other people. Perhaps this is the sense of objective calmness that enfolds some at moments close to death. I was being unwound, wiped clean – though emptied, not purified.

It wasn't so much that I could do nothing; it was that I had become nothing.

And it's as though I write of another person, someone spawned in that car journey. What happened didn't happen to me, but to the person I became. I can't view it now with anger or fear, far less with penitence, but only with a dispassionate clarity – she was abducted, she was abused and beaten in captivity – but in that cold wasteland, in that stripped-down world in which she was denied any of her customary points of reference, she found a new life in her, a new person, capable of acts she couldn't have imagined. She feels guilty that she can scan those days and collate hideous events without the slightest catch in the throat, no gasp, and that her hands stay steady as she talks of them.

It happened to her, you see, not to me.

We drove urban streets for perhaps half an hour. I heard no talking and my breath became damp and muggy around my hooded head. Some movement on the seat beside me heralded a fresh intervention, and I was pulled up by the shoulder, my head following trunk like the lagged response of one roused from sleep. The hood snatched off like a magician's reveal and a wordless, dark young man next to me, holding a small plastic cup to my mouth, the size of a tablet dispenser. He pinched my nose with a reversed hand, the palm covering my eyes and I ingested the contents of the cup. It was viscous liquid and tasted like a bad soda I drank on that last night in Sudan. The hood rustled back; I was less a falcon being returned to blind calm than a parrot being put to sleep in its cage. The arrhythmic road had straightened and I vacated myself, neither asleep nor now fully conscious but in a parallel peace.

So I can't say how long I was in that car, nor even properly when I left it. I believe I can remember some stairs, though that seems like it was longer ago, which either I negotiated well, leading my mysterious escort party like old friends, or up which I was partially carried, my feet tentatively exploring where they might find some purchase.

I was asleep for a long time, I think. I could have slept for ever and I don't think anything awoke me. My room came to me in episodes. There was a radio somewhere and it had been playing long into my consciousness, a man's voice telling me in Arabic how good minted fluoride was for the gums, maybe. Or it may be that the voice was occupying my head, as the tongue I located in it, which had clearly been up and about its business before others of my components had awoken, was exploring the remains of the viscous film behind my teeth.

It was tranquil, like sleeping in as a child, the sun shining insistently through a high window beyond numb feet, covered absurdly with a candlewick bedspread. Fingers still played at the base of my throat and I heard unrestricted airflow through my nose, expelled air from a dormant windpipe. I recognised the fingers as my own, raising the index and middle to tap at my chin. There was some gluey stickiness around my mouth and I supposed I'd been gagged.

Above me, a hexagonally tiled ceiling. I felt no desire to move, ever again, until a deep breath, perhaps even a raucous snore catching the back of a dry throat, raised me to consciousness properly and the sun had passed the window.

This time, my head moved to my right side and my eyes followed. The bed was a divan, wooden framed, and against a distempered wall to my left. The floor was a beige-brown rope-cord carpeting that had been neatly cut against a thin skirting board, painted magnolia. The room was twenty-two feet by twelve, because I paced it out in the early days when I thought the detail might be important in any subsequent debrief. It was the kind of room an estate agent might describe as a single bedroom, or even ambitiously as the study. The only window was the high little one to the right of my feet, more of a skylight really, through which the sun now shone what I guessed to be its afternoon tone. The door was at the opposite end of the wall to my bedhead and flush with it. There was a small alcove, no more than a recessed fitted cupboard really, at the foot of the bed. Nothing on the walls, no other furniture.

Swinging my legs and sitting up without having made any real decision to do so, I saw a black length of fabric-reinforced duct tape on the floor beside the bed, about eight inches long and still curved from the shape of my chin. My gag, still sticky. I picked it up.

Instantly, I needed to pee. It was time to tell Dad I was awake. I called a "Hello", rather cheerily under the circumstances.

The air of human presence and the changing blink of shadow on the wall indicated the arrival of the young man who I presumed served my in-flight cocktail in the car. Tidy dark beard, sleeveless navy shirt, fashion combat pants, late-twenties I'd guess and re-assuringly unarmed. He looked at me blankly.

"I need the toilet," I said like a child, ridiculously, and he indicated the alcove to my left with an upturned palm, expressionless and without judgement, a simple declaration of direction.

I stood gingerly and my head expressed alarm, like a conning tower in fog. Through slightly tunnelled vision, I saw the alcove contained two white enamel buckets, a pitcher of water covered with a coarse grey towel and two large white linen napkins. I squatted over a bucket and then laid one of the linens over it, like an altar offering. The young man reappeared by and by, collected and returned it empty, without speaking, as I sat on the bed.

It never occurred to me to ask where I was. It was both obvious and irrelevant. It wasn't, anyway, a question that could be answered with a geographical reference. I was in my own clothes, I noted, but my watch and wrist-purse were gone and, of course, my mobile phone. I propped the single, foam-filled pillow against the bed-head and watched the cast of the sun across the room's corner.

A little later, he brought me some sustenance on a small, orange plastic tray. Some flatbread, hummus, an oily salad of leaves and a tourist bottle of fizzy water with a flip-cap and teat. Wordlessly he dealt with my ablutions again. A single switch lit a central ceiling bulb with a round paper shade. After a while I turned it off, just to see if it worked and was under my control, and let it grow dark. I could hear the drone and sliced air of fast traffic somewhere, but no voices. I lay on my back, my fingers plaited together on my abdomen and thought of the feeding station in Sudan and the weeping doctor. There was no point in considering my own circumstances; the effort was pointless, like starting out in a desert for a location over the horizon, without a map. It wasn't even worth starting and it would be mortally dangerous to do so.

Morning brought a fresh aspect to the room, the sun lighting the window only by reflection. It would only, I learned, start to catch the sills directly at around what I calculated to be midday or early afternoon. The bearded dead face brought me slices of orange and dates.

Sweat in the night had started to chap the inside of my thighs where my trousers creased, so I moved awkwardly. I stretched against the bare wall and called out facetiously for the window to be opened for some air.

"It's too small to climb through!" I reasoned loudly.

The bed couldn't help me reach it as it was screwed to the wall with brackets and an upturned bucket didn't provide the height. No answer. I had tried the door handle with a gentle and silent turn of the wrist. So far as I could tell, one simple bolt on the outside.

I'd been awake, I thought, perhaps two or three hours, when the motionless day and the rhythms of a solitary bluebottle was fractured by the clatter of new arrivals beyond my door, male voices in the clacking beat of Arabic and dull thumps of furniture supporting the weight of human and metal cargo. The bolt turned and a burly man ambled in, with a head like a waxen orb, long pale shorts with sandals and a light flak jacket. He inspected me as he walked an arc across the room, drawing on a cigarette and watching me, as one who would inspect a second-hand car before purchase.

A younger man, almost a boy, followed, a gun slung over his shoulder, then a troll of indeterminate age, black-toothed and sweating, their driver perhaps, I thought. He wore a loose, rust-coloured turban, that trailed at the back. Odd colour, I thought.

"Hello," said Burly at last, flatly.

I nodded neutrally. I was striking a balance between truculence and compliance. He stood over me.

"How are you?" I didn't answer, just stared at the wall. "Do you have all you need?"

"I need to be in Jerusalem," I said. "There's a conference I'm attending, you know. They'll miss me."

He smoked. "I want you to know that you are of no value to us," he said, in good English. "We only need you for a little time, maybe to serve a big purpose. Or maybe a long time. Short time, long time, it doesn't matter. We will use you and throw you away."

I was looking at his stomach, straight ahead. His shirt was made by a French designer.

"Are you Hamas?" I said pathetically. It was like I was networking at the conference. Silence on his part.

"What do you want me to say?" I said, I hoped tonelessly. "That I'll cooperate or something?"

He squatted down to look me in the eye and I caught the acrid breath of tobacco, the sweet kind, not the dusty foliage of truckers. He took the pace from his voice, so the words just rode the air from his throat hoarsely.

"We're going to make you a movie star, Christian lady."

His eyes darted between each of mine, looking for reaction. Looking back, I now know this was the only moment that I felt the knot at the base of the sternum that precedes crying. The cold fear of physical violence, even the prospect of immediate death, never gave me that feeling again, not this simple room, nor in the other rooms of the flat. I could handle the serious stuff. It was being patronised with the simple imagery of schoolgirl dreams that nearly did it.

"What is this?" he said suddenly, pointing at my eyebrow.

"It's a scar," I said.

"Scar? How is that?"

"In a sword-fight," I said. "You should see the other guys."

He paused and contemplated me. Then he snorted a laugh and put his hand on my knee to support himself as he stood and the moment passed.

"You know you should never have come back to Palestine," he said as he turned his back, the boy and the Troll parting to let him out. Then they followed him. The lock snapped and I looked upwards to the ceiling to clear the moisture from the lower lids of my eyes and realised I was praying.

"Dear God," I was whispering over and over again. "Dear God." It became a chanted litany as the hours ran from day to night. "Deargoddeargoddeargoddeargod." A rhythmic, gibbering appeal because there was nothing else to ask, because there was nothing to be understood.

But in the still of that night there was the call of another thought. From a remote hill somewhere, another voice was shouting a single question into the wind. "Deargoddeargoddeargod." Yet a further, more insistent petition was pressing me: why "back to Palestine"? Why "back"? How much these people knew of me was the background noise to my exhausted despair, like the endless faint dog-bark that carried on the breeze to my high window.

Time passed again and this was to be the routine of my

existence in that room over days that turned into weeks – torpid longueurs punctuated with intense engagements, interludes of heightened reality, then endless isolation, with only feeding and defecating events, while voices in the next room affirmed that I was never alone. I wondered if I would ever be able to wash properly; I dreamt of washing my hair in a mountain stream.

The low sun shining on to my tiled ceiling showed it was late afternoon when they returned some days later. It was the Troll who opened the door and the boy swung in like a bellhop with a letter.

"This way," he directed and seized my upper arm as I passed him, needlessly pushing me through the door. This must be what it was like to have been hanged in Britain, I remember thinking dispassionately, as I left my condemned cell for the first time.

The next room was only slightly larger than mine. It held a square, dark wooden table, some plastic easy chairs and a heavy door facing the one I came through, with two heavy bolts across its cross-beams and a single mortice lock by its round handle.

My heightened consciousness took in the metal-framed window with its short and dirtied coral fabric curtains, through which I could see the top of a wall that might mark the boundary of our building and some roofs in a parallel line beyond, implying a narrow street or an alley. We were, I guessed, on the second floor. There was an open arch to my right, to a space with a stove and a fridge, also bathed in natural light from another window. I assumed this had a bathroom to its rear, next to my room. We were in a one- or two-bedroom flat.

This front reception room had five men in it. Burly, the Boy and the Troll, who had been joined by two others, a youngish man who could have been the boy's elder brother, who was talking in

Lebanese to a more European-looking man in maybe his forties. This one was tinkering with a camcorder, wired by telephone spring cable to a laptop on the table.

This table was being shifted, leading to an altercation between the technician and the European. The young men were simultaneously climbing into dishdashes and arranging turbans above dark cowboy-style neckerchiefs. Sheets of paper with Arabic slogans were taped to the wall opposite the camera and I was manhandled on to a stool in front of them.

The boys, dressed, picked up automatic weapons and flanked me.

I can follow Lebanese patois rather more easily than Palestinian, so I gathered it was proving difficult to frame me with the slogans and the militia boys. I was stood up and sat down again as the chair was moved forward and back. Then the camera tripod was pulled back hard against the opposite wall, with its operator deploying its autofocus while holding the laptop in his spare hand. The cable jumped from its socket and he swore.

I suggested – first in English and then in pidgin Arabic – that the cameraman should use the extra range afforded by the kitchenette. There followed a pastiche of the clifftop just-one-step-back routine, a silent-movie slapstick. At one point, Burly laughed, a grunted guffaw that acknowledged, I thought, that I was directing the shoot.

After a while, the camera stood at a slight angle in the cooking area. The boys now stood at my shoulders with legs braced and guns across their chests, in the internationally recognised pose for terrorist propaganda videos. The room was hushed and, with Burly standing aside, the Eurocrat began reading a script towards the laptop.

As I stared ahead, as instructed, it began to dawn on me that I might be about to die, that this pantomime was about my videoed execution. My response was neither cold terror nor warm resignation, but rather a sense of humiliation. I felt pathetically compliant, assisting in my own destruction because they were stronger than me and I needed to please them.

I'd seen it in the wretched footage of executions before, from the Nazis to the Chinese. The obedient kneeling, the facing patiently towards the self-dug grave. If I cooperate, if I just play this game your way, you might approve of me and I may thus be acknowledged momentarily as part of this world, rather than merely its waste product. It's this instinct, this final hope, I think, that makes the condemned play their parts so dutifully in the drama of their own deaths, instead of raging against the darkness of their killers' intent, spoiling the show, like a defiant Christ who spits in the eye of Pontius Pilate and takes one Roman centurion down with him.

For me, I was acknowledging my captors' control, their total domination in the two-roomed universe that they had created to contain me. So naturally I would play their game by their rules, help them to the best camera angle so they could murder me most effectively for public consumption.

As I sat and tried to listen, almost politely – the Jews were this and that, the state of Israel was something else – like the guest speaker at speech day, the crippled girl at school swung her wheelchair briefly in front of me. I felt sorry for myself not because I was about to die, but because my instinct had been to make common cause with my executioners, because the desire to join in to avoid any further, unnecessary suffering overcomes any conviction of your own autonomy. I'd stepped in for Sarah. There was no one there for me now. It was lonely.

I wondered briefly who would see this video. The Ruperts in their riverside offices, freeze-framing my rag-doll moment, that final affirmation that I was commoditised meat. I have no family to speak of, but I hoped Adrian wouldn't see it. I didn't want to be his paschal lamb. And I didn't want Hugh to see it either. He wouldn't get the joke. Perhaps it would make YouTube. Perhaps they could play it on a loop at General Synod, and the new women bishops could lay garlands on the lino at my still-twitching feet.

I could pick out some of the hurried Lebanese, delivered in a monotone rap, like a languid recitation of someone else's audition piece. The Western oppressors of Islam were as guilty as the killer Jews, apparently. Mr Euro turned slightly to address this passage to me, and the boy to my right laid the cool blade of his curved kukri, or agricultural machete – I'm no expert on weapons of dismemberment – across my breast.

I glanced down, as if a waiter had dropped something in my lap. Burly shouted and left the wall, into the light of our stage area. Talking colloquial Arabic too fast for me to follow, he grabbed the handle of the blade, then my hair, and yanked my head back so that I blinked into the white light of the ceiling bulb, like Joan's final vision at the stake of St Margaret.

Burly was still babbling at the boy and I realised he was giving directions in how to slit my throat. Mad as it sounds now, a paralysing calm consumed me at this point, as I winced into the light. I dreaded the pain, for sure, and I could feel my blood pound, so I knew it would spurt under some pressure. And it hurt now as he gathered a firmer clump of hair and pulled on the roots, but imminently I was to be no longer part of this room, nor of this foul human charade, with its cock-strutting politics. It all began to fall away and that was soothing, in its way.

I started, before I even recognised the formation of the words, to whisper the Nunc Dimittis. It's odd to think of now, because I'm not sure I'd know the words that well, in Cranmer's version anyway, if I was asked for them in, say, a taxi.

But these words moved my lips then in what I assumed would be their last articulations.

"Lord, now lettest thou thy servant depart in peace, according to thy word."

Burly stood aside, handing my hair to the boy, who held it more gently, and Mr Eurotrash was talking, the last other voice I would hear, I presumed. The words popped noiselessly on the breeze over my lips.

"For mine eyes have seen thy salvation."

On which word, I wondered, would Simeon's prayer end? I suppose every martyrdom leaves the fragment of an unfinished prayer, but I didn't count as a martyr, I wasn't dying for the Lord I now professed, I was dying for a Hamas promotional video. The sort of motivational tool that's used in motels on Beirut's *périphérique* and becomes the sordid currency of prurient schoolboys on social media. Decapitation. Would my brain know when it hit the floor?

"To be a light to lighten the Gentiles."

The boy, it came to me, had dropped the hacking sword to his side and had let go of my hair, like a schoolchild who had completed his role in the nativity play. I rocked my head forward, away from the light, celebrating my intact neck, and looked the camcorder dead in the eye. Then Burly was in my face. There were minty toothpaste notes to the twist of tobacco on his breath.

"What are you saying?" he asked.

I switched my focus to his right ear, the blur of his sun-leathered skin becoming suddenly sharp.

"I was naming my children," I said.

He straightened and said something about taking the camera out, then indicated that I was to be returned to my cell. The younger one to my left took me under the armpit and, more roughly this time, swung me to my feet and around in a cruel parody of a square dance, and through the door. Burly followed. As I stood on the rope carpet, he looked at me with a sort of palsied face and his shoulders dropped.

"We don't kill you today," he said without expression, then turned and left. I heard the bolts shift on the outer door to the street. The boy and the dark young man remained.

"You like it?" said the boy, his top lip parting from his upper teeth.

"Do I like what?" I said, as benignly as I could muster. I genuinely didn't know what he meant. He swung up his arm and handed the other his automatic weapon, then rushed on me, pushing me hard up against the wall, a forearm across my throat, his other hand working the buckle of my trouser belt ineffectually. He was gurning at me and I hung limp against the wall, as I think you're taught to if attacked by a bear. The fumbling hand slowed and he glanced at his friend in an appeal for assistance, but he stayed at the door.

"You won't like it," I said softly. He was still and I fixed his dark eyes. "I'm bleeding."

I held the stare. It was a point of information, no more.

He whisked his arm away in a grand gesture of jettisoning me and staggered into the middle of the room as if drunk, snapping his head from me to his friend and back again.

"Huh," he went and "Huh" again, then a chuck of the head and a grin. He took his weapon back and, rather spoiling the effect of his desperado exit, gestured an "after you" to his partner, before slamming and locking the door behind him without looking back at me.

I stayed against the wall, breathing in the solitude of the room. This was my space. After a few minutes like that, I took the steps to my bed and lay on my back, breathing evenly and deeply. My limbs felt heavy but didn't shake. The palms of my hands spread over the sheets, which had stiffened from my night sweats.

I realised, curiously, that I had slept for a moment or two when my left knuckles slid into the narrow gap between the bed and the cool of the wall. There was a fissure in the wood, following the grain into the body of the bed and forming a point at the corner, on which I caught my palm. It was a splinter at its end, but it grew into a heavy shard down its fractured length. My fingers played against the spring of its pointed end, pushing it towards the wall, before it snapped back against the sprung pressure of its attached base.

That distant voice from another hill was calling to me again, but I couldn't make out what it was saying. But it shouted every time I twanged the lumpen splinter on my bedstead. It was a comfort, a gift, a sign. When it had my attention, it whispered.

"We're going to take action, you and me. We're going to lead events, not be their victim. We're going to try not to die here. This isn't Golgotha. The wood of your cross is splintered, Natalie. Break it. Take it. It's yours."

I ran my hand down the length of the split wood, collecting tiny shards in my fingers. I played with it a while like this, also scratching and lightly puncturing my palm, like a stigmatum, until I slept properly.

13

I can occupy my space, what's directly around me and about me. I can pull it into my head and live safely there. And so that's what I did. They can't touch you if you go inside, right inside, and mark your own time. They can watch but they can't join in, you see? Because everything is inside my ball, and they can do what they want to Natalie out there, but they can't get in here. In here, there's only me, and while I rock and hum, there's nothing, nothing in this world that can come close. I'm bored in here, but it's a blissful boredom, full of grace and peace. They can do what they like with Nat, but they can't get in here. Here, where no voices crowd in, where I can watch but no one can see me, where there are no secrets to be told because there's no one to tell.

The wood broken from the bed began to form. But I didn't know what it was for. Really. I watched myself make it, carve it, fashion it from its pointy pointless form into its new identity. It was now a thing and things have purpose, if only I could find out what it was.

I expect it was about a week after I broke it off, maybe more, but less than two, that about two-thirds of the length of that jagged splinter lay sharpened into a stiletto. In another world, it would have been just a good piece of kindling, spitting and spluttering, its thin tip aflame first. It lay between the bed and the wall, whence it came, but now that it was a thing, now that it was something that had a mysterious purpose, it had a marked place, because everything has its place and this one's place was taped securely to the bed with the length of that duct tape they'd gagged me with when they first brought me here. It was a perfect artefact, modelled by the purest boredom, the kind of stasis that is entirely free of order and planning and ambition.

I suppose a therapist would say that it was also a small act of self-determination, a defiant little secret. They had given me a loose abaya to wear and watched as I stripped and put it on. My lavatory was a bucket and they took it away. There was nothing they didn't know about Natalie here. But there was one tiny element that wasn't known to those in the next room, and it was this sharpened thing with its bulbous butt that I'd shaped to my right palm. I was my own secret Lady Macbeth.

The days had fallen into a vacuous routine. The boy and the Troll took the night shifts. The film crew had not returned. The silent one was always there in the day, sluicing my buckets, bringing me fresh fruit for breakfast, flatbread and olives and tomatoes in the middle of the day, usually nothing at night but water, sometimes chicken or lentil soup. I presumed my diet was designed to avoid the least bucket cleaning in the night, calculating that my bowel movements would be confined to the early mornings, when waste was cleared. I wasn't getting hungry in a room that took four paces to cover. I'd lie on my back on the floor in the morning and cycle my legs in the air to keep circulation going.

It was the fizzy drinks that led to my secret wooden spear. One day, early on, when the passage of the hours still sometimes bothered me, I'd mimed to the silent one with a hiss and a pop that a drink other than water would be agreeable. I'd trembled from lack of sugar and needed the rush or I feared I'd faint. Incredibly, the next day the plastic tray had a can of cola on it and thereafter various orangey carbonated drinks arrived. I said some wine would be nice too, but that was lost on Mr Silent.

With the edge of the first can, I scratched a small cross in the plaster of the wall under the window, conducting my own little ontological experiment under controlled clinical conditions. I knelt before it, sitting on my ankles, and emptied my head.

"Be still and know that I am God."

"However deep the pit, God's love is deeper still."

During priestly training, I'd heard others talk of letting the Holy Spirit take vacant possession of your mind, like a squatter. But nothing came, of course, except a cramp in my ankle.

Then I toyed with mental images. I'd lay at the foot of the cross before me what I imagined to be my despair – though I had yet to experience anything that I could truly call that. And I prayed that the burden of this captivity would be borne for me. Good vocabulary, I thought.

I'd read years ago of a Beirut hostage who had fallen to the floor of his dungeon, never before or since a believer, begging for release from despair, even the release of death. The next moment he was dancing in a trance of ecstasy. He'd never sought to explain this radical mood swing in terms of deliverance, but as a professional Christian I calculated that I might be able to generate something similar.

But nothing. No still small voice nor answering host, no hope, least of all a sure and certain hope, as promised by scripture. Just my improvised cross, mugging at me from the wall. I was being stonewalled by God.

So by way of distraction, I'd wrapped the ring-pull from the drink can around my finger and, almost idly, like I'd cut myself in the old days to check that I was still there, I'd pushed the curled leaf of it into the finger next to it until it bled. The same blood that they would spill in their video sequel, I fully expected. I watched it closely, as a child might examine a caterpillar crawling between your fingers.

A while later, a plan to fill the empty hours had formed. I was a woman with a purpose again, a small narrative to fulfil. The radio was playing in the next room and I waited to hear the bathroom door shut next to my room. About an hour later, maybe more, it did so. I bent over my bed and took hold of the splinter. The flush sounded – a solid overhead cistern, and there was the noise of the flow and the plumbing that ran under my room as it rushed into an extended gurgling flood. I was braced across the bed now, holding the nose of the large splinter with both hands above the level of the sheet on the bed, taut to breaking point at its broad base.

A second flush from the bathroom and I pulled hard and sharply. It just sprang against itself and I fell forward with it, but with a progressive final pressure before the cistern filled it began to give, not with a crack, but rather a melee of rustling disintegration as it parted at the base in a bush of sharp fibres. I'd moaned in the effort, I realised, and as the cistern's burble quietened so did I, holding my kindling log tightly in its place in case I'd been heard. But the radio played on.

I wish I could tell you that I began to whittle another cross, or a figurine of the Blessed Virgin. No, I'm afraid the merchant of death needs the tools of his trade. Half-wrapping the ring-pull in one of the linen cloths and wedging it between my fisted fingers, I could pull it along the narrowing length of the wood perhaps a dozen times before the ring-pull folded up and presented no cutting edge. In this way I gradually sharpened a plane that led to a slender but strong point.

So my time wasn't entirely wasted in Cousin Derek's shed. The shavings went in my pillowcase. Olive stones went in the empty cans to simulate the rattle of complete ring-pulls. And Lady Macbeth had her dagger.

The routine grew slightly easier. The Troll never left the front room, sitting with the expression of a surprised sea lion who'd just been served an extra side-order of sardines.

The key to the lock on the front door, I noticed, hung on an identity card around his neck. I saw this because my door was now left open and though I was rarely allowed to leave my room I was now permitted to use their bathroom, with its half-decent lavatory with a noisy cistern that needed double-flushing, a shower with a Perspex wall and a basin unit. The plumbing was efficient; the flush on the loo turned out not to be an old chain-pull, but a big handled affair.

The window of this bathroom was on the same wall as my room, also high. The frame opened from the top and stopped within six inches at a locating bar. No prospect of an exit and the Boy and the Troll left me to my toilet.

I'd long dispensed with underwear, but was chafed by the trousers I still wore during the day to make the abaya last at night, and by the lack of hygiene, so I needed some soothing in the groin. There was soap. The place, I realised, was in a state of disrepair, but wasn't old. A flat with one bedroom, which was mine. The caretaker's accommodation above a block, maybe, or student digs. An anonymous remote little block that would attract no attention. But I knew if I was taken there again, I'd know it instantly.

Whenever I left the bathroom, the Troll stood to cover the street-facing windows in the kitchenette and the main living room, one arm extended like a portly usher, as if I didn't know the way to go. Stupid slug. But, by doing so, he did confirm that there was a street or some other sort of thoroughfare out there.

And then my dream started. Don't think that it will be easy to tell. Real dreams never are. They never make sense when you're awake.

I made friends with the Boy, won his trust. That's the truth. The only truth. It's the kind of verity that lies like a bloodstain on a white marble floor. I cover it with the underlay and shagpile of all that's happened before and since, but it's always there, the sin that can't be absolved, don't even ask. No point in dwelling on him, for he's well out of it, but I'm the living expiation of guilt, the devil's work in progress.

Actually, it's a commonplace to say that there's a bloody stain on a marble floor. It's the easy way out to go for a curse, to say that there's a bloody stain on a marble floor, like in a fairy tale where a thousand maids can't scrub it clean and the queen orders it covered with the finest damasks, but still its dull, accusing shape comes through.

It's not like that at all. In truth, the Boy is a cheeky pixie of a memory and I can be thinking of something workaday, thinking of what to eat or what to say, and he'll pop up, just surface in my memory pool, and swish the water from his hair and smile in that way of his and laugh, teeth clean and set, and strike out for a certain shore like any young man finding his way.

This is what happened in my dream.

He began bringing me tea, a clear brew in a glass mug with a red plastic handle and frame. I remember such detail. It may have been some kind of atonement for the violation of our first encounter, but I doubt it. He was just curious and bored and he spoke some English. So I asked his name.

"Hamal," he said.

"Where are you from, Hamal?"

He just grinned that grin that was the raising of his top lip.

"I need something to pass the time, Hamal. Something to read, something to look at, or I'll go out of my mind."

I pointed at my temple. He seemed to misunderstand, I don't know whether deliberately, and made a pistol-kick gesture with his fingers and left to watch the television that I could hear had now replaced the radio, with the Troll.

But he brought a trashy magazine the next night, a compilation of sickly romances in Arabic, with repainted photos of princesses and brigands, and a deck of playing cards. They had no suits that I recognised and the numbers only rose to seven, but there seemed to be a repeating pattern of spirits and animals, so Hamal fetched a low stool and we sat on the floor and we played a crude form of Top Trumps, then a game I knew from the Sudan camps called Spit, a cross between Patience and Snap and quite aggressive, and I watched to see if it flipped Hamal's nasty switch in his head. So I set the cards out and showed him the order, numbers up or down, which needed to be expended on the two piles we built between us. The winner of each round took the smaller pile and the aim was to rid ourselves of all our cards on the opponent. And like a good girl, I lost. And drew him slowly in.

As the distraction of the cards wore on, his English expanded.

"How long will we be here, Hamal?"

He shook his head. "I don't know."

"Will I die here?"

He looked at me and the top lip raised.

"Maybe," he said.

He always brought his gun with the tea, a stocky little semi-automatic, or so he told me, propping it as insouciantly against the wall as if it was an umbrella. He'd stay maybe an hour, before quiz shows in the Troll's company beckoned. He was not to be an emasculated Arab boy.

The tea turned to coffee, because he preferred it, and he brought a backgammon board which he tried to teach me, but he didn't really know the rules himself, so we turned it over and played the checkerboard on the other side, or draughts as I called it, which inexplicably made him laugh. Checkers was the American word he knew.

He offered me a cigarette for the first time and I took it, and we flicked ash into a bowl from which I'd eaten tomato and cheese.

"Where are you from, Hamal?"

"From Dayr al Balah."

"Gaza?"

He nodded. We were sitting on the floor, coffee cups as makeshift ashtrays between us.

"Is that where we are? Gaza?"

Hamal laughed and flicked ash.

"Is that where we are?" I repeated and leaned in a bit, joining in his fun, not interrogating.

"No," he said with a little, sad shake of the head. And I believed him.

"Then are we in Lebanon?" This I knew was far more likely, not just from the patois of the video cameraman but for purposes of their own security. Hamal just laughed some more, as if he was being teased, and looked at the ceiling, the back of his head against the wall, blowing smoke.

"Good dates in al Balah, I hear."

"Not any more," he said.

"What do you do when you're there?"

"There's nothing to do. I fight."

Early on in the hours I'd spent staring at the ceiling, I'd concluded with some certainty that I was the hostage of a Hamas cell in Lebanon. I'd stated the logic of that in hours of isolation and simply accepted the proposition I'd given myself.

"Who do you fight, Hamal?"

He laughed more uneasily now.

"Your people," he said, looking at the floor.

As time passed I started to be able to make Hamal laugh with almost anything I said. I amused him with talk of Americans, trying to put some distance between the US and me, mocking their ridiculous baseball caps – though he seemed to like those – and their burgers and debit cards.

But there remained something simply carnal about him and the top-lip grin was less a characteristic than an affectation of disdain, because he continued to look at me from under lowered lids, like a boxer would intimidate an opponent. Though perhaps I seek to dehumanise him now, because of what I did to him.

One night, when he brought cigarettes and coffee, I asked archly if I could touch his gun. After the barest of pauses, he said, "Sure," and leaned over and picked it off the wall. But he moved round so that he sat next to me and we pointed it away towards the wall. So I can't turn it on him, I thought, even if I know how.

It felt lighter than I expected. I played the girlie.

"Is it loaded?" I cooed, though I knew the answer from his acquiescence and his body language.

"No," he said. That top lip. He put finger and thumb into his top pocket and pulled out two rounds on a clip, sleek and polished, the smooth silver of the cartridge casing offsetting the deeper bronze of the head.

"Show me," I said, thrusting the rifle back at him.

He swaggered a bit as he revealed the loading chamber just above the rear handle. He thumbed one round through the lid, against a spring, then the second. I puckered up and blew air in a silent whistle. Whoa. I hoped I looked impressed.

"Is it ready?"

"No."

He slid an oblong wedge just above the chamber forwards with the same thumb.

"Safety catch."

He exhibited no shame, no sense of irony, that he might be demonstrating the tool of my eventual execution. He swung the muzzle towards me and I palmed it away with an exaggerated cringe, though in truth I really did feel my stomach knot.

He pointed it at the wall and made two "pee-ow" noises with

faux kickbacks. I took a step forward so we were both holding it and gave a little childish give-me tug on its stock.

"Nah," he top-lipped at me and pulled the short magazine from the bottom of the weapon, returning the two rounds to his breast pocket. Replacing the magazine with a snap, he made to pull the gun from my hands, but I held on.

"How old are you, Hamal?"

"Twenty-two," he replied, with a toss of his head.

I'd guess he was adding a year or two. I pulled him in close with the gun and leaned over it and kissed him hard, locating that errant top lip. He was surprised but didn't recoil and I took my hands off the gun and cupped his face to keep it there, while separating momentarily to look at him, as if admiringly, I hoped.

He swung the gun away against the wall and pushed me backwards towards the bed, but without the aggression of his useless attempted rape of some weeks before. I put my palms against his chest, feeling the little cylinders of bullets in his top-left pocket between my fingers.

"No, Hamal. Not yet."

He did what he did, just smiled with his lip in free flight, ran his hand down my backside, then picked up his gun, the cigarettes and, with an uncharacteristic house pride, the coffee cups, and left the room, as ever without looking back.

I had no plan. I'd obviously decided to work on Hamal, but I really didn't know what I was going to do. If I had known, if I'd formulated it as some kind of strategy, then I'd never have been able to do what eventually I did. At least, I like to think I wouldn't be able to.

My seduction of the boy just seemed some form of progress, or the instigation of a change that might generate some progress. Perhaps he'd tell me something. Perhaps he'd help me. Perhaps he'd persuade someone to let me go. But, no, I had considered none of these outcomes and they certainly formed no part of a conscious plan. If I had thought about it, it seems highly unlikely that I could have thought that establishing some human intimacy with my captors would improve the situation.

If I'd really been considering consequences, I might have acknowledged the possibility of being raped by the Troll, so I really can't have been planning at all. Maybe I was just whoring some new living privileges. But I hadn't even thought about that either. Sometimes, I have to confess, Hamal was just something to do.

But the following morning began to shape a purpose for my folly. Hamal and the Troll stayed longer than usual, their telly coming on a little earlier to replace the radio, an indication that they were expecting to wait. My door remained locked, but I was by now familiar enough with the ambient sounds to know when Mr Silent arrived with Burly. The television went off ahead of a short and earnest exchange, before the cast moved into my room, Burly unlocking and leading, the other three following, appropriately armed to show off their diligence to their boss.

"Get up," said Burly and I did.

He was carrying a flat little pile of white cotton, which he dropped at the foot of my bed as I moved away from it. It was a gown and shawl, I discovered later, along with the white undertrousers that unmarried Muslim women often wear, the gown high-necked, tied and buttoned at the front. It was not unlike being admitted to hospital.

"It seems your people don't want you," he said, standing in front of me with his hands on his hips. I said nothing. What was there to say? But I felt intensely lonely.

"So it's time to be rid of you, missionary. Put some Arab clothes on."

He indicated the pile. I was to move from black abaya to white – quite a transformation, night to day.

"You like? Tomorrow you meet some different Arabs, yes – different Arabs. Maybe they make their own video, yes? You understand?"

He chuckled and turned to share the joke with his staff, but it turned out this was just a manoeuvre to give his shoulder and right arm enough swing. He brought that arm up in one complete motion, swiping the back of his hand across my head with such deft force that only my head snapped to my left and hit the wall, my body still erect and the stagger only coming a moment later.

I felt nothing at all, no pain, but there was a buzzing and I couldn't see from my right eye, as if a large cushion had been pushed against that side of my head. A moment or two went missing and my head grew heavy and pendulous as I turned back to the room. Only the left eye was processing images and I was looking at the crocodile motif on Burly's shirt, a line of vision that was lower than I expected. I was crouched, I realised, but not kneeling, much as high-Anglican priests pray over the Eucharistic elements. There was some chatter in the room, but my buzzing ear was covering it.

As snow flies from a windscreen, my vision was gradually restored and I looked past Burly's chest to Hamal. He was leaning to his left to get a better view. As I made eye contact and held it, the top lip lifted into the leer and for some reason I was disappointed, I think, as I'd hoped that I wouldn't have to hate him, because that would be a waste of energy. The Troll was animated, joshing and jabbing Hamal at his side. Burly held me up by the shoulder of my shirt.

"We will send you and your kind to play with your fool in Hell," he hissed and momentarily I thought he was deliberately playing a pantomime villain.

"Get dressed in your Arabic clothes, priestess, because you stink, you hear? Your pussy stinks."

He let go, I fell back across the bed and they bundled from the room. My room. And here's the weird bit: I smelt myself. I ran my palm across my crotch and smelt it.

And so I reflected, flat out, in my own clothes. It was true, they smelt, but the shower had kept me reasonably hygienic inside them. I realised that I had hardly worn the abaya, only when the room had grown oppressively stuffy. The underwear had long gone – I'd left it in the bathroom, I think, and I suppose the Troll had binned it – but I wore my jeans as a defiant identity. I was like Joan of Arc, putting on my heretical male clothing and inviting the contempt of my captors.

The evening was darkening now, the television was chattering, like an irritating neighbour. My mind was clear and I deconstructed my situation with a clarity that must have originated from the potent combination of an austere nun-like diet, solitude and physical violence. It was this last component, as the flesh around my temple swelled into a numb tumulus, that I imagined had had a catalytic effect on hitherto undiscovered powers of analysis.

It had been between two and three weeks, I calculated – I should have scratched the wall every dusk, I cursed myself now –

since the video was shot. I imagined that it had been sent to news outlets, first to Al Jazeera in Cairo. From their scoop, it would have been on the European and possibly American networks, through CNN and the BBC. The pompous British newspapers would have been sorting it out to their own satisfaction, mostly online but also in hard copy, putting a picture of me and the boys on the front page initially and a leader comment inside; the right-wing press would have been saying that I should never have been put in harm's way and blaming the liberal-left's indulgence of Palestine, while, for their part, the papers on the left would claim that I was the consequence of everyone dragging their heels on the peace process, an implication that Israel's very existence made the Middle East insoluble. Then they'd all turn to sport.

The foreign secretary, possibly the PM too, would have been saying that all that could be done was being done, the new news makeover of "we will never negotiate with terrorists". Special forces may have been briefed, I speculated, if they had a clearer idea of where I was than I did – "We presume she's in Lebanon, sir" – but I could only anticipate emergency rescue if the politicos calculated that they would come out of it smelling of roses, the peace process intact or enhanced, whether I was alive or dead. And from where I was lying, that was the point: a bungled early rescue would doubtless mean the Troll or Hamal putting a bullet through my head or chest.

The alternative was months in this or another room, or the sordid little execution-by-video from which I had previously been acquitted. All three options led me to the same course of action: early intervention on my part to change the narrative, radically.

If I left my fate to negotiation, I could still be dead at the end of it. Or dead at any stage during it, come to that. If I disrupted the process of my own demise now, it was also likely that I would be killed, but it would at least be a consequence of my own initiative, rather than of my inaction. And there was a slim possibility that, if I changed the course of events drastically enough, something entirely unpredictable might occur. If that was to unfold, then I needed to bring forward my end to an unexpected place, endeavour to make my end a new beginning. That was it, really. I was going to die to this life and see what happened: ignominious oblivion, or an exit of my own choosing. I developed an intense sense of my own mortality and simply invested it in the lives of those who held me captive.

My room had darkened, but I didn't turn on the light.

With clarity, I saw that it hardly mattered that it was my head or torso that was discovered by a roadside and made the early evening news, affirming those newspaper leader lines. It had to be some-one's body, after all. It might as well be mine. "Cowardly and bar-baric," I could hear the foreign secretary saying.

No, I'd kill my way out this night. It was worth a try and better to be killed by the Boy or the Troll than in some piece of jihadist death-porn posted on the web. And, either way, in my attempt I'd die to this life.

They might come in the night for me but, like Joan, I wouldn't change my clothes. They'd have to strip me and put me in them to spill my Christian blood. Splash themselves. And seeing me naked would hurt them. I would not go as a lamb to the slaughter. This room wasn't my Gethsemane. It was my Temple and it was here, on this altar, that I would make my blood sacrifice. I would wipe my slate dirty.

I allowed one little warm patch of nobility to soak into the fabric tapestry of my story. This way, no one would really be clear how or why I'd died. A mysteriously dead former aid worker was less likely to screw up the prospects of a peaceful settlement than a public execution. That was a prospect that comforted me. Death is always better as a mystery.

And so it started. I cleared my head. And I found a song there.

I met my boyfriend at the sweetie shop . . .

I left the bed only to put the Arabic day clothes in the corner of the room. When I heard Hamal's key in the door, I glided to the facing wall and leaned against it, breathing hard to keep still.

The light was off. Hamal needed to know from the top that tonight was different. The door opened a little and stopped. For an instant, I thought the dark might act as a block, startle him away. That might offer me a way out, this cup would pass from me, I'd be left there in the dark wondering if my dream was just the first manifestation of a madness born of incarceration.

"Hamal?"

The door opened. I had called him by name. I'd started it and there was no way back.

"Where are you?" he said.

"Here."

He reached for the light switch and turned it on. He was carrying the Thermos of coffee and two cups, his fingers wrapped into their handles.

But no gun, I noticed. Did he always leave it outside? I suddenly couldn't remember. Like a dizzy girlfriend afraid of alerting her father, I waved an arm forward at him mockingly.

"Turn it off!"

He obeyed, rather touchingly.

"Come here."

I was growing accustomed to the dark. The room was flooded with a blue glow from a light night sky, and I moved towards him to put my arm around his neck, the Thermos and cups clattering awkwardly at his side.

"Listen, Hamal, we have tonight. Go get the checkerboard and tell him you'll be a while. Lock the door when you come back." And I bit his ear lightly. Silly, but I realised then I'd never known the Troll's name.

Hamal grinned and set down the Thermos. I'd wanted to tell him to bring his gun, but could think of nothing to make that sound plausibly like foreplay. I'd thought about how to get him on the bed and slipped my trousers off and slid under the single coarse cover.

I heard the lav flush, some words outside and the volume of the television rise slightly. Then he was in the door.

He paused again and I said, "Over here."

He turned into the room, locking the door and palming the key, and a hunched shoulder revealed that he was carrying the weapon. There is a God.

"Come here," I repeated.

He bought me ice cream, he bought me cake . . .

He stood by the bed, looking down at me, and I imagined his lip was high. I whispered further encouragement, swinging open the bedcover in invitation, but he didn't move, just stood there. It occurred to me that I didn't know Arabic form, what his father might have taught him to expect.

I swung out of bed and stood against him, ran my hand up his cheek and kissed him urgently. That lip, I noticed, was lowered, resting on his upper teeth, and I thought he wasn't responding. But he dropped the gun against the wall and clutched my bare back with both hands, and we stood there for a moment, turning our heads like dancing birds to get fresh purchases on each other's mouths.

"I want you now," he murmured.

Perhaps he'd watched some Western porn. It was the last thing I heard him say.

I let out a short little breath of emulated hyperventilation, rested my forehead on his chest and started to rub his groin. Its hardening cargo took shape and I sat on the edge of the bed, unzipped him and he flopped out forward, like a salami from a carrier bag. He moaned and I left off for a mischievous "ssh", my index finger across my lips. Perhaps that's why he said no more. I resumed the salty work of preparation, but he pulled away and pushed me back on the bed, gripping my right leg behind the knee and pushing it aside.

"No, Hamal," I hissed, "no, no, no," but that only fired him up and he pushed into me and I gasped. This wasn't going to last long and I had to move quickly. My head was pushed against the wall and I feigned an uncomfortable crick, crying out softly and arching my back, pushing my hips down and him out. Close to his head now, I nuzzled his ear and caught it roughly with my hand, making out that the throes of passion had made me lose all decorum. He moved to the side ever so slightly to extricate his ear, and I used the movement to swing his shoulders bedwards, down the wall, and laid his head on the pillow.

He brought me home with a bellyache . . .

Deargoddeargoddeargod . . .

I swung a hand in indication and he shifted his legs on to the bed and I straddled him. With one hand by his head on the pillow, I used the other to help him and he did the rest with a short upward thrust. I rocked my hips on him and guessed that he wanted the dignity of being serviced.

I needed him at his most vulnerable if I was to succeed and the moment I had only vaguely anticipated had arrived. He was offering himself up. The sacrificial lamb.

Mama Mama, I feel sick, call the doctor quick, quick, quick . . .

I delivered the usual verbal encouragements over his face and I felt an aggression well up in me.

"Show me, Hamal." And he started to pump rapidly, as I pushed my fingers over his chest, running across the stubby pencil shapes in his top pocket, my quarry. I threw my head back and entreated him and, as the young do, he responded.

"Come on, Hamal," I whispered and he quickened like a sewing-machine needle, his soft breaths growing staccato.

That meant I could place the palm of my left hand firmly across his mouth and I grimaced a further "ssh". I could feel him expand in me and I pushed my hand forward as I cupped his mouth, as if lost to the moment, raising his chin and forcing his face away from his neck. He began to shimmer and shake and his thrusts became stabs. I reached into the gap beside the bed. The duct tape came away with a rasp and the wood block flipped up against my knee. I cupped the thick end in my palm, its fashioned point running down my wrist.

Doctor, doctor, will I die? Count to five and stay alive . . .

I wish I could say that I can watch myself in that act objectively now, rationalise it, tell myself I did what was necessary. But I still look through the same eyes and I see it. And I can feel the ungainly sex that set the stage for it. And I remember the crystal-clear concentration of making the cleanest cut, like a Halal butcher. Like the execution of a prince, there could only be one blow.

I raised the stake to shoulder height, in the fisted gesture of the revolutionary. I brought it down as one might the handle of a spade, just above the ball of his clavicle and below and to the right of his Adam's apple.

The point of the thin blade entered his neck like a sheath and further and quicker than I could have imagined possible. His arms shot up my chest and grabbed at my face. He bucked as I rode him, pushing into him as he pushed into me.

So I leaned in hard with my left arm, swivelling the palm of my hand to push with all my body weight against his chin, I suppose in some frantic hope that his neck would break.

It meant too that I never saw his eyes. He convulsed under me, expelling an extended snort through flared and bloodied nostrils. His left arm suddenly flailed away to the right of the bed, hitting the wall with a thud that could have alerted the Troll.

In that twist, his neck moved aside and around on its axis as if pulling away from the impaling and that afforded a chance to yank on the butt end of the makeshift stock, pulling it to one side as if trying to free it. Something gave and a dark fountain splashed over my forearms, his second discharge.

Then he was still.

But still stiff, one arm straight out to the side, fingers cupped in supplication and his legs quivering as his manhood withered. I held him there for more than a moment, listening to the sounds of the room, a pounding silence, my ratcheting breaths, the gurgle in his throat accompanying the bubbling up of lifeblood, the stream a dark maroon in the moonlight, crude oil bubbling from a well.

I took my hand from the stock and it lay like a great goitre at the base of the neck. I dismounted and stood by the bed and tried to still my breathing to hear whether the door was being tested or banged on.

Nothing, so far as I could tell through a strange tinnitus that was crackling in my ears. I pulled a length of the candlewick bedspread from beneath his calf and wiped globules of thick blood from my arms, another to wipe the stickiness from my thigh.

One, two, three, four, five . . . I'm alive . . .

With a struggle, I began to focus forward again, on what must happen next, wiping each finger quickly, then with a fast and steady hand felt for his upper left pocket and tore back the felt fastening.

There was a lined second pocket and for a moment I could feel the shells through material but couldn't reach them and, in an instant of frustration and revulsion, my upper legs filled with a soiling sensation of panic.

Steadying myself with a deep breath, I took my hand out and found the deeper rear pocket and felt the cool metal and removed the clip, dropping one of the bullets and having to wipe blood away again.

I took the gun from the wall and slumped cross-legged to the floor, the weapon across my lap. I found the loading flap and pushed a round through it.

The flap just swung lazily, no sprung resistance and the cartridge didn't locate and just flopped out. Again, a nervous chorus in my thighs.

I forced concentration, lowering my forehead and breathing heavily. So I pulled back the cross-hatched thumb switch. There was a snap and I tried again. This time the chamber was alive with sprung resistance.

The first round clunked into place; the second harder to push, but then swallowed crisply into the maw. I laid it gingerly on the carpet, stood and glanced at the body of the Boy on the bed as if I feared it would move. I felt nothing at all. It was if it had nothing to do with me, as if I was observing the body from a distance. It was resolutely still and dark, but for the luminescence of the flaccid fish extending from the trouser zip.

Dragging myself back into the moment, I started to pull my trousers back on, hesitated, pulled them off again and grabbed one of the linen cloths on the bucket, wiping as much blood as I could from my legs.

Think, girl!

Then I pulled on the white Arab day-wear, standing away from the widening pool of blood and wiping my feet harshly on the rope carpet and a linen towel. The under-trousers and smock first, then the shawl at the shoulders.

Picked up the gun again, held it in both hands firmly, pulled back on the handle. Couldn't remember if it was live with button forward or back.

Think, girl.

Forward, I think. Picked up the checkerboard with the other hand and stepped to the door. My legs felt loose and detached. I stood there, listening to the TV, trying to discern where he was sitting.

I rattled the pieces in the closed checkerboard and called something brightly, forcing what was meant to sound like a chuckle but came out as a light cry from my dry throat.

I turned the key, wincing as the door disengaged with a clunk. My right arm pinned the gun to the wall by the door jamb and I opened it, trying to delay shakes.

The Troll was sitting behind the table to the right, a wrap in his hand, some cans in front of him. Also, a pistol. I couldn't see the other automatic weapon.

"How do I look?" I said, trying to be bright, but it came out as a tremulous quaver, like I was crying.

The Troll had his mouth open for a bite of wrap and looked dead-faced at me, trying to process the information before him.

I took one step into the room. No one else there – I couldn't have been sure – and let my right arm with the weapon swing through to join me, still smiling a rictus grimace to maintain perhaps a second's continued confusion in the Troll's slow mind.

What must have been the familiar slap of its leather sling on the metal drew his eyes down to the gun and he started to rise.

I took two or three steps towards him – it's as vivid as if I was making a witness statement – holding the weapon in front of me like a child offering it to him and curling my finger into the trigger guard.

There was a thud that seemed to reorder the air in the room and a piece of the Troll's upper left breast to the shoulder flew away and a lump of plaster fell from the wall by the door.

As I looked through the mist, the Troll had disappeared backwards over his chair, but was rising to his feet again. I pointed it over the table and pulled the trigger again.

Nothing. I pulled at the cocking lever and the second live round ejected from the side.

The Troll was up, wide-eyed, slack-jawed and taking a step towards the table with an atavistic groan, the chair tangled between his fat legs.

I threw the rifle at him and grabbed for the pistol, fumbling it round at him in hands slippery from blood and sweat.

I hadn't time to wonder if it was loaded. I just didn't want him getting to it first if it was. But his expression confirmed that it was. He stopped on his front foot, shook his jowls and opened his mouth to cry out, pieces of wrap spilling out.

Holding it with both hands across the table, I pulled and turned my head away, as if pulling a cracker. A much louder bark this time that bounced off the walls and back into my head, kicking my arms up and throwing me back on my heels. When my forearms fell down in front of me, clearing my vision, the Troll wasn't there any more, just a stippled pattern of crimson across the door and half the window beside it.

I moved crab-like, making whinnying sounds, round the table and his bulk lay motionless on its back. I threw the gun aside – stupid – and moved to the head of this island of flesh.

The eyes stared sightlessly in the way I'd seen in feeding stations and one side of his checked summer shirt was turning deep and dark and wet.

The neck sash suspending the door key hung into the dry

armpit. I grabbed it, clearing the sash from the back of his head with a jerk.

The two bolts on the door came back easily enough, but the key in the mortice only seemed to turn one way and to no effect, the door remaining resolutely barred, until I paused, took a grip, took a step back from delirium and realised I was double-locking, so moved it to the middle and tried the handle.

The door moved back towards me and all I wanted in the world was to be the other side of it. Whatever was on the other side, whatever greeted me, hell or eternity, I'd shot my bolt, it was finished – so whatever I met, more guards, a hail of bullets, rabid dogs in searchlights, whatever, it was OK, if only I could be out.

A rush of cool air and I was at the top of a flight of stairs that doubled back on itself into a front yard. Of course, the stairs; I saw them as if from a dream.

An indoor light turned on in a window to my right, perhaps in response to the sound of gunfire, perhaps the door was alarmed, perhaps not.

I started down the stairs and into the yard. No lights on the ground floor, but I expected, kind of knew, that I'd be grabbed at any moment by unseen hands.

There was a baby crying somewhere, I remember.

A front gate, metal vertical bars. A combination spring-lock and a high, neatly painted corrugated fence on either side, framed with brick.

Back down the side of the house. High waste bins, maybe two metres high. Up on to the rim of the first one and I could see over the side fencing.

Some kind of vehicle port. I dropped over the fence into the forecourt, past some parked cars, and stepped over a low wall and into a tidy street, newly built, with security gates shielding the maisonettes similar to the one I'd just emerged from, with parking areas next to them.

Streetlamps and two figures walking my way on the pavement. But not running.

I couldn't be found here.

I crossed the road and walked briskly away from them. I heard music from one house, saw a family eating in another.

Maybe five gates down, the unbroken line of housing gave way to an alley between the buildings. I took it, as this would be the direction my room's window had faced and the sound of distant traffic. I also knew from the direction of the sun on that window that it faced west.

I had no particular desire for west, I suppose, but west would eventually mean sea and ports, east meant mountains and trouble.

The alley opened behind the houses on to a small, railed viewing bay, the backyards of the houses on either side. I'd been kept in a room that faced out to open country. Of course.

Away below, I could pick out the lights of vehicles on the road, but not many. I swung over the rail and on to the ground and picked my way carefully into the dark, aware that a torch would have easily picked me out in my white clothing. An easy shot.

The ground started to fall away fast, shale, or a slate outcrop. I started to glissade down, like a cartoon cat on marbles, then sitting to take the tide of the small stone avalanche I'd started.

Occasionally there was a large rock that I had to pick around. The ground levelled, a small brook, some barbed-wire fencing.

The road was close now and I began to follow its line, staying in the dark on mushy and mossy grass; south, I reckoned.

But the soggy ground and the rocks slowed progress, and I had to make for the roadside, lying flat down its bankside when headlights appeared. It was an open, hedgeless highway and I could spot the lights of vehicles when they were still far off, long before they illuminated me.

Maybe a couple of kilometres of this and the road rose on an escarpment, some larger rocks lower down to my side. I glided down and between them and rested my head, while lorries thundered by above.

It was only then that I started to shake, my whole body trembling, great swings of my forearms with no autonomic nervous control, as if in the trauma of a hospital admission after a road crash.

I gibbered in the cold, salivating down my chin, muttering like a drunk, speaking in tongues of men and angels. I knew I was in some kind of withdrawal, a detox from the intensity of a short window of absolute trauma, maybe no more than half an hour, in which I had changed the world. So I squatted there, dribbling and shaking, unable to address the enormity of what was happening. The rocks offered a kind of sanctuary; the headlights were like passing comets in the sky and from time to time a trance-like sleep wrapped me.

14

First light revealed mists on the meadows under the crags, between which I'd fallen from the scene of my crime. I could see from my rock sanctuary that the length of the road I'd walked formed a gradually falling left sweep around the little mountain I'd descended and it grew craggier as the road fell away – I'd been lucky to come down where I had.

I forced myself to concentrate, to put mental distance between the house way up beyond the crags and my rock of ages. I calculated I had about three or four hours of daylight, from dawn to around nine, before the shift changed at the house and the bodies were found, assuming that the gunshots hadn't been investigated.

So I needed transport early, before anyone came looking for me. I heard dogs barking as soon as I could see across the sheep meadows and I imagined my trail being followed and shivered the great jaw-rattling shake of the dangerously exposed.

There was something else: I wasn't just fully awake as soon as the sky turned mellow, but I felt real again, not the imagined creature of the night hours. I had woken from my dream.

One, two, three, four, five. . . Think, girl, get a grip.

I checked my legs and arms; there were scratches and one deeper gash on the back of one calf, caked now with dried blood.

My arms were pinked with my own as well as the Boy's blood. The overtrousers were torn and the back of the smock was wholly scuffed with slate dust, but I'd just have to explain that away somehow. I washed in the brook and, clocking that the sheep that had started their dawn bleating were downstream, I drank a little as it looked cool and clear, living water that soothed my sickened stomach.

That dawn, I guessed, I was in the foothills of the Chouf mountains, but I'd need a road sign or a talkative driver to get some bearings. So I straightened up and patted down my incongruous clothing and scrambled up the bank to the roadside. There was a utility bin, grit or sand perhaps, away down the road and I strode down purposefully to sit on it.

Only one vehicle, a coach of sorts, passed in the opposite direction. Sitting on the bin, I let a lorry pass, then another, while pretending to examine an imaginary smartphone in the palm of my hand. A lorry has connections, professional curiosities.

Then a suave executive car. I didn't stand, but offered an inquisitive palm, such as a professional stuck in a wilderness might offer if their car had broken down and they were wondering what to do next. It too passed.

I became keenly aware of the risk I was taking. Mr Silent might take this route to his work as my janitor, or Burly, or any of his mates might already be out on the road looking for me. I'd be picked up, driven up a track somewhere and despatched. If I was lucky. Women who behaved like men could be particularly brutally treated. Raped and stoned, maybe; there were enough rocks around.

I thought of taking off across country again, but the crags rose sharply on the other side of the road and this was wild country. I had to take the chance of a car ride.

I remember them all. A station wagon, a van, a woman with children. The children looked at me, heads turning as the car passed. It must have been past seven, or even later, a school run. I'd soon have to think of hiding again.

I became more demanding. I stood, stuck out my thumb. Would that be recognised as British? No, thumb in Lebanon, flat palm in Syria, I recalled. Several more cars between the lorries. The working world was waking.

Then a red flatbed arrived, the sort with the maker's name written large across the back, the kind we used in the desert. I saw sun-wrinkled skin, a white singlet, grey stubble. I felt his gaze focus on me from within the cab, like I was a sign. So my head followed its passing and the brake lights came on, its nose dipping slightly, dust rising from the kerb.

I should have a bag to pick up, I thought, as I ran to catch up, surprised that my legs were working so well. The passenger window was down and a wiry, bronzed little man, probably late forties, but dried up by the sun, like a prune, was leaning across, his bright blue eyes the only colour in the cab.

"Hi," he said, leaning his fist on the rug of the passenger seat. Popeye's Mediterranean uncle.

Dust and earth and cigarette packets on the dash, a long-extinguished air freshener swinging from the rear-view mirror. Placed there optimistically by a wife, maybe? It was shabbier and it smelt of bricks, but it reminded me of Yusef's truck, the same sense of enclosed safety, nothing to do but wait and watch, the sun winking from behind the windscreen struts.

"Thanks," I'd said girlishly as I fell in, like a cowgirl.

Then a bit too quickly, "I'm a relief worker with the UN. Been doing a tour of camps on a sanitation inspect. Just broke down. My truck was just taken away."

"Yeah?" he said, grinning and wincing forward.

He wasn't engaging with that narrative and I concluded that he wasn't with my captors. I was motoring away and I wanted to go with that presumption, away from glassy eyes and sticky blood and the condemning silence.

"Where you going?"

"Just down to the border," I said.

I hadn't thought that far yet. I was still concentrating on departing, getting away, not on arriving anywhere. I started to build an assumption that border guards would be sufficiently bureaucratic to turn me in to the authorities, where I could contact the UN Mission and maybe the British consulate. Just a dippy relief worker who had got separated from her team. Even if they recognised me from the TV bulletins, they'd pass me up the line. They'd not want to get involved.

"Border?"

He chuckled softly to himself and rested just one hand on the top of the steering wheel. He looked out through his open window and shook his head a bit.

"I know," I said, trying to enjoy whatever the joke was. "I need to check some supplies coming in."

As casual as I could be. Keep it vague. I guessed he was a Lebanese builder, busy over the years with the rebuilding of the Beirut suburbs and the bombed south.

"Border," he said again. "Is that what you call it now?"

I didn't understand. The road was black and new. I stayed silent and he drove quite slowly, that one brown arm holding the top of the wheel, the other hand cupped in the slipstream outside his window.

"I'm going down to Jericho. Which side will I drop you?"

Still I said nothing. The Lebanon/Israel border was long closed, a militarised zone. Very few passed that way and only with the highest authority. He couldn't possibly be passing in a builder's truck. I didn't want to direct the conversation towards my lack of papers or passport.

I felt the swing in my stomach as I started to lose control again. It was like one of those fantasy games where you can't escape your dystopia, always ending up back in the same place. A truck passed. Something about its licence plates? I was finding it hard to concentrate.

Then a road sign, growing larger, like a dawning idea. It was coming to me gently to tell me something. A direction on to a slip-road, two lines, two languages. One Arabic. One Hebrew.

I pretended to be lost in thought. The road was straightening out from the hills and we were looking out across a plain.

"Remind me of the name of that village, that town, where you picked me up? Where I broke down. I'll need to tell them to pick up my truck."

He shrugged and stuck out his bottom lip. "I don't know. One of the developments. A new one, I think."

Some more traffic, passing too quickly for me to catch details. What did Lebanese plates look like anyway? How did it look when Yusef was driving me? Come on, girl, get a grip.

"Where are we, I mean, how far to the border . . . to the . . .

barrier?" I couldn't think of the words. "To the wall. Roughly, from here."

"We're only twenty minutes, maybe half an hour from the checkpoint now," he said calmly. He hadn't baulked when I said "wall". Why had I said wall?

"You have papers, yes?" He looked at me only for the second time. I was carrying nothing. This could get him arrested.

"Bumbag," I said uselessly.

A larger sign, blue across the road, which now widened into traffic lanes. Hebrew again. Oh God. I felt sick with madness, everything rocking, not just the car. I wanted to say to let me out now, here, deal with this panic attack on my own, hyperventilate beside the road with my head between my knees. Is that prayer?

The traffic filter was to another trunk road, a big town from the size of the sign, just eight kilometres away. Hebrew again. Oh, Jesus Christ. It says Nazareth.

"Drop me here," I said. Then, pathetically, "We have an office. I just remembered. It'll be fine. Please, just pull up before the exit."

I sounded urgent, distressed, panicky. Not good.

But he flicked his indicator arm, glanced at his wing mirror and channelled. He must think I'm a mad bitch. Or is this where he pulls a gun, parks up beside a smarter van. In it is sitting Burly and the Troll, maybe Hamal in the back.

I'd be glad to see him. In a strange way, it would make everything OK.

"Just stop, please. I feel sick."

He cupped his hand up to indicate that it made no difference to him. "It's easy. I'll drop you at the roundabout. Better for lifts."

Suddenly it was all true and I'd readjusted all sensory perception. This is where I am, I thought. This is reality. The road to
Nazareth.

I needed time to think. I'd killed my captors. I had to come to
terms with that. But here was the shock of the new: I hadn't been
held in Lebanon by Hamas. I hadn't even been held in the occupied West Bank. I'd never left Israel. I needed to absorb that
knowledge, or let it wash over me like a rising tide. I needed to
know what it meant for me, for what I'd need to do next.

In the end, he drove me nearly into town, where the traffic
started thickening and telephone wires criss-crossed the road.
There were boys on bicycles. A petrol station.

He grinned from the driving door as he drove away, made
a sweeping pass with his hand. Onward and upward. He had
flicked a radio on when we'd left the freeway and I suddenly
felt bad that maybe he'd been expecting to talk more, have some
company.

He swung the truck around in the road. He was just a regular
Palestinian – Muslim? Christian? – going about his business. The
simplicity of that encounter made me want to weep by the road. I
couldn't really remember a time when I'd related to anyone who I
didn't think might kill me and I wasn't ready for the shock of
human kindness.

I was now severed from my previous life, when I'd known
human warmth like that as ordinary. But I had a kind of freedom
again. The road rose before me and I could walk into Nazareth
from here.

✣

I sat on a low white wall on the edge of a square, on the edge of the Latin Quarter. On the edge of a wall again, as I had by the leaning tree at Jerusalem University with Toby an eternity ago.

But I'd fallen back into my old familiar bubble like an old armchair. All around me crowded in, jostling for space, coming too close, but nothing and no one could touch me in my own world.

Watch but don't touch. The cyclists ramming past, the tourist coaches schlepping up the hill into the old city, some stalls selling oranges and bananas between palm and plane trees, the sun pinking the tarmac between their creeping shadows.

The people of Nazareth went about their chores and I didn't think of them or me. I just sat, I suppose for some hours, not thinking but only watching. No one in the world knew I was here. Just being, I think you'd say, conscious, breathing steadily, watching without really seeing.

The sounds pressed in too, the sound of motor engines, the voices, the footsteps. But I was set to a different rhythm, a more somnolent metronomic tick. I was in my own little viewing gallery.

I knew I had murdered two people since the last moon. I had stabbed one to death with a crude weapon I had fashioned and shot the other twice in the chest with two different guns. Before then, weapons of choice had been my voice, my knee and a carpentry circular saw. I'd graduated.

But these thoughts took no purchase, like gulls flying into glass, and they just fell away. So I sat in silence, with no judgement made or received, just waiting, until a time came not to do so.

Beside me on the wall was the peel of an orange that had been tossed to me by one of the market boys. He'd held it up and called in Arabic to me as I crossed the square. Maybe because he was

Palestinian. Maybe because of my clothes. I had shrugged in a manner that was meant to convey something between not being bothered and having no money, and he'd lobbed it to me and I'd caught it and smiled. I hadn't wanted to attract any attention and dropping it might have done so.

Then there had been a skip, full of building materials for recycling, by one of the eternal building sites that pepper Israeli towns, patching up the flimsy buildings that hang between the international construction. There was a short length of copper piping among the cluster of plumbing detritus in one corner, and I slipped it into my sleeve as I passed between skip and plastic sheeting that hung like curtains around a wounded patient.

As ever, I can't claim to have had any plan, but knew vaguely I shouldn't have thrown my murder weapon away. The little piece of tap piping, about the length of a child's geometry ruler, now lay under my orange peel, and I sat waiting for the reason I'd taken it to come to me.

I know all about wordless prayer – you don't need words to pray; Yusef's mother-in-law had shown me that – and so I waited for direction. It's good enough to acknowledge there's a plan, but you don't need to know what the plan is.

What I did know is that I had more time for my enemies than my friends. More time for the dead Hamal and Troll, even Burly, and for the people that ran them than for those who had let them take me.

I slid my backside from the wall before I knew I was leaving it and I had a sense that I'd started an enterprise. Here we go. I slipped my copper tube back into my sleeve, then crossed the square confidently and directly, invisibly, to the cafe opposite, up two tiled steps, a narrow terrace where two men had been playing backgammon for as long as I could remember sitting on the wall, and into the cool of the bar.

There was a stocky young woman who I'd watched serving at tables. A taller young man had left as their customers dwindled, probably for a nap, I thought, or to buy food in the market for the evening shift. A Jewish family working an inherited franchise hard, I'd guessed.

She turned from wiping cups, showing her teeth but not smiling. She had expressive dark eyes – deeply loved by the man in her life, I supposed. They flicked me up and down, not rudely, almost imperceptibly.

"I'm so sorry," I said in Hebrew, then in English: "I've lost my phone. I'm afraid it may have been stolen. I've no way of contacting my boyfriend to pick me up. Could I possibly use yours, just for a second?"

The briefest of pauses, then her face broke into a broad and effortless smile.

"Naturally."

She started to disentangle a landline from below the shelf of the bar, then gave up and picked a mobile out of a breast pocket, from behind her order pad. I sighed that this was too gracious, apologetically, and she waved in dismissive generosity. The global sisterhood for needy phone calls to errant boyfriends trounced any curiosities she may have harboured of this Westerner, with poor Hebrew, in Arab clothes.

I pointed to the terrace and she said, "Sure," in English. In the Jewish way, she'd gone for the whole hospitality sketch and had decided that I wasn't going to run off with her mobile.

I didn't need to gather myself; perhaps I'd done that on the wall. A swift internet search reminded me of Toby's office switchboard number and I punched out his direct extension line with a jabby forefinger. I recalled it without pause. Prayer without words.

It rang out and gave me Toby's voicemail, more serious in tone than he really was. I was committed, I knew that, and after the beep I didn't miss a beat.

"Hi, Toby, it's Nat. Remember me? Call me on this, why don't you."

I snapped the phone shut. The girl was standing in the door, wiping her hands.

"He'll call me back," I said, holding up her phone. She didn't take it.

"Sit down," she said. "I'll get you coffee."

I half-laughed. "I haven't any money. Stolen too."

"Pay me next time." And she disappeared inside.

I sat down, the borrowed mobile in front of me. How quickly could they trace it? Do they have that sort of technology anyway?

I figured I'd sit for about half an hour, then move on. That way they'd only find this girl and her phone. And I'd try from some-where else.

Suddenly I wasn't sure what I was doing; I wanted Toby to come for me, not a hit squad. Pulling that off depended on how I floated my fly on their water. But I knew now I couldn't trust my friends any more than I could give myself up to Burly and his pals.

The girl brought olives and figs and coffee in a small percolator. I didn't wait long. Perhaps eleven minutes. Approximately. Who am I kidding, I counted them. The screen lit with the number I'd dialled. I answered but stayed silent, the girl watching me.

"Nat?"

"Who is this?"

"Bloody Nora, Nat, where've you been? We've – I've – been worried sick."

That's exactly what he said.

"Listen, Toby, listen very carefully. Don't screw this up or I'll never see you again, you understand? I'm in Nazareth." He started to interrupt and I talked across him. "I want you to come and pick me up. But only you, Toby. Got that? Only you – and you tell no one, absolutely no one, that you're coming. That's really important, got that, Toby? I'll know if you do and you'll never see me again. Know that."

"What's going on, Nat. You OK?" I suddenly wanted to cry, a great wracking sob welling up inside.

"Not dead, Toby."

I started to spit down the phone, my voice breaking.

"Not fucking dead. So you get here now. Alone. I'm in the square behind the Mennonite church, on the Latin side. Park opposite the building site next to the palm trees. It's Giuseppe Market. You come alone in your little silver car, all right? Or – listen to me, Toby – the whole bloody thing goes off and we're all dead."

"Giuseppe Market. Nat, tell me—" But I hung up, weeping softly.

The girl was standing in the doorway. This time she looked severe and turned away. Oh, sod it, I thought, I give up, do your worst, call the police or Mossad or whatever. I'm finished. Spent.

But she returned almost straight away, with two glasses and a pichet of white wine, some bread and a pack of cigarettes. She sat, took a cigarette and pushed the packet towards me, without a word.

"I'm Esther," she said after a while. "What's your name?"

"Maria," I said. I wanted to protect her.

I stayed more than that half an hour. Toby was on the case and I'd blown my cover, as I believe the argot has it. He'd had time, before he called me back, to speak to colleagues and record the conversation. I estimated that it would take him less than an hour and a half to collect his car and drive to Nazareth. He'd drive up the road that followed the exclusion wall of the Occupied Territory. That was certainly the way I planned to return. No papers for the West Bank.

Esther had gone back inside from time to time to collect small coffees and biscuits for the passing afternoon trade. She was from Haifa. Her brother owned the cafe, not a husband as it turned out, but she was deeply loved. I was right about that.

His wife had been unwell and had to spend time in a clinic in Tiberias. She'd had a hysterectomy and had lost a lot of blood. Esther had come to help and had stayed. Her sister-in-law was getting better, but her brother practically lived in Galilee now. But the cafe was going bust. She didn't know enough about running it and her brother had to look after his wife. The bank was calling in the debt on the property.

But she moved about among tables like she owned the place. The afternoon sun was harsh now and she adjusted the awning to give us some shade.

"Hide the sun till dark," she said to herself with a smile. Her phone played the opening bar of *Star Wars*. She picked it up and rocked it between her thumb and finger at me.

248

"For you? I think? Your boyfriend?" She laughed.

The text said, "Hold tight. Coming. T."

Yeah, you and whose army, I thought. Still, maybe Esther would be my witness. I moved inside and sat at the window and watched the square. I watched it to see if its character changed, whether more police turned up, any heavies in shades. I couldn't see anything that might indicate a security presence, but then I wouldn't, would I?

The fruiterers smoked. The tourists took photos. The women came and went, talking until it was time to go. The square continued its turnover.

Esther was sitting opposite me, smoking but not drinking.

"Some terrible things have happened to you," she said.

"I've done some terrible things," I replied, looking down.

"That's what I said. Terrible things have happened."

Neither of us spoke. She poured me more wine.

"Whatever it is, Maria, you can be made clean again. It's OK."

"I don't think I've ever been clean, Esther. But thanks."

She looked at me for a few moments.

"You should be washed. We have tvilah. Jews wash away their sins. Makes us pure again."

"Show me where to find those waters," I said. It was a scriptural reference and I couldn't be sure if she knew it. She was silent and watched me.

"There's nothing that can't be washed away," she said at last. "You've been among the dead?"

"Yes."

"We wash ourselves clean again when we've been among the dead. It gives us life, pure life, again."

I couldn't go where she was taking me.

"I'm so lonely," I said suddenly. I remembered the doctor in Sudan. "And tired. I'm just so bloody tired."

"I know. Wash it away."

"Thanks, Esther," I said and tried a brief smile. "I'll try to remember that."

It was only with a languid curiosity that I watched Toby's silver hatchback pull slowly into the square, over Esther's shoulder, its red brake lights flickering querulously along the line of palms as if he was looking for his date. Or kerb-crawling.

He put two tyres on the kerb and stopped. Was he phoning? But a moment later, he got out, hoiked up his trousers, looked around like a batsman at his crease. He'd had his hair cut, I noticed. He took off his cotton bomber and opened his back door, hanging it over the back of the driver's seat.

There was no point in waiting any longer. If there was a team covering the square, they'd find me soon anyway. If someone shot me from an upstairs window, it might as well be now as later. A blissful calm washed over me, as if I'd chosen my ending.

He – they – may not know what I was wearing. And they may not take the risk of a shooting in a busy Nazareth square. I was in control again. And I can't deny I was enjoying the feeling. Always have.

I took a long drag on the last of Esther's cigarettes and stubbed it out. She smiled that broad smile. She was leaning back on the bar now, arms crossed under her perfect cereal-bowl breasts.

"I'll see you later," I said. "I'll come back and pay."

She crossed and kissed me on both cheeks, holding my arms.

"I don't think so. But God go with you, Maria," she said.

I suddenly felt a sharp pang of shame that I'd lied to her.

"Natalie. My name's actually Natalie."

"Maria to me. If anyone ever asks, I'll tell them Maria."

Her mobile chirruped its text signal again and she shrugged with a laugh.

"You'd better go. He's chasing you."

"Thank you, Esther."

I hugged her. I suddenly wanted to stay with her for ever, hide in her cafe, snuggle down in a tiny room upstairs, mop the floors at dawn. But life can never be like that.

I wrapped the shawl over my head and across my face in the Arabic day-style and stepped on to the terrace. There were pedestrians passing Toby's car continuously in both directions. Sufficient cover if I timed it right. I fell in behind two women with laden shopping baskets, a young man overtaking swiftly on our right. It was perhaps only seventy or seventy-five metres or so. I walked briskly behind the young man – we could look like we were together. He was going to walk around the offside of Toby's car. That was cool. If Toby was watching his wing mirror, he'd see the white shirt and jeans of the young man, some Arab woman in his wake.

A whole narrative can fit into a single thought, I know now. And, as I stepped off the kerb behind Toby's car, I had several of them competing in my brain, complete and concurrent premonitions in a single synapse snap. The back door would be locked. Toby would have thrown the central locking, of course he would. He'd hear me try the handle, swing out of the driver's door and stand before me, watching me dragged to the ground by the heavies he'd fixed.

Esther would be watching and would see that and that would be sad.

Or he'd stay put and loads of little, tight-suited men would run up and bundle me in the car, or pin me to its roof. Or they'd simply shoot me with silenced guns, the thuds of rounds entering my chest and abdomen. Or they would swing a hood over my head, like Burly did, my throat constricting again, unable to breathe. And I was breathing fast. I wouldn't last long before suffocating, bowels opened.

But the door handle came up on my fingers, it opened effortlessly and I swung in, one easy move. The car smelt of polish, newly valeted; well done, Toby.

He was turning round, first left to cover the door opening, then right as I took the back seat. I swung a hand around his head and cupped his forehead as his hands came up and dropped the copper piping down my left sleeve.

I had to keep it away from his mirrors, so pushed it firmly between the headrest and the palm of my hand, while pulling his head back hard with my right hand, my hand in his hair, like I'd learned in my hostage video.

The pipe pushed into his neck just above the collar.

"Shut up, Toby, just bloody shut it, Toby, or I swear to God I'm going to blow your head off. I can do it, Toby, I can kill, and I'll just pull this trigger, do you hear, and you'll be dead and I'll be dead and it'll all be over, Toby."

"Nat, for fuck's sake, what the hell are you doing!" His hands were over my forearm but he wasn't pulling, the cold copper on his neck had frozen him and I felt his whole body tense. I took his phone from his top pocket. I noticed my hand was steady.

"Shut up, Toby." Yank.

"Nat, what . . . Jesus Christ—"

"Just listen, Toby. Listen hard and we'll both stay alive."

I looked around quickly. No one at the doors. Just people passing, middle-distance staring.

"Just drive very slowly and calmly out of the square straight ahead. Don't turn round, Toby. I'm serious. Or I'm pulling this frigging trigger. Just go."

He slowly lowered his hands, as if balancing, and leaned forward obediently, bringing a shaking arm under control to start the car. Good.

"Lock the doors."

We pulled away, behind a freezer van. I pushed the pipe harder into his flesh at an angle. I wanted him to feel the edge of the barrel. Toby was making little grunts.

"Nat?"

"Follow the main road. Down the hill."

"Nat, take it easy. Please just be calm. Let's talk."

"Just keep driving."

We pulled up at lights. Cars beside us. Businessmen. Families. I began to feel rather less conspicuous, rather more stupid. Had I really just said "Drive"?

"Shut up. I'll tell you where to go."

I looked behind. What was I looking for? Maybe a car would pull across in front of us. The road widened to the edge of town as it became light-industrial, with warehouses and shuttered whole-sale shops.

"Now fork left," I said, like I knew where we were going.

The road rose again gently, some houses and a school on the

left, a pile of tractor tyres to the right. I looked behind again. A soft-drinks float. Really?

"Turn right."

A recreation field. The drinks float has gone straight on.

"Pull in here. Turn the engine off."

My arms ached. I so wanted to let go now. But I pulled Toby's head back again and pushed the piping.

"You didn't expect me, Toby, did you? You didn't think you'd see me again."

I was hissing in his ear.

"I've killed, Toby, I've just killed grown men, blood all over my hands, and I can kill you. It'll be so bloody easy. I'll just pull my trigger and your throat will be all over the windscreen. Is this where you're going to die?"

And all the time he was saying: "Nat, what are you doing, why are you doing this, Nat, what's going on?"

"You and your bastard little friends, Toby. How was it arranged? What was the plan? You fucking threw me away, Toby."

"I don't understand, Nat. I don't know what you're saying. I don't know what's going on. I just don't understand."

I could see in the rear-view mirror that he'd started to cry. Softly, resignedly. Like the boy Jon at school. I looked at myself in my own right eye, below and slightly behind his. I looked minx-like and he just looked blank, hopeless, staring unseeing over the bonnet of the car.

Holding him, I watched us both in the mirror for a moment. We could have been a zany couple in a photo booth. I listened to our uneven breathing, arrhythmical, out of time.

I could see it now, everything made sense. No need for charades. I fell back into the back seat, broke the spell.

"Oh, sod you, Tobes. It's only a bit of pipe."

And I threw it into the front passenger seat.

15

There was something of a tristesse in the air as Toby leaned on his forearms across the table from me. We were in his flat in West Jerusalem. Modern, a sort of designer version of the one I'd been slammed up in. Net curtains over floor-length windows leading to a tiny balcony. Utilitarian and very male.

I remember wondering, for the first time, if he might be gay. A small hall, this sitting room, a low red sofa against the wall facing a flat-screen TV and this table against the window, a tiny kitchen behind Toby, a small bedroom, I guessed, behind me, which would have a neatly made bed smelling of washing powder, a half-read thick novel and a bottle of mineral water. A room his mother would recognise as his.

We'd driven down from Nazareth without saying much. He was still feeling shaky and resentful, evidently, and was trying to regain some dignity. I played with his mobile phone. I wasn't sure if he could use it to call his office without me knowing and I wanted to answer it if it rang.

I'd told him I'd tell him everything when we got to Jerusalem and made sure he wasn't planning to drive down through the West Bank.

I'd said, "I'll bring you up to date," like a schoolteacher or a sales rep. It sounded administrative.

It would go like this: As far as my time allocation has gone, Toby, I've spent the last month or so largely incarcerated in a room in a village that's a bit like a settlement in northern Israel. I was led to understand that I was taken hostage by Hamas extremists who had taken me into Lebanon. They were going to kill me, I was sure of that, so I killed the two who guarded me overnight and escaped.

Has anyone ever done that before, Toby?

No, of course I didn't tell him that. Anyway, he hadn't taken my little drama with the copper piping well at all. I thought the sheer release of nervous energy would have made him laugh. But no. He just slumped against his car-door window, which he lowered slightly, breathing heavily and eyeing me like a punch-drunk boxer in the mirror.

"Sorry," I'd said. "I thought you might have come to kill me. Or turn me in."

I told him not to call the office and, when eventually he spoke, he said he'd only told them he was going out for a doctor's appointment, because I'd told him not to grass me up. As we sat there, some Jewish kids playing football on the recreation ground beside us, he didn't look like someone who was briefed to turn me in, or indeed turn me over.

"Let's go back," I'd said, and climbed into the front seat, tossing the copper pipe into the footwell to make it look like a game.

And so here we were, mid-evening, the remains of some chicken and rice that he had microwaved and I had wolfed down, while Toby rolled a cup of the leftover broth between the palms of his hands and stared at the table.

I had thick black coffee now and was gnawing at a mango. I'd told him most of it, as if in bullet points. They bundled me in a car. They drugged me. They made a video, threatening to kill me.

I paused at that bit. The video I had fondly imagined had run on a loop on the 24-hour news channels, from Al Jazeera to CNN?

Toby just shook his head. "We've seen nothing. No such thing."

He even sounded a bit bored.

I went on. They kept me in a room. Then they said they were transferring me, giving me over to a different crew. I said that sort of thing, anyway. At the end, I just said that I'd fought my way out and left it at that. I don't know why. Killing now seemed strangely banal in this suburban, yuppie flat.

"Here's the thing, Toby, I was in Israel. I never left it. One of the new developments, somewhere up near Haifa. I wasn't even in the West Bank."

Toby stared at me. Then: "Would you find it again?"

"Well, of course. Probably. But there'd be nothing there now."

I looked at him hard as he studied his broth.

"Where did you think I was, Toby?"

"We thought you'd taken off with some aid friends. The conference was over. It happens."

He fetched a couple of cans of beer and a half-empty bottle of red wine, with a stopper. As soon as I drank, I started to fall asleep.

"They were going to kill me, Toby."

I wanted him to ask who "they" were, but he didn't. He just said: "We'll tell the office in the morning."

"No!"

"We'll have to tell someone I've found you."

"No. I don't know. I thought I was safe with you, Toby."

"You are. Safer than I am with you, as it happens."

"Have you told the office you've got me?" It must have been the twentieth time I'd asked him.

"No. Why would I?"

"Did they talk to you about me?"

"They asked if I'd heard from you a couple of times. They thought you'd gone off with your friends."

"Why didn't anyone want to know where I was?"

"I told you," he said wearily. There was a pause.

"Will you promise not to tell anyone I'm here, Toby? At least until tomorrow?"

"I promise."

Another pause for effect.

"I believe you."

I threw my head back and looked at the intertwined bamboo lampshade hanging from the ceiling and I wanted to cry again. So I stood instead and fell on to the sofa.

Some time later, Toby came with an unzipped sleeping bag and a quilt, which he spread over me and put a foam-filled pillow by my head. It did indeed smell of washing powder. He turned the lights out without a word – I think he thought I was asleep – and left the room softly.

Then I heard him turn a key in his door and I tensed, eyes popping open wide in the dark. A gasp that I realised was mine. But street-light was falling across the room and the nets lifted lazily to a crack in the sliding door, and I knew this was a very different room to the last one that was locked on me.

With a smile, I realised Toby was locking me out, not in.

I was expecting night terrors, a sweaty and fevered half-sleep in which recently buried images of the Boy's and the Troll's torsos would erupt like cheap-movie zombies from a grave. But I slept as I did as a child.

Yes, it disturbs me now, or at least when I think about it. I recognise I have the capacity to rip a boy's throat out as I screwed him and gun down his dumb sidekick, in order to survive myself, and then sleep like I've just had a hard day at school and my mum has made everything all right.

I barely moved before morning and had only pulled up the cool nylon of the sleeping bag into my cheek as a kind of comforter. When I woke, it was light and the sounds from the kitchen could have been a parent fussing.

My body had that stillness in which you can feel every fibre of it but you're not sure you can move anything. When I did stir, just to awaken my hips, Toby brought me Jasmine tea.

I showered in his little en-suite – I must have stunk. He lent me some pants and we actually laughed, like students in digs. It was our first shared levity since my crazed stick-up. He had some colour back, I noticed.

"Are you going to work?" I asked.

"It's Shabbat," he said. It was quiet outside, I noticed now.

We sat at the table again, as if it was the morning after a party.

"I'll drive you to your place," said Toby. "I have a pass key."

"They won't be there."

"Who won't?"

"It doesn't matter."

"We may as well check it out anyway."

"I don't want to be found, Toby. I don't want them to find me."

"It'll be fine. Really."

He was handling me, managing me. I was a high-maintenance guest and he wanted rid of me. But he was probably scared that I might repeat some version of the Nazareth performance.

So we drove across Jerusalem, quiet and Saturday-still. Up the Bekaa Valley road that skirts the old wall, the Temple of the Rock high on one side, Gethsemane and the Mount of Olives on the other, the terraces of white-marbled graves, the lucky first who will be raised when the Messiah comes.

I made Toby stop at the end of the road of the low-rise apartments where I'd stayed weeks before, but an age ago. It looked as it always had. Like I'd come out of an illness and was being returned home. I had changed since I was last here, but this looked the same. How could it? Or it was like visiting a childhood home and finding it unchanged.

It felt like déjà vu, but I had to remind myself that I really had been here before. I could have been visiting a set for a short film of my life. There was no one sitting in cars, nobody patrolling the pavements, though I imagined that any surveillance would be conducted from a flat opposite, or next door.

"You OK?" said Toby, after we'd parked up.

"Yeah. You go first, there may be somebody inside."

I watched him as he climbed the steps and, intriguingly, he did ring the bell and pause, before using his pass key. I wondered what would have happened if Burly, or anyone else for that matter, had answered the door. I'd drive the car off, I supposed.

But I glanced across and Toby had taken the ignition key. Of course he had. My copper piping was still in the footwell. Toby was back only a minute later.

"Do you want to come in then?" he said through the open car window.

I turned the lights on in the apartment, because Toby hadn't and I wanted to see if the electricity had been cut off. The first thing I noticed was that there were a pair of tights on the floor where I'd stepped out of them.

The conference programme was open on the round table, an empty glass tumbler securing it against draughts from the window I'd closed before heading for East Jerusalem on my errand of weeks before. A mug had blotches of mould on the remains of some coffee in the kitchen.

It was all a shrine to my former life and I could picture my ghost moving in the room, busying myself with those matters from another time, another world, like they were important.

It was a time I'd mysteriously abandoned. The bathroom was musty, dust gathering at the waterline in the bath. There was an abandoned stillness everywhere. This place had just gone on, impervious to events, like a church. This little flat was my *Marie Celeste*, floating emptily on into a future that no longer contained me.

Ridiculously, I opened a wardrobe first. No one had stolen my clothes. Then the drawer in the fitted cabinet by the bed. My passport and UN Blue Card. I held them, flicked through the pages in case – I don't know – my face had been changed in the photos or something, like my identity had been airbrushed away, while Toby stood watching me from the door.

Something fell from the passport and I bent to pick it up. I inspected the little plastic rectangle, turning it in my fingers.

"What is it?"

"It's my debit card." I turned to show Toby.

"No burglars then."

"No. But I didn't leave it here. I wouldn't have done. It was with me in my bag."

"Evidently not."

"I wouldn't have left it here, Toby."

He didn't answer. Just walked away towards the front door, signalling that it was time to go.

"Wait," I said, and pushed past him again into the living room. There was a little teak table by the television, near the power plugs. I stood, staring at what was on it, as though cherishing the sight of something precious that has been lost and found.

Toby joined me and followed my line of sight.

"What is it?" he said.

"It's my mobile." I picked it up, pulling the charger from its base. The screen lit.

"Probably some texts from me," said Toby. I was turning it round in my hands. It had the cracked cover of The Fed that I'd always kept on it. Contacts. There was Hugh. There was Adrian. There was "Home".

"I didn't leave it here, Toby. It was with me. It was the first thing they took."

"Well, you've got it now," he said. "Come on. We can clean up later."

"I want to change," I said, returning to the wardrobe.

Toby said he'd wait outside. When I came out – trousers, shirt, light cardigan, another change of clothes in a plastic supermarket bag – Toby had started the car and I jumped in lightly next to him.

"Did anyone come looking for me here when I was away?" I asked as we swung round in the turning circle at the dead end.

"I don't think so, no. Not on my watch."

Yes, they did. Of course they bloody did. But there was no point in arguing.

Toby kept insisting that we went to his office. Why?

It all had to be reported, he said, but he didn't sound convincing.

I wondered if he'd been phoned about the two bloodied corpses up-country, my grotesque abattoir. "How could she have done this?" Perhaps he had.

He was strangely calm in my company if he knew about that. Perhaps it was time to tell him. But I made him drive into Bethany, turning right at the entry roundabout, away from the tidy Jewish bit and into the Palestinian side, rougher but safer for my purposes. Toby bought kebabs from a cafe. I asked for fizzy water, but he came back with two paper cups of milky coffee as well and we sat on a bench.

"Am I getting you into trouble, Toby?"

"Why?"

"You can't harbour me without telling your people, can you?"

There was a silence.

"Have you told your people?" I stopped eating. "Have you told your office, Toby?"

"Yes."

A long pause, while we ate.

"I don't mind. You had to. Why haven't they come for me?"

"I don't know. They're busy."

"Why haven't they tried to kill me?"

He sighed. "Why would they want to do that?"

"Come on, Toby." I stared at him. "Why haven't they rounded me up?"

I'd hardened my tone and he looked agitated. Maybe it brought back memories of Nazareth. We'd gulped the coffees and now swigged on the bottles of water. I let the question hang.

"The Desk just says you disappeared," he said eventually. "Went to East Jay and just vanished. They weren't unduly worried. Your visa was fine and you know lots of people in the region."

I snorted.

"So I run an errand and just disappear. Come on, Tobes. Didn't anyone want to debrief me? Didn't anyone come looking for me? Wasn't anyone worried? About the document exchange, if not me. Weren't you worried?"

"Let me take you to the office. You can ask them. They can help."

"Isn't it shut weekends?"

"There are always pastoral staff we can contact."

Pastoral? Then he turned towards me.

"You need help, Nat. Let us help you."

It was a tone I'd heard before, but I couldn't place it for a moment. Then I had it. Dr Gray. Therapy. My neck began to prick with humidity and anger. I shook a little. I realised he didn't believe any of it. You don't believe me, Toby.

But I didn't say it, just carried on drinking my water and staring across the road at a shop that appeared to sell second-hand electrical goods. Toby had now been assigned, or maybe assigned himself, to look after the nutcase who had disappeared after the conference.

He was still talking.

"There are people who can help you. You need a good rest after all you've been through. There's a lot you need to get out of your system."

"Horseshit," I said and screwed up the box the kebab had come in. "It's a free world, isn't it, Toby?"

I was feeling sick and my breath was short and quickening. I stood and felt my thigh shake lightly. There was a bin attached to a telegraph pole and as soon as I reached it I was neatly sick into it, this little emetic episode suddenly lightening me.

I drew the back of my hand across my mouth. Toby handed me a large navy-blue handkerchief, but said nothing.

"Toby, what's going on?"

He was flicking the nail of his thumb.

"You're a danger to yourself," he said. "You're not well."

"It's not me who's the danger. Who is telling you this? Your people?"

"Not my people. Not any people. You just need help. You've had some sort of breakdown."

Yeah, that's what they'll have told him, I thought.

"And who are you and your people? Don't bullshit me any more, Toby."

"You know who we are. Don't be silly."

He could have been speaking to that sister he didn't have.

"Yes, but what office are you working in? Who are you working for? Come on, I'm tired of this."

I really was. Suddenly I was really tired.

"Toby, when I phoned you from Nazareth. . . it rings out then transfers."

266

"It transfers to my mobile. It's no big deal," said Toby. "Or it shouldn't be. We're working out of the American embassy."

"What do you do?"

He looked at me like he didn't understand. Perhaps he didn't.

"Come on, Toby. What's been going on."

"Nothing. Really. It's all as you were briefed. The conference and everything. All legit. It's just led by the Americans, not us. It wasn't led out of London, that's all. It's Washington."

"US money?"

"I guess."

I didn't care. It wasn't the biggest lie in the world. But there must be something else. So I waited, but nothing more came. Toby lit a cigarette and offered me one. I refused. My mouth tasted of tin and I was breathing hard.

"Toby, I need help."

"I know. I'll take you in." He was suddenly more kind. "You do need help. They say you need medical help."

"What do they want to do with me, Toby? Am I a security risk?"

"No, they're just worried about you. And London wants to know what's been going on."

"But, Toby, I've killed people, I really have."

"Stop it, Nat. Relax. Tell them all about it in London."

"Someone must know about the bodies." I was shaking again.

"Natalie, we can get you home quickly. When you've seen a doctor. Back to London."

"Did they tell you about the bodies, Toby? Did they tell you they'd found them?"

I was speaking calmly and rhythmically, I thought, staring across the road for certainty, but everything was rattling inside, like being pushed in a pram over cobblestones.

"There was a boy in the back room. I seduced him, stabbed him in the neck and he bled to death. Then there was a fat guy in the lounge I shot."

He paused, not shocked or anything, just patient.

"We can get you back to London. There are people there who can look after you. Help you. Nat, we're here to help. We'll get you home safely."

I sat down again next to him.

"Toby, do you think I'm dangerous?"

"No, I don't."

"Are you afraid of me?"

"No, I'm not."

I sighed deeply and my voice broke. I peered up at the sky to stop the tears running out from the bottom of my eyes. "I could tell you such things."

"It's OK, Nat. We're going to look after you."

"Why don't you just take me in? Have me arrested, locked up or whatever? I've done such terrible things, Toby."

"There's no need for that."

I was feeling stronger again, calmer. Maybe the kebab had just been too much.

"OK, Tobes, I give up. Take me in. Let's go."

I sat in his car with my head against the window. Toby drove back towards the city in silence. I knew I was unwell. I was tired again, beyond measure. I wanted a bed and I wanted comfort. I wanted to be talked to and I wanted to be believed. My breathing was shallower again and I was calm. Little pinpricks in the backs of my hands told me that I was sweating, tackling a mild fever, maybe. My immune system must be really weak, I thought.

But as my breath clouded the window glass, I started to think more clearly again. I could see where I was. I thought back to the little room, up north, beyond Nazareth. It would still be there. How did it look now? How did it sound? What voices filled it? "You should never have come back to Palestine." Why back? Think, girl. And now I was being taken back again. Toby's little car taking me into the city of Jerusalem, the blood sacrifice to the Temple.

The obedient handmaid of Toby's elders. Time to be given up, to give up, a time to rest. Let them take over. Let them look after me. That's what Toby had said. But I still had strength if I conserved it properly. They needn't rewrite my story. Think, girl. Time to take control again. One more roll of the dice.

Traffic had built up now as Jerusalem anticipated the second dusk of its Sabbath. Every few hundred yards, Toby was pulling up at lights, or stopping as the traffic thickened. I watched as he was penned into a middle lane, two cars behind the front one at the traffic lights as they turned red at a junction, not exactly gridlocked, but moving very slowly with frustrated drivers swinging between lanes.

Barely lifting my head from the window, I opened the door as if to be sick again and with a casual, "See you, Tobes," I was out and among the cars.

There were some Nat-come-backs from Toby as I found the pavement, which were then drowned by a crescendo of blaring horns. I calculated that Toby would balance chasing me against causing a huge scene in traffic in a diplomatic car. As I found the depths of a crowd, I knew I was free and I felt strangely strong, despite my sickness.

I reflected on how easy it was to shake off an escort. You just get out of their car.

I kept looking behind me to check if I was being tailed – maybe Toby had been working with minders in a car behind us? I walked up beside the Western Wall and into the Jewish Quarter of the old city, climbing the wooden ramps. I'd stop suddenly and walk back into the faces of pedestrians behind me, but that made me feel foolish and any mild hysteria seemed to start the sweats again.

I stopped at a cashpoint in a little booth. What was my PIN number again? Come on, girl, get a grip. There was a risk the cash machine would just keep the card, but I figured it would be better to find out that way than by trying to use it in a hotel where I could be seized.

And I stared at my reflection in the steel and glass of the bank, searching anyone who dawdled behind me. They were either very good and imperceptible, or Toby was the sum total of my security and he'd just lost me.

In every sense, I checked my balance. My debit card hadn't been blocked. The float was still there, minus a couple of debits from before the kidnapping, nothing since.

So I checked into the Damascus Gate Hotel on the north side of the old city. Standing in its reception, I texted Hugh on an impulse.

"Huge – what's up? Tell me all, Natter x."

It was suitably ambiguous; if they'd heard of my disappearance in London, I'd get the whole "where have you been" scene. If not, it was just an innocent, catch-up, gossipy text.

The hotel was all plastic crystal chandeliers and yellow

bottle-eye glass in arched window frames, what Palestinians do when they want to channel the *Arabian Nights*.

I took a pot of hot chocolate from the seated lobby area up to the roof terrace, which was really just an asphalted flat roof with some awnings and garden furniture between television cables. And I sat in the lowering sun and tried to think about what to do next.

It was the first time I'd thought beyond the next hour or so since I'd escaped. Killed and escaped. How easy it was to say that. So I murmured it to myself as I looked out over the parapet of the roof at the walls of old Jerusalem turning from olive to ochre in the early evening sun.

My illness – food poisoning? – was creeping up on me, only announcing its presence when it had arrived. I began to realise there were recurrent pauses between my episodes of sickness, each one incrementally worse than before. So there were phoney periods when my mind relaxed and assumed that my perception was normal. Then it started to tell me that something was very wrong and the nervous system kicked in, breath quickened, sweat pricked.

The edge of my vision began to blur, while the centre, what I actually looked at, grew the more intense. I watched my arm put my hand on the edge of the table, tried to touch the handle of the cup, to make it normal. I could feel the long draw of breath expanding my chest, apparently no longer an involuntary action. I stood to see what my legs could do and wandered in one short direction on the roof, then another.

I needed to stay away from the parapet wall, or was I drawn to it?

I thought I saw my frame falling from the roof, lying by the old

271

paperback stall down there, burgundy blood, those staring glassy eyes, mouth open in the death-dribble of sleep. But joined in one chorus with Hamal and the Troll. Sleep-dribble of death. Words chanted in my head. Back in my bubble, everything on the outside, but crowding in on me, trying to get in.

I stumbled through the staircase door and down to my room, if I could find it. Yes, I remembered where it was, so I must be OK, mustn't I. OK? I watched my hand shaking and I was amused, distracted, as it tried to get the card in the lock, as if it wasn't mine. Red to green. In.

Sat for a moment on the bed, head between knees, thought I was going to be sick and went to the bathroom, paced about some more, gasping as if I'd forgotten to breathe, but careful not to hyperventilate or I might faint, hand grasping at an invisible chain of pearls. Splashed some water on my face. Opened the window and closed it again – the body on the pavement, cheek pushed to the ground like a baby asleep, raising a lip in a curl.

I sat on the edge of the bed again, glancing around the room, everything slowing down, retreating from me slightly, my fevered face cooling. The pressure off my face and chest. I wondered if this was what a heart attack was like. Picked up my phone and stared at it as if I hadn't seen it before. It had received a text. I didn't care and threw it aside. No time for that now.

This was worse than when I was cowering in the rocks after I'd escaped. But my room was now returning to some sort of natural focus, one of the breaks between attacks. And I knew I needed to get out again, just to keep moving, away from a floral bedcover and the drugstore print of the ruined temple at Eritrea. I composed myself, taking control. I leaned on the desk and looked at myself in the mirror. I was a bit older now. But the eyes – is that how I looked at other people?

I sat on the lav and emptied myself. There was that faint but persistent tinnitus in my ear again. I started to look around me, as if it was all new. The tiles were black, cool to the touch. My knees were more pointed than I'd noticed before. Everything was surprising me. The fan sucked air out and a cobweb that the maid had dislodged swung like seaweed in a current before it. Terms of reference were returning.

Again I picked up my phone. My hand was steady, though still cool with sweat. I needed to be among people, lost among them.

In the lobby, it was strangely serene. I sat cross-legged at the end of a sofa, by a huge pot plant, needing no magazine. I watched hotel guests arrive and leave and declined the offer of a drink from a waiter with a wag of a forefinger.

I rotated the gold band on the finger of my left hand, recognising with detachment that I was still married. I thought briefly of Adrian, wondering less where he was than whether he really existed anymore. It had never occurred to me to contact him. Why would I? Why would he contact me? I pondered this while I stared at the suited ankles and black heels of two men checking in.

One was Arab, already showing rich, dark stubble on a face that had been shaved that morning. The other was European white, with a slim valise, no real luggage. Perhaps it had gone up before him. He strolled from the concierge desk, shaking his head. They had been checking out something for him that was wrong, I thought. He was smiling with that self-assurance that everything could be so much better if only the world was run by his executive colleagues. He walked to nearly in front of me.

"Hi." American. "Never book through Amex."

I half-shook my head, indicating that I maybe knew what he meant, but also that I didn't care.

"You staying here?"

"Yes, I am."

"Like it?"

"It'll do, I guess." Oh, there you go, I'd started talking American already.

"Been here long?"

He was sitting now, on the padded armrest of the sofa opposite me.

"Rather too long. Unexpectedly."

I wasn't looking at him. I sounded irritated and I didn't mean that, and actually it was helpful to have some human engagement. I just couldn't let him in my bubble.

"Miss a flight? I tell you, the organisation here is third world. Our major market in the Middle East and it may as well be South-east Asia."

I said nothing, but feigned a half-smile. If I was polite perhaps he'd go away.

"I'm here maybe four, five, six times a year and I have more trouble here than in any other developed region we travel to. It's not just the security at Ben Gurion – Abu Graibion, I call it – it's the whole financial services thing. Trouble is, it's run by Arabs and Israelis. No one knows what they're doing. How was it when you were banged up in your little room, missy, playing checkers with the brown boy?"

Now I was looking in his face. He was leaning across the aisle, smiling.

"What did you say?" I tried to sound calm, but I stammered.

"Only I wouldn't let my staff here, because you have to know their ways, don't you? But actually I love it here for all that. Have you eaten in the Armenian Quarter?"

"What did you say to me?" I repeated. His smile flickered.

"You can eat best, I think, in the Armenian Quarter. If you know where to go. But I guess it's hard to eat when you've ripped a kid's throat out as you fucked him."

Everything now was moving slowly, really slowly. I heard my own words echo in my ears, down a cavern.

"Who are you?" I sounded calm and I was surprised.

I wasn't scared, even if he was going to kill me. But if he was, he wouldn't be talking, he'd be killing. What occurs to me now is that I was mildly excited, comforted even, that apparently someone knew what had happened to me, that someone had at last come for me. Even if he was what Hugh would have called a potty-mouth. I smiled at that thought.

"My name's Jim. I'm from Connecticut originally. What's your business here?"

"I assume you know that."

"Oh," he said, leaning back and pausing. He looked at me harder now.

"Oh," he said again in a more knowing way. "Are you looking for work?"

"Why are you saying these things?"

He just sat and looked at me.

Eventually he said, "Maybe we could get a drink later. Get to know each other a bit better. We're gonna make you pay for what you did to our friends, you bitch."

"What?"

"I said I'm happy to pay to be friends. I'm rich."

You clever bastard.

"Excuse me," I said and jiggled my mobile at him.

"Sure, do what you have to do. I'm in Room 305." But already I'd left him.

I walked down a pebble-dashed corridor with jewellery cabinets, away from the lifts, towards a dining room. There must be toilets, I thought, but there weren't. Two girls were stripping blue table-cloths from long tables. I sat for a moment, shaking, and pretended to check something on my mobile. I forced myself to think in an ordered way.

Had to find Toby again – should never have left him. I called his number. It rang, then there was that longer tone that indicates a switch to another extension. A woman's voice answered.

"Who am I speaking to?" I said and, absurdly, thought I should have said "to whom".

"This is the British Consulate in Jerusalem."

"I thought I'd phoned Toby Naismith's extension."

"Toby Naismith doesn't work here any more."

I paused to absorb this information.

"When did he leave?"

"Oh," she said, "I'm not sure. Would you like me to put you through to that department?"

"No. Yes. Please."

Another pause. Another, younger woman.

"Is Toby there?" I tried to sound everyday and sing-song. Like an aerobics teacher, maybe.

"Who's speaking?"

"It's Nat." What the hell.

"From?" Damn, she was good. Or maybe she hadn't been briefed. How very British.

"Connecticut," I said.

"Toby Naismith doesn't work here any more."

"Oh?" Pleasantly, as if we hadn't been in touch for a while. "When did he finish?"

"Ooh, I couldn't say."

"And where did he go?"

"I don't have that information. You'd need to speak to his department. Can I put you through?"

"No, not to worry, thank you."

There are revelations you can't approach because of their scale, we were taught at college. You simply concentrate on how they "form" you. It's a type of obedience, I suppose. The Yank sent to rattle me in the lobby, who pretended he thought I was a whore. Toby wasn't working at the consulate. These were not to be examined or questioned. What they did to me was what was important.

Breathing was coming hard again and my hairline cooled with sweat. The beast was returning and it was going to be a bad one. I stood and one of the waitresses moved as if to help me. No no.

I made the lift and my room before my arm shook too much to handle the key card. And I lay on the bed. Maybe this time I would die, maybe this time my heart would stop. My knee was moving up and down and I couldn't bear the repetition. I stood and considered the window again. So easy and it would be over.

I was clutching at the window handle, whether to get air into me or me into the air I'll never know, when I heard the lock on my door lift with a clunk. I turned and moved into the short passage before the door.

"Who is it?"

But the question was lost in the crash of the door bursting open. Something, someone dark and huge, swung me and pinned me to the cupboard door. I wilted in the embrace. I was done. It's finished. Take me.

Another huge figure passed into the room and I heard a shouted single word. What was that language? My head was too fevered to process it.

A man's face withdrew from next to mine. Slavic features. Dark, kind eyes.

"Sorry," he whispered and smiled slightly.

His colleague was closing the window, a semi-automatic weapon slung at his waist. The man who had been holding me had one too. I was shaking properly now.

But there was a third person, to my right, standing in the door. Leaning on a stick.

It was Sarah Curse.

16

High ceilings to stare up into, with dewdrop pargeting. Cream and gold upholstery with silk throws. Double doors topped with marble, Moorish ogees. Embroidered wall drapes of Ottoman warriors. Pale brown marbled floors with Persian rugs. French windows to a terrace, with the longest net curtains I'd ever seen, furling like smoke in warm night air.

I was in an enormous velvet recliner, where I'd slept for I don't know how long. Sarah was beside me, holding a straw from a cool yoghurt-tasting drink to my lips.

I'd stopped shaking.

Sarah was stroking my hair from my forehead with her other hand. A smart, wiry young man stood behind her.

"I'm so sorry, Nat. I never in a million years meant this to happen."

I shifted slightly in my sit-up lounger and felt the tug of a cannula on my forearm. There was a clear bag hanging from a metal stand next to me. Sarah followed my eyes.

"It's saline," she said. "We're flushing you out."

"What was it?"

"We don't know yet. The toxicologist can find out. But from your reaction, Alexei reckons it was maybe a bastard cousin of phenothiazine, maybe mixed with opiate. Massive delusions, hallucinations, altered reality. Most people die when they think they can fly."

The young man looked up. This was Dr Alexei.

"What a junkie I've become," I said, and closed my eyes again. I thought of the American guy in the lobby, probably telling his mates about the mad chick he'd met. "Did you pay my hotel bill?" And I heard her breath as she smiled.

Sarah had spoken with a quiet urgency in that hotel room, taking control as she always did.

"Nat, listen to me. Look at me, Nat. You're in huge danger but I can protect you. But we have to go now, this instant, do you understand? We have to go right now. Let me take you somewhere safe."

She threw a rug from somewhere around my shoulders and she loped as I stumbled with the big men out of the hotel, like I was some kind of protected celebrity. Down the corridor and through a fire door and down a metal staircase. Through a backyard belching steam from kitchens. I heard someone say in Arabic that I was ill. Outside there was a huge silver 4x4 with black windows.

More men. One of them tried to help me in by guiding my head.

"No!" I shouted and kicked out.

"It's OK," said Sarah, who had swung in the other side. "It's OK."

I collapsed into her side and gave in to the shakes and sweat. My arm was lifting up and down of its own will. Sarah reached around my shoulder and held it firmly.

"I've done terrible things, Sar. I've done such terrible things," I gibbered.

"It's OK, we're safe now," said Sarah and kissed the top of my head.

"I'm going out of my mind."

"No, you're not."

We drove out west from Jerusalem on the 386, apparently, in to the hills and glades and out beyond the moshav Even Sapir, one of the Israeli agricultural cooperative experiments, then up through woodland on some kind of private road and eventually through guarded gates.

There were tended lawns and views out across the plain. The house was dazzling white with a Palladian portico into whose shade we drove. And Sarah took my hand and led me to the sanctuary of pillows and cool sheets. They gave me something and I slept.

When I was stronger, I left my recliner and the intravenous drip, and was shown to a guest bedroom on the first floor. A small balcony and a wet room. It was like a Dubai hotel. Then I looked for Sarah outside, where I could hear calm voices in the still air. The colonnaded terrace had huge, throne-like wicker chairs, and beyond there were steps to the lawn. It swept down with palm trees to a lake. There were swans. A classical statue of a goddess.

Sarah walked up the lawn with her available arm outstretched. The other held a light wooden stick, not the big metal one with a forearm-support that she used in town.

"Look at you," she said.

"Yeah, look at me."

We sat on the terrace and avoided questions. I ate the mezze that the staff brought, and when a bottle of white Burgundy shedding chilled tears of condensation hovered over my glass, I instinctively looked to Sarah. She nodded and we sipped.

Emboldened by the hummus and wine, the time had come for questions. The elephant on the terrace could no longer be ignored.

"Where are we, Sar?"

"It belongs to the Russia Centre," she said without a pause, as though rehearsed.

"Does that mean it's a safe house?"

This time she did pause.

"Well, you're certainly safe here."

"What happens next?"

"We need to get you safely home."

We walked and talked in the sunshine some more, resuming the avoidance strategy. We spoke of Israeli agricultural policy, of rush plants and the expense of tending a grass lawn in the desert.

At early evening, we went through different French windows off the terrace into a library, or perhaps a large study. There was dark wood here as well as marble, bookcases with Russian titles on the spines, between them paintings that may have been by Impressionists.

"This is where a lot of the networking is done for the Centre's investment in the peace process," said Sarah, as if she was a tour guide.

I picked up a small vase with an Egyptian frieze.

"By that I take it you mean that this is where your boss manipulates the Zionists," I said.

"Damn," said Sarah. "I suppose you were never going to be an easy house guest."

I didn't wait and spoke firmly without looking at her.

"Thank you, Sar. Thank you from the bottom of my heart. I know you've saved my life. Thank you and I love you."

But I didn't move closer to her.

"'sOK," she said eventually with a girly little shrug from a perch on the end of a chaise longue.

"This is Sarapov's home in Israel, isn't it," I said, looking at the vase again.

"If you like."

"I do like. Very much." And I laughed a little to release the tension.

"I married him, Nat."

Now I looked at her.

"I married Sergei," she added, as if I'd asked for clarification.

"That's not the sort of thing to tell me when I'm holding a three-million-dollar vase," I said and put it down.

"It's not worth anything like that," she said.

"Whatever—"

"He's not the enemy, Nat. We're not the enemy."

"Whatever it takes," I said. "When's supper?"

We sat on the terrace, listening to cicadas grinding their legs in the gloaming, while kufta kebabs were brought to us from a barbecue.

"Don't you want to know what happened to me?" I asked when we'd eaten.

"I figured you'd tell me when you were ready."

I sat back. Go for it, girl.

"I was taken to a settlement north of Nazareth where I was a prisoner. They beat me and made a hostage video, which they never showed. I murdered my two guards to escape."

"I'm so sorry, Nat."

"Do you believe me?"

"It doesn't matter what I believe. And it doesn't matter what happened. What matters is what happens from here."

"No. I need to know what happened, Sarah. I need to know who did this to me, and I need to know what made me do what I did. Or I'll go mad."

"We had nothing to do with it, Nat."

"Nothing to do with what?"

"You being taken, your disappearance, or whatever happened to you."

"But you knew about my job, right? You knew what I had to do over here?"

"The intelligence exchange. Yes."

"So you set up the envelope switch. You set that up and that set me up."

"We had an interest in the exchange of information. But we didn't set you up."

I wasn't dry-eyed, but I was calm.

"What was in the envelopes, Sar?"

"Don't be angry with me, Nat, but it really doesn't matter."

"It bloody well matters to me, Sarah. I was banged up, bloody near murdered, and I had to shag and kill my way out. So don't bloody tell me it doesn't matter."

My voice was raised but lost in the silken dark of that place. The staff at the barbecue didn't turn or look up. I wondered if they spoke English.

Sarah looked like she was going to make a concession in the face of this emerging rage.

"I don't know, Nat. That's the truth, Nat. You were just meant to make the exchange. We'll find out."

But I wanted as much as I could get.

"Who was Toby?"

"Don't worry about Toby. He's a drone. They wouldn't tell him what's going down."

"Why didn't they just round me up when I got back to Jerusalem? They could have just. . . taken me out, or whatever they do."

"They were gaslighting you, Nat."

I sat back with a gasp of exasperation and threw an arm in the air theatrically. It was good to feel it working again.

"What the bloody hell does that mean?"

"If they'd picked you up, it would have made it look like you were important to them. As it was, you were an unstable associate who'd had a massive breakdown. The only harm that would come to you is what you did to yourself."

"And Toby knew this?"

"No, as I say, above his pay grade. But he was told to look after you, I expect."

I was quieter now, acknowledging that Sarah was giving all she could.

"How about you, Sar, how did you know all this?"

"We have people working with them. That's how I found out you were in Jerusalem."

"But how did you know I was in that hotel?"

"Our people were picking up more from Toby's office – they knew where you were too. That's why I was in such a rush to get you out."

"Do they know where I am now?"

"No. You've just disappeared again. Like magic. Except this time it's not their magic, it's ours."

"Doesn't the hotel have CCTV?" I was struggling to find a weakness in her case.

"Oh, please, Nat. . . it's always crashing, and guess what? It crashed just before we arrived."

She looked at me reproachfully. I could tell she was trying to lighten the tone.

"What happens now?" I asked, defeated, Sarah's junior again.

"We've got to get you home safely. The important thing is to make you safe."

"How do we do that?"

"I don't know yet. Friends are working on it. More in the morning. Let's walk by the lake. It's really lovely in the moonlight."

Down by the lake the velvet darkness of the water absorbed rather than reflected the stars, as if heaven had been pulled to earth. A bat jinked across it like a fallen angel.

"Where's Mr Sarapov?" I asked.

"Vienna. Then New York. You should meet him. You'd like him."

"Any husband of yours is a friend of mine," I said. "Do you have a cigarette, Sar?"

"Back at the house."

We turned to go back up the lawn.

"I don't know who I can trust any more," I said. "But I do trust you, Sar."

Sarah sighed. "I wish you had a choice," she said.

From early morning, I could hear Sarah on her mobile and laptop, in snatches of Russian, Hebrew and Arabic. When I joined her, she was sitting among untouched plates of fruit, yoghurt and meats, drinking thick black coffee. I ate a little and waited for her to stop tapping.

"Well encrypted, I hope?" I said when she paused.

"Yes, but no one's looking here," she said. "I'm on Russian trade lines."

She shut the laptop and looked at me. The melancholy of the night before had evaporated in the hot morning air.

"We're going to get you out and home but we're going to do that by arousing no suspicion."

"Out to where?" I said through a mouthful of brioche.

"London."

I put down the coffee pot. "Why will I be safe there?"

"We're going to make you safe. We're going to give you stuff to make you safe."

"Like a Russian tank? Or a Palestinian suicide vest?"

"Shut up, Nat, and listen."

So I did. She outlined her plan and then got on to travel arrangements.

"We have a jet. We can't fly direct to Europe from here – too dangerous, they could pick us up on customs and immigration. We'll take you out of Beirut. But we can't fly direct there. So we'll take you to Amman. That's easy, we do it all the time. Then you fly scheduled Amman to Beirut, you'll not get picked up on that. You have your passport?"

"And UN Blue Card, yes."

"You won't need either of those. We have a brand-new Russian passport for you. And visa. You're with the Centre now. In fact, you have been for . . ." She looked at her laptop. ". . . eleven years. Congratulations. I have your old one to be safe."

She picked it up and waved it. "So please don't say you have a British passport again."

"Who am I, Sar?"

"Maria. Maria Koltsov. Masha for short. You'd like her too, as it happens. We use her all the time."

"Maria. How funny." I thought of Esther. "But I don't speak Russian," I said.

"It's fine. Nor does she. She's from Detroit. But no one will ask."

She looked at me in her authoritative way. "We go this afternoon. I'll meet you in Lebanon. At Yusef Nasser's place."

She was going too fast and I held my arms out, palms flat.

"Whoa, Sar. You know Yusef?"

"I know who he is, yes. Sorry for the intrusion. Go to him. He's your other friend."

17

The anxiety only started to kick in again at Amman airport. Until then, the day had been like a business trip. Sarah had hand luggage with soaps and creams, bless her, and changes of clothes: brand names, light and loose tops, a bra at last. She promised warmer things for London.

Another 4x4 waited and we drove down on to the plain, and there was an airstrip with a few light aircraft and a small executive jet with its engines idling. Two guards peered into the car, but seemed to be expecting us.

"I'll see you there, hun," said Sarah, and kissed me. "Two or three days at the most."

And then we were airborne over the top of the Dead Sea, just me and one of the Russian staff, a big but nice man who just smiled reassuringly in my direction. We taxied into a kind of private jet enclosure at Amman, then through two lounges where my escort showed passports and visas and spoke Arabic with a dense accent.

He left me with my tickets on landside, pointing at the departures board and I waited less in anonymity than pseudonymity, trying to see the world as Maria would.

You have to fly through Jordan to reach Lebanon from Israel.

Amman airport is plastic and inauthentic. All that Arabic vaulting that tries to look like palm trees, reflected in mirrored black flooring that was meant to look like marble but was some kind of veneer, no depth in its reflection. Just a transit point, somewhere to travel from, not to. As it would have been for the magi, it's a point to the east that's much less important than your destination to the west.

Waiting for my connection – a cute little earner for Jordan – the anxiety returned and I trembled slightly, but no sweats, nor shortening of breath. As I sat on a marble-style bench, I wondered again if I was being followed, whether someone even now was checking me out from the passing travellers or from the mezzanine balcony of cafes and bars.

I played around with the things I knew for sure to calm me down. I'd been a game-changer since I killed to escape. But they hadn't wanted to bring me in, arrest me, shut me up. If they'd wanted to kill me, they could have done, easily. But they'd left me with Toby, poor sweet Toby, who I prayed wasn't any part of this, even if he had spiked my coffee.

I wondered what had happened to him. But I was no longer disappointed or even surprised to recognise that I didn't care. I was too tired emotionally to care about anything. If they were leaving me in the wild, it was because I could lead them somewhere. I'm afraid I didn't care about that either. Where else had I to go?

All my explorings were leading me to where I began, to recognise the place for the first time. But that was only part of my internal poetry. I was recognising myself for the first time, watching my little token as I moved it in the game. Looking at the little hunched figures in the mock-marbled mass of the transfer hall at Amman, I realised I was formed now entirely by events. Taken at their flood, they were washing me back where I'd come from.

I once went back to my school not long after my dad died. I suppose, with him gone, I'd wanted to check how much of my childhood was real. I wanted to know if it looked any different without him around.

Sometimes you expect a place to wait for you, to keep its memories fresh for your return. But it hadn't done that. It looked just the same, but it wasn't part of my story any more.

The corridor where they'd laughed at Sarah had been repainted with a gloss magnolia over the two-tone institutional light-blue and brown of our schooldays. It seemed to shrug at me and didn't care that I hadn't been there. Many other girls had laughed and cried through it since. It had moved on without my memory's permission. We don't own places. They own us and then they throw us away.

It was a bit like that when I arrived in Beirut. When I reached the camp, I noticed it had a new parking area at the foot of the incline. The washing had been edged out of the way to make room for satellite dishes, like Arab figures huddling from soldiers.

The water channel still ran down the centre of the passageway, but it didn't seem so steep now, like I'd been a child when I was here before, and the way was shorter than I remembered, meaning I had to walk up and down it twice to be sure I was in the right alley.

But then I found the house as if it was an old friend waiting patiently to be recognised. It was shuttered, but the car seat was still outside, though covered in a tarpaulin and bright orange

blanket, which had made me hesitate in case I was standing before
something similar but not the same.

A young neighbour, tall and scrawny – had I seen him as a boy?
– told me that they couldn't be far, and I walked up the hill a bit to
where some lads were playing basketball on a cleared terrace. I sat
on a bin, in the shade, idly watching them for about an hour I
suppose. When I wandered back down, I was pleased, though not
exultant, to see that the windows of the house were now unshut-
tered. There were new stringed beads hanging as a curtain across
the door. I just walked in. I was home, after all, and I simply called,
"Hello?"

Yusef emerged from the back rooms. He was wiping his hands
on an old stretch of towelling. His hands were oily – I thought for
an instant that he might be mending a bike for Asi. But, of course,
he'd be all grown up now. He had been mending a washing
machine, perhaps. The old lady's chair was gone, I noticed, along
with the painting of the Madonna. In its place was an old L-shaped
leatherette sofa, cream-coloured and cracked, and a low glass
table, which Yusef would have plundered from a college somewhere.

He had pulled up short, just looking at me. I suddenly felt
relieved. His tummy was only slightly looser, I noticed, and a few
white hairs flecked his stubble.

"Yuse, I'm in trouble," I said. He just took the three steps forward and, still holding the rag to protect me from the oil, hugged
me in the way that I'd forgotten he'd hugged me when I left years
before.

He cooked lamb and I told him my story. Part of my story. I
didn't tell him about the Boy and the Troll. Not what I'd done to

them anyway. I was neither ashamed nor afraid of Yusef's reaction, but – and here's the weird thing – I didn't think it was relevant. I'm aware now that I've put that episode – no, that event – in its own compartment. I have killed two people. I stabbed one in the throat and shot the other. Twice. There. But why tell Yusef? That's not why I was here. But later he extracted part of the truth from me.

"How did you get out?" he asked as we sat on the car seat again, like the old days, even if we sat there as different people.

"They were men. They wanted to do things to me that men do. The young one did."

"He raped you?"

"I raped him."

Yusef said nothing more and I was grateful for that. And that was it.

After a while, watching his cigarette smoke spiral into the dark like incense, Yusef turned to me. "Who knows you're here?"

"Only Sarah, I think," I said. "I'm sorry, Yuse. I had to come. I'm so sorry."

"It's OK, it doesn't matter."

"I don't think I was followed. But they may have the flight trail. I don't know."

"It doesn't matter," he said again. "Everyone knows where I live anyway."

"Sarah Curse does. How does she know you, Yuse?"

He just smiled and resumed his smoking, blowing rings now.

"You'll sleep here. You'll be safe."

And I did. In what I guessed had been his boy's room.

"He's just finished college now," is all Yusef said. "Army next."

"I don't want to get you into trouble, Yuse," I said pathetically.

I don't know what I was imagining. Some American drone taking out his house and half the neighbourhood, maybe.

The next morning he brought me coffee and fruit and crisp-bread, and he was energised, like he had a plan. I wondered if he'd been awake all night, whether he'd spoken to Sarah.

He stood out in front of the house, on a mobile, smoking hard, then just stood for a long time looking at the ground, hand on hip. He had to go away, he said, when he came back in, he'd be about a day, back tomorrow anyway, probably later in the day, maybe thirty-six hours. It was important, he said, and he thought he could help.

"Trust me," he said needlessly. I was to go nowhere. Someone – it sounded like Aysha – would bring me food. But I had to promise that I would stay in the house.

"You'll be safe here," he said. "But you'll only be safe here."

I wanted to stay in Yusef's house anyway. Just try to get me out, I thought. When he'd gone, only a little while later, I began to melt into a tranquillity I hadn't known for what seemed a lifetime, one I couldn't remember ever having felt. One I haven't known since either, if I'm honest.

Yusef's concrete house in its maze of little alleyways enfolded me. I lay on that nasty Seventies sofa, smoking his cigarettes and staring sightlessly at the ceiling as if my bones had sunk to the bottom of a sack-like body. In the distance, a radio played Western pop. The sun in the alley shifted listlessly. Occasionally children shouted. I felt remote, untouched, lost in Lebanon. How could I have thought I was in Lebanon when I was a prisoner? This was Lebanon. And I was out of the game at last.

It turned out Aysha was a young girl, maybe fourteen. She

brought meatballs and salad and water on a tray, and just smiled innocently and scampered away, her bright pink headscarf fluttering.

My reverie wasn't even really broken by Uncle, more hollow-eyed now, a little gaunt, when he looked in to roll a ciggie and pat my knee, just to see if I was true, I think.

When he left, I wandered outside with him and two men straightened up against the wall opposite. They were very much like the young men who had departed into the night with Yusef when Asi had disappeared as a boy. They grinned and raised a hand, whether to Uncle or me I wasn't sure.

I dreamed lazily back on the sofa, halfway between waking fantasy and sleep. I dreamed that Yusef drove me again, down through Israel somehow, my thonged feet on his dashboard, my elbow out of the window. I don't know how he'd managed the border, he's clever like that, and on we drove, the pop station in the house melding with his car radio, down the coast road, with bougainvillea in the central reservation and the sea washing up in endless white strips beside us, down through the posh suburbs of Caesarea, down past the verdant fig orchards of Gaza, where Hamal waved as we passed, and we pulled in only for diesel and a wash in the salty sea, Yuse smiling under his mirrored aviators as he put me back in his truck and drove on, taking me away, down south, to the desert lands, across into Egypt, where we would never be found, between palm fronds and pyramids.

I hardly knew night from that day, or light from dark. Later, I should have been turning restlessly under the single clean sheet Aysha had put on the bed. I should, it occurred to me in wakeful moments, have been sinking just under consciousness where ghosts awaited, then jerking awake with an ecstatic gasp, my blank eyes staring into an invisible face. But I didn't. I slept gently in swan down, on soft eddies of the night's tide.

Speak to me with silence, I had said, and a voice in my heart had picked up its rhythm: "be still, be still, be still".

This was wordless prayer again, I knew that, but it brought no gift of tears, the kind the old mystic women relished. I pushed at a garden door to bring my own gift, my own jar of nard. But, looking down, there was blood in the cups of my hands, blood I'd spilled in a back room probably not a hundred miles south of here. I was kneeling now, dropping tears on the boy's lifeless feet, drying the blood from around the white-faced Troll's head with my hair.

But I knew I couldn't bring them with me, up here, to lay on a catafalque, dignified in my memory. I couldn't bring them, for they are dead and I had put them in another place. Be still, be still, be still, the insistent beat. The swan turned the sky above me. I was asleep now, I knew that, but I hadn't abandoned this house, Yusef's boy's room, and I could stare with open eyes at the ceiling sky and it sparkled the reflection of my swan lake.

I'd watched the sky like this as a child, I remembered. Not long after my mother died, my father had set to work in the garden and made me help him, clearing the foliage of a spring that had run unchecked while Mum was ill. I think he wanted to keep me busy, distracted. But I was listless in my grief, half-heartedly pulling at dry shoots, swinging meagre armfuls that fell across the lawn between me and the wheelbarrow.

Dad wasn't reproachful – there was a moratorium on parental discipline at that strangely liberated time. And when he had filled the barrow he told me to sit on its chaotic contents as he wheeled it to where autumn's bonfire was building. I fell back as he wheeled it, spreading my arms to clutch at the spilling weeds.

I watched the sky then, its lighted white winking at me through the branches of suburban border trees. At the foot of the garden he left me there, peacefully comfortable as I was now, while I traced his movements in sound, the abrasive plunge of a spade in loose earth in the vegetable patch, or the clack of shears restraining the privet's incursion.

Still I watched the sky, the arc of clouds turning in the orb of a single opened eye. And I knew – be still, be still, be still – that all would be well with us, whatever happened when I left my barrow, however much it seemed so very far from well.

As I lay in Yusef's spare bed, I recalled that garden now and the dry and rotting smells of sap and nettle and string. The stars were winking at me from the same sky now. No, I didn't need to bring Hamal or the Troll or any of the lives I'd abused, or taken, snuffed, despatched. They were already here and all was well.

Yusef returned in the middle of the afternoon the following day. The girl had been in, bringing fresh coffee and food, smiling as if she was servicing a hotel chalet. I was waiting for nothing now. I was an anchoress and I could have lived in a hole in the wall in that refugee camp, this girl and other passers-by handing me their victuals on metal plates, through a hole.

He seemed satisfied, drank some tea, ate some cake, smoked and turned the radio up. Had I been comfortable and received all I needed? I had. More than he could know. We'll talk later, he had said, and lit me another cigarette. To the girl, he asked if anyone else had come to the house. No, she affirmed, with a detached shrug. Only Uncle, I pointed out, and he smiled like that wasn't what he meant.

Yusef cooked beautifully that night, stirring a large pan of yakneh, pearl barley and goat, as it gave off swinging clouds of steam like a tiny industrial plant. A cold box of beers came from somewhere, though we didn't drink much. Lovely as everything was, Yusef had an agenda and this supper was a prelude, not an end in itself. I waited. What could possibly be the rush, after all? Yusef had cooked and it was good. This was now. Be still.

We ate sitting on the squeaky-leather sofa, off the low table. After the stew came pears and mangos, great fibrous slithery lumps that we nuzzled and snogged off the inverted skin. Then it was done and Yusef cleared, brought a little percolator of coffee, no wine.

He lit up and I refused. Yusef was smoking hard, too much, I thought. Get me, worried about someone's health. Then he leaned forward, forearms on his knees, cigarette wedged between fingers, his thumbs and forefingers pressed together as a priest protects her fingers for the sacrament at communion.

"Natalie, listen to me, I want to tell you something, something very important. I think you're in very great danger. Even more danger if you stay here with me, actually."

I smiled like I kept being told that. He looked at me for the first time since the start of this little speech.

"You understand what I'm saying?"

I frowned and turned my head slightly.

"Natalie, I've been to see some friends. Important friends. Friends who know a lot of what goes on."

I lowered my forehead in a "go on" sort of way. He was being very earnest and I wanted to show serious attention. He was also very sweet and I wanted to grab him.

"Natalie, when you were taken away, when you were locked up . . . My friends are very important, Natalie. They know everything. Natalie, there was no operation at that time."

"Operation?"

"No Arab operation."

"No Arab operation," I repeated, like I was eliciting a confession.

"You understand?"

He looked hopeful. I leaned back, as if taking something in. I didn't want to disappoint Yusef, he was my friend – no, more than that – and I didn't want to hurt him.

"You mean Hamas, Yuse? Or do you mean Hezbollah?"

I thought I saw a flicker of acknowledgement, or it may have been relief.

"My friends know everything."

"I'm sure they do, Yuse, I'm sure they do. Why do you think I'm in danger now?"

He was very calm and his shoulders had slumped. He was speaking to me as if I was an intimate, I realised, and in that moment I knew that he'd never done that before, not with me. I was both excited by the thought and a little saddened that it meant all the time I'd known him he'd been keeping his distance. He looked at me now with no defence.

"Because if it wasn't an Arab operation, whose was it?"

He wasn't expecting an answer, just sharing the thought.

He went on: "It was meant to look like you were taken by Palestinian freedom fighters. But you weren't. What does that tell us?"

I didn't care. All I could think wildly was that Yusef believed me. I was believed. He knew I'd been held in that room. I just wanted to hang round his neck and be rocked.

But I said, "I don't know. What does that tell us?" My mouth was dry.

"It means someone was trying to make it look like us. It means that someone wanted to make it look like Israel's enemies had taken you. Maybe even had killed you."

I was watching his face closely. He looked more serious than I'd ever seen him, even more than when Asi had gone missing.

"Yuse, there's something I have to tell you."

I reached out and took his hand.

"I killed two of them to escape. The two who guarded me at night. I stabbed one and I shot one. It's made me sick in the head."

He fixed me with dark eyes and his hand gripped mine. Now his eyes were flitting between mine, examining me. Then one side of his mouth curled up in a smile and he blinked slowly as if it was a bow.

"You are a great soldier," he said. I didn't laugh. "And you need to be protected."

"You believe me, Yusef? That I did that?"

He spoke slowly and carefully now: "I know that you did."

"Do you? How?"

"I just know you did. It's the truth."

The relief broke over me like a wave. I let out a little sob and lowered my head, my spare palm covering my mouth, while I still held Yusef's hand.

"Why haven't they killed me already, Yuse, or why haven't they taken me in, arrested me, I don't know, loads of sirens and police cars when I reappeared?"

I'd let go of his hand now, so I could put hands to my eyes.

"They don't need to. You're not a big enough danger to them, yet. Maybe you're more value to them like this – they want to follow you, see where you go. Maybe they followed you here. I don't know."

"Yuse, I'm really sorry," I said for about the twelfth time, but this time imploringly, my head to one side, craving absolution. "It was Sarah who told me to come."

"Don't be sorry. It's OK. They know enough about me anyway."

"Know what about you." Like that, not a question, more of an acknowledgement.

"It doesn't matter. Well, it does matter," he shrugged. "But only because I can keep you safe."

I had to break the weight of his seriousness.

"I get to stay here for ever? Oh, Yuse, I thought you'd never ask." But it didn't work.

"No, listen, Natalie. We can give you something that'll keep you safe."

"And keep you safe?"

He looked down again.

"There are lists. Lists of names. The rest of what you swapped in those envelopes in Jerusalem. It's what they want more than anything. There are many many lists."

"I'm sure there are. Let's have a drink, Yuse."

And we talked into the night out on our car seat, with great drafts of Lebanese deep red peasant wine, Yusef finally relaxing, the stars slowly turning above us, as if we were lying together staring up at the sky from a flat roof, or a hay rake, or from the back of a swan on a dark lake, or from a wheelbarrow full of weeds.

I slept with Yusef that night. It was inevitable and understood. When the bottles were empty and the night was as still as a promise that there would never be morning, we moved inside, slipped from clothes and between the coarse linen of his bed. It was a large bed and there were heavy ruby drapes hanging the full length of the wall at its head. I wondered if this had been his marital bed, but it didn't matter.

We lay kissing gently and only occasionally, a smell of fresh wine on both of us, the rustle of bedding tracing gradual and uninsistent body movements. I think both of us dozed for a while. The sex just progressed in its own time, not ours, and the room was glowing with the first of dawn when I finally took his weight on me, running fingers up through the tight hair on his chest. He was beyond gentle – it was almost as though we absent-mindedly made love, or as if we dreamed it.

Looking back, I have wondered whether it ever crossed my mind that I would suffer some flashback horror, panic, push Yusef away, cry as I saw that back room and little divan again. But I had a different body now. I was on a flood tide.

It didn't even really feel like sex. It was an act of union, a somnolent progression to the inevitability of the night hours. Yes, it was a communion. When he rolled away beside me it was as if my sleeping face in his neck was one and the same act. I watched a ceiling that had now lost its power to be the sky. We were in that firmament now. We were bonded by our common cause, just the two of us, and not because we were lovers. Lovers? What did that mean?

When the room had awoken, when light distinguished it from the mystery that had gone before, he got up and fetched a bottle of mineral water, then coffee. I padded about naked on the rope carpeting, visiting the outside loo, rewrapping myself in linen. Strangely, I knew there would be no peace for me in this house any more. Not like the day before. I must shake the dust from my heels again. I dressed and moved to the living area.

"Sit down," said Yusef, suddenly but not unkindly. And I obeyed.

"It may be better if you don't fly from Beirut."

"You don't say . . ."

"You can be tracked too easily. They may decide . . . you might get taken again."

"I'm hoping I could get taken again anyway."

I weighted the words to express their puerile ambiguity.

What could he mean? I couldn't schlep back into Israel. Syria was out of the question.

"Do you want me to take the train?" I said at last.

"I could get you to Egypt," said Yusef.

Now I really did laugh, genuinely. A huge release of tension. I wanted to tell him about my dream, but I wanted to laugh at him more.

"Seriously, Nat. By boat."

No, not seriously, Yuse. Not remotely seriously. I'd taken my chance with Beirut. I'd survived Israel. I had a mission. That morning, I felt invincible.

Then Aysha stuck her head round the door. Someone was here for us. A lady. Sarah appeared behind her and just walked in.

"Yusef?" she said and held out her hand to him. So she hadn't met him before, and I was glad.

There was very little small talk. Sarah was working, I realised. The three of us were at a meeting and there was a single item on the agenda: my transfer to the UK.

Yusef's Mediterranean cruise was summarily dismissed. It was to be another private flight, another identity. I looked at the Lebanese passport Sarah gave me. Republique Libanaise. Black and shiny. Pages of Arabic, French and English. The fat, squat cedar tree on the front. Crisp but not new. And my picture on the main page again, a different one this time. Sarah's file on me must have damn near crashed her laptop. It was stamped with a faded officialdom. It felt like mine.

"It's OK," said Yusef. "It's safe. I said I'd keep you safe. We do this often. You'll go out our way."

We? Was it Yusef that Sarah spoke to on her smart Israeli terrace? I didn't like that thought so much and shut it away.

"She is part of a language-teaching delegation that flies regularly between Italy, Britain and Beirut," cut in Sarah. "There will be six of you. You're invisible."

That wasn't quite true. But my visibility had disappeared behind the name in the passport. Huda Serrano.

"Why can't I stay here?" I asked and I meant it. "If it's so easy to get a new identity, why don't I just disappear here?"

"Now you're not in Jerusalem they wouldn't have to explain you away," said Sarah. "Mad or dead, they're not bothered."

"But you took me out of Jerusalem."

"They were on your case, Nat. It would only have ended in tears."

"So tell me how I'm meant to be safer in London? They'll find me easily there."

"We're going to give you something to protect you," said Sarah.

"So Yusef tells me," I said and I was conscious of lining up with Yusef against Sarah.

"We're going to give you a list of names—"

"Oh God, not again," I said. "I'm not being your go-between. I'm not being your little postman. Look what happened last time."

"But this is different. Names of those working for the Quartet in Palestine."

I paused to absorb this.

"But they know who they are. They're their own people," I said blankly.

"They don't know we know. And they'll keep you safe," said Yusef. I clocked that for him it was all about keeping me safe and I liked that.

"But that was what I was swapping in Jerusalem in the first place. That was the whole point. Mutually assured blown covers."

Sarah looked at Yusef. Then she looked back at me.

"Those envelopes were empty," she said. "Decoys."

Yusef sucked air through his teeth. I felt the wave break over me. Nobody spoke.

"So it was all. . . only about me," I said eventually to no one.

Sarah just looked at me.

"I won't pretend that you aren't doing us a favour by taking this back to London. There's no exchange this time. Just telling them we know. But it will keep you safe," she said.

"If anything happens to me, you publish the list?"

She just looked at me, then down at my passport.

"Will you do it?" asked Yusef.

"I don't suppose there's much choice," I said to the window. "Who do I tell?"

"You don't have to tell anyone," said Sarah. "You'll just need to forward an email to the Centre when you arrive and they will take care of everything. You're just the fence. No one will touch you. But it has to come from you."

"OK," I said.

But I was already forming another plan. And I wasn't going to share it with Sarah. There was unfinished business and there could be no redemption without it.

Yusef drove me to the airport the next morning. I'd said that if I'd been followed, then they'd know who he was taking, but Yuse just shook his head firmly.

"They don't know where you are."

Funny, he'd picked me up at the airport when I first arrived in Beirut. He hadn't had much English then. He seemed more remotely Middle Eastern. My courier, I'd thought, good. I'd hardly looked at him, though I thought I was friendly enough, asking about local matters, how the job would shape up. Now here he was dropping me at the same airport, his sometime lover, with a forged passport, saving my life, apparently.

I tried to calm down, distract myself, by wondering who Huda Serrano really was. What she might look like, if she wasn't being me. Whether she had ever been anyone. Yusef had just chuckled when I'd asked.

"She's no one. And everyone. She is you now."

I wore a blue scarf around my head, as I had in the photograph.

I was a Muslim convert, making some of the travel arrangements for the delegation, which she'd flown in with two weeks previously.

"Who was she when she came in, Yuse? Where is she now?"

"It doesn't matter," he said from behind those mirrored sunglasses.

He took his hand from the gear lever and held the inside of my elbow briefly, but didn't say anything else. The subject was being closed down.

"There is a guide in the group who will check you all through."

At the airport, he parked as he must have done a thousand times before. In the departures hall we were joined by a large Arab in a light grey suit and pale skin, a dark and hairy mole on his left cheek.

"Mr Serrano," said Yusef and Hairy Mole's fat lips parted in a smile as Yusef handed over the passport. We joined the small group, a mixture of Lebanese and Europeans, bags on trolleys, small pieces of cabin luggage, one of which Hairy Mole passed to me.

Suddenly the scene started to slip away from me. My self-protective bubble was taking me, but I wasn't going to let it yet and I fought to stay outside it, so I turned towards Yusef. He just blanked me and shook his head imperceptibly. I felt a twang of resentment.

We'd lain in bed the second night I'd spent in his house, coiled together, but he hadn't even kissed me, just the breeze of his breath on my forehead. I understood now. He looked at Hairy Mole and shook his hand firmly, then flicked a salute at me with the palm of his hand and turned and walked briskly away. The back of his neck needed a shave, I noticed. He didn't walk away slowly. He wasn't giving me a chance to catch him up.

The little group busied itself, but none of them looked at me. Only Hairy Mole did, whose name was Mo. He was pleasant enough, it turned out, and moved with a reassuring ease as my consort, showing me to my seat on the plane – a rather bigger jet this time, but unmistakably the cramped and rarefied chariot of the elite – and then sitting in his, some six rows in front.

He had alleviated some fear, placing a hand firmly in the small of my back as we were waved through immigration. No, the fear I had came from elsewhere.

As we approached Heathrow, I couldn't displace the thought that the man sitting behind me and across the aisle in a brown blazer was my tail from Beirut. Rationalising didn't help, the idea that it was absurd that my erstwhile captors could have infiltrated a flight chartered by Sarah's Centre. But I clenched the balls of my fists between my thighs and held a rage inside that wanted to spit in his face and claw at his eyes.

But there was a panic I felt of another kind as we pitched in to Heathrow, and I realised it was a kind of response to bereavement. This was a country that I'd lost, had died for me, and now it was resurrected, unrecognisable but the same, the life outside my tomb, a zombie town.

It was summertime in London, but it was still cold and bleak by comparison and darkness encroached even the brightest of streets. You could see the denial of this truth on implacable faces. So here was home again, with its permanent hum, its pointless arrogance, its business of self-entitlement. I watched it as a ghost might watch its former world go by, trapped by despair in the places of its former life, following death. The only evidence that I was really there were the little interactions with the show's set pieces – the

Polish émigré at the coffee counter, the boy lawyer's sharp shoulder, the concierge at the hotel, a tourist asking the way.

I'd felt this way once with an extreme hangover. It had been the morning after arriving back from the feeding stations of Sudan and sixteen weeks of watching babies die, so my consciousness may have been attenuated then too.

I stopped once to give a penny-whistler a five-pound note. I don't know why and I don't care. I lied that I already had the magazine he was selling from a pile behind him. God bless you and have a very good day, he'd said. He was groomed and scruffy at the same time, the way you are when you're clean but in scavenged clothes. Maybe I just needed to make human contact with someone around me, to prove I was there and not some spectre at London's eternal feast.

I checked into a Babylon of a hotel in Shepherd's Bush to which Sarah had directed me, one of the transit camps for Heathrow airport. I was glad – I didn't want to be central, too cramped, enclosed and expensive. And, anyway, it felt like being outside the city walls. Masha's debit card worked when the cashier swiped it and I wondered wistfully whether my balance was not only being watched but managed, topped up by an indulgent uncle subsidising a wayward, orphan niece. Well, Tiffany's next, and I smiled.

It had a "Business Centre", so a code for an hour of internet took me to a mezzanine with a row of PCs where young women with hair extensions and power tights were convincing themselves by booking venues that they had careers in marketing. I opened the fresh email account I'd been assigned.

The name looked strange now I saw it on screen. I stared at it for maybe quarter of an hour. Incoming messages: 0. Sent Mail: 0. Outbox 0. Drafts 0.

I opened a browser, ludicrously ran a search on Israeli settlements. And there they were, their smart little white boxes, clustered new towns on the plains and downs of the West Bank.

The soft rustle of the lift took me to my room. 119. A recovery cubicle for the commercially sick, with a window that locked open at four inches, a little acknowledgement that at least some of its occupants would want to throw themselves out of it into a defiant oblivion, write themselves off the balance sheet, form that crazy shape in the car park.

I'd taken an apple, a supple red like all the rest, from a display in the mezzanine cafe, put it on a small plate, taken a knife from the grey plastic container with four pods for knives, forks, big spoons, teaspoons, which made the same crunch when you disturbed the cutlery, like beach stones on a tide, as the ones we had at school did. Now I sliced my apple, coring the segments with my knife into a little white towel from the bathroom that reminded me of the linens that the silent boy brought me over my buckets in that Israeli room.

It was too blunt to skin the apple and the serrated inch on its curve too clumsy, so I lay the four little segments side by side on the glass-topped table by the London tourist magazine, like boats in a harbour.

Yes, and with an electric-cold shiver I ran the blade gently up the soft underside of my forearm, from the wrist to the pit of the elbow and my body buckled in welcome.

Come pierce me, make me pay. A little more pressure on the next stroke and I had the dry line of a scratch. Then with a grunt of welcome the slight serration went in, in, in, a furrow ploughed between sinews, dimpled blue veins giving way like sapling roots, or weeds in a pond, with the great unreachable prize, the great lazy pikes of arteries somewhere much lower and safer, in crimson depths. Life blood bubbled up and eagerly ran the little circumference of my arm and dripped into the white towel that I would leave in the little sanitary bin for tampons.

The pain was distant, not mine, and I cut again, across this time. A cross. It was some kind of justice. Some recognition of both my worth and worthlessness. And, oh, you can't believe, that's so good to confess. I had to clench my thighs to stop myself wetting at my own confession. I dripped blood. I was both mortal and alive. I could slice my vile body and it would shed, you see? For you, for me. I was flesh and blood.

18

I was being watched. I was convinced of that now. I couldn't stay in my room; there was a tiny red bulb in the ceiling corner, a little light on the air-conditioning unit above the bathroom door that looked fibre-optic and a television on a short metal arm that I turned to face the window. All the time I rocked, with my own voice telling me that they weren't watching me through anything glass and electric. It was like trying to locate my own cry, a call that would haul me back from stupid, mistaken presumptions. I struggled to be rational.

I still had Masha's debit card. Sarah had said it was better to stick with Masha for money, even on Huda's passport. But maybe they all knew about Masha in London? I knew I had trusted Sarah because I wanted to. That's the only reason anyone ever invests trust. Trust in God. I'd checked into the hotel she'd told me to, hadn't I? But the receptionist had paused at her screen, maybe to check me into this room specially? So I could be watched? And around my head the doubts went again.

It was me that was ahead of the game, I kept telling myself, not them. But how-could-they-know kept seguing into how-did-they-know. Fear of surveillance gives you a physical reaction. I was telling myself that I was on my own; I'd breathe deeply, but I still turned my back to the little blinking lights and the TV. I sat on the edge of the bed, facing the en-suite wall, and shook a bit. Until I thought there was an audio monitor of some sort in the bedside lamp, tracking my breathing.

So I left the room again, banging against the walls of the long corridor. Probably drunk, I saw a room-maid think, as I tracked the wall past her trolley. Now I was watching myself as through CCTV, the grey figure in staccato little freeze-frames, like those shots of murdered teenagers or robbed newsagents.

I made it to the lifts, but then couldn't get in a lift that was occupied. A man and a woman, dressed as tourists, probably Scandinavian. They looked concerned, but I was thinking it was strange that such people would come for me. I dashed for the stairs and back down to the Business Centre. The pumping of blood made my forearms tingle along the weals the fruit knife had made, now coagulated.

I had less fear of the PC there, for some reason. Perhaps because it took my password, obeyed my command, you see? I was looking outwards through it, you understand, and no one could look back at me. I felt clammy sweat cool on the backs of my hands.

One received mail. I sat and stared, without opening it. Another delicious anticipation. Also cherishing imminent relief and delaying disappointment – suppose it was just a welcoming message from the provider? But it was real. Yusef was there for me. I was connected, across the multitudes of Europe, across the Balkans, across the eastern Med, connected to the place that had nearly killed me, with someone – even there – who loved me, who had sent this gift of grace, who had reached out in my loneliness and touched me and made me real.

The title box just said "Message" beside the paperclip of an attachment. From an email address that was just a jumble of numbers and letters, an Arab tramp hitching a ride with this gleaming great Western railroad of internet mail.

I moved the cursor across with a now quite steady hand and clicked. There was, of course, no message, just a PDF. I opened it and the screen filled with white nothing. I scrolled. Some Arabic emerging from the right that I didn't recognise, then some numbers in Roman numerals, like filing references. At the bottom, a crude stamp – a raised arm, clutching an assault rifle, the emblem of the Shia military that had constituted Hezbollah – and a date. It was nearly eleven years old. From about the time I was first in Lebanon with Yusef, I thought, and smiled.

The marketing maidens had long gone about their functions, but I still reduced the page to a tab and walked away out to the mezzanine landing that overlooked the lobby, leaving my jacket on the back of the chair to show the place was taken. I know, it's stupid and embarrassing, but I was suddenly thinking that the Business Centre was being monitored too.

And I dialled Roger Passmore's number on the mobile Sarah had given me only for contacting the Centre, only for contacting her. I was disobeying her for the first time and I felt a momentary twinge of sorrow for that, which I swept away. I had known since Yusef's house that I was going to do this. This was my time now. All mine.

The stiff, bored voice of his PA. It was like I'd never been away. A pause, some music. I pictured the scene. Young men and women, perhaps, being turfed out of Roger's office.

Then: "Natalie. How good to hear you. Is everything all right?"

I didn't reply immediately. I couldn't. It was like continuing a long-dead conversation, one that had started years ago. Strangely, it was also like hearing someone I thought was dead.

"Hello?" he said and I feared he was going to do that cradle-tapping thing that people only do in movies.

"Hello, Roger," I said at last and was surprised by the flat calm of my voice. I presumed I was going on tape.

"Natalie, what's been happening?"

It had that false breeziness of someone unqualified to deal with a wild animal. And I laughed, a dry little airy chuckle, gen-uine, not for him, a release of anxiety, I suppose. Isn't that what they say about comedy, about timing? I had rehearsed what I needed to say.

"I need two things, Roger. I need your email address. A private one. A secure one. I'm sure you have one of those, yes? And I need to see you, alone, at eleven thirty tomorrow morning."

"I'm not sure I can do that."

"Oh, you will. Trust me. Give me that email."

"Can you tell me what this about?"

"Give me an email and sit in front of it now."

I collected myself and lowered my voice.

"I want you to have it now. Are you in front of a computer?"

He answered slowly, like he was looking at someone else.

"I can use my tablet, yes."

"So give me your fucking address. I promise it'll be worth it."

I returned to the PC. Another pause from him.

"OK, Natalie. Keep calm. Are you taking this down? It's rogerrabbit21, all one word, with numerals . . ."

Somehow that moment made it all worthwhile. His email tag was rogerrabbit. And I'd never have known if I hadn't gone through all this.

"Make sure you get the double-R in the middle."

"Got it," I said. "But only the twenty-first, Roger. Aw."

That would be fun on the replays, office juniors smirking. But maybe he'd have it edited out.

"Never mind," I said as I tapped in his address. Send. "There."

And after a moment: "Has it arrived?"

But I knew it had. Silence his end. I hung up and turned off the mobile.

I lay across the cover of another bed, my head just below the cheap and over-inflated hotel pillows. I'd had to move fast and couldn't believe how stupid I'd been to leave my bag in my room. I'd grabbed it from the first floor, no trouble with the lifts, and ran from the hotel.

I made the sanctuary of the Tube and took the eastbound Central Line. It was nearly empty. There was only a fair and pretty girl with a dark boy in a pushchair sharing the lift – a nanny, I guessed. No one looked at me. But I got off at Oxford Street – plenty of exits, always crowds outside – to watch my back, just in case. Nothing, so I carried on to Liverpool Street and found a small budget hotel on the margins of Shoreditch, built of mock-sandstone with a glass corner. I checked in again, this time using cash from Masha's card. A moment's concern again as the cashier stared at the screen, but then she smiled up at me.

"Would you like an early morning call?"

On the bed five minutes later, I realised I was relaxed again for the first time since I'd left Yusef's bed. It felt a little post-coital, like Yusef had just rolled away. I wanted lazily to turn the mobile on, to see the numbers coming in, to see if Sarah had called, as she promised she would, using the cover of her switchboard through the Centre. I wanted to see if there were numbers starting with the international +44 or just marked "blocked" or "private number" because they would surely be from Roger's office. They'd be trying to catch up. And I wondered if Sarah already knew I'd betrayed her, betrayed her trust by going my own way. I'm sorry, Sar.

But I'd said all that needed to be said in that last call. I felt in control, even if they found me now and took me in. Whatever, I was safe now. I'd disobeyed orders by presenting my calling card myself, my "life assurance", as Yusef had called it. But I reasoned it was the same deal, whether I did it or the Centre did – now no one would want me dead, not yet. And, this way, I was finishing the job myself. Well, finishing my job.

I wandered downstairs, ordered half a pizza in a bar, drank espresso, had a long bath back in my room, thinking of nothing in particular, feeling little other than a frisson of anticipation for the next day. The night deepened and the hotel stilled against the traffic that streamed around the road junctions outside. I felt no real need to sleep, but did anyway, naked, between sheets that I knew now weren't going to be bathed in my blood.

In the morning, I was up like I had a regular job. Bizarrely, I stretched my back and legs against the desk cabinet and tried some sit-ups, the palms of my hands behind my head. I wanted to be stretched, able to move easily. Again, no need to check out – I wasn't coming back.

The Arab scarf wrapped around my head, I walked to Bank – I don't know why; something about not using the same station twice? Crossing the roads regularly, dawdling, doubling back across pedestrian traffic lights, always checking my tail. I'd grown accustomed to this behaviour, this street-craft, self-taught. Nothing that I could see.

On the platform, there was a loose crowd to weave my way through. I jumped off the first two Central Line trains that arrived, just as the train doors were closing. No one followed from other doors. Everyone on the platform left with the train. At Bond Street, I walked up through subterranean shops to the surface. It felt good. I was alone. And then south through Mayfair. It was nearly 10.40. In Burlington Arcade, the Dickensian Olde London shopfronts bulged like overfed bellies constrained by corsetry.

I hailed a cab, heading east on Piccadilly, asked for St Paul's, turned the mobile on again and called Roger. He answered directly this time.

"Good morning, Roger. Here are your joining instructions. Please come to Brown's Hotel in Albemarle Street at eleven thirty. Ask for me at the desk. And please come alone."

No harm in being polite. I left the mobile on and pushed it hard down between the armrest and the seat. It amused me that if they were getting excited about tracking the phone, then they'd be following a black cab all over Greater London – maybe even out to an airport. That might tie up some Ruperts while I spoke to Roger. We were stationary in traffic at Piccadilly Circus and I said there had been a change of plan, pushed a fiver through the partition to the cab driver and set off back down Piccadilly.

Now I had to separate Roger from any minders. Assuming he came to the hotel and didn't just send a courier to collect whatever was at the concierge. Maybe he'd send Toby, if he was back. I rather hoped he would. I could complain about his coffee. But I guessed he'd come himself, if this had all been his own operation. He had to keep his own secrets, if no one else's.

Brown's straddles a pair of parallel streets that lead north from Piccadilly, each with an entrance, each running northbound traffic. I'd been there for a fundraiser and watched Americans leave via Albemarle, while the Brits and staff left by Dover Street.

I guessed Roger would know that. It might just make it tricky for him to cover at short notice. It might also further split up those on my case who weren't by now following the cab. But I didn't know. I was guessing.

I asked the concierge for paper and an envelope and scribbled a note for Roger and left it at the desk, like a worried daughter. Then I left by the Albemarle entrance, walked briskly round the block and back in through the Dover door, picked up a newspaper and waved away a waitress. Outside I could see cabs on the Dover Street rank. Good.

At a little after 11.30, I saw Roger arrive by the Albemarle door, as I anticipated he would. He looked in the dark little coffee lounge and I watched him, distorted through bevelled glass, darkly, rather as I had once watched Adrian through a bathroom door. I feared he was going to search the ground floor and stood to leave for the Ladies.

But, as instructed, he approached the desk, a pause, an envelope and he was leaving again by Albemarle to cross Piccadilly to the east and down St James's Street to the old wine merchant where the note told him I'd be waiting. He pulled a mobile phone from his breast pocket, I noted.

I left by the Dover entrance and jumped in the cab at the front of the rank. "St Paul's cathedral," I said again and "can we go via Pall Mall – there's someone I have to pick up on the way."

Down Hay Hill, left into Berkeley Street, and I forced calmness on myself at the pedestrian crossings. The driver had all the time in his world. As we were held at the lights on Piccadilly, I saw Roger cross in front of the cab. Alone – perfect.

As the cab swung right into St James's Street, I said: "There he is, could you just pull over beyond him?"

The cabbie drew up, pulled the handbrake to unlock my door, and I swung the door open into Roger's stride.

"Hello, Mr Rabbit," I said, "get in."

He looked back up the street, so I said quietly: "Get in, or your entry wound will be just below the hairline. Loft window across the road. I've made some dangerous friends."

He smiled thinly. I don't think he believed me. But he got in. And I knew I had him.

I figured we had about fifteen minutes, twenty tops, but maybe a little longer if we caught traffic on the Embankment.

"Where are you taking me, Natalie?" he asked as we pulled into the traffic heading for Trafalgar Square.

"St Paul's, Roger. It's where I work, y'know."

I looked behind us, more for his benefit than mine. I wanted him to know I was still watching.

"So are you going to tell me what all this is about?"

He was taking control. I had to stop that.

"Don't be silly, Roger. You know why you're here. Why else would you have come on your own? And at a moment's notice."

"I've been worried about you."

"Do you want the lists, Roger?"

I realised I was trembling. My voice was too high-pitched. Get a grip, girl.

"What lists, Natalie?"

"Oh, I think you know. You'll have properly inspected the cover I emailed you yesterday."

Better. I'd said it slowly. I tried to breathe evenly.

"I have to tell you I have no idea what that was. Or what this is."

I turned and addressed his profile. I was surprised at my own anger, for once, not just my ability to suppress it.

"You left your desk as soon as I called to be run around the West End. So don't shit me around, Roger. You sent me into East Jerusalem to pretend to swap your little list, you tool. Well, surprise surprise, I have it after all."

The fountains splashed in Trafalgar Square.

"What list would that be?"

He stared straight ahead, as if he was driving. I realised that he might be wired for sound.

"But it didn't work out that way. Funny how there's always a different strategy going down. What is it that makes God laugh, Roger? People making plans?"

He said nothing.

"Was it you or your boss who had me kidnapped, Roger?"

I hoped that "boss" was wounding. He half-smiled. I felt the rage begin to roll inside me.

"Tell me, Roger. Was the swap of names too much like a peace process? Too much like slowing the escalation to war?"

He raised his eyebrows slightly and shook his head in an attempt at theatrical bemusement.

"I really don't know what this is about."

"Well, let me speculate," I said. We swung on to the Embankment. "Suppose we were collecting the names of those who were working for Hamas in the UN, with the big aid organisations. And what had we offered in return? The names of those who worked for us? Just at a wild guess, Roger, I'd say those Palestinians who had been turned."

He was still, silent, but I could tell he was listening, because his eyes flickered across the cab's windscreen. So I went on.

"But that's too much like a negotiation, isn't it, Roger. Like a negotiated settlement. Too much like peace – like an Israel settled within its old borders, eh? Just like the good old days before 1967. Before the magical mystery tour."

I leaned in to him.

"And what better way to stop that than have a British priest kidnapped and killed, when the time was right. Was that your idea, Roger? Or theirs? But things don't always work out as planned, do they . . . Roger."

I spat his name. He turned to me for the first time. His neck and lower cheeks had flushed slightly and I could see that he was angry.

"Come back with me, Natalie. Let us help you."

I ignored that and it was my turn to look out of the cab.

"Who did you make me kill, Roger? Were they Israelis? Or were they just turned Palestinians? On the list, maybe. Did they even know what they were doing? Or were they just another bunch of sad suckers doing a job for a few American dollars?"

He looked at me now, not unkindly, sighing and letting his shoulders drop, cocking his head to one side.

"You're a fantasist, Natalie. Let me help you. I don't know what's happened to you. But I do know you need help."

I looked from one pale eye to the other. I could have cried.

"Who did I kill?" I asked again, barely audibly, I think. He was still watching me and I looked back at him.

"You killed no one, Natalie. Come back with me. Let me help."

It was a staring match now. I lost and looked out of the window again, through the black iron railings to the lawns at the Temple.

"What happened to Toby?" I asked, as one might inquire after a school friend.

"Why do you ask?"

I gathered myself.

"It doesn't matter. You wouldn't tell me the truth. I have the lists. And if anything happens to me – or to anyone I love in the Middle East – let it be understood, Roger, they get published. Understand that, Roger. WikiArabs, WikiJews, Wikibollah."

I'd altered the rhythm and there was silence. He was waiting for more. We were at Blackfriars, where this had all started.

"But there's something else," I said, moving my agenda on.

He turned his chest slightly towards me and stared at the cab's light grey carpet to indicate he was listening.

"There's still cash in that development budget you sent me out with. My cover, wasn't it?"

"Please, Natalie, you're not well. You need rest."

I talked over him. "You'll invest it after all. You'll distribute it just as we said at the conference. But you'll keep me informed and I'll have final clearance on where it's spent. And specifically you'll put a million dollars into an organisation I'll give you the name of."

"I thought this might come down to money," he said, exhaling.

He was trying to provoke me, distract me with the venal, the perceived blackmail. I took his hand on the seat, cupping my palm over his loose fist as a child might play that game, wrapping a rock with paper to win, the fragile beating the rough.

"Roger, we're going to have such fun. I'm going to make you plant new fig orchards in Gaza. Oh, and we're going to invest in a cafe in Nazareth, by the way. No, not invest – we're going to save it."

He jerked a single laugh of scorn, but nodded a kind of acquiescence.

"And I'm going to write my story, Roger. Change the names to protect the guilty. And you're going to get it published for me. And if anything happens to me, the real names get published."

We were on Ludgate Hill now, passing that coffee shop where I'd decided to go to Jerusalem. I could see myself inside, sitting back in my chair, already weary, Toby all bouncy. We were crawling past it up to the western facade of the cathedral. My wailing wall.

He didn't take his hand away, but moved his other across, topping mine, joining the game. He had decided it was over. Whatever he'd come for, he'd received. Or he was giving up.

"You're an extraordinary woman, Natalie. Our recruitment is good, but we must have had no idea what we were taking on with you. I hope we can work together again soon."

He dropped his eyes and took his hands away.

"Take care, Natalie. Take very good care of yourself."

It was a threat, of course.

"No, Roger," I said and I leaned in much further. "You're going to take very good care of me."

It was intimate in a creepy way. I broke the spell. "Drop me here," I said to the driver, as we pulled level with Paternoster Square. "I'm sure the gentleman doesn't mind paying."

I closed the door and stood at the window a moment.

"What a glorious day the Lord has made," said Roger, smiling now, resigned.

"Let's rejoice and be glad in it," I said and let go of his door.

I stood on the edge of the cobbles as the cab swung around. Roger didn't turn to look at me. I let him slip down the hill, disappearing among buses, before I turned my back and headed towards the Chapter House.

Epilogue

I suppose it's a commonplace to say that we spend too long on the past. But we do.

We try to live with it by suggesting that memory is unreliable or that others see it differently, or that it can come back and surprise us, or that we simply make our own history. But it's all an avoidance strategy, because our future is entirely unmanageable too. Nothing turns out as we expect it to.

I know that people always say that, but they don't really know what it means. They mean the course of their lives is unpredictable, or that some episodes don't turn out as they might have done. But I mean something different: nothing, nothing at all, absolutely nothing turns out as you might expect, because we're remade by every new event that unfolds. So that means that our expectations are always on the change, and subtly, imperceptibly, develop like the appearance of lines on a face.

I understand that now, my relationship with my future, and it's not too late for me. As the man might have said, the future's another country, we'll do things differently there.

I told you at the start that I'm writing my life assurance and I still am. But it's my confession too. Near the same window seat where I began, I'm now set up at a helpful little trestle table that makes it easier to type at the laptop. Let me just tell you about the day I started to write all this down.

It wasn't an epiphany and I didn't suddenly have an urge to make a record of what had happened to me and what I'd done. That would imply that I was joining in, engaging with others, and it wasn't like that. It was quite the reverse; it was because I was, for the first time, truly alone and I realised that I was.

I've never felt more alone. Not in my little backroom prison in northern Israel, not with the dying in Sudan, not being married to Adrian. No, I was never more alone than when I stood in the late low winter sun of Oxford's South Park, holding my baby son.

I was standing about three-quarters of the way up the hill, looking down to the river and across the town, and though the odd cyclist passed and some adolescents in baggy black tracksuit trousers were kicking a football about not far away, as they had on a rec ground in suburban Nazareth, their cries carrying through the oily membrane of what I might once have called my bubble, I seemed to be the only one here, with all the world over there, where the godly towers popped up from the melee of roofs, as they may once have done in Jerusalem.

I was deliciously alone, feeling my stretched body, like the flesh of fruit, held compactly by firm skins of clothing, the outer layer a dog-tooth coat of some vintage I'd bought for five pounds in a charity shop with Hugh.

Absurdly, I still wore the headscarf Yusef had given me – a link to him, I suppose, the man I would never see again – and it now completed the retro-forties anachronism that stood on a metalled path, a ghostly figure, looking like she was wondering how to spend her ration, her simple husband killed in a distant war some-where.

Alone, not despite my baby in the crook of my elbow, but because of him. We were, we are, one body, he and I, and standing there, as one, we were complete, independent of anyone. He, this tiny child, has done more than anyone to burst the bubble in which I existed, more than the kindly doctor lady that I now see twice a week, and to put me in the world. There is nothing like being put in the world for feeling so totally alone.

He was wrapped, in a similarly absurd counterpoint to my head-scarf, in a little pink cot blanket, because Hugh had been so sure that he would be a girl. In the three days since his birth, his face had unfolded like a flower and now his shiny nose had reddened slightly against the cold and the waffle-weave was folded down over his forehead like a cap, concealing his cloud of dark hair, the only visible clue to which were those jet lashes that now sealed his eyes in sleep, the quiver of a lower lip, hidden in the tiny fold of his pout, the surface sign of the ticking, thrumming little body of life in the bundle. Other than the button-like interruption that is the redoubt of that reddening nose, his skin was a creamy caramel. It looked like it could be scooped and I will wait and watch as its depths darken.

But I should tell you why I was there. My beautiful boy – still unnamed then, as I recall us standing alone on that hillside – was born at the John Radcliffe Hospital early on a February morning. It had been a relatively quick delivery, they told me, quicker than I'd feared and in all honesty the pain's not all it's cracked up to be.

He arrived in a slither of lilac, "a little undercooked", the nurse said, and Hugh, whose forearm I gripped throughout, wept like a woman. They put him straight on my breast and then he slept like he'd just come from a sweaty day in the fields, and Hugh threw the blanket over him, stammering something silly about the dangers of being gender-specific. And we cried and laughed some more.

They put him under a lamp because he was a little jaundiced, so we were stuck there for a day or two. But as soon as Hugh was gone, I just wanted to get him and me out and away from there. They tried to make us wait. I filled out forms and on the line about parents I just wrote "Father unknown", because it was right.

We were meant to see another doctor, but on the morning of the third day, while it was still dark, I packed my little bag – yes, the same little bag – and we left, catching a bus into town, the old women in the queue cooing and nodding knowingly and me smiling proudly.

On Headington Road, I won't say I panicked – God knows, I don't do that now – but as the city approached I knew I needed to get out, I knew we had to be on our own, to have some time on our own. So there I was in the park, holding him, and I don't have to imagine myself back far to know the woman who stood there.

She had landed back in Britain feeling like a stranger reoccu-pying an alien existence, like a Palestinian coming home. She knew no one any more, but they behaved as if they knew her. And now it was as if the gash in time that had accommodated my life in Israel and Palestine and Lebanon had healed over, leaving only scar tissue. It was a subcutaneous scar and one that no one need really notice, but I could still feel it, like an old injury that wasn't spoken about in polite company.

I saw Adrian twice and then no more. I doubt we'll ever meet again. I'd borrowed the master keys from the Chapter House and the house was dulled by human absence, not unlike my apartment in Jerusalem. Adrian had vacated, computer and clothes gone, and surprisingly little space was left by his departure. I phoned his office like I was calling a utility service. I didn't even have to pause before making the call.

We met at the house, but he didn't come in – just returning his keys, he said. I didn't ask where he was living and he didn't ask where I'd been. Then I called him at the office again when I knew I was pregnant. I don't know why. I took him some post and a Hungarian language course he'd left behind. We met at a coffee house near his office. He snorted derisively when I told him, but he didn't ask who the father was, so I couldn't tell him I didn't know.

Dean saw me in his rooms again and murderers, rapists and the like must give off noxious fumes that only someone of his sophistication can detect, because his nostrils flared like someone had served him a dog-mess sandwich at a General Synod fete. I told him I'd been to see the Bishop – I made the appointment as soon as I got out of Roger's cab – and had asked for a new job.

The Bishop had said he would see what he could do, but in the meantime I should take some time out. Go on retreat. Get my strength back. He was his old kind self and treated me pastorally like someone who'd had some kind of breakdown. I wondered what his security-service friends had told him, if anything.

I wasn't about to tell him anything – I'm tired of being treated like I'm mad. Dr Shirley here in Oxford doesn't treat me like I'm mad, not like old Dr Gray.

The Bishop said that when I was refreshed, I was to speak to him again. My ministry wasn't to be wasted, he said, and the

Church of England needed a bishop like me. So perhaps he knows nothing of what happened in Israel. I have called him. I took a bit of a gamble and said that I doubted he wanted a divorced (well, as good as) woman bishop with an illegitimate, mixed-race son.

"You mean a single mother," he said, "with an adopted Middle Eastern child."

So he knows something, but no more than I could have told him. I've been lucky to have him. Blessed am I among women, eh?

So I came up here, to Oxford, like a Victorian woman in a delicate condition, awaiting her time. Hugh has these dear friends at the uni, he a Philosophy don, she a psychiatrist. Dr Shirley I call her, and I have their old nanny's flat at the top of the house. And that's where I'm writing – have now written – this, my confession.

My son sleeps quietly in a carry-cot through the bright-white folding shutter doors that are always open over the warm and expensively rough oatmeal carpet.

I may take him out in the buggy later. We can go down into the town and I may buy him something in the market, some woollen bootees, a little plastic ring of hoops for him to focus on as he kicks his legs out and sucks his knuckles.

He's the future now. Best not to dwell on the past. That's what the lady of this house tells me. I know she meant it kindly and, while she doesn't know what she's talking about, she is a little more right than she realises. What happens next is all that matters. That's the truth.

About the Author

George Pitcher is a journalist by background and a vicar in the Church of England. *A Dark Nativity* is his first novel.

Acknowledgements

As journalists know, it can take a long time and a lot of people to stand up a story. And this story took more than most. First of all, thank you to Unbound, which has come up with the astonishing concept for the publishing industry that books can be published that have not been written before by someone else. So to the team at Unbound: Thanks to Dan for being my first supporter (in every way), John for not remembering me, Mark B for the video, Phil for making it work, Georgia for the campaign, Rachael – ah, especially Rachael – for listening to Nat and understanding what she was trying to say, Anna for the ruthless timeline, Mark E for the cover, Justine for the copy-edit, DeAndra for the rigour of the proofs, Charlotte for the suave PR, Penguin Random House for the distribution and all the bar staff at the Narrowboat.

Also: Jo Goldsmith for telling me what Nat did as a foreign-aid worker and for playing Nat in the video, because she didn't want to, our daughter Eddi for explaining how Nat talks and Mobbs for losing me to the study. Thank you, Natalie, for letting me into your world and, finally, thank you for buying this book or, perhaps, just borrowing it.

Supporters

Unbound is a new kind of publishing house. Our books are funded directly by readers. This was a very popular idea during the late eighteenth and early nineteenth centuries. Now we have revived it for the internet age. It allows authors to write the books they really want to write and readers to support the books they would most like to see published.

The names listed below are of readers who have pledged their support and made this book happen. If you'd like to join them, visit www.unbound.com.

Ian Anderson

James Anderson

Christine Armstrong

Martin Baker

Charlotte & Bill
  Bannister-Parker

Josh & Sophie Bayliss

Jon Bennett

Neil Bennett

William Bonwitt

John Booth

Jean-Claude Bragard

Richard Bridges

Matthew Butler

Tomas Carruthers

Andrew Carson

Anne Cheng

Robert Chote

Roger Clark

Anthony Collins

Daniel Colson

Joseph Connolly

Richard & Alison Cundall
Jonathan Acton Davis
Caroline Delmonte
Malcolm Doney
Patrick Donovan
Mark Dubbery
Stuart Elliott
Julie Etchingham
Steve Falla
Carmel Fitzsimons
Sheila Fitzsimons
Tiago Fonseca
Ben Frankel
Gilli Fryzer
Christine Goodair
John Griffiths
Loyd Grossman
Kirstie Hamilton
Bridget Hargreave
Michael Harris
Neil Hayes
Stephen Heard
Simon and Diana Heffer
Gary Hicks
Alexander S Hoare
Julia Hobsbawm
Lucinda Horton
Ian Irvine
James Irving

Carole Irwin
Steve and Caro Jacobs
Joanna Jepson
Philip Johnston
Julia Jones
Sarah Jones
Simon Jones
Paul Kafka
Henrietta Kelly
Sian Kevill
Urmee Khan
Dan Kieran
Neal Lawson
Aideen Lee
William Lewis
Tim Livesey
Mike and Heather Love
Sarah Macdonald
Caroline Macfarland
Amanda Mackenzie
Stewart Maclean
Adam Macqueen
Jon Magidsohn
Tito Manto
Melvyn Marckus
Keith McDowall
Beany McLean
Ian McManus
Zoë Mezin

Dominic Midgley
David Mills
Victoria Mitchell
John Mitchinson
Harry Morton
Vazken Movsesian
Kathryn Mullaney
Carlo Navato
Nigel Newton
Alice & Ed Newton-Rex
Kate Nicholas
Lindsay Nicholson
Cristina Odone
Robert Phillips
Polly Pitcher
Tom Pitcher
Justin Pollard
Eve Poole
Hugh Pye
Jeff Randall
Mathew Rea
David Reed
Ben Rich
John Ridding
Daniel Rogers
Gill Roles
David Sceats

David Shepherd-Cross
Clive Stafford Smith
Stuart Smith
Stefan Stern
James Storm
Ruth Sunderland
Nicholas Taylor
Robert Taylor
Peter Thermer
Tilly Vacher
Anna Vaught
Patrick Walsh
Richard Warren
Sir Kenneth & Lady Warren
Martin Webb
Guy Weston
Simon Whale & the Luther
    Pendragon team
Michael White
Andrew Wilkins
Peter Wilson
Lisa Wong
Charles Melville Wright
Martin Wroe
Teresa Wynne
Kimia Zabihyan